By Midnight

By Midnight

A RAVENWOOD MYSTERY

MIA JAMES

GOLLANCZ

LONDON

The right of Mia James to be identified as the author of this
work has been asserted by her in accordance with the
Copyright, Designs and Patents Act 1988.

First published in Great Britain in 2010 by Gollancz
An imprint of the Orion Publishing Group
Orion House, 5 Upper St Martin's Lane,
London WC2H 9EA
An Hachette UK Company

A CIP catalogue record for this book is
available from the British Library

ISBN 978 0 575 09552 6 (Cased)
ISBN 978 0 575 09553 3 (Export Trade Paperback)

3 5 7 9 10 8 6 4 2

Typeset by Deltatype Ltd, Birkenhead, Merseyside

Printed in Great Britain by Clays Ltd, St Ives plc

The Orion Publishing Group's policy is to use papers
that are natural, renewable and recyclable products and
made from wood grown in sustainable forests. The logging
and manufacturing processes are expected to conform to
the environmental regulations of the country of origin.

www.orionbooks.co.uk

To Fin

Prologue

She was dying. He could feel her life slipping away between his fingers. He had tried to ignore the signs, tried to pretend it was just the night cold making her face so white, but now as they paused in the pool of gaslight he could see the grey circles under her eyes and the dark blood on her lips. He was no physician, but he still knew what it meant, he had seen it too many times before. Her flesh was hot to the touch and there were bruises flowering on her slender neck. Death had marked her; it was only a matter of time before he collected.

'I'm sorry,' she panted. 'Just a little rest and then I'll be fine.'

'Of course,' he said, setting her down in a doorway. 'As long as you need.'

The young man's handsome face was pinched, pained. *She looks so beautiful, even now*, he thought. *How can God take her away from me?* Suddenly he looked up, searching the dark alleyway behind them anxiously, his blue eyes scanning the thick, swirling fog, his nose flaring reflexively even though he could smell nothing above the rancid stench of London.

'They're coming,' he whispered to himself. 'We can't stay here.'

She moaned softly as he lifted her into his arms. Glancing around, he increased his pace, his cloak billowing behind them. He skidded and almost fell on the cobbles as he turned from the narrow side street into the main thoroughfare. It was still busy despite the late hour and he felt a little hope steal into his heart as he saw the tall grey spire stretching up towards the moon. If he could just reach the church, then, perhaps, there was still a chance. God could not fail him. Veering across the street, dodging a carriage and ignoring the cursing driver, he charged up the steps.

'Open the door!' he shouted, his fist hammering on the heavy oak. 'For pity's sake, let us in!'

Still holding the girl tightly, he allowed himself to look back across the road. He could see nothing in the darkness, but he knew they would be here soon, their claws and teeth bared. Nothing would stop them from claiming their prize.

'Help us!' he yelled again, slamming his palm against the wood. 'In Christ's name!'

'And what do you know of Christ?' said a voice. The door creaked open a fraction and the black barrel of a pistol poked through the gap. 'Get away from here, you devil. I know what you are.'

The young man looked towards the door, his eyes blazing. 'I don't ask for sanctuary for myself,' he said. 'I ask for her.' He lifted the girl, the small silver crucifix around her neck glinting dully.

There was a long pause and then the pistol was withdrawn. 'Bring her in. Quickly.'

The cleric looked young, or as young as anyone could look in his line of work. His back was bent and his face creased, but his hair was not yet completely grey. He had the same smell of death about him as the girl did, he noted as he watched the priest bolt the door.

'This way,' said the priest, holding his lamp as high as he could. He opened the door to a small but cosy room lit by candles, a meagre fire burning in the grate. 'Here, put her on the cot.'

Once the girl was settled, the cleric turned his lamp up and held it close to her face. Her skin was sallow in the harsh light, her lips blue-tinged, sweat beading on her forehead. He shook his head. 'There's nothing we can do.'

The young man grasped the priest's arm, squeezing hard. 'There must be something – some prayer or incantation? Please,' he asked desperately.

2

The cleric spread his hands helplessly. 'She's too far gone. Only God can help her now.'

The young man turned to him, his gaze intense and unwavering. 'Then it's up to me.'

The cleric's eyes widened. 'No, no, I beg you!'

'What else can I do?' growled the man. 'I tried to save her, I tried to get her away from those demons, but she's dying. Dying!'

'Damn you!' cried the priest. 'This is a house of God.'

The man pushed the priest from the room. 'Then go and pray for us,' he hissed.

Locking the door behind the priest, he slowly knelt by the cot and gently brushed the girl's damp hair back from her face. The blood was bubbling in her throat now and her eyes were flickering open and shut.

'It's time, Lily. It's time,' he murmured, stroking her pale neck tenderly. 'Now we'll be together.'

He lowered his head, his lips parting as if for a kiss. Painfully yet determinedly, the girl turned her head.

'No,' she whispered. 'I can't. I *won't*.' A tear slid slowly down her face.

'But this is the only way,' he insisted, panic in his voice. 'Join me and you'll be cured. I can't bear to lose you.'

She gave a weak smile, her teeth stained pink with blood. 'What we have is special, my love,' she replied, her eyes clear and sure. 'Don't ruin it like this, with this evil.'

'What I did was for us,' he said softly, stroking her cold cheek.

'But if you do this, if you kill another human being, God will never forgive you and you will be lost for ever.' She saw his stricken face and tried to smile. 'We'll be together again, I promise you,' she said.

A crash echoed from the front of the church.

'They're here.'

'Don't,' she said, gripping his wrist fiercely. 'You're not like them. Promise me you'll stay strong.'

He nodded sadly. 'I promise. Only the one who made me like this – he will pay.'

'Then you will be free?'

'Yes, darling. And then we can be together.'

Suddenly she was wracked with a terrible coughing fit.

'Don't worry, our love will endure,' she gasped into his ear. 'I will be with you again.'

Her chest jerked upwards, once, twice, and then her limbs went rigid. Her eyelids trembled and her lips parted.

'I love you,' she whispered. And she was gone.

'NOOO!' he roared, pulling her body to him, clutching at her hair. 'NO!'

He lay like that for a few moments, his tears falling on her pale cheek, then he slowly rose. Outside, he could hear thuds and splintering wood. With one last look towards the bed, he threw off his cloak and opened the door.

PART ONE

Chapter One

The first thing she saw was the fox. Peering up through the rain running down the car window, she could see the copper weathervane on top of the church spinning in the wind, endlessly chasing its tail. Although the church spire must have been a hundred feet tall, April was sure she could hear the unoiled squeak as the animal whirled around.

'Why would anyone make a church weathervane in the shape of a fox?' she muttered to herself. 'Not very religious, is it?'

'Hmm? What's that?' asked her father, looking up briefly from the wet road.

'Nothing.' She sighed, beginning to bite a chipped fingernail. The last thing she wanted was one of her dad's fascinating lectures on the history of religious buildings. No, that wasn't quite true: the last thing April Dunne wanted was to be here, squashed into their tiny car as it struggled up some hill five hundred miles from home. Given the atmosphere between her mother and father during the latter half of their eight-hour drive from Scotland, she had a feeling it was mutual. As they turned the corner, April could see the rest of the church: tall and grey with high windows and, above all, *old*. April shook her head slowly. Ancient and boring, just like everything else around here, from what she could see.

'Are you sure this is it?' said April's mother, rubbing irritably at the steamed-up windows. 'This looks more like Lincoln than London.'

For once April was in agreement with her mother. She glanced over at the older woman, so sophisticated and chic

7

with her designer wardrobe, buttery-blonde wavy hair and high cheekbones. *Where are my cheekbones?* she asked herself, miserably glancing at her mousy hair in the window's reflection. 'They'll come,' her mother always said, 'and anyway, you're pretty as you are.' Tell that to all the boys who had failed to ask her out.

They were crawling along the High Street and, pressing her nose against the condensation, April took in the fifties-style chemist, the dusty window of the jeweller's, the bent-backed pensioners – *are they all pensioners?* – fighting against the wind as they struggled home or wherever it was old people went on a Sunday night.

'It looks so ... dreary,' said April.

'Well, it won't always be raining,' said her dad, flashing her a reassuring smile in the rear-view mirror.

'Never mind, darling,' said April's mother as she flipped open a Chanel compact mirror and touched up her lip gloss. 'You'll see all your little friends again in the summer. Look at it this way – we're only a few Tube stops from Piccadilly Circus.'

Eleven, April thought miserably. Ever since her father had announced that the Dunne family was moving to Highgate in north London, she had been studying the escape routes. Of course April understood that when her dad lost his job as an investigative reporter on the *Scotsman* newspaper he would have to find another job, but why did they have to leave Edinburgh, why did they have to leave all her friends? She was English by birth, but having spent all her teen years in Edinburgh she felt no attachment to the south and had absolutely no affinity with this gloomy-looking place, that was for sure. What annoyed her the most was that she had just been about to start an A-level course at Leith College, a cool modern place with funky architecture, no uniform and loads of boys. *Loads* of boys: proper grown-up boys with cars, boys who didn't remember you as a gawky eleven-year-old with braces. But that was all gone now, wasn't it? She had tried her best to persuade them to let *her* stay, at least – with her best friend Fiona or one of

8

her parents' friends, even boarding school – but all her suggestions had been shot down as they insisted they couldn't move without her. So instead she had been forced to hang around at her old school until they were ready to move and now they were carting her off to some horrid posh place in a tiny suburb a million light years away from everyone she knew. And what was worse, they were plonking her in halfway through the term: could she stand out any more? April looked around with a start as her mother snapped her compact shut.

'We're here!' she trilled. Her mother – *Silvia*, as April liked to think of her, as that way she could pretend her mother wasn't her mother – had loved the fact that April's dad was a respected man in Edinburgh and she had enjoyed the snobby dinner-party circuit, but she had hated Edinburgh with its drab granite buildings and its unrelenting weather. She had lived in Belgravia and Covent Garden when she was growing up and used to joke that if she ventured further north than Hampstead she'd get a nosebleed. But much as she had detested being stuck in a provincial outpost, she hated William Dunne's loss of status more. She had been giving April's poor dad an incredibly hard time ever since he'd announced he was losing his old job and that he had been offered a new position on the local Hampstead paper. Even more of a hard time than usual; it wasn't like April could remember a time when her mother wasn't at Dad's throat about something. This time, however, it had been much worse. According to her mother, Dad's new job was a 'major step backwards' and 'completely beneath him'. If they were moving to London, Silvia thought he should be 'shooting for editor' on one of the prestigious broadsheets like the *Telegraph* or *Times*. 'Am I supposed to tell people you're reporting on the local garden fete?' she had heard her mother yell in one of her parents' frequent rows. April had hoped that her proximity to the centre of things would make her mother a little less spiky.

April had been gutted too when her dad had lost his job. He had the coolest job of any of her friends' parents, who all worked in IT or in banks. There had been perks as well:

9

free books and occasionally tickets for gigs at the Playhouse or press screenings for movies that had yet to come out; Dad's friends on the arts desk were always happy to pass them on to him. His name and photograph always accompanying his *Scotsman* stories meant that William Dunne was a somebody, and that stopped April from being a nobody.

Her dad swung the car around to the left and into a wide square with a sort of park in the middle, pulling up in front of a narrow house with a bright yellow door. To April, it looked as if the houses on either side were squeezing it upwards. *Bullies*, she thought.

'Well?' said her dad, when nobody moved. 'We've been in the car for most of the day – does no one want to go inside?'

They flung the car doors open and dashed up the stone path through the rain, the wind snatching at their hair and coats. They huddled together in the small porch while her father fiddled with the unfamiliar keys and then they all burst inside.

They were faced by a narrow corridor dominated by a long flight of stairs. It was dark, dusty and, frankly, creepy.

'Isn't this nice?' said her dad, forcing a smile and nudging April's arm. 'Home sweet home, eh?'

April's mother sniffed the air like a dog. 'Wait until I speak to Tilda,' she said, her mouth in a fixed angry line.

April's dad caught her eye and gave a playful wince, which momentarily lifted her spirits. Tilda was one of Silvia Dunne's closest friends, some sort of society player her mum had known since they shared a dorm at their posh girls' school back in the eighties. Tilda now worked for a prestigious estate agent and had offered the Dunnes a 'once-in-a-lifetime insider deal' on the house, swearing it was the best thing she had ever seen in the area. April hated Tilda and all of Silvia's friends with a passion – horrible stuck-up snobs, the lot of them – but she had revised her opinion when she had offered Silvia such a great deal on the house. Now, as they gingerly walked down the corridor, April wasn't so sure. Shadows crept into the rooms from every corner and there was a damp, slightly earthy smell. April flicked on the lights but they did little to push back the gloom. The living room was large with a high ceiling, but it still felt cramped and claustrophobic.

'Tilda did say she hadn't seen the property in a while,' said Silvia, unable to keep the disappointment from her voice. 'She's very busy.'

'Why don't you both go and unpack? The removal men put the boxes in the bedrooms,' said William, walking over to the large marble fireplace. He had been down earlier in the week to arrange the furniture and belongings. 'I'll get a fire going, make it all cosy while you two go and explore.'

April knew that her dad was just trying to see the positive side – as always – but this gloomy welcome had done nothing to alleviate her homesickness for her friends and her life back in Edinburgh. Sighing, she followed her mother through the dining room and into the large kitchen at the back of the house. At least here it was well lit: fluorescent light bounced off the marble worktops and the shiny red Aga stove. Silvia pulled open the large American-style fridge.

'I knew Tilda wouldn't let me down,' she said, reaching in and pulling out an expensive-looking bottle of wine. 'Right then, glasses ...' she muttered, opening cupboards impatiently.

'I'll just go and look around by myself, shall I?' said April, knowing that her mother wasn't listening. 'Maybe do some drugs, or go into the cellar and get chopped up by the mad axeman, okay?'

Silvia waved a vague hand. 'Yes, darling, that sounds nice.'

April didn't find any axemen, just a rather tired-looking Georgian terrace house with several dingy bedrooms and a lot of very creaky stairs. She had decided the small room at the top of the house would be her bedroom, partly because it had a view across the roof to the village and partly because it was the only place she could get a signal on her mobile. The room was full of cardboard boxes stuffed with her possessions, but at least someone – her father, when he had been down the previous weekend? – had made up the bed with white sheets and an unfamiliar duvet. She sat cross-legged on the bed and speed-dialled Fiona.

'Hi, this is Fee, you know what to do ...' said the sing-song message, followed by the beep. April was disappointed her best friend wasn't there to listen to her moan about her new home, but it still made her smile a little to hear her breathy, enthusiastic voice. Fiona Donald – 'a good, solid Scots name', she always liked to point out, while making gagging motions – had kept April sane since they had been allocated desks next to each at St Geoffrey's five years ago. 'Just imagine how wrong it could have gone if they hadn't seated us alphabetically,' Fee had said just before April left for Highgate. It was the only time April could remember feeling grateful to her parents. Without the quirk of fate that brought them together she might never have bonded with Fee over their love of low-quality pop music, and they might not have then shared everything from hair-dye disasters to doomed crushes ever since. April couldn't imagine life without her best friend, but now she was going to have to try to cope.

'Hey, babes,' said April into the voicemail, 'just arrived. It's raining and everyone is old. Yep, that just about sums it up. Call me when you get this, okay?'

She snapped her phone shut and lay back on the bed. She could already hear raised voices downstairs – big surprise. From up here she could only pick out odd phrases from her mother: 'Why didn't you accept it?' and then, 'He's only trying to help,' and from her father: 'Christ, Silvia, is it a crime to provide for my family?'

April knew exactly what that was all about. Tomorrow she was due to begin at the prestigious Ravenwood School on the far side of Highgate. They weren't even giving her a single day to unpack and acclimatise to her new environment. From the little April knew about the school it sounded like some sort of freak show, one half stuffed with maths geniuses and chess masters, the other half made up of some of the richest kids in London, all there because they had been tutored within an inch of their lives or their daddies had made some generous financial gift to the school. It sounded completely intimidating and the drive past it on the way to the house had done nothing to reassure her. A huge grey Gothic monstrosity on the edge of Hampstead Heath, it had obviously been an important stately home a couple of hundred years ago and looked like it was still haunted by the original owners. But it wasn't even the creepiness of the place that bothered April, it was the students. She could just picture the scene tomorrow: people being dropped off in Ferraris while she clumped up in her trainers. That was the big problem, of course, and the cause of the argument downstairs: Ravenwood wasn't cheap and, given their reduced circumstances, her parents would struggle with the fees. Her grandfather Thomas, Silvia's dad, who owned an impressive house in the backstreets of Covent Garden and had put Silvia through the best schools in the land, had offered to pay the fees, but William had refused point blank and her parents had been arguing about it ever since. So, since she was going, she assumed her dad had used his once-great name and maybe a few highly placed contacts to swing it. It wouldn't make her mother happy either way, given the irony of the situation: finally she was getting the opportunity to shop till she dropped, and just as suddenly couldn't afford it due to the sky-high school fees.

Sighing, April walked over to the window to look out at the village. The rain seemed to have stopped and the moon was now shining down on the wet roof tiles, although she could see that funny fox weathervane on top of the church still being jerked back and forth by the gusts.

'Chill out, Foxy,' she whispered.

To the left, she could see across the square and beyond that to the top of the High Street. *If the dark clouds lift*, thought April, *it might actually be quite pretty*. As she scanned the view, she saw movement in the little park – three figures walking slowly under the big trees, then perching on a bench. April squinted – definitely two boys and a girl. Her heart leapt: young people! They looked to be about her age, although she couldn't be sure from this distance. She snatched up her phone and ran downstairs.

April walked into the living room to find it transformed. Her dad had a glowing fire popping and spitting in the hearth and had lit a load of big church candles which were dotted all over the room. It actually did look as warm and inviting as he had promised. He was already ensconced in an armchair pulled up in front of the fire, papers and open books spread all around him, stabbing angrily away at his laptop. It was no surprise to find her dad hard at work only minutes after moving into the new house, and minutes after finishing a big fight with her mother. Nothing stopped her dad working. She couldn't remember a time when he wasn't bent over a book or a paper or barking questions into a phone. Actually, now she came to think of it, she couldn't remember ever seeing him sleep. If he wasn't working on some story about a corrupt government department or a drug company scandal for the paper, then he was beavering away on his books: heavy non-fiction books debunking conspiracy theories that sold almost no copies except to nut-jobs and university professors. From what April could tell, her dad's books involved highly technical scientific explanations for ghosts and UFOs and the abominable snowman. Something like that, anyway. April was more into chick lit.

'I'm nipping out,' she said, pulling on her favourite coat.

He looked up from his laptop. 'What's your hurry? You must have taken three steps at a time back there.'

'I've spotted signs of life in the village.' She smiled.

'If you're going out, can you post a letter for me?' he said, turning to the cracked leather briefcase next to his chair.

She watched him with grudging affection as he pulled out handfuls of paper, plonking them down in haphazard piles. She didn't like to think of her dad as handsome but she knew he was; all her friends' mums fancied him. No doubt his looks were what had attracted Silvia to him in the first place; April couldn't think of any other reason. Silvia was privileged, snobbish and superficial, whereas William was hard-working, cynical and academic. And under that dishevelled, disorganised surface, her father had a big heart. Anyone who had put up with Silvia for so long *had* to have hidden depths. And despite all April's annoyance at the upheaval of moving down here, she knew it was her dad who had suffered most in all this, being pushed out of a job he loved and forced to start again. Having a surly teenager and a disapproving wife in tow couldn't have helped much either.

'Thanks, Dad,' she said, as he handed her a creased envelope.

He frowned slightly, cocking his head. 'For the letter?'

April smiled. 'Yeah, for the letter.'

As she opened the front door and ran down the path to the gate, the wind whipped up and blew April's hair into her face. Pulling it back, she looked up – and that's when she saw him. A tall, dark-haired boy standing on the other side of the road. He was staring straight at her.

Wow. He's good-looking, she thought, with a mixture of excitement and nerves. Tall and slim in dark jeans and a navy pea coat, he looked as if he had just stepped out of an Abercrombie & Fitch advert. His hair was swept back off his forehead and she looked into his deep-set black eyes. Just for a moment, there was a flicker of something in his face: recognition, perhaps? Surprise? She stared back, mesmerised by his eyes, so dark and intense; so intense, in fact, that, after a moment, April had to look away.

Who was he? Was he one of the people she had seen on the bench earlier? And why was he staring at her?

'April?'

She turned around to see her mother standing in the doorway, arms crossed. Silvia had changed into white skinny jeans and a thick cream cashmere jumper that looked completely inappropriate for unpacking boxes. 'Where do you think you're going?'

April waved the envelope. 'I'm just going to post a letter for Dad.'

'Inside,' snapped Silvia impatiently. 'You've got a big day tomorrow.'

April glared at her mother. Why did she always have to interfere? She was only going for a walk, for heaven's sake.

'Mum ...' she complained.

'Now! I mean it,' said her mother, taking a few steps down the path.

April glanced back at the square. The boy was gone. The square was totally empty, as if no one had ever been there. She frowned; where had he vanished to so quickly? Reluctantly, April walked back up the path.

'What's the big deal?' she asked sulkily as she reached the door. 'Why can't I go out?'

Her mother looked over her shoulder at the spot where the boy had been standing, then up and down the street.

'I'll tell you why,' she said, pulling April inside. 'There's been a murder.'

Chapter Two

'Dad. What's this about a murder?'

April stuffed a piece of toast in her mouth as her father walked into the kitchen. It was 8.30 on a Monday morning and her mother was hovering by the door, jangling the car keys.

'Don't start him off,' said Silvia sarcastically, shooting a dirty look at her husband. 'We have to leave in about thirty seconds if I'm going to give you a lift to school.'

Yeah, like I'm going to rush for my first day at freak-school, thought April. Right now she would welcome the distraction of one of her father's stories, especially one about a grisly local murder. Last night, when Silvia had pulled her back into the house in full view of that totally fit boy, she had just muttered something about 'something on the news' and 'dangerous streets', then sent her upstairs to unpack. Then Fiona had phoned back with the latest gossip, which had put all thoughts of murder from her head. Apparently Fee had just seen Miranda Cooper, one of April's classmates at St Geoffrey's, at the cinema with Neil Stevenson, the boy April had been nursing a crush on for the past eighteen months. Neil was an Orlando Bloom lookalike whom April had slowly managed to befriend over the past year. He was sporty and cool, one of the popular clique at Marshgate Boys, and normally their paths would never have crossed, but as luck would have it, Neil's mum was one of Silvia's cronies. Consequently, whenever Silvia 'popped by' Neil's house to drop off something at the weekend or on the way to school, he and April would be forced into each other's company. 'Just go and chat to Neil for five minutes, darling,' she would say, waving a hand. 'Listen to a CD or something.' It had always grated on April that her mother clearly trusted her to go into some random boy's bedroom unsupervised; did she really think her daughter was that unattractive? Anyway, the upside was that after the initial awkwardness, she and Neil had bonded over their mothers' respective failings as parents and started to get to know each other. April hadn't exactly rated her chances with Neil, even after he invited her to his seventeenth birthday party in a pub on Princes Street, but a girl could hope, couldn't she? April had borrowed her mum's Gucci peasant dress, the only thing she could find in her wardrobe that didn't make her look about fifty, and had gone along with Fee and another friend. When they had bumped into Miranda on the street a few hundred metres away from the party, they had invited her along too. *Big mistake.*

'The murder in Dartmouth Park?' said William, draining his coffee. 'Thought you'd know all about that by now.'

'Why would I?'

'Well, the bloke who was murdered was in that band, Belarus.'

April's eyes widened. *'Alix Graves* was killed?'

Unlike half the girls in her class, April wasn't a mad Belarus fan. They were a bit too morose, the lyrics too dark. Half the tracks on the last album were just too *experimental* – or so one reviewer in *NME* had described them. But Alix Graves was sexy. She knew at least three girls who would have to phone the Samaritans when they heard he'd been found murdered in his London home. Fee for one – she had been known to kiss his picture before retiring for the night.

'Who's Alix Graves?' said Silvia, fastening the belt of her silk trenchcoat a little tighter.

'He's only one of the biggest rock stars in the country,' April gasped, incredulous. '"Moon Cry"? "Dark Angel"?' She looked at her mother's blank face with amazement. 'You've really never heard of him?'

Her father smiled. 'Your mother prefers Sting. Anyway,

Alix's house was in Dartmouth Park, which is a fair way from here, so you don't need to worry too much. The police are evidently still baffled by what happened and who might have done it, though. The latest thinking is some crazed fan but no one really knows.'

April pulled her phone out and speed-dialled Fiona as her mother gave a theatrical cough.

'April,' said Silvia impatiently, 'it's late. Do you want me to give you a lift or not?'

April shot her mother a withering look. Didn't she understand that this was earth-shattering news? Alix Graves had been murdered and, what was more, it had happened down the road! She had to talk to Fiona. She would be wearing a black veil around Edinburgh for the weekend at least.

'Off you go, love. We'll talk later,' said her father. 'I'll see what the guys at work know about it. But don't worry and don't let it ruin your first day at school, okay?'

'In the meantime I want you straight back here after school,' said Silvia briskly. 'I don't want you wandering around when there's some maniac on the loose.'

'And how am I supposed to make friends if I'm trapped in here?' said April, in her mind changing the words 'make friends' to 'meet boys'.

'Join the chess club or something,' replied Silvia absently.

'*You are kidding*?' asked April, looking pleadingly at her father.

'I'm afraid I'm with your mother on this one,' said William sympathetically. 'Just until we find out what's going on.'

April shook her head and grabbed her bag. 'Well, I think I'll walk to school – is that okay? You don't think I'll be murdered in broad daylight, do you?' she said sarcastically. She stalked to the front door, angry at her parents – how could they even consider grounding her at such a crucial time? – but also glad that walking would delay her arrival at her new school for those crucial last few minutes, because it was the last place on earth she wanted to be going. Right now she reckoned that being stalked by a killer would be less scary than Ravenwood School.

'God, Fee, it's like I'm a prisoner here,' she said. 'I seriously think they'd rather lock me in the cellar until I'm old enough to be married off than let me make a decision for myself.'

April had rung Fiona as soon as she was out of the house. Her parents would never understand what massive news Alix Graves' death was (although their generation never stopped banging on about John Lennon, so they should) and they certainly wouldn't get how hard it would hit someone like Fiona, who had posters and cuttings of Alix plastered on every available surface in her room.

'Yeah, it sucks you've been grounded.' Fiona sighed. 'But at least you're alive.'

'Oh, Fee, I'm sorry,' said April, wincing. 'I was so mad with them, I didn't think. How are you doing?'

'I'll be okay.' Fiona sniffed. 'I'm not sure it's actually sunk in just yet. Do you think I'll get away with wearing black today?'

April smiled to herself. She was right about her friend – she was genuinely shocked and upset, but she would also relish the opportunity for drama. The St Geoffrey's uniform was a horrible battleship grey with burgundy trim and was strictly enforced. Heaven help the girl who dared to turn up in a skirt above the knee – she risked the wrath of their formidable headmistress Miss Batty. April had once been on the receiving end after wearing shoes that were deemed 'inappropriately high' and she still shivered at the memory.

'Good luck with that,' said April. 'I can't see Miss Batty letting you wear black if your whole family had dropped down dead, let alone ...'

She tailed off as Fiona began to sob. 'Sorry, Fee, I didn't mean ...' April felt the miles between them stretching away into the distance. 'Oh, honey, I wish I was there to help you through this.'

'Well, if your dad can find out anything more about it, you know, *details*, I think that would help.'

'Sure, I'll ask him, but it is his first day at work.'

'No, no,' said Fiona, blowing her nose loudly. 'Quite right, the show must go on, that's what Alix would have wanted. Perhaps I can just wear a black hat to the school gates or something, some small gesture like that.'

'That would be better.'

'Anyway, that's enough about me,' said Fiona. 'It's your first day, you lucky thing.'

'Lucky? I'm dreading it. All those freaky brainboxes and rich kids, it's going to be a nightmare.'

'No uniform, all those new boys, it's going to be amazing!' enthused Fiona, recovering herself. 'Just imagine, loads of boys actually sitting next to you in class, talking to you in the corridor, holding doors open for you – it'll be heaven.'

April smiled. It was amazing what five years of private education in an all-girls school could do for your imagination. Since her place at Ravenwood had been confirmed, Fiona had blown the school up into some sort of romantic Jane Austin-era fantasy where elegant gentlemen cast furtive but earnest glances at you from beneath their top hats.

'I'm not sure it's going to be quite that exciting, Fee.'

'Of course it is,' insisted Fiona. 'There will be boys with *titles* there – real-life lords.'

'I don't think ...'

But Fiona was still talking. 'And I bet they all drive Range Rovers and call their mums and dads "mater and pater". God, you must call me as soon as you get out of there, I need to hear everything!'

April didn't think it was going to be exciting at all, in fact she was dreading setting foot inside the gates. Even worse, all Fiona's talk of boys had immediately made her think of Neil. Her stomach turned over. The last thing she wanted to do was meet new boys who would waltz off with the first flirty blonde who fluttered her eyelashes in their direction.

Fiona was clearly on April's wavelength.

nyway, you don't have to worry about Neil—' she began.

'Neil?' said April quickly. 'What about Neil?'

'You'll never believe this, but—*sskkizzzzopp*—aid Miranda wa—*kkzzzunnngg*—'

Dammit – her phone was breaking up! 'Fee? What? Who said what about Miranda?'

Silence. April looked down at the screen of her phone. One bar! And she was only about two miles out of central London – how did that work?

'Hello? Can you hear me? Fee?'

'Listen, you're cracking up a bit,' said Fiona. 'Give me a call at—'

Her last words were cut off. *Damn, damn, damn.* April looked down at her phone, then up at the street and sighed. 'Cracking up is right,' she muttered and set off down the hill.

Walking towards the Heath in the bright October morning sunlight, April actually found it hard to feel too gloomy. Red and golden leaves peppered the pavement under gracefully sagging autumnal trees and she had to grudgingly admit that the whole village looked rather lovely; the tall stone houses with their clipped gardens, the view of London in the distance all covered in a blanket of rust and red. They had never really had autumn in Scotland. In fact she and Fiona often joked how Edinburgh was under a weird spell of permanent winter. Sure, they had a few weeks of weak sunlight in high summer, but then it was straight back to bullet-hard rain being blown directly into your face. She looked down at her coat; it was stylish, but it was still heavy wool. April's wardrobe consisted almost entirely of things made of wool; it was the only way to keep warm in Scotland. Secretly she actually enjoyed wrapping up in scarves, hats and thick jumpers as she didn't particularly want anyone staring at her body, which she always felt was too lanky and boyish, a world away from Miranda Cooper's sexy Kelly Brook curves. And April certainly didn't want anyone looking at her today of all days. Even so, she had been up especially early that morning to choose an outfit, excited and nervous about her first day at a school without a uniform. She had discussed it with Fee for weeks, but it was impossible to second-guess what would be considered the 'right look' at Ravenwood, despite the fact that the school had sent through a forbidding-looking list of rules, including a dress code that specified height of shoes, length of skirts and so on. Even so it was liberating – not to say terrifying – to be able to choose 'real clothes' to wear to school. She had carefully picked out something stylish but still neutral and safe; the navy skirt and cream cowl-neck jumper hardly marked her out as a fashion pioneer. It was more like camouflage; her plan was to sink into the background as much as possible ... but until she got there she had no idea if this outfit would help her blend in or make her stand out.

She walked down Swain's Lane, a steep road that followed the contour of the hill on which Highgate was built. It was clearly a very old road, with ancient stone walls on one side and old iron railings on the other, through which she could glimpse Highgate Cemetery. When April had researched the area – hoping, she supposed, to find a loophole that would let her stay in Scotland – she had been intrigued to discover the range of people spending eternity in the graveyard. Famous figures like Karl Marx rubbed shoulders with Radclyffe Hall, little-known author of a book called *The Well of Loneliness*. April looked around. *Loneliness. That's about right*, she thought, then almost jumped backwards as something broke cover from the undergrowth and sprinted across the road. Her hand flew to her mouth, her heart pounding as she tried not to cry out.

'A fox,' she gasped, slightly embarrassed by her reaction. 'Only a fox.'

She knew that foxes were a common sight in many cities, of course, but she'd never seen one in Edinburgh's less forgiving granite landscape.

'Stupid,' she whispered, but she still looked nervously over her shoulder and increased her pace a little.

Ravenwood was impressive in the light of day. The sun wasn't quite out, but the rain had made the slate roof glisten and the puddles in the quad in front of the grand pillared entrance reflected the brightness. As she turned into the wide gates she had to dodge around the line of cars stopping in front of the school.

April had to stifle an incredulous laugh. It looked like the Oscars – lines of limousines and black prestige vehicles dropping their A-list cargo onto an imaginary red carpet before purring away. In her direct line of vision she could see two grey Porsche Cayennes, three Bentleys and six black 4x4s of assorted sizes, all with tinted windows, all stopping briefly on Ravenwood's wide gravel drive. April offered a little prayer of thanks that she had avoided the humiliation of letting her mother drop her off in their little hatchback. She could only see the backs of the students getting out of the cars but she recognised the red soles of the strictly non-regulation Christian Louboutain shoes, not to mention the assortment of Louis Vuitton and Mulberry totes masquerading as school bags. *God, this is going to be hell*, she thought. Taking a deep breath, April joined the stream of pupils walking into school, assuming they knew where they were going. There were a few curious glances from younger pupils, but she guessed that, to them, a senior was a senior. She pulled a letter from her bag that said she had to register in room thirty-six at 9 a.m., wherever room thirty-six was. There was nothing for it – she'd have to ask. She tapped a girl walking past her on the shoulder. April pulled her hand back at the touch of the coat. Fur – *real* fur. The girl spun around and thick blonde hair bounced over her shoulders. Her face was exquisite, like a Russian czarina's – wide-spaced pale blue eyes, pale skin like marble and a cool, haughty expression that matched her icy beauty perfectly. April opened her mouth to speak but no words came out; the girl stopped and gave April a curious look, as if she wasn't entirely sure what she was seeing. Then she smoothed the arm of her silky-haired black coat and turned away, having clearly dismissed her from her thoughts.

April heard giggling behind her.

'Heaven help she who touches the black rabbit.'

She spun round to see a short girl with a dark bob and a mischievous grin.

'You look lost.'

'I am.' April nodded, blushing. She watched the fur-coat-wearing student disappear through double doors at the end of the corridor. 'Was that coat really black rabbit?' she asked in a hushed voice.

'Disgusting, isn't it?' said the girl. 'It was white mink last winter. She's the only girl allowed to wear fur to school, for some reason. Then again, Davina's father is practically the richest man in London so I guess normal rules don't apply. I'm Caro Jackson, by the way. Who are you?'

'April. April Dunne.'

She was distracted briefly by a gorgeous Indian boy walking into school, his suit so neatly pressed it looked as if it had sharp edges.

'What are you in for?'

April turned back to Caro. 'In for?'

'Your gift.' Caro grinned. 'What got you locked up here? You know: maths, physics, telekinesis – what's your *speciality*? You know Ravenwood caters specifically for the academically gifted.'

Her last word was dripping with sarcasm. April examined Caro again; she was the only person she'd seen who deviated from the *model student* of either sort, neither the type who looked like they digested algebra over breakfast nor strutted the catwalk over the school holidays. April noticed that Caro's jumper was a little bobbly and that she had black nail polish – something April knew was strictly forbidden in the school rules.

'Nothing special about me, sorry, but I'm joining the Lower Sixth. I think my dad pulled a few strings to get me in here and, I don't know, they must have liked something about me as my GCSE results didn't exactly mark me out as gifted.' She shrugged. She had been quite pleased with two A stars, four As and three B grades, but knew they'd be laughed at by some of the brainboxes here. 'Are you in the sixth form too?'

Caro nodded, then took an apple out of her bag and bit into it. 'Miss Holden's my form teacher.'

'Great! Me too,' said April, feeling a sense of relief. 'I've got to find her in room thirty-six – could you tell me where it is?'

'I know where thirty-six is,' said Caro casually. 'I've been here since I was thirteen. Come on. We need to go through the refectory.'

April obediently followed Caro down a corridor. A distant noise became louder and louder until Caro swung open a pair of double doors that led into a glass-roofed atrium. It was an impressively high open space, but when crowded with pupils laughing, yelling and calling out to each other, the acoustics were deafening. April tried to take it all in: a bank of drinks machines stood along one mahogany-panelled wall; along another was a long antique table on which pairs of pupils were playing backgammon. Gaggles of beautiful people lounged on the black leather sofas while younger pupils scurried through as if they had no business being there.

'I can't believe people are playing backgammon before school,' whispered April.

'So you've spotted the geeks.' Caro smiled, nodding towards them. 'Those are the eggheads, mostly pure maths, some quantum theorists. Don't try to talk to them unless you know pi to twenty decimal points. A lot of international students, for some reason – in fact you'll find Ravenwood is very multi-cultural. North London society is very rich, present company excepted.'

April frowned. 'What do you mean?'

'Me. I'm the odd one out, as one of the scholarship kids here. Mum's a hairdresser, Dad's a window-cleaner, which makes me like a Martian or something.'

April nodded and smiled. She had only just met this girl, but it was nice being included in something, even if it was as an outsider. Now Caro indicated a group by the vending machine gathered around a handsome boy with floppy blond hair. They were all highly groomed and slightly regal-looking.

'Who are they?'

'Those are the rugby boys. Most of them are planning to read law or something equally serious at uni and they spend all their time studying philosophy and international affairs with a view to their inevitable political careers.' Caro shot April a wink. 'It goes without saying, don't trust them.' She followed April's gaze and gave a wry smile. 'And before you ask, the pretty boy with the blond hair is Benjamin Osbourne. You should trust him the least.'

Just then, the boy next to Benjamin turned around and looked straight at April. A lazy grin spread slowly across his face and he nodded at her. April almost gasped out loud. It was the dark-haired boy she had seen in the square the night before. She could feel her heart start beating faster.

'Uh-oh,' said Caro, taking April by the arm and turning her around. 'Come away.'

'What do you mean?'

'Gabriel Swift. You're wasting your time with him,' said Caro. 'He's one of those unattainable, too-good-for-us-regular-humans types. I think he must be dating older girls, because I've never seen him with anyone here.'

April glanced back and was disappointed to see that the boy was no longer looking at her.

'And who are they in the middle?' asked April, nodding towards the sofas in the centre of the room. Five or six drop-dead-beautiful girls were draped across them, pristine in their state-of-the-art designer wear.

'We call them "the Faces",' said Caro with a grim smile. 'The "popular" girls. That's "Face" as in "two-faced". Basically Ravenwood is split in two – either you're academically brilliant or you're from money. Those girls are the richest of the rich and they're the scariest clique at Ravenwood. Although I'm guessing every school has something similar, right?'

April nodded. Even at St Geoffrey's there had been a clique of snooty, pretty girls who dressed in the latest fashions and looked down on everyone else, casually spreading rumours and gossip about people for their own amusement. In Edinburgh, where such posturing had seemed ludicrous, April and Fee had

27

been able to laugh at their pretentions, but the Ravenwood girls looked frightening and other-worldly with their beauty and casual confidence.

'The net worth of those kids on the sofas is about forty billion quid,' said Caro. 'Family money, of course, but still.'

'There's the rabbit-coat girl,' said April, recognising the mane of golden hair. As she watched, the tall blond boy moved over and sat next to her. 'Wow. Is that her boyfriend? Lucky cow.'

'Brother.' Caro smiled. 'Davina and Benjamin Osbourne. Their father Nicholas is one of those mega-rich Eastern Europeans, made a fortune in chemicals, all very shady. Funnily enough, though, Davina doesn't tend to date other rich boys. She's more into brains. See that guy to her left?'

April nodded. He was cute but not stunning and he was clearly ill at ease in such company.

'That's Jonathon, her latest geek-du-jour. I think she goes for the smart boys to make up for her own complete airheadedness.'

April tried to absorb this information while she sized up her new companion. Caro didn't fit into this picture, with her wry outlook, always watching, always searching faces. It made April feel a little better; she wasn't the only outsider at Ravenwood.

'So what's your speciality, Caro?'

'Oh, chemistry, biology, physics, all with a creative twist. The rather boring ambition is to write books about science, like Stephen Hawking but without the funny voice.' She grinned.

'Oh really? My dad is a writer,' said April. 'He used to work for the *Scotsman*.'

Caro looked at her wide-eyed. 'Your dad isn't *William Dunne*, is he?'

April nodded.

'Oh my God, I love him,' said Caro enthusiastically. 'I think I've read everything he's ever written. That thing he did on Area Fifty-One was awesome. His books are so definitive, so well argued. He mixes pop culture with science like no one else I've ever read.'

April smiled politely, but inside she was cringing. Trust her to talk to the one girl in the school who had heard of her father. Caro put her hand on April's arm.

'Sorry,' she said sheepishly. 'I'm gushing, aren't I? It's just I wish I had any sort of role model in my own family. The best we've managed is Uncle David who owns a dry cleaners.'

Then the bell rang and everyone began to move. April and her new friend began to walk out of the refectory, joining the crush.

'Actually, I think I might have a story for your dad, if you want to meet me after school?'

'Okay,' said April warily. 'What's it about?'

'This place,' said Caro, just a hint of a smile on her face. 'I think it's a giant conspiracy to take over the world.'

Chapter Three

Mr Sheldon was a tall man, probably somewhere in his forties, although his white hair made him look much older. In fact, along with his grey three-piece suit and heavy silver-framed glasses, he looked exactly as April had always imagined a distinguished college professor would look. The fact that he was also the head teacher at Ravenwood only added to his air of importance. Headmasters didn't normally take classes, of course, but April was quickly learning that Ravenwood was some way from the usual definition of 'normal'. Mr Sheldon strode up and down in front of the philosophy class, telling stories of long-dead Greeks and Germans that should have been deadly dull, but he somehow made them fascinating; it was like watching a particularly good documentary on TV. But still ... something wasn't quite right, April thought, as she sat at the back maintaining her 'head down, stay off the radar' policy. There was something about Mr Sheldon, something in the picture that didn't quite fit. He put her on edge, for some reason. Maybe it was just that she wasn't used to actually listening to a teacher. Not just hearing their words and picking a few relevant sound bites out of the drone, but really *listening* to what they were saying, then really thinking about it. It was certainly a new experience for April, especially as there were plenty of distractions. The gorgeous blond boy, Benjamin, was sitting three rows in front of her and kept turning to whisper to his friend. Every time he did, she could see his slightly wicked smile and his cheekbones and his ... Hmm, now what had she been saying about concentrating?

'So how many of you have seen *Star Trek*?' said Mr Sheldon

in his deep, honeyed voice. A few arms tentatively raised – *not as many as you'd think, given the geek factor in this school*, thought April. Mr Sheldon was obviously thinking the same thing as he smiled. 'I suspect a few of are hiding your light under a bushel,' he said, eliciting some guilty laughs.

'All right, so how many of you have seen *Back to the Future?*'

A lot more hands were raised, mostly by eager pupils in the front two rows.

'So what's the main idea behind it?'

A boy in the very front row put up a hand. April realised it was Jonathon, Davina's boyfriend.

'Time travel,' said Jonathon confidently. 'Marty McFly travels through time – past, present and future – in the mad professor's car, which is a sort of time machine, fixing various problems in order to save his family.'

There was another round of giggles, and Mr Sheldon nodded.

'Very good, Jonathon. That sort of story is generally described as science fiction, but in reality, there's very little science involved. We don't have the technology create a "flux capacitor". Consequently, it's more accurate to say that *Back to the Future* is actually philosophical fiction. When Marty changes the past, it changes events in the future.'

April was glad to see other people around her frowning too.

'Which leads us to the central problem, when you're writing about time travel,' continued Mr Sheldon. 'Can anyone tell me what it's called? Benjamin?'

Benjamin didn't even look up. 'The Grandfather Paradox,' he said in an offhand tone, as if it was obvious.

'Excellent. The Grandfather Paradox: what if you built your own time machine, zipped back seventy or eighty years and killed your grandfather when he was a boy? If Granddad was dead and never met Grandma, that means one of your parents would never have existed and therefore you wouldn't be around to build that time machine.'

Mr Sheldon looked at the furrowed brows of the class and laughed. 'Don't worry, I'm not testing you on your movie knowledge, I'm simply using it as an example of philosophy in action for the benefit of our newer class members.'

Oh God, thought April, *don't point me out, please.*

'Those of us who have been studying this for some time know that the beauty of philosophy is that for any given phenomenon – time travel, the existence of God, free will – you can come up with several hypotheses that will seem to explain it just as well as the accepted explanation. As we've discussed before, there are no right answers in philosophy. Although please note that doesn't mean you will automatically get an A for turning up to your exam.'

Everyone laughed.

'Okay, let's consider another age-old conundrum: the chicken and the egg.'

He lifted one hand and pointed to the back of the class. April's heart jumped as she thought she was going to be asked to speak, but the teacher was pointing to the plump girl with rosy cheeks sitting next to her.

'Emily. Which came first, the chicken or the egg?'

'The egg,' answered the girl confidently.

Mr Sheldon nodded. 'Very well. Why?'

'Well, in nature DNA can only be modified in the womb, or in this case the egg. So as evolution is a series of genetic mutations, it must have happened before the chicken was born, which means, in the egg.'

Mr Sheldon clapped his hands. 'Splendid. A perfect scientific answer. But this is a philosophy class, so what's the problem with this theorem?'

He paused and let his eyes sweep around the room. 'How about you, Miss Dunne?'

With a lurch, April realised he was looking straight at her. How did he know she wasn't paying attention?

'April, can you tell us what's wrong with Emily's rather straightforward, by-the-book answer?'

She glanced to her side and saw that all of the rosiness

had drained from Emily's cheeks and she was now glaring at April.

'Wrong?' stuttered April.

'It does seem to address all the possibilities, doesn't it?' said Mr Sheldon, stroking his chin. 'Evolution, mutations – it all sounds very straightforward, I suppose.' Mr Sheldon shook his head slightly and turned back to his eager students at the front. 'Perhaps someone else can—'

'Evolution,' blurted April.

'I'm sorry?'

'Well, uh, Emily's explanation assumes that evolution is correct.'

Mr Sheldon chuckled. 'It seems we have a true Christian in our midst, ladies and gentlemen,' he said, raising more laughter. 'No, no,' said Mr Sheldon, raising his hand to silence the jeers. 'Enough. She is quite correct. Emily's scientific explanation assumes far too much. And April is at least thinking for herself.'

April felt herself blush.

'Of course, before we give her a round of applause, we should consider how *narrow* an answer hers is,' continued Mr Sheldon. April felt the blush increase as she realised that Benjamin Osbourne had turned to look at her. He turned back to his friend and whispered something and they both laughed.

'Miss Dunne may be thinking for herself,' said Mr Sheldon, 'but she's still thinking along conventional lines. Just because you have seen one chicken emerge from an egg, can you assume that the same will be true for the millions of eggs produced every year? Is that logical? Does that make sense? If you see a chair with four legs, does that mean all chairs have four legs? No. The reality is that *in absolute terms*, we know almost nothing about eggs, where they come from, what they are or whether they are related to chickens. This is what philosophy is all about: turning lazy thinking on its head and questioning everything you see, everything you think you know.'

April was now glaring at Mr Sheldon, but the teacher had moved on.

'Consider this: what do you really know about the people around you? What do you know about your mother, father, brothers and sisters? Does your brother take heroin? Is your sister a virgin?'

There were a few nervous titters, but Mr Sheldon wasn't smiling.

'What about the person beside you?'

April wasn't inclined to look at the girl next to her; even without turning her head she could tell Emily was glowering at her. Instead she looked the other way – and her breath caught in her throat. Gabriel Swift was staring directly at her from the end of the row, his eyes narrowed. April looked away quickly, her blush now approaching pillar-box red.

'What do you really know about your classmates?' Mr Sheldon was saying. 'Just because they come to your school, sit next to you every day, you assume they are benign. Perhaps they are. Perhaps they're not. Perhaps they're planning on blowing up this class. Perhaps they're planning something worse.'

There was more strained laughter. April glanced up at Gabriel again, but he had sat back in his chair and another pupil was blocking her view.

'But that's what I want you to consider in this class, in this *school*,' continued Mr Sheldon. 'This is Ravenwood, people. Here we expect you to look at things from a different angle. Probe, think, question, investigate. The world is much more interesting that way, I promise you.'

The bell rang and the students began to scrabble their books into bags. Mr Sheldon clapped his hands and opened up a cardboard box on his desk.

'Okay, class, before you disappear, your homework is to read this book,' he said, waving a thick volume in the air. He began to hand them out as the students shuffled past. There was some groaning as they looked at the heavy tome.

'Don't worry, this is the author's complete works, not a single novel. Read as many as you wish, but I only require you to read the short story "Random Quest". It's easy to read and has everything you could want: war, romance and time travel. Imagine Brad and Angelina in the lead roles if it helps. We'll discuss it next lesson.'

As April filed past the teacher, he handed her the thick book. 'Good thinking there, April,' he said in a low voice, 'I'm pleased.'

Before April could react, Mr Sheldon had turned away to shout at two girls poring over a magazine.

'Now this is what I'm talking about,' said Mr Sheldon, snatching the offending mag and dropping it into the waste-paper basket next to his desk. 'Celebrity culture has played a confidence trick on you, people. God frowns on the worship of graven images, ladies, haven't you heard? Think for your-selves!'

'But it's got the last interview with Alix Graves in it,' complained the taller of the girls.

'Alix Graves is dead, Lucy,' said Mr Sheldon. 'I'm sure you'll have found someone else to obsess over by next week.'

April looked up, surprised both by the insensitivity and the fact that a teacher would even have heard of Alix Graves. As she did, Gabriel barged past her, sending her spinning, and she dropped her books with a clatter. As she bent to scoop them up, she heard giggles and felt all eyes on her. *Great, just what I need*, she thought. *So much for staying under the radar.*

'Are you all right?'

She looked up into Benjamin Osbourne's blue eyes. He bent to help her up, his face concerned. *God, he's good-looking*, thought April.

'Yes, yes, fine,' she muttered as she quickly gathered her belongings and moved into the corridor. She glanced back and saw that Benjamin was still watching her, a smile playing around his perfect mouth.

'You're sure you're okay?'

April nodded and almost ran down the corridor. But she wasn't fine, far from it. She had been humiliated and laughed at, she'd felt out of her depth and ... well, Benjamin must think she was a clumsy, stupid new girl with a bright red face.

But that wasn't the worst of it. No, the thing that had upset her most was that strange boy, Gabriel, barging into her. She couldn't swear to it, but she was fairly sure he had whispered something to her as he pushed past. And it had sounded very much like, 'Get out.'

Chapter Four

April was lost. After Mr Sheldon's philosophy class, she had fled. She needed to get out, find somewhere away from the prying eyes of her classmates. All she had wanted was to get through the day without making a spectacle of herself, but no – she couldn't even manage that. *What the hell's wrong with me? Why can't I ever avoid making an ass of myself – especially when boys are watching?* She sat down on a bench and took a deep breath. Now her embarrassment was fading a little, April began to get annoyed. Why did everyone here have to be so nasty? Mr Sheldon had known it was her first day, so why did he feel the need to single her out and then ridicule her answer in front of the class? That Emily could take a running jump, too. Benjamin had at least tried to help her, but what was that boy Gabriel doing barging into her? She'd only laid eyes on him a couple of times; what had she ever done to provoke him?

'I hate this school,' she whispered. She looked down at the book Mr Sheldon had handed out. A John Wyndham omnibus. Never heard of him. She turned to the contents page and her heart sank. The first story was *Day of the Triffids*: she had definitely heard of that one, something to do with giant man-eating plants, if memory served. April loathed science fiction with a passion, all those stupid aliens and lasers and stuff. And those nerdy boys who were into it tended to be weird and a bit, well, hygienically challenged. She ran her finger down the other titles: *The Midwich Cuckoos*, *Chocky*, *The Kraken Wakes* ... Opening the book at random, she read the first two lines of *The Midwich Cuckoos*. *Wow. Dull*, she thought. No, make that dull *and* old-fashioned, full of dusty language and polite ideas: everything seemed to be 'agreeable', 'curious' and 'queer', although April did manage to smile when she discovered that the hero was called Richard Gayford. She shook her head. Even more than sci-fi, April hated it when teachers tried to be trendy but missed the mark by about three decades. Sighing and deciding she would worry about it later, she shoved the book in her bag and headed back the way she'd come, certain that her class must all have gone by now. She took the staircase down to the main hall and asked a younger girl for directions to the front entrance, the only way out of the building she knew of. The girl was polite and helpful, giving her detailed directions which April immediately forgot. In hindsight she should have known she was having her leg pulled, especially when the first instruction had led her into a service corridor, but April had a stubborn streak she assumed she'd inherited from her father and ploughed on despite her misgivings. Now she had lost all sense of direction. She knew she was on a lower floor, but beyond that she was hopelessly confused. Annoyed with herself, she pushed her way through a door marked 'exit' – and walked straight into somebody.

'Hey! Watch out!' said an angry voice, as April became aware of eyes on her. There were two stunning girls lounging against railings. A third, with whom she had collided, had almost dropped a bottle she'd been drinking from and was wiping her mouth.

'Don't you look where you're going?' she demanded.

'Sorry,' muttered April, trying to skirt around her and get up the steps. *Drinking alcohol in school?* She knew she was in trouble; they wouldn't take kindly to being caught, even if she wasn't a teacher. April had almost made it past them when one of the girls stepped out in front of her. With a sinking feeling, April realised it was the beautiful girl with the rabbit-fur coat she had noticed before school. Davina, sister to the gorgeous Benjamin.

'So you're the new girl,' she said, her blue eyes running

over April like a scanner. April couldn't help but feel a little uncomfortable being observed so closely.

'I suppose so,' said April lamely. She glanced at the other girls and could see they were waiting for Davina's lead. After a pause that felt like an eternity to April, the girl smiled and held out a slender hand.

'I'm Davina,' she said simply. 'This is Layla and Chessy,' she said, pointing to her two friends.

'I'm April,' she said.

'I know,' said Davina. She stared at April for a moment, then beckoned her up the steps. 'Come on, I bet no one's shown you around here, have they?'

'Uh, no, no they haven't,' stammered April as she followed. The other girls fell into step behind them.

'Don't worry, we'll look after you – won't we, ladies?' She smiled. 'So I hear you're from Edinburgh. I just love Edinburgh, it's so romantic. My mother is involved with the Festival, so I fly up most years. Don't you just adore the Scotsman?'

'My dad used to work for them. He's a writer.'

Davina shot her a confused look, then laughed. 'No, silly, I mean the Scotsman Hotel. They have the best spa in the city.' She stretched out her thin fingers. She had a huge diamond ring on her index finger and April didn't doubt it was real. 'I could so do with a manicure right now.' She sighed and linked her arm through April's in an unsettling gesture of intimacy. 'Mmm ... what's that heavenly perfume?' she asked.

'Um, just soap, I think,' stuttered April and Davina laughed a tinkling laugh.

'You're so funny,' she said as they turned a corner and found themselves walking parallel to the front of the school, passing in front of the gymnasium.

'So tell me, April,' Davina said in a conspiratorial whisper. 'Are you single?'

April giggled nervously.

'We'll take that as a yes,' said Layla from behind them.

'We must see what we can do about that,' said Davina coolly. She stopped and turned towards April, her eyes narrowing as if she were sizing her up. Suddenly April felt horribly self-conscious, knowing she looked dowdy and fat next to this sleeker, better groomed specimen.

'Well, I think we can certainly make a few adjustments that will help,' said Davina, touching the collar of April's coat, then pulling her hand away as if it was unclean. 'I've got a beautiful Chloé dress you'd look amazing in and if we gave you smokier eyes ...' Seeing April's expression, she smiled sweetly and giggled. 'Sorry, April, I'm doing it again, aren't I?'

'What?'

'Oh, I'm always doing this, getting carried away. Here we are, we've only just met and I'm already giving you a makeover. When I decide I like someone, I just jump right in and ... silly, isn't it?'

'No, no, it's nice,' said April quickly, nervously pulling her coat around her. 'Honestly, it's fine.'

Davina beamed and squeezed April's hand. 'I'm glad,' she said. 'Listen, do you want to come over to my ...'

But suddenly April wasn't listening. Her gaze had been drawn over Davina's shoulder. It was Gabriel. He was walking fast, his face fixed in a scowl, and he had turned the collar of his jacket up against the cold.

'What's wrong?' Davina asked.

'Nothing,' replied April. 'Just that boy. I saw him last night. I think he lives near me.'

'Gabriel?' Davina rolled her eyes. 'Don't even think about it. I mean, he's like my brother's best friend and everything, but he's so *moody*,' she said as they watched his hunched back disappear through the gates and across the road. 'Rumour has it he's not that interested.'

April frowned. 'What do you mean?' She heard Layla and Chessy giggle.

'Sex, darling, sex,' said Layla. 'Don't they have that in Scotland?'

They all turned as they heard a cough behind them. Caro was standing there, swinging her bag back and forth.

'Not interrupting anything, am I?' she said tonelessly.

April noticed an unmistakable look of dislike pass between Layla and Caro. She was reminded of two cats meeting on a garden path. They didn't actually hiss at each other, but the sentiment was the same.

'Caro,' said Layla coldly, then turned to April. 'I'll probably see you tomorrow. I think we've got English together.'

Davina pulled a beeping mobile out of her pocket. 'My driver is here. I'm off too. Chess – you coming?'

'Made some new friends?' Caro said sarcastically to April once Davina and her posse had left.

'No. Yes, well, I just met her. I was lost, you see ...'

Caro started striding away and April had to trot to keep up with her.

'Sorry, Caro, is there a problem?' she asked.

'Hey, it's no business of mine who you choose to hang out with,' she said, not looking up.

'I'm hardly hanging out with them. I just bumped into Davina and she collared me.'

Caro stopped walking and turned to April. 'Aren't you the lucky one?'

'What's your problem?' asked April, confused. She was beginning to think that everyone at Ravenwood was a bit unhinged.

Caro looked angry. 'They're witches,' she said. 'They'll suck you in, turn you around and then ... Oh, never mind!' She stalked off again.

'Caro! Please!' cried April, grabbing her arm. 'Just tell me.'

Caro looked at April, her green eyes probing April's. Slowly, her intense expression softened and she let out a deep breath.

'Look, I'm sorry,' she said, shrugging. 'It's not you, it's her.'

'I get that,' said April with a slight smile. 'So what's the problem between you two?'

Caro looked as if she was about to say something, then shook her head. 'Those girls are evil. Pure, black-hearted, evil witches.'

April blinked at Caro for a second, then burst out laughing. After a second, Caro joined in.

'Sorry.' She grinned. 'I get a little carried away when it comes to the Faces. Okay, maybe they're not actually the spawn of Satan, but seriously, watch out for them.'

'I will.' April smiled. She paused for a moment, then said, 'Caro, can I ask you something?'

'Sure, what?'

'Have you read *The Da Vinci Code*?'

'I have – why?'

'And do you watch *24*? *Prison Break*?'

They both burst out laughing again.

'Okay, so I like a conspiracy,' said Caro. 'But that doesn't mean they're not out to get me.'

As they left the school grounds and slowly walked back up to the village, Caro explained her hatred of the Faces. She and Davina's sidekick Layla had once been best friends, hanging out together, obsessing over boys, sleepovers, all the teen clichés. Then Davina had arrived, and taken over. She had instantly become the centre of attention and Layla fell under Davina's glamorous spell. Layla was invited to join the Osbournes on a break in their summer home by the Black Sea. When she came back, she was transformed: slimmer, super-groomed and equipped with an immaculate wardrobe.

'Which was cool, but she'd changed in other ways as well,' said Caro, shaking her head. 'She used to have a wicked sense of humour. Now she's ultra serious, terribly upright. She just wasn't ... well, she was a different person. A clone. Seriously, April, stay away or they'll turn you into one of them.'

'Thanks for the warning, but they honestly don't seem so bad,' said April carefully. 'I mean, okay, they're a bit catty and look down on everyone, and I don't approve of Davina's fur coat but—'

'Okay, let's just leave it,' said Caro sulkily.

April's heart sank. She really hadn't meant to upset Caro – after all, this was the one girl who seemed to want to be her friend and who had been kind enough to help her through her first day, and yet here she was contradicting her about people she obviously knew nothing about.

'No, I'm sorry,' said April quickly. 'I clearly don't know what I'm talking about, I've been here all of five minutes. Ignore me, okay?'

Caro shrugged. 'Okay.'

'We can go to my house if you want,' said April, eager to change the subject.

'Will your dad be there?'

'Doubt it. It's his first day at work. He'll probably be late.'

They walked a little way further. April couldn't stand the silence.

'So what's your conspiracy theory?'

Caro just carried on walking. April puffed out her cheeks. She'd tried, but it seemed her new friend was a whack-job. Finally Caro stopped dead on the pavement and spun around.

'I haven't quite nailed it, but there's something going on at school. Something bad. I know you probably don't want to hear all this on your first day but I'd feel bad if I didn't tell you and then something happened to you.'

'I don't understand.'

'Well, for a start, the school's incredibly private. No one knows who's behind it. It's some sort of educational trust set up about ten years ago, but beyond Hawk there seems to be no hierarchy or management.'

'Hawk?'

Caro smiled. 'The headmaster, Mr Sheldon. It's his nick-name. You know, the way he looks at you as if he's deciding whether to swoop down and eat you?'

'Oh, I get it. But how do you know? About the manage-ment, I mean.'

'I did a little digging. Well, make that a lot of digging, but I can't find any information on how the school is funded. And no one seems too bothered by that.'

'That's not exactly evidence of a cover-up though, is it?'

'I know I sound like a mad conspiracy nut, but I'm convinced of it. I mean, have you seen the staff? The teachers may look like the usual losers with patches on their elbows, but let me tell you, most of them are geniuses. Pick any one and Google them, they've all come from Oxbridge or Ivy League professorships, they're the best in their fields. And they have to be; they're about the only ones who can keep up with the kids. I asked a few of the teachers why they're here and they made a joke along the lines of "they made me an offer I couldn't refuse". Obviously private schools have a lot of money, but we're talking a serious wedge here – and that's before you start getting into the NASA-standard computer and science equipment they have in the basement.'

April thought it through. 'But that doesn't mean there's a conspiracy, does it? I mean, it could be funded by some eccentric billionaire, like that Microsoft guy, who wants to keep his name out of it.'

Caro slapped April on the back, making her stumble forwards a few steps.

'Ha! I knew you'd get it!' She laughed. 'Yes, I thought of that – maybe it's even a corporation like Coca-Cola wanting to make money from the science breakthroughs or whatever. What do you think?'

'It's interesting – odd accounts, supercomputers and all. But I don't see the scandal.'

Caro held up a finger. 'The scandal is in the vanishings.'

'Vanishings?'

'People are disappearing. Not just from the school – although eight kids have vanished in the time I've been at Ravenwood.'

'Vanished where?'

Caro shrugged. 'The official line is that those kids returned home, Korea, India, Russia or wherever, or moved out of the area. But I knew three of them, and I could never get in contact with them again.'

'So what do you think happened to them?'

'I think they got them.'

'"They"? Who's "they"?'

Caro paused dramatically then leant forward and whispered, 'The vampires.'

April laughed, but the smile faded when she realised Caro wasn't laughing along with her. *Is she serious? Surely she's winding me up?* She waited for a moment, hoping there was going to be a big punchline, but Caro just looked at her, her expression completely serious.

'The vamp—' began April, but her phone rang. She fumbled it out of her bag and looked at the screen. It was Fiona.

'Sorry, Caro, I've got to take this.'

'That's okay. I've got to get home anyway and that's my bus,' she said, pointing towards the bus stop. 'Maybe mention it to your dad, eh?' she shouted as she sprinted across the road. 'It'd be great to discuss it with him.'

April smiled and nodded, waving as Caro turned the corner.

'Hi, Fee,' she said into the phone.

'Hi, hon. How's things?'

'Okay. I think.'

'I wanted to check on you. I've been feeling crappy all day for telling you about the Neil Stevenson and Miranda thing when you have way bigger things going on.'

For a second April wondered what she was talking about. After today, life in Edinburgh felt so distant and removed.

'Oh, *that*. Forget about it, life moves on.'

'Okay then. Tell me all about Ravenwood!'

April watched Caro get on the bus, forcing a smile as she waved from the top deck. 'You're never going to believe this, Fee,' she said. 'I'm surrounded by loonies.'

Chapter Five

Sometimes, thought April, *being bad feels pretty good.* She grinned as she clanged the front gate closed behind her and skipped across the road, swinging around an old-fashioned streetlamp and across the square. She felt a slight pang of guilt knowing that her parents had banned her from leaving the house after dark, but when she arrived home and found her mother not yet back from her long lunch and her father still at work, she had figured it would do no harm to nip out for a while. It wasn't as if Highgate was South Central LA, was it? And anyway, she had to admit it was the fact she was sneaking out that made it so much fun. She had spent the last few weeks – the last sixteen years, now she came to think about it – having everyone tell her where to go, what to do, what to think. For once she was free, going where she wanted, no one knowing where she was.

April crossed the square and passed the Highgate Literary & Scientific Institution: built in 1839, according to the carving under the eaves. April imagined a group of mad professors sitting around smoking pipes and discussing poetry. *Dad should join*, she thought with a smile, *he'd fit right in.* She glanced at her watch. It was six-thirty on a clear autumn evening and already April could see a bright, three-quarter moon in the sky. As she walked down Swain's Lane, retracing her route to school that morning, she wondered if it was the unusually luminous moon that had sent everyone in Highgate a little loopy.

She mulled over her day as she walked, breath steaming in the cold air in front of her. Okay, so there had been the incident in Philosophy class, but then Mr Sheldon had been pushing them, trying to get them to think about the subject properly and open their minds. And he had said something nice to her at the end, too. Not that Gabriel Swift had done anything to help, barging into her, whatever his problem was. But still, to be honest, her first day at Ravenwood hadn't been too awful; she had two new friends – acquaintances, at least – and that couldn't be bad, could it? Better than being the weird new girl no one wants to speak to. Davina was a little over-familiar, but then maybe that was just her way, and April liked Caro, even if she was full-on and kinda crazy. Funny but odd. Fiona had laughed at April's description of Caro and said, 'She sounds just like your dad.'

April peered through a gate to her left where she could see the church roof shining in the bright moonlight. *It's just a church, not a haunted castle*, she thought, smiling. It was Ravenwood that looked like Dracula's house – from the outside, anyway. Inside, it was the other kids rather than the narrow corridors that had unnerved her. They actually seemed to be there to learn; no giggling at the back, no note-passing, everyone fully engaged in the lessons. April had to admit she had been swept up in it too and had actually come away from school feeling inspired and enthused about her subjects, which was something that had rarely happened before. *So what's wrong with that?* she scolded herself. They might be geeks with enormous brains, but for a school for the academically gifted, they weren't too freaky. At least someone there had heard of Alix Graves.

The dead singer, of course, was the real reason she was out here in the first place. She'd been trying to convince herself she was just taking an early evening stroll, getting some air and checking out the neighbourhood, but the truth was she wanted to see Alix Graves' house and find out a bit more for Fee. It wasn't that she wanted to see where he was killed – unless the windows were splashed with blood, she wasn't going to see much anyway – it was more the fascination of seeing what a real rock star's house looked like. How big was it? Were there gargoyles on the roof? Stained-glass windows? *God, I've been watching way too many horror movies*, she thought with a wry smile. Dartmouth Park was supposedly full of big, spooky old houses like that, although for all she knew Alix had lived in a super-modern angular glass and steel bachelor pad. Either way, she wanted to take some photos to send to Fiona; might help her get some closure and ...

What the hell was that?

April stopped and held her breath – she was sure she had heard a cry. It was almost fully dark now and the air felt still and cold and, other than the distant sound of the main road at the bottom of the hill, all was quiet. The ancient brick walls surrounding the cemetery loomed on either side of her. She listened, her head cocked, her ears almost twitching.

There it is again. What is *it? A baby? A cat?*

She walked back up the lane to the black wrought-iron gates she had just passed – the entrance to the cemetery. April had noticed it earlier in the day because there was a curious little gatehouse just inside, but it was different now: now the gate was open. *Was it open a minute ago?* she wondered, frowning. *But surely I'd have noticed? Or was it the creak of the gate I heard?* Certainly from the leaves piled up at the bottom, it looked as if it had been a long time since it was last ajar this way. Edging closer, April strained to see through the uprights of the gate, but the low light was casting crazy shadows and she couldn't see anything.

Suddenly a sharp cry went up, making April skitter back a few steps. This time the sound was unmistakable: a creature – a person? – in pain. Then she heard a quieter sound, like sobbing. It was close, too, just inside the gates.

'Hello?' she said, trying to force her voice to sound strong. 'Is anyone there?'

Now there was another cry, softer this time, weaker.

'Do you need help?' she asked. Despite her fears, despite her parents' dire warnings, April couldn't run away. What if someone was really hurt? What if they needed an ambulance?

She walked forwards again, close enough to touch the gates,

and reached out and pushed the one hanging ajar further open. It creaked inwards and, in the shifting shadows, April could see something lying in the centre of the overgrown path ahead. A small body. As her eyes adjusted she could see it was moving, its side heaving up and down.

'Are you okay?' she said softly, taking a step inside the gates. As her body brushed against the metal the gate it creaked loudly and the shape jumped, trying to struggle to its feet. Now April could see what it was. A fox. It was trying to get up, but it couldn't.

She crouched down a few metres away from the animal, but immediately leapt back to her feet. Her hands had touched something warm and wet on the grass. She held her fingers up and in the milky moonlight she could see a glistening black liquid on her fingers. *Is that blood?* she thought, her heart leaping. She looked back at the fox. It was lying still as a statue, but she could still hear a whimpering coming from its throat.

In the dim light she felt uneasy being so close to this wild animal, but the fox sounded so distressed she couldn't just ignore it.

'Who did this to you, little guy?' she whispered. 'What's out there?'

She peered into the darkness. Just trees and gravestones, nothing except … And then something caught her eye. A shadow that wasn't a shadow.

She gasped, her hand jerking to her mouth. There were eyes looking at her. Dark, piercing eyes, staring out from the shadows. She began to back towards the gate, the fox forgotten, but found she could barely move her legs. Then there was a deafening roar and the rush of wind, as if something was coming straight at her. She tensed, expecting to be knocked to the ground, but instead she was lifted into the air and yanked backwards, her legs kicking out uselessly. She barely had time to register the sound of the rusty gate screeching wide open before she looked up and found herself lying bruised in the middle of Swain's Lane.

What the hell … ?

'Go! Quickly!' whispered a voice in front of her. Scrabbling to her feet, April looked towards the voice, but all she could see was a silhouette framed in the shadow of the gateway.

'Get out of here!' hissed the voice. 'Go on – run!'

As the figure turned, the moon caught his face and April felt her head swim. It was the dark-haired boy from the square, from school: Gabriel Swift.

'GO!' he shouted, slamming the gate shut. April turned and sprinted up the hill as fast as her feet would take her.

April had been under the shower for ten minutes, turning the heat up into the red, but she still couldn't drive the cold from her bones. Her legs were still shaking from her full-pelt dash up the hill, and her teeth were chattering despite the clouds of steam in the room. She stepped out reluctantly and wrapped herself in a towel, sitting on the edge of the bath until she felt the shivers leave her body. She tried to make sense of what had just happened. What had she seen out there? Was it just a dead fox? Or two dead foxes? There had been an awful lot of blood for just one. Had it been hit by a car? Had it been attacked? Why was the gate open when she was sure it had been chained shut earlier in the day? So many questions whirling around her head and no answers, especially not the one she really wanted: what was Gabriel doing there and why had he yanked her out? Had she been in danger? What on earth had possessed her to go into the cemetery anyway – was she mad? She shook her head, admitting that for once her parents had been right. She'd been an idiot to go out alone, in the dark, in an area she barely knew. She dried herself and dressed quickly, then grabbed her phone, speed-dialling Fee's number.

'It's me again.'

There was a pause. 'What's up?' asked Fiona, worry in her voice.

'The weirdest thing happened to me when I went for a walk around Highgate.'

'Okay, switch over to the webcam,' said Fiona urgently. 'I need to see your ugly mug.'

Fiona had always been a bit of a computer genius – she'd had wireless before most people had broadband – and when April had told her she was moving south, Fee had promptly turned up at her house with a gift-wrapped webcam. So sweet. But as April fiddled with her laptop, she had the time to pause and think about the events in Swain's Lane: what had she really seen? She'd seen an injured animal and been shouted at by a strange boy. When it came down to it, she didn't really have a clue what had happened out there. At last Fiona's face flicked up on the screen. It was fuzzy and jerky, but it was so good to see her that April wanted to cry.

'Come on,' said Fee sternly, 'tell me what's the matter. And don't leave anything out, I can see you now.'

'Well, I heard this strange noise,' started April slowly. 'It was coming from the cemetery. So I went in to see and, well, it was a fox.'

There was a long pause before Fee spoke. 'That's it? That's the weird thing?'

'Then I fell backwards,' she offered, realising how stupid it would sound to tell her friend that she thought she had been lifted off the ground. 'And there was this boy there and he yelled at me to run.'

'Well, I think I'd want to leg it too if I saw a half-dead fox in a spooky graveyard,' said Fee. 'But who was this boy? Why did he shout?'

April began to backtrack. 'It was probably just some practical joke or something. I suppose what with Alix's murder being just down the hill and everything, I'm a bit jumpy. It was probably nothing.'

'I guess,' said Fiona, not sounding convinced. 'But you don't need to get too worked up about Alix. I've been following the story all day and they're saying his murder's probably a crazed fan or something to do with his private life. It's terrible, of course, but it's one of those one-in-a-million things. It's not as if a bloody murder happens every day, is it? Or aren't I helping?'

April laughed. She could feel a bit of the tension in her shoulders easing.

'No, you're helping a lot,' she said. 'And it's brilliant to see you.' She looked at her friend's face. 'How are you feeling anyway?'

'Oh, bearing up. I tried to wear a black scarf into school and Miss Batty went mental. I mean, it's not as if I was dressed like Queen Victoria, or something.'

'So did you get detention?'

Fiona laughed. 'No, just the opposite. Turns out she's not a big music fan, so when I told her I was in mourning for Alix Graves she assumed that he was a relative and went into sympathy mode. Apparently her door's always open, if I just want to go in for a cry.'

April's eyes widened. Knowing her friend's love of the dramatic, that was like a red rag to a bull. 'Fee, you didn't take her up on her offer, did you?'

Fiona pulled a face. 'I'm not that daft. She'll find out who Alix is eventually and she'd go ballistic if she thought I'd been taking advantage of her good nature.'

April laughed and shook her head. She missed Fiona and her uncanny ability to get in and out of trouble. There was rarely a dull moment when she was around.

'So what are you up to tonight?'

'I was just going out actually,' said Fiona. 'Me and Sophie are going over to Juliet's to talk tactics. She wants to get back with Iain.'

April felt a sudden pang of jealousy. She wanted to be up there plotting with her friends, spending hours deciding the perfect wording for a text, working out what to say on the phone. Doing normal, everyday things, not like here ... Suddenly the image of those dark eyes blinked into her mind. She shuddered.

'April? You still with me?'

'Yes, yes, sorry.' April realised that she hadn't heard a word of her friend's last sentence.

'I can see that you're busy,' said Fiona, pointing at the boxes still piled up in a corner of the room. 'I'd better let you go. I miss you, you know.'

'I know,' said April sadly. 'Have a good time at Juliet's. But not too good a time, eh?'

Fiona laughed. 'Promise.'

April closed the laptop and looked around her little bedroom. It was small and a bit cramped even without packing crates taking up all the space. It certainly didn't look like home. She got up and walked to the window, half-hoping to see a lone figure with dark hair standing in the little park, but the square was empty. Or at least she was pretty sure it was empty; maybe one of those shadows wasn't all it seemed. No, that was silly; what she had seen in the graveyard must have been a trick of the light or something. Sighing, she walked downstairs and wandered into the kitchen. Her father was home, sitting at the breakfast bar munching on some cheese on toast.

'When did you get in?'

'A couple of minutes ago,' he said, pouring her a cup of tea from the pot. 'Hungry?' he asked, offering her a slice of toast.

April shook her head.

'How was school?'

'Interesting,' she said. 'How about your new job?'

'Interesting.' He smiled. 'Where's your mum?'

April shrugged. 'She left me a note to say she was meeting friends.'

William grabbed two books that were in front of him and got up to leave. 'Well, back to work.'

'Sit back down for a minute at least.' April laughed, pushing him into his chair. 'You're such a workaholic.'

April had noticed that he had already set up his study opposite the living room; books and papers, files and more files, she didn't know what drove him. Perhaps it was a desire to have a book hit the best-seller charts; one of his old university friends was a big newspaper editor who had a lucrative sideline in popular history books and April could always hear the trace of envy in her dad's voice whenever he got in touch. But then maybe her dad was simply trying to provide Silvia with the

53

kind of life he knew she wanted: a nice home, a fast car and a social life packed with glamour. *Yeah, like even that would make her happy.*

'So what are you working on this time?' she asked her father.

He ran a hand across his stubble. 'I've got to get a proposal in to my publisher by Friday. My agent thinks we might be able to get a decent advance this time. Maybe some film interest, too.'

'Fantastic.' April smiled, feeling guilty for challenging his work ethic. At least he tried. 'What's the big idea?'

'It's the London East End book I was telling you about on holiday. My theory about the plague pits.'

She shook her head. 'Sorry, Dad, but you can't expect me to keep up. One minute it's Egyptian cults, the next it's human trafficking.'

He laughed. 'Sorry, I didn't realise quite how boring I've become.'

'Not boring,' said April affectionately. 'Confusing.'

He pulled a long string of cheese off his toast and pushed it around his plate. 'Actually, it's connected to this area. If your mother knew about it, she definitely wouldn't let you out at night.'

April felt her skin prickle and looked away, glancing at the window, now running with rain.

'What's the matter?' he asked.

'Nothing, it's just ...'

'What?' he said, touching her hand. 'What is it?'

It's just I saw a monster with glowing eyes and got covered in blood, she thought to herself.

'I was walking up Swain's Lane and I thought I saw something. But don't worry – I think I'm just a bit nervy because of the Graves murder.'

'Swain's Lane? When was this?' he asked sternly.

'Oh, after school, but it was getting dark,' said April quickly, suddenly remembering she could get into trouble for breaking her curfew. But she was sure her father's expression had changed the moment she mentioned Swain's Lane. 'Were you alone? What did you see?' he asked.

'I'm not sure, I just ...' she stuttered, wondering whether to tell him. She so wanted to share it with someone and who better than her conspiracy-theory-debunking dad? After all, a man who wrote books about the abominable snowman would surely believe her when she said she'd seen a ... a what? What *had* she seen, exactly? A spook? A spirit? A zombie? It was ridiculous when you thought about it.

'I saw an injured fox,' she said lamely.

William chuckled with a note of relief. 'I thought you were going to tell me you'd seen someone hanging around or something.'

'What sort of someone?'

He tapped her hand reassuringly. 'No one, darling. Highgate is one of the safest suburbs in London.'

'Not for Alix Graves, it wasn't.'

'No, but then it looks like his murder was an isolated incident. The police think it might have been connected to his business interests – you know, his record label and that Full Moon Festival he used to organise, they think it might have something to do with a shady financial investor. So I doubt that has anything to do with the area.'

William was smiling now, but April wasn't convinced. There was something about the way her father was talking and avoiding her eyes.

'But who would be hanging around here?' she persisted. 'Someone from another school or something?'

'No, no, the schools in this area, Ravenwood, Highgate School, they're far too posh for knife-wielding teens, darling.'

'So what made you think there might be?'

'Footpads and brigands are a bit on my mind at the moment,' he said, tapping one of his books. April craned her neck – the top one was called *The Dark Victorian Age*. He shrugged. 'Just a bit of research for the new book. Back in the Victorian period, London was an absolute cesspit of thieves and murderers cutting each other's throats for a swig of gin.' He paused and held up a finger as he noticed April's look of distress. 'But that was a hundred and fifty years ago, remember. They had no police force to speak of, people were incredibly poor and London itself was crammed into a few square miles around the City and Covent Garden. Back then, anything beyond the city walls was countryside.'

'Even here?'

'Well, yes and no. No: Highgate was a separate village built around the school; it's been here for four hundred years. Yes: they chose to build the cemetery here because there was land and because the graveyards in London were overflowing and poisoning the water supply. Which is what this book's about, more or less.'

April felt another chill. 'Graveyards?' she asked.

Her father leant back and looked up at the ceiling.

He's avoiding my eyes again, thought April. *What's he not telling me?*

'A bit. It's more about disease – plague pits and sewers and so forth,' he said vaguely.

'What, no monsters this time?' she asked.

'No, no monsters, darling.' He laughed, but when he finally looked at her, his eyes were serious. 'There's no such thing.'

Chapter Six

There had been a time when April could lose herself in magazines. She would pore over red-carpet pictures and soak up celebrity gossip, then swap it with her friends as if they all personally knew the actresses and singers they were reading about. She would read the problem pages and horoscopes, half-believing that they had some sort of sound advice to give her about boys or exams or how to tell if you were a good kisser. Now she couldn't even work up much excitement about a scandal involving an A-list actress getting caught necking with both girls and boys in a seedy Soho goth club. She threw the magazine down onto the bed and flopped back onto her pillow, staring at the ceiling. The digital clock by her bed said it was past midnight but April just couldn't sleep. She was anxious, on edge, and there were endless things going around in her head. It had been a pretty weird day, all in all. A first day at school was traumatic enough, but seeing ... whatever it was she had seen was enough to keep anyone wide-eyed. She began to reach for her phone, but then stopped herself. Who would she call so late? She could go online, but where was the fun in that when she knew all her Edinburgh friends would be in bed or, worse, out having fun? She lay back and stared out of the window; the sky was almost purple and she could see the moon peeking through a gap in the rain clouds. She remembered how her dad had pointed to the night sky when she was little and said the man in the moon was watching her.

'See?' he would say. 'He's smiling at you.' Tonight it didn't look like the man in the moon was smiling. Tonight it looked like a sneer. April turned over and wished she could go back to those carefree days, back to when her dad had commuted to work every day and he and Mum had seemed, well, *in love*. April remembered it as a series of hazy snapshots: riding on her dad's shoulders as he walked through wavy waist-high grass, or squatting next to a stream glinting in the sunshine, scooping tadpoles into a jam jar with a net. April smiled at those memories, however cheesy they now seemed. It was as if she had picked her childhood from a Laura Ashley catalogue. And where was her mum in these sepia photographs? Trailing behind in her wafty Pucci kaftans, her head covered by one of those huge bee-keeper's hats, complaining about wasps and pollen and skin cancer. Back then, Silvia's grumbles were only half-serious and her father would laugh along with her, joking that he would give her the kiss of life if a greenfly landed on her. April giggled to herself. They weren't all bad, her parents, not really. Maddening, yes, frustratingly narrow-minded, but she supposed she did love them. Well, most of the time.

It kept nagging away at April, the way her father had reacted to her walking alone down Swain's Lane after dark. There was obviously something about it that had worried him. What could it be? The only thing of interest on the higher part of Swain's Lane was the gate to the cemetery; lower down it was all houses. Why would he be concerned about the cemetery? Perhaps it was something to do with this disease thing he was working on, or maybe the fox? She hadn't seen many of them, but they were definitely wild animals and she was almost certain they were riddled with horrible germs. She shivered and looked at her hands. She had scrubbed them meticulously in the shower, but you could never tell what nastiness might be lurking there unseen. Suddenly, she felt itchy and uncomfortable. She jumped up and, pulling on her dressing gown, padded down the stairs to the kitchen. She knew her mother would have a little bottle of that antibacterial hand gel in one of the cupboards, although it was probably too late for her by now; she probably had listeria and scabies and things they hadn't even discovered yet crawling all over her. The house was in darkness and, as she reached the bottom of the stairs, her eyes were drawn to the stained-glass arch above the front door. She hadn't noticed it before. Lit up by the streetlight outside, she could see a picture of a deer being chased by hunters. It was an odd scene for such an urban house. Over the threshold of a country manor, perhaps, but here in the centre of London ... Then she remembered what her father had said earlier: it hadn't always been part of the city, but it still seemed incongruous, wrong somehow. Seeing the glass up there suddenly made her feel exposed and unsafe, as if the front door was flimsy and insubstantial, unable to keep out whatever lurked in the dark. It was silly of course – the door was solid, and it was locked. Still, she shivered as she swung around the banister and trotted into the kitchen, opening cupboards and drawers looking for the hand gel, finding it and slathering her hands with the tingly green goop. Feeling a little better, she took a Diet Pepsi from the fridge and popped it open. *The last thing I need right now is more caffeine*, she thought. *I need something to knock me out.* Seeing her school bag, she picked it up and rummaged for the book Mr Sheldon had handed out in class.

Sci-fi homework, great, she thought with an ironic smile, *perfect to send me to sleep.* 'Random Quest', the story he wanted to discuss, seemed to be about a man called Colin who woke up after a laboratory accident to find himself in a parallel universe where the Second World War never happened. More importantly, his dead wife was now alive and married to someone else and he was married to a completely new woman called ... *Oh God, I was right first time!* April thought. *This is super-dull.* She threw it down and picked up *The Dark Victorian Age*, the book her dad had left lying on the side. Now this was more like it, she thought as she flicked through. It was full of tales of ladies in amazing dresses who poisoned their husbands and gangs of pickpockets fighting in the streets. As she turned a page, something fluttered to the floor. April smiled as she bent to pick up a passport-sized shot of her from a school-photo session when she must have been about six; her dad had been using it as a bookmark. She looked very cute with her long, thick hair – April had always had thick hair, even as a baby – and a gap where the Tooth Fairy had visited in the night. April felt a little embarrassed that her dad still thought of her as a little girl, but also pleased that he had held on to the photo for so long. She was just putting it back when she noticed a line on the page the photo was marking:

A memorable note was received on 16 October 1888. It accom-panied part of a kidney alleged to be from a recent victim with the assurance, t'other piece I fried and ate it was very nise.

'Ugh, gross,' whispered April to herself. *Who is this, Hannibal Lecter?* Reading on, she discovered it was a chapter about vari-ous 'sexual deviants' from the Victorian era – most famously Jack the Ripper, the supposed author of the letter about the kidney. April read on for a while, unable to drag herself away from the morbidly fascinating crimes. Apparently Jack the Ripper had been running around London's East End in 1888, which didn't seem all that long ago, really. Her dad's words came back to her and she realised what had been bothering her all this time: he'd said his new book had a connection to this area, and that Silvia definitely wouldn't let her out if she knew about it. But not even *her* mother could use Jack the Ripper as an excuse to keep her locked up indoors. So what was going on? She walked down the hall to her dad's study and gently closed the door behind her. She wasn't sure what she was looking for, but she hoped there would be something here to explain why her dad was so evasive about the nature of his book, and so jumpy about Highgate. April sat down at his desk: it was a tip. Piles of papers, stacks of books, Post-it notes stuck to every surface, all with scrawled lines like 'Roman link?', 'Call FG, ask to find Ott. txt', or '23.11.88 – 14.02.93 – signif?' That made April stop: the last date was her birth-day. In fact, Valentine's Day 1993 was the exact day she was born. What other significance might it have? She opened his laptop as quietly as she could and winced; in the silent study, the whirring of the fan as the machine woke up sounded horribly loud. She glanced at the door, straining her ears for any sounds of movement, but the house was as still as before. She turned back to the screen. Much like his real desk, her dad's computer desktop was a mess, crowded with files and folders, most of them with titles like 'Myths' or 'Ancient Relics', next to his work files: '*Scotsman* Features' or 'Human Trafficking Project'. She clicked on one: 'Mythology' held sub-folders labelled, predictably enough, 'Greek', 'Roman', 'Norse' and 'Celtic'. It was all as she expected, apart from a folder with a strange jumbled title: 'J-M569mp'. Clicking on it gave her a prompt window asking her to enter a password. She tried a few guesses, but nothing happened. She shook her head. Probably just porn, she thought, then immediately regretted allowing the idea into her head. 'Eww ...' she whispered to herself. 'God, I'm going to need more of that green gel.'

Then she had a sudden inspiration. She went to 'Recent items' and pulled down the list.

'Here we go,' she said, scrolling down to a file named 'Highgate'.

It popped open on screen. It was clearly still in note form: some bits obviously cut and pasted from elsewhere, some single random lines, all very jumbled. But there was one longer piece of writing headed 'Foreword'.

There is a deep, dark evil within this city ...

'Evil?' she whispered.

... An evil so ancient, it is almost beyond the reach of history. Perhaps it has always been here; perhaps this darkness is the real reason men chose to settle on the banks of the great River Thames. This evil, however, is not some supernatural force lurking in the shadows. It is something far more mundane, much more everyday. It is its very ordinariness that makes it so dangerous and its universality that has kept it hidden for so long. It surrounds us still, cloaked in myth and fantasy. It

*has grown much more dangerous in this modern world where
technology isolates us, playing into this contagion's hands, allowing it to spread further and faster. However, it is today's
technology, today's new ways of thinking and communicating,
that may eventually defeat the evil, by exposing it to the light
where it will turn to dust.*

'Bloody hell,' said April in a low voice. *What was he saying
about no monsters?* She quickly scrolled down, but that was all
her dad had written so far. She went back to the 'recent items'
list and opened another file. 'Chapters?'

It was a list, which read:

*The Plague
The Great Fire
Unexplained Outbreaks of Violence
Riots and Rookeries
Jack the Ripper
Dr Crippen
The Krays*

'What *is* this thing?' she breathed. What had her father discovered to link all of this together? He'd mentioned the plague,
hadn't he? Now April was feeling distinctly unsettled. She
closed the laptop and began to sort through the things on the
desk. There was a pile of buff cardboard folders stamped with
the words 'Ham and High Archive, Please Return'. Inside she
found yellowing old newspaper clippings attached to boards
– some of them very old indeed. The *Islington Chronicle*, the
Hampstead Weekly News, the *Camden Bugle*. Stories of crowds
attacking policemen, unprovoked attacks on clergymen, gangs
of youths on the rampage, all in north London, all within
miles of her home. One cutting about murder – a woman was
found with her throat torn out on Hampstead Heath – was
disturbingly close, but it was dated 1903. The more she read,
the more uncomfortable April felt. There were many more
stories of horrible slayings; torture, decapitation, even mass

graves. Individually, these incidents just looked like disturbing but unremarkable events, but if there was something gluing them all together, then that was extremely worrying, especially if it had something to do with the area where she now lived. She carefully put the cuttings back as they had been and tried the desk drawers. The large right-hand one was locked, but the middle drawer slid open. Her father's diary was inside, each day crammed with appointments, phone numbers and doodles. Under that, she found a battered old notebook. Now this was more like it – her dad's spidery handwriting filled pages with random thoughts and ideas he had jotted down as he'd been doing his research. *I need to look at that in more detail*, she decided. Putting it to one side, she picked up a large reference book called *A Topographical History of London*, which had loads of coloured Post-its sticking out of the top marking various pages. The marked pages were old maps of London, some of the streets, some of the sewers; one was a map charting the course of the River Fleet, which passed through Highgate on its meandering journey down to the Thames. She turned over a few more pages, finding another map with pencil notes in her dad's handwriting. It was dated 1884 and showed the expansion of the Tube – the Metropolitan District line and the East London line stretching into the East End. Her father had drawn a ring around Whitechapel Station.

'Hang on,' murmured April. She switched off the light and, picking up the notebook, tiptoed back into the kitchen. Once there, she consulted *The Dark Victorian Age* book on the counter. Yes, she was right – Jack the Ripper had been running about killing women in 1888. *Are the two things linked?* But that was absurd, how could people building the Tube be connected to Jack the Ripper? It made no sense. But then, according to the book, there was such a huge network of tunnels, sewers, canals and rivers, even secret passageways and roads under the City, that nobody actually knew how many miles of pipe there were under the ground. Things could move around without anyone suspecting. Had Jack the Ripper escaped detection by nipping down the sewers? Or was there more to it than that?

April had seen the Johnny Depp movie using the conspiracy theory that the Ripper was linked to the royal family. Were they infected by this disease too?

'April?'

She screamed.

'Woah, woah,' said her father, holding up his hands. 'It's okay, it's just me.'

April's heart was beating rapidly, partly from the surprise, but also because she had almost been caught red-handed. In fact, she had been. Her dad's notebook was still in her hand.

'Dad, I—'

'WILL!' came a roar from the top of the stairs. 'What the *bloody* hell's going on down there?'

William took a step back towards the kitchen door.

'God, woman, don't be so dramatic, it's just us,' he shouted. 'Go back to bed!'

April stuffed the notebook into her school bag while he was distracted.

'Sheesh,' he said. 'It's a good job they don't allow guns in this country. She'd have been down here blasting away at imaginary burglars.'

'Sorry, Dad,' said April, 'I couldn't sleep. Came down for my book,' she added, showing him the John Wyndham omnibus.

'They're working you hard already, aren't they?' he said with a smile.

'I don't know how I'm going to have time to do anything else. You should see the reading list they've given us for English Lit, it's huge.'

Her father grinned affectionately and put his arm around her, leading her back towards the stairs.

'Well, you'd better get back to bed, or you won't be awake enough to read anything tomorrow.'

April nodded gratefully and they began to walk up the stairs. They stopped on the landing and she leant in to give her father a kiss. Just as she was turning away, he put his hand on her arm.

'How did you find it?' he asked.

April's heart jumped. *He knows*, she thought, *he knows I've been snooping*.

'What do you mean?' she asked, as evenly as she could.

'School, darling. How did you find it all? Didn't really ask you earlier, it must have been difficult.'

'Oh, school. It was okay. Why wouldn't it be?'

'Well, you're up at one o'clock in the morning, so I'm thinking maybe you've got something on your mind. No one's giving you a hard time for being the new girl, are they?'

'No, not really. It's a bit of a worry, I suppose, especially starting right in the middle of term. But actually I've already made a couple of friends. One girl I think you'll really get on with – she's just like you.'

William pulled a face. 'Not too much, I hope.' He smiled.

'There's worse things to be, Dad,' she said, and ran up the stairs.

Ripper – who? Victim of his environment. Infected? Disease released from underground? Possible, but why such violence? Royal link? Part of cover-up?

William Dunne's handwriting was so bad April was amazed he'd managed to make a living as a journalist all these years. Maybe he could read it. She flipped over another page of his battered and closely written notebook and cocked her head, listening for any movement. There had been a brief fight in her parents' room as soon as her father went back to bed: 'Up all hours, it's not natural.' 'Give her a break, she's just started a new school.' 'Whose fault is that?' – all the usual things, but they had quickly blown themselves out and now all was quiet. April turned back to the notebook. It was just a scrawl in some places and, as the notes were meant for himself, the meaning of much of it was frustratingly unclear to April.

Whitechapel branch, plague pits – Def. Roman remains under Spitalfields – connection? What about the coffin/West

65

End rumour; possible urban myth? Another royal connection with Ripper murders?

One word was written in the middle of a page in big letters and underlined a number of times: '*DISEASE*'.

'A disease?' whispered April. That was what her dad had said in the kitchen, but how could a disease make you go on a killing spree? How could it make Jack the Ripper hack up all those women? It sounded pretty far-fetched; after all, if there was some virus floating around turning people into homicidal maniacs, wouldn't it make the news more often? Anyway, even if there were some truth to it, it still didn't answer the question that had brought her to this point: what was the local connection? If her dad thought that the Underground network had spread this disease, that didn't really make sense in Highgate – the highest point in London wasn't the ideal spot for digging a tunnel, you even had to walk to the bottom of the hill to catch the Tube.

Underneath the word '*Disease*' were a number of arrows pointing to words and phrases: 'bleeding gums', 'pale skin', 'hypersexuality'. Her dad had circled them and drawn another arrow to one word.

'*Vampires.*'

April laughed out loud, despite herself. 'You're kidding me …' she whispered. 'Caro will love this.'

Actually, April felt a sense of relief. She had been getting herself all worked up, convinced her father had uncovered some plot to poison the Tube or something, but no – he was back on the usual stuff: beasties and werewolves. She frowned. So why had he told her he wasn't? 'No monsters', that was what he had said – but why lie about it? And then she turned over the page and felt her skin go cold. Written at the top of the page were two words:

Highgate Vampire.

Chapter Seven

April wasn't having a good morning. She had woken up with a pounding headache and the worst case of Bed Head Hair in the history of sleep; she looked like she'd spent the night in an eighties metal band. She also had a vaguely unsettled feeling, as if she had been having nightmares she couldn't remember. Worse, at breakfast it was immediately clear that her parents weren't talking – if it wasn't for the black atmosphere they were generating, she might have been impressed that they had managed to slot in a full-scale fight before their cereal. Still, hearing them hissing at each other had given her time to slip into her dad's study and return his notebook. Strolling into the kitchen, muttering something about an early start, April had grabbed some toast and tried to make a run for it, but her dad caught her at the door.

'April, it's raining,' he had said firmly. 'I'm giving you a lift. Besides, I don't like you walking about around here until we know a bit more about what's going on.'

For the first few minutes they sat in silence, listening to the *swoosh-swoosh* of the windscreen wipers, neither keen to discuss or acknowledge the cloud slowly descending on their family. April dearly wanted to grill her dad about the vampire thing, but she could hardly say, 'Hey, Dad, so I was going through all your things last night, and I was wondering ...' She still couldn't get her head around why he had lied to her about the book. Why wouldn't he tell her the truth? After all, he'd written stuff about crop circles and Bigfoot. What was so different about this? She gazed through the window at the grey houses and dark road. So drab, so depressing, she'd almost welcome a bit of supernatural excitement. And the atmosphere in the house was becoming unbearable.

'Listen, April, we need to talk,' said William finally.

She looked at him with alarm. Was he reading her thoughts?

'I know you don't want to hear this, love—'

Oh God, no, thought April, fixing her gaze on the car in front, *it's the divorce, it's the divorce! He's going to tell me Silvia's having an affair with her tennis coach and that I've got to choose between Dad and Roger Federer.*

'—But there was another murder last night.'

April looked up sharply, curiously disappointed that her father wasn't announcing a domestic upheaval.

'Where? Here?' she asked. 'In Highgate?'

William Dunne looked at his daughter warily, then nodded. 'I'm afraid so. One of the lads on the news desk called early this morning to talk over the new edition. Your mother wasn't too pleased to be disturbed, as you can imagine.'

Ah, so that explained the frosty atmosphere. Silvia wouldn't have been impressed that Dad's 'silly little rag' had needed to rewrite its front page, plus her mother had some loopy idea that the morning light was bad for her skin and she was always furious if anyone dared to interfere with her beauty sleep.

'But I thought the Alix Graves thing was just some shady business deal gone wrong or something,' said April, a strange sinking feeling in her stomach.

Her father glanced over at her again. 'That was the theory. But it's possible the two murders may be linked.'

'You're kidding ...' April could feel her sinking feeling going *Titanic*. 'So who was the second victim? Not another celebrity?'

William shrugged. 'No, no. A young woman. We don't have all the facts yet, but it seems there are a few similarities. And, well, it was a little closer to home than Alix Graves' house.'

April shifted in her seat. 'Closer? How close?'

William Dunne hesitated for a moment. 'She was found in

Highgate Cemetery, just by Swain's Lane. The police received a tip-off phone call last night.'

April felt as if someone had shoved her sideways. She grabbed the armrest and squeezed her eyes shut. *It can't have been!* she thought. *It can't have been a murder, it was just a fox, wasn't it?* Then another thought hit her and her eyes flew open. The blood! She stared down at her hands. Could it have been that *girl's* blood she had touched? *Oh please God no ...*

'April?'

It was only then that April noticed her father had stopped the car.

'Dad ...'

Soundlessly, William pulled April into a tight hug. She began to shake as she realised that if she had taken another step into the cemetery, if she had arrived there a moment sooner, she might have been able to help that poor woman, she might have ... she might have been dead, too.

'Honey, what is it?' he was saying softly, stroking her hair. He was concerned, but still calm, still reassuring. 'What's upset you?'

'Oh God, Dad, I think I saw it,' she whispered, her damp eyes searching his.

'Saw what, honey?'

'The blood,' she said. 'I think I was there when that girl was killed.'

The headmaster's office was surprisingly untidy. Considering that the rest of the school was state-of-the-art, all polished wood and steel, the head's lair was reassuringly chaotic. The furniture was still grand and expensive, but the drawers of the filing cabinets were so overflowing with papers they barely closed. In fact, Mr Sheldon's desk itself was the only surface not completely covered with books, files and toppling towers of A4 paper, and that was mainly due to the huge bulk of the headmaster's ancient desktop computer. *Where did he get that?* wondered April. *The Antiques Roadshow?* She had been expecting gleaming chrome and glass, leather chairs, possibly a wall of TVs all tuned to satellite news stations. She could barely believe that this was the office of the head of a top private school, let alone of the Bond-villain genius behind a massive global conspiracy. Caro was going to be so disappointed. Her new friend would, however, love the fact that April had been summoned to the headmaster's office on her second day at the school. Okay, so it was through no fault of her own – if you ignored the fact that she had defied her parents' orders to stay indoors, of course – but it certainly looked edgy and rebellious, especially with the police on their way. It was just the sort of intrigue Caro would approve of. She glanced about, hoping to spot some scandalous titbit or piece of evidence to support Caro's mad theories, but the walls were lined with glass-fronted bookshelves holding dusty books with Latin titles; nothing to suggest international intrigue. She glanced up at the clock. She'd been sitting there for ten minutes already. When April had told her father what she had seen the previous evening, he had immediately insisted that she speak to the police. 'It sounds important, April,' he had said gravely. 'And even if it's not, the police need to know everything they can about last night in order to stand a chance of catching this monster.'

He had called a contact on the force who had told him they would interview April at the school – understandably, they didn't want to wait until April got home in case she had vital information. 'Plus it's less traumatic than dragging her down the nick,' he'd said.

Policemen may know all about catching murderers, but they don't know much about schools, thought April ruefully. A summons to the headmaster's office was bad enough, but when Mrs Bagly, the headmaster's secretary, had come to collect April from Chemistry, stage-whispering the words 'the police need to see her' to Mr Fitzpatrick, the teacher, it had prompted a hiss of gleeful muttering around the classroom. April was sure the school grapevine would have her down as a global drug trafficker by now.

'Sorry to keep you, April,' said Mr Sheldon as he strode in, his sharp eyes scanning her. He sat down behind his desk and steepled his fingers. 'Now then, I hear you've been in a spot of – uh – unpleasantness. Can you tell me what you saw, exactly?'

April shifted in her seat. She didn't like the way Mr Sheldon was looking at her – sort of a mixture of distaste and curiosity – and she wasn't sure if she should be telling the headmaster things that only the police should hear.

'I'm not sure I actually saw anything.'

Mr Sheldon frowned so deeply his grey eyebrows knitted together over his nose.

'But I was led to believe that you had seen this poor unfortunate girl lying in the cemetery?'

April froze. She hadn't told anyone except her dad about it yet and the press hadn't released the story either.

'How did you know I was in the cemetery?'

Sheldon's face softened. 'Extrapolating the facts, Miss Dunne,' he said. 'Plus, I do have a few contacts within the police. You have to with a job like mine, although I might add, we experience very, very little trouble here at Ravenwood.'

She wasn't sure if he was making a sly dig at her or not, but fortunately he was distracted by the ringing phone.

He snatched it up, barking, 'Yes?' into the receiver and listening briefly. 'It appears the police are here. Early,' he said to April with some disapproval.

The teacher stood up and walked around his desk just as the office door opened and a serious-looking man with grey hair and a younger, slightly plump woman walked in. The woman was scowling and wearing a badly fitting dark green trouser suit, while April thought the man looked like a marine sergeant from a Bruce Willis movie – the sort who gets killed in the first half-hour.

'Mr Sheldon,' said the man, offering his hand, 'I'm Detective Inspector Ian Reece and this is Detective Sergeant Amy Carling. Thank you for letting us use your office. Would you mind if we talk to Miss Dunne on our own?'

'Well, as April's parents aren't here,' said the headmaster smoothly, 'I think it would be best if I stayed—'

'No, that's okay, Mr Sheldon,' said April. 'I think I'll be fine.'

'Don't worry, sir, she'll be safe with us.'

'I'm sure,' said Mr Sheldon, backing towards the door. 'Let me know if you need anything.' He glanced at April meaningfully and lowered his voice. 'School files, that sort of thing?'

'Yes, of course, sir,' said the inspector, shutting the door firmly and turning to April. 'Now then, Miss Dunne, thank you for contacting us. Would you like to tell us exactly what you saw yesterday evening?'

'Everyone's looking at me.'

Caro bit into her crisp and Marmite sandwich, dropping crumbs all over the refectory table. 'Well *of course* they're looking at you,' she said between munches. 'You're the prime suspect in a shocking murder investigation. They're all looking to see if you've still got blood on you.'

The Ravenwood students were not the sort to openly gawp, but whenever she looked up April could feel eyes flicking away from her and hear comments being whispered from the sides of mouths.

'Don't listen to her, sweetie, it's her overripe imagination,' said Simon kindly. 'They're probably just looking at Caro's latest dye-job.'

Caro gave him a withering look and April smiled. Simon Oliver was the closest thing Caro had to a best friend at Ravenwood; they had gone to junior school together and spent their early years playing Barbie and dressing up, but with the onset of puberty their relationship had become more spiky. 'He's such a diva,' Caro had complained over lunch the previous day. 'You never know what he's thinking.' Reading between the lines, April suspected there was an element of unrequited love on Caro's part at least, not helped by the fact that Simon Oliver was exactly Caro's type with his pale skin, dangling emo-fringe and collection of Belarus tour T-shirts. There seemed to be an assumption he was gay, but Caro wouldn't hear of it. 'He's just Simon,' she said defensively. Either way, he was an expert at bursting Caro's bubble. Without his balancing influence, April might well have believed every one of Caro's wild theories.

'But I'm not a suspect – am I?' She turned to Caro for reassurance, but her friend only grinned.

'Everyone's a suspect,' she said with relish. 'Especially someone who—' she held up her fingers to form quotation marks '—"stumbles across" the body.'

'I didn't stumble across anything,' said April desperately. 'I didn't even see her body.'

'No use telling the coppers that,' said Caro, starting on a Penguin biscuit. 'Statistics speak for themselves. Top suspect in any murder is always the husband, second is whoever found the body. And you have to admit you did have blood all over you.'

'Fox blood,' corrected Simon. 'And if you'd listened, April said she didn't find the body. Someone else called the police, remember?'

Caro held up her hands innocently. 'Hey, it's not me she has to convince. I believe your story, especially the bit about the shadow with the dark eyes.'

April bit her lip. She knew it sounded ludicrous, but that was what she had seen. Or was it? She wasn't even sure herself any more. One thing was certain: she needed to talk to Gabriel Swift as soon as she could – she had to know what he had seen. Did he see the body? Did he see the murderer? How was he wrapped up in all this? She couldn't keep on with this 'strange shadow' story – she had seen the look of dismay on the police officers' faces when she had come to that part of the story. She could sympathise; it wasn't as if you could translate her description into a *Crimewatch* photofit.

'Listen, Caro,' said April, casting her eyes about and lowering her voice. 'What you said yesterday about the school, who's behind it? Well, my dad—'

'Yeah, sorry about that,' said Caro quickly, glancing at Simon with an embarrassed look on her face. 'I was speaking figuratively or metaphorically or something – and anyway, it's just an idea. I've got a million of 'em. Maybe don't tell your dad that one, I'll look like a loony.'

And then again, maybe he'd agree with you, thought April. She still wanted to tell her new friends what she had read in her dad's notes, but Caro was right – in the cold light of day, the idea that some sort of underground disease or, even worse, a vampire, might be responsible for all the violence in London did sound a little loony. 'A little loony' was something April was used to with her father, of course, but it wasn't necessarily something she wanted to share with the world.

'Don't worry,' said Simon, seeing April's troubled expression. 'It's not like you actually killed that girl, is it? You were only trying to help and you told the police everything you know.'

April felt a wave of guilt and looked across the room to where the Faces were sitting. She didn't really know why, but she hadn't quite told the police everything. She had left out the part about seeing Gabriel there, about him pulling her out of the cemetery, about him telling her to run home. She had meant to tell them, she honestly had, but when it came to it, something had stopped her. Fear? No, somehow she didn't sense any evil in him. Loyalty? Hardly – she barely knew him. Across the room, Gabriel was talking intently to that bitchy girl Layla; he didn't seem to have noticed April at all. The truth was she didn't have a very clear picture of what had happened the previous evening and that bothered her. Why was Gabriel there? Had he called the police? April just didn't know what to think. Maybe it was her father's genes, maybe it was just morbid curiosity, maybe it was pure guilt that she hadn't done more to help that poor girl – whatever it was, April knew she couldn't relax until she had found out what had happened that night. If she had given the police Gabriel Swift's name, the chances were she never would.

'Do you really think I'm being treated as a suspect?' said April seriously. 'Okay, so I was in the area, but why on earth would I want to murder anyone?'

Caro shrugged. 'Drug deal gone wrong? Crime of passion?

Hey,' she said, waving a stick of celery at April, 'perhaps you were lesbian lovers.'

'Well, it's nice to see someone's enjoying all this,' said Simon sarcastically. 'I mean, it's not like anyone's been killed or anything, is it?'

Caro giggled and threw her celery at him. 'Can I help it if I *love* being at the centre of a murder investigation?' She smiled playfully. 'Besides, look at all the attention April's getting. Yesterday she was just the new girl, today she's one half of Bonnie and Clyde.'

April smiled despite herself. It would have been so easy to give in to paranoia and fear, but her new friend's irreverent take on events put the whole episode into perspective. Especially the slightly silly part about those dark eyes.

'Hello, here comes trouble,' said Caro, nodding towards the far side of the room. April looked up to see Davina Osbourne making a beeline for their table.

'Hi, April,' she sang, giving them all the full sixty-watt smile. 'I heard about last night, honey,' she said, pouting sympathetically. 'It sounds so horrible. I just wanted to come over and check that you're okay?'

'Your concern is so touching, "honey",' mimicked Caro.

'Thanks, Davina,' said April quickly, 'but I'm fine. I just heard some noises in Swain's Lane last night and—'

'Oh my God,' said Davina, dramatically covering her mouth. 'Did you hear Isabelle getting killed? Actually getting killed? Screams and stuff?'

'No, I just heard a few noises, the police aren't even sure if I was in the same place—'

'Who's Isabelle?' interrupted Caro.

Davina glared at Caro and then turned her attention back to April.

'Didn't you know? Her name was Isabelle Davis, she was a student here a few years ago. A friend of mine at the Royal Opera House knew her quite well, lovely skin, great hair – such a waste, don't you think?'

April couldn't reply. Somehow knowing the girl's name made the whole thing seem all the more real.

'You okay, A?' asked Caro, touching her arm.

'Oh no, I haven't made things worse, have I?' said Davina. 'Do you want some Evian? Why don't you come and sit with us while you calm down? I think Chessy's got some of her mum's Valium.'

'Why don't you just leave her alone?' snapped Caro. 'She was fine until you got here.'

'No, please, I'll be okay, I just need some air,' said April, getting to her feet. Both Caro and Davina moved to help her, but she brushed them off and headed for the door. 'Thanks, but I need to ... I need to be alone for a while,' she said as she left.

April pushed through the refectory's double doors, aware that every eye in the room was watching her, and burst out into the corridor. *I will not cry, I will not cry*, she said to herself over and over again. She ran blindly down the halls, turning corners at random, finally coming to a stop next to a mercifully abandoned cloakroom where she sat down on a bench. 'Breathe,' she whispered to herself, pulling in air through her nose and letting it out through her mouth. She tried to remember what you were supposed to think of to calm yourself down – cool wet grass, was it? She was finding it hard to think of anything except those dark eyes.

'Ah, Ravenwood's latest bad girl,' said a voice. 'I was wondering when our paths would cross.'

April looked up. Benjamin Osbourne looked down at her through his mop of blond hair and gave her a sardonic smile.

'Sorry, I have terrible manners,' he said, offering April a slight bow. 'We haven't been properly introduced. I'm Benjamin. I believe you know my sister, Davina?'

April could only nod. Without taking his blue eyes from her, Benjamin tilted his head slightly to the left. 'And this is my friend Marcus Brent.' April saw another tall boy behind him, this one with dark brown hair and pronounced eyebrows that gave his eyes a rather hooded look. She had seen him staring at her earlier in the refectory – in fact 'glaring' would be a more accurate description. Clearly Marcus was one of the students who thought the new girl was bringing Ravenwood into disrepute.

'Come on, Ben,' said Marcus impatiently. 'We're already late.'

'Don't mind him.' Benjamin smiled. 'Beautiful girls unnerve Marcus.' He allowed Marcus to pull him away, calling over his shoulder as they went, 'See you soon.'

April sat there in shock. Had the sexiest boy in school just called her beautiful? Or was he like that with everyone? Probably. That sort of good-looking wealthy boy thought they could charm the pants off any girl they liked. Well, he wasn't going to have that effect on her. No way. She stood up, then sat down again with a thump, her knees having turned to jelly.

'Whoa …' she said, rubbing her temples. Maybe Benjamin's charm had worked after all. She walked into the Ladies and looked at herself in the mirror; her cheeks were distinctly flushed. Nothing to do with Benjamin, she assured herself, nothing at all. Although, he was really good-looking. But she wasn't about to go gooey over a boy, not after Neil. No way.

That'll teach me to go out on cold, damp nights, she scolded herself as the bell rang and she walked to her next lesson. *I must be coming down with something.*

Chapter Eight

April had spent the rest of the week just trying to keep her head above water. By Friday, she was surprised to find that she was actually enjoying coming to school for the lessons rather than the social life. At her old school, she'd liked a few subjects, but she had never been able to see the point of half of them. Chemistry? It was so dull. Geography? I mean, who cared about oxbow lakes? Lessons had felt like unavoidable pauses between spending time with Fee and her other friends. But at Ravenwood it was different; the lessons here were interesting, even stimulating, and she found that she was actually reading the course books *before* the lessons. To begin with her father had teased her about it, but when he saw how engaged she was he had simply smiled and said, 'A chip off the old block.'

The truth was that reading the books in advance was the only way April had a hope in hell of keeping up with the other students. They used words like 'moreover' and 'emphatically' and seemed to already know as much as, if not more than, their teachers about any given subject. More shocking, the adults actually seemed to respect their students' opinions. Now *that* was definitely a first. This morning in History, for example, the tutor Miss Holden didn't seem interested in teaching them names and dates; she was more focused on promoting a discussion that pushed their notions of what history was – not a fusty list of births, battles and deaths, but a fluid, organic entity whose whole interpretation could be changed by a speech, a book or even something as nebulous as the fashions of the day. Even so, April found her mind wandering during the lesson. She was haunted by the feeling of unease that the walk down Swain's Lane had left her with. Images of Gabriel, glaring eyes, shivering foxes, even the disbelieving faces of the police officers who had interviewed her were all whirling around, jumbled up in her head. She gazed down at her open book, intending to make copious notes, but instead she found she'd been doodling pictures of weird creatures and strange abstract shapes in the margin. What *was* going on in the village? And why was her dad researching the Highgate Vampire? Her father had kept her up to date on the police investigation, but they seemed to be floundering for lack of proper evidence. There was a question mark over exactly how Isabelle Davis had been killed and whether or not her death was linked to the Alix Graves murder. 'The police are releasing very little information,' said William, 'which usually means it's either something pretty unpleasant and they don't want to trigger any copycats, or the circumstances are sensitive and they don't want to scare off witnesses.'

Caro, predictably, had seen conspiracy written all over it. 'They're not releasing details because they don't want to rock the boat,' she had said confidently. 'It must implicate some prominent businessman or celebrity, maybe even someone in the police, so they're closing ranks. It's got bloody fingerprints all over it, you mark my words.'

April had no theories of her own, but she did find the whole episode disquieting, especially as she was no wiser regarding Gabriel's involvement. For some reason, she simply couldn't get him out of her mind. Sure, he was sexy, but it was more than that; April couldn't say why, but she felt there was some sort of connection between them. When she had looked into his eyes, there had been almost ... she shivered and shook the thought away. She knew nothing about him and she really had no idea how he was mixed up in the murder. Had he called the police? What was he doing there anyway? For about three seconds, April had entertained the idea that Gabriel might have had something to do with Isabelle's death, but just as quickly dismissed it as too far-fetched. After all, she had been there by accident, there was no reason why he couldn't have just been passing too. Either way, Gabriel hadn't been in school for the rest of the week and when she had wandered around Highgate Village after school, half-hoping to bump into him, half-hoping she wouldn't, she hadn't seen so much as a shadow of him, and the longer it went on, the longer her imagination was left to run riot.

'April?'

She looked up sharply. She had been lost in her thoughts, wondering if Gabriel had in fact been protecting her from some unseen killer, when she became aware that everyone was looking at her. Again.

'April?' prompted Miss Holden. 'The Renaissance?'

'Oh, uh, yes? What about it?'

A twitter of giggles went around the class and Miss Holden's expression changed to one of undisguised annoyance.

'Miss Dunne, if you're not up to taking the lesson, please excuse yourself and visit the nurse *before* we begin. Uninterested pupils may well be the norm at whatever school you previously attended, but at Ravenwood we take education very seriously.'

'Sorry, I didn't sleep very well—'

'I am not at all interested in your nocturnal activities,' snapped Miss Holden, to more titters. 'What I *am* interested in is the concept of the Renaissance as a rewrite of history.' She turned away, dismissing April, and addressed a lanky boy to April's left. 'Now, Mr Frazer, perhaps *you* can tell us ...'

After that April followed the lesson much more closely, taking notes diligently, but also sparing a moment or two to plan a few horrific acts of revenge on Miss Holden for humiliating her in front of the entire class. Now not only would she be seen as a freak and an outsider, she would be seen as a bad student, too – something she had a feeling was a greater crime in a school for the academically brilliant than out-and-out delinquency would be.

'April, stay behind, please.'

The end-of-lesson bell had rung and her classmates were all filing out, chattering and laughing, when Miss Holden stepped forward and stopped April. She closed the door behind the last pupil and motioned for April to sit as she perched on the front of her desk, her lips pursed. She was in her mid-thirties with shoulder-length red hair in tight ringlets, smartly dressed, but with a boho feel – wooden beads around her neck, a floral-print blouse and Roman sandals – but the soft lines did nothing to take the edge off her severe stare.

If she doesn't stop frowning like that, April thought, *she's going to need a bucketload of Botox.*

'I can sympathise that you might be feeling a little lost here, April. A move and a new school would upset anyone.'

April nodded gratefully. 'Yes, I—' she began, but Miss Holden cut her off.

'But that doesn't mean you can bring your emotions into my lessons. I can't allow disruption.' She waited until April was looking at her and said, 'I'll say it again, because this is important. Ravenwood is not like your old school, April. Not in any way.'

April frowned. There was something about Miss Holden's emphasis on that last line that seemed significant. 'Not in *any* way.' She searched the woman's face, but she was already speaking again.

'What we teach here is very important. *Very* important. Some might say it's a matter of life or death.'

Oh please, thought April. *It's only history.*

Miss Holden caught April's sceptical expression. 'I know this may look like a school packed with over-privileged nouveau riche snobs and, yes, there is an element of that here, it's the nature of the beast – when Mummy and Daddy pay for the best education for their little darlings, they get what they've paid for – but let me tell you, there are still a lot of pupils who have worked exceptionally hard to get here and they continue to work damned hard to stay here. For them, getting into a top university, Oxford, Cambridge, Harvard, is their sole focus and if they don't make it, then … well, let's just say there will be consequences.'

'Consequences?'

'Yes, consequences,' said the teacher, a brief flare of anger in her eyes. Miss Holden sighed and folded her arms. 'Look, April, I know your background. At this moment you might only be interested in music and boys, but the facts remain that you're intelligent, pretty, grounded, you're an all-rounder and I'm sure if you apply yourself you'll do just fine.'

April looked down at her hands, embarrassed.

'But there are kids here who simply can't do anything else. Maths, physics, science, these students are brilliant in their fields, but they are specialists. Put the biology student in an English class and they are average at best, so imagine what life's going to be like for them if they don't get where they're supposed to be. And think of the bigger picture – if that happens we might be denying society a cure for cancer, or the ability to breathe on the moon.'

She regarded April for a moment, seemed to be weighing up something in her mind. 'And, more importantly, we need to make sure they don't fall under the wrong influences.'

'The Russians?'

Miss Holden burst out laughing. 'No, April, not the Russians,' she said with a wry smile. 'The Soviet threat is well and truly over, dear.'

April could feel her face go bright red as Miss Holden turned serious again.

'But you can appreciate that students with such incredible potential are very vulnerable. We need to keep you all from being corrupted too early – it's part of our job.'

April thought she might be joking, but she looked completely straight-faced. *Why do adults always spend so much time worrying about our morals?* she wondered, eyeing the teacher's beads and sandals. *Like you've never rolled a joint in your life, you hypocrite.*

'And speaking of corrupting influences, it's also an unofficial part of our jobs to keep an eye on you and the people you're spending time with.'

April looked up, suddenly feeling angry. Had she been spying on her? 'I think you know who I'm talking about.'

'Caro?'

'No, not Caro,' said Miss Holden impatiently. 'Caroline Jackson may have discipline issues and a unique way of looking at the world, but she's fairly harmless. I'm talking about the so-called "Faces" and their self-appointed leader in particular, Davina Osbourne.'

April could barely believe her ears. How dare a teacher tell her who she could and could not hang out with?

'I thought your jurisdiction ended at the school gates, Miss Holden,' said April defiantly.

'No, April, it goes a lot further than that. And I know I'm not telling you anything you don't already know or sense: Davina Osbourne is bad news. I'm merely pointing out the obvious – that if you continue to spend time with her and her friends, you're going to find yourself in trouble. And trouble seems to be following you, doesn't it?'

'That's not fair,' said April. 'It's just bad luck. I can't help it if something happens right in front of me, can I?'

'Can't you?'

April started. 'What's that supposed to mean?'

'We make our own luck, April, both good and bad, and you have to be aware of your own power to influence events.'

'What, you mean I should have done something different? What? What was I supposed to do?'

April felt a bubbling anger towards the teacher. How *dare* she? Was she saying that April should have run back into the cemetery and fought a mad killer with her bare hands? It was ridiculous! She was only a sixteen-year-old girl, not some superhero.

'Are you saying that if I'd done something differently,' asked April, barely controlling her voice, 'that girl Isabelle wouldn't be dead?'

Miss Holden didn't speak. The teacher shook her head slightly and stood up, smoothing her skirt down. 'Just be careful, April, that's all I ask. As you mature into an adult, you'll have choices to make. Some of them will be very important, more important than they may seem at the time.'

Condescending cow, thought April. But she knew that arguing with a teacher would only land her in yet more unasked-for trouble, so instead she stood up and forced a smile.

'Thanks for the advice, Miss Holden,' she said, trying her best not to let sarcasm drift into her words. 'I'll think about what you've said.'

Miss Holden touched her arm. 'Do,' she said. 'Please.'

Note to self, thought April as she closed the classroom behind her. *Never daydream in class again.* She walked down the corridor and out through the main entrance, feeling the bite of the cold air in her lungs.

'Hey, sweetie,' said a voice. April almost jumped out of her skin.

She turned to see Davina right behind her. It was almost uncanny, given that Miss Holden had just been warning her to stay away from her. Well, she wasn't about to let that cow tell her what to do. April was so mad with the teacher, if she'd told her not to play in traffic she would have run across a motorway.

'Davina,' she breathed. 'I didn't hear you.'

'I get that a lot,' said Davina, smiling. Standing next to her was a Chinese girl with shoulder-length hair and glasses.

'This is Ling Po,' said Davina. 'She's a new girl too, aren't you, Ling? I thought I'd introduce you two as you're both in the same boat.'

The girl smiled awkwardly, casting her eyes down.

'She's shy,' said Davina, 'but we'll soon cure that, won't we, Ling? Anyway ...' Davina linked her arm through April's and led her towards the gate. 'What kept you? I was waiting for you after History. We were worried, weren't we, Ling?'

'Oh, Miss Holden wanted a chat,' said April.

Davina paused a beat. 'More questions?'

'No, something about how I'm holding everyone back because I'm not hanging on her every word.'

Davina laughed. 'That's typical of that witch. She's always sticking her nose in where it's not wanted. Don't let her get to you, she's just jealous of us.'

'Jealous? Of us?'

'Clever, pretty girls like you and me, April. And Ling, of course,' she added, with a glance back at the girl trailing along behind them. 'I mean, have you seen what she wears? Like some old hippy throwback, and not in a good way. She's old before her time and she hates to see fabulous young people having fun.'

'I suppose ...' said April, not exactly surprised that the dislike between them was mutual.

'I'm telling you. Old and bitter. Anyway, talking of beautiful people having fun, that's why I was waiting for you. Milo's parents are away this weekend so we're throwing a Halloween party on Sunday.'

'Sunday?' said April, knowing what her parents would say about going out the night before a school day, but Davina wasn't listening. Clearly that sort of thing wasn't important in her rarefied world.

'It's going to be so amazing I can't even begin,' continued Davina. 'Only the best people will be there and everyone's going to look stunning – dress code black, of course. Say you'll come?'

April nodded. 'Of course, I'd love to if I can. Why don't you text me the details, my number—'

Davina held up a sleek black phone. 'Already got it!' she sang.

April smiled to herself. How could Miss Holden have thought these girls were dangerous? Davina was an airhead, yes. A little smug too, and she certainly didn't have any problems with her self-esteem: Davina clearly thought she was just about perfect. April hadn't seen her in any classes, but there must be a brain underneath the socialite act, otherwise she would never have qualified for Ravenwood, no matter how rich Daddy was. Or maybe her speciality was gossip and social networking? Either way, to suggest that the Faces could be a malign influence was crazy. They just weren't that clever.

'I can't decide what to wear,' gushed Davina, as if to prove April's point. 'I'm thinking about a gorgeous chiffon Dolce minidress I saw in Harvey Nicks, but maybe I should go for something more grand like vintage Dior or even a McQueen ball gown. What do you think? And then there's shoes and bags and I'm going to force Mummy to lend me her Cartier earrings for the night. Oh, it's going to be such fun!'

'I can't wait,' said April, and was surprised to find that she was telling the truth.

'She said I was *harmless?*'

'*Fairly* harmless,' corrected April.

She suppressed a smirk as Caro spluttered with indignation. They were sitting in the Americano Coffee Bar on Highgate High Street and April had just related the story of her encounters with Miss Holden and Davina earlier in the day.

'Fairly harmless? That's worse than plain ordinary harmless!' she shouted. 'Like I'm even mediocre at being harmful! What do I have to do to be seen as disruptive?'

April laughed. 'I suspect you're going to have to rethink your plan of anarchy.'

Caro shook her head in disbelief. 'It's just not fair. You find a dead body—'

'A dead fox,' said April.

'Whatever,' continued Caro, 'and just like that you're edgy and cool. I've been cultivating this image of the school rebel for years, then you come along, fall asleep in a lesson and all of a sudden you're Che Guevara. There's no justice.'

'You could always fall asleep in *more* lessons, or stink-bomb the staff room,' suggested April.

'Don't you think I've thought of that?' She sighed. 'If I thought it would look good on my Oxford entrance papers, I would.' She stared morosely into her coffee. 'So, on the subject of disruption, any plans for the big night?'

'What big night?'

'Halloween,' Caro said, lowering her voice an octave.

April shook her head. 'Oh, I don't think I'm going to go.'

'What? You have to go!'

April frowned. 'I thought you were going to forbid me to

mix with all those fakes and give me a lecture about going over to the dark side.'

'No, no, don't you see? You *have* to go over to the dark side. It's the only way we'll ever find out what's going on!'

April laughed. 'Not you too,' she said.

'What do you mean?'

'Miss Holden. She seems to think the Faces are some sort of dangerous paramilitary organisation hell-bent on world destruction.'

'Well, I wouldn't underestimate their desire to crush everything before them,' said Caro. 'But mainly through withering put-downs rather than out-and-out violence.'

'So you don't think they're dangerous?'

'No, but their friends and relatives are. The party is at Milo Asprey's house and his father is hot stuff in the energy industry. He's also super-tight with Davina and Ben's daddy, Nicholas Osbourne, who heads up Agropharm International, no less.'

'Agropharm?' April whistled. 'Even I've heard of them. They make aspirin, don't they?'

'Aspirin, paint, plastics, explosives, chemical weapons ...'

April's mouth dropped open.

'But don't get Mr Osbourne wrong – he's not all bad, he does a lot of work for charity. He's the chairman of Airlift, the big charity for refugees and war-zone relief. He gives with one hand and takes away with the other, just like all good politicians.'

'How do you know all this?'

'I have my sources.'

'Is this part of your conspiracy thing?'

Caro shrugged. 'I said it before, there are no records of who runs the educational trust behind Ravenwood, but Mr Asprey is very active in fund-raising for the school and best of friends with all the governors, who seem to be in awe of him.'

'That doesn't necessarily make him Mr Big, though, does it?'

'No, but it does make him a great place to start.' Caro grinned. 'Which is why we need to get you spruced up for your big night out.'

Chapter Nine

April had to admit it, there were times when she could have strangled her mother, and shopping this Saturday was one of them. She had lost count of the occasions she had closed her eyes and imagined Silvia stepping into an open lift shaft or walking out in front of a speeding truck. She wasn't proud of having such thoughts, but then she figured it didn't make her a homicidal maniac, just a normal teenager. *Not that you could be a normal teenager with parents like mine*, she thought as she watched her mother mixing with the Saturday shoppers on the ground floor of Selfridges. One parent had never outgrown Scooby Doo and spent all his spare time chasing UFOs and zombies; the other had never outgrown Barbie and spent all her time trying to have the best outfit/car/princess/castle.

'Oh, now *this* is just fabulous,' said Silvia, holding up a huge turquoise confection with puff sleeves and a silver net overskirt.

'Mum, I'm not five. I don't want to look like the Little Mermaid. And the dress code is *black*.'

'But it's Moschino, darling. Cheap and chic?'

April shook her head firmly. 'I want a classic little black dress, nothing too showy. I want to look nice, not weird.'

'But it's the only label I can find here,' said Silvia, looking around with distaste. 'Can't we go up to the designer floor?'

'No, Mum,' said April. 'We can't afford designer dresses any more, remember?'

Silvia sighed. 'Don't remind me,' she muttered. She picked up a pink miniskirt, looking over at April hopefully, but April pulled a face.

'*Black*, Mother.'

Silvia sighed again. 'But black is so unflattering on your complexion, darling.'

'Mum. It's a Halloween party, remember? Witches and vampires?'

'Your father's favourite time of year.' Silvia reluctantly resumed her search. 'Ah, now I think *this* fits your somewhat limited requirements. And it's on sale too.'

She pulled a dress from the rack with a flourish. It was black, shimmery and looked very expensive.

'Okay, I'll try it on,' said April in a sulky voice, but she could already tell that it was going to be perfect. Looking in the changing room mirror minutes later, she could see her mother had chosen well; it was a classic little black dress – fashionable, not frumpy and not too revealing, stopping just above the knee, but still sexy. She had to admit, with her hair up and some gothy make-up, she would look sensational. Her mother had come up trumps. Not that she was going to admit that to her.

'Oh yes,' said Silvia, peeking around the curtain. 'The boys will be queuing up.'

'Mum!' protested April, but Silvia just chuckled.

'Right, Ms Conservative,' she said, grabbing April's hand. 'Let's see if we can spice this up with some drop-dead heels.'

Laden down with bags, April struggled into the taxi.

'I don't see why we had to get a cab,' she grumbled as she flopped into the seat. 'It's only a two-minute walk to the Tube.' She had no particular desire to fight through the crowds with her shopping, especially as it was beginning to rain, but it annoyed her the way her mother casually wasted money when her father was obviously struggling to make ends meet.

'Well, my feet are killing me,' said Silvia, as the cab slipped into rush-hour traffic. She pulled off a shoe and rubbed her toes, sighing dramatically. 'Besides,' she added, with a sideways glance, 'I wanted to talk to you before we get there.'

April rolled her eyes. Not the 'don't take drugs, don't get

pregnant' lecture again; she had to put up with it every time she went to a party or out on a date. Not that *that* happened very often. It was bad enough that she had to hear words like 'condoms' and 'spliffs' coming from her mother's mouth – especially considering Silvia behaved like a sulky teenager herself most of the time – but today's timing was particularly bad. To her surprise, April had enjoyed having a day out with her mother and she didn't want any misplaced 'counselling' ruining their bonding session. They had gone to Nails Inc. for pedicures and manicures, then to Carluccios for lunch – April loved their wild-mushroom risotto more than anything – and then on a mammoth shopping spree from Marble Arch to Piccadilly. Most of all, though, April had loved seeing her mother back to her old fun-loving caution-to-the-wind self. Their time in Edinburgh had made her spiky and moody, but back in the capital she seemed to come to life again. So one of Silvia's toe-curling 'advice' sessions was the last thing she needed right now, especially after Miss Holden's talking-to. *Lord save me from hopeless, well-meaning adults*, she thought.

'Now darling, I know you're sixteen—' Silvia began.

'Mum, please, I'm old enough—' protested April, but Silvia held up a hand.

'Yes, I know, and that's why I'm telling you this. You've got your father's mind, God knows, but sometimes you don't understand everything that goes on between adults.'

Uh-oh, this isn't the 'don't drink vodka Red Bulls' lecture, thought April with a lurch. *They're not getting divorced after all, are they?*

Silvia took a deep breath and looked out through the window. 'You know your father and I haven't been getting on so well lately,' she said quietly, 'and I wanted to tell you that none of it is your fault.'

I never thought it was! thought April indignantly.

'Couples can sometimes go through difficult patches now and then and … things happen. But we've made a fresh start by coming down here, the new job and your new school, the new house.'

She looked over at her daughter and April was appalled to see that Silvia had tears in her eyes.

'Don't worry, baby. Everything will be fine,' she said, her voice trembling. 'It *has* to be.'

April didn't know what to do. It wasn't as if her mother was cold and unemotional, far from it. She periodically threw huge temper tantrums when April's dad wouldn't give in to her demands and she would often go into long dramatic sulks over rows or imagined slights. But the genuine, adult emotion she seemed to be displaying here was alien to April. She'd never seen her mother cry before. Scream and yell, yes. Bucket-loads of crocodile tears as she wailed that 'no one cared', plenty of that. But this? April was at a loss. Should she offer reassuring advice? A warm sisterly hug? But before April could do anything, her mother banged her fist against the window.

'Damn that man!' she whispered. 'Damn him.' Then she shook her head, reached into her Prada bag and pulled out a tissue, blowing her nose loudly. 'Don't worry about me, darling,' she said briskly, leaning over to pat April's leg. 'I must have had one too many Manhattans at lunch, that's all. But I would appreciate it if you didn't mention any of this when we see Grandpa.'

Ah, so that's what this is all about, April realised, her sympathy for her mother's plight rapidly drying up. Silvia didn't want Grandpa Thomas knowing that she and William were having marital difficulties. April's grandfather was an imposing man, originally a Romanian immigrant who had made a fortune by unspecified means in the sixties and now lived in a huge house in Covent Garden, which was dark and full of strange ornate furniture and exotic smells. To April, as a little girl, Grandpa Thomas had always seemed like the ogre in the fairy tales with his wild white hair and crazy eyebrows, but as she had grown older she had begun to understand that his ways were those of the Old Country, where family and tradition were of huge importance. Not that it had stopped him changing the family name and doing his best to hide his accent and background as he clambered up the social ladder. In private, however, Thomas never tired of reminding them that their family were Eastern royalty – although he was always vague on the specifics. He also never tired of hinting that Silvia's behaviour had always fallen short of the princess he'd wanted her to be. April guessed that marrying a lowly writer, William Dunne, had been Silvia's greatest act of rebellion and thus any suggestion that their union might now be shaky would only light her grandfather's already short fuse. But she still resented being asked to cover for her mother. She looked out of the window, watching fat raindrops swim down the glass.

'It's not like I'm going to bring it up, is it?' said April. 'And considering we haven't seen him in six months, I expect we can find something else to talk about. I know Grandpa can be a bit insensitive at times, but I can't even imagine him asking what the atmosphere's like at home.'

'I know, darling,' said Silvia, a pleading note in her voice, 'but you know how easily upset your grandpa can be, especially when it comes to your dad, so let's try and keep this nice and light, shall we? It's been ages since we've seen him, just the two of us, so let's just enjoy it.'

April looked at her mother. Like every other teenager in the country she was used to seeing her parents as 'Her Parents', people who did nothing except gripe about the tidiness of your room and moan about your supposed 'attitude'. It was rare you got to peek behind the curtain to see the real person, and she wasn't sure she liked what she was seeing. Her mother looked different; older, tired. April knew she was being manipulated, but it was hard to resist when her mother had let her guard down so much.

'Okay, I won't say anything.' April sighed as the cab pulled up outside her grandfather's house. 'But can you try not to argue about Dad for once, please?'

Her mother tried to smile, but fell some way short. 'I'll try, darling,' she said, 'I'll try.'

Even in his old age, Thomas Hamilton was still intimidating. At six foot four he was a huge bear of a man, with a big head and hands like tennis racquets. His house was equally impressive, with a pillared entrance hall floored with black and white marble. A sweeping staircase led up to dozens of bedrooms and bathrooms. It was unfathomable to April that anyone could live in a house so big, especially in the centre of London where a Portaloo cost a king's ransom. But despite all the splendour, April was shocked to see that Grandpa Thomas had aged in the six months since she had last seen him – his back was more bowed, his face more lined – but he still towered over Silvia as he bent to kiss the top of her head.

'Poppa,' she said, brushing him away. 'Don't, please.'

'What? I can't even kiss my only daughter now?' he said, spreading his huge arms in a gesture of outrage. 'Has it become a crime to love my family?'

'Of course not, Daddy,' said Silvia, 'just don't … fuss so.'

'Can I help it if I'm happy to see my best girls? You never phone, you don't visit …'

'Okay, okay,' said Silvia testily, putting her bags onto a leather chesterfield sofa. 'We're here now, aren't we?'

Thomas shrugged and shifted his attention to April. 'Ah, my princess!' he boomed, effortlessly scooping April up like a grizzly bear grabbing a fish. He squeezed her until she thought her eyes were going to pop.

'Hi, Grandpa,' she gasped.

'Too grown-up to give your grandfather a kiss?' he said.

'Of course not, Gramps,' said April, kissing his leathery cheek.

'That's better. Now let me have a look at you,' he said, stepping back to inspect her. 'Ah, you have my good looks, Princess.' He chuckled. 'You're growing into a fine woman, just like your mum, huh?'

'Poppa, you're embarrassing her,' scolded Silvia, although April could see she had enjoyed the compliment.

'Embarrass you?' he roared, squeezing April's cheeks with his paw. 'Why should my girls be embarrassed that they're beautiful?'

A thin, familiar figure in a dark suit appeared at Thomas's

elbow. 'Afternoon tea is served, sir,' he announced in a subdued voice.

'Ah! Thank you, Stanton,' replied Thomas, turning and putting his arms around the two women's shoulders. 'Shall we have some cake?'

He led them through the wide entrance hall and under an archway into the drawing room. It was just as remarkable as the rest of the house, with a high ceiling, elaborate plaster mouldings and a carved mahogany fireplace, above which hung a huge portrait of a man looking remarkably like Thomas, only he had a moustache and was sitting proudly astride a rearing horse. Her grandfather caught April looking at the painting as they sat down in armchairs arranged around an elegant walnut table formally laid with crisp linen and polished silver.

'Do you remember you were always frightened of that picture as a girl?' Thomas laughed. 'You would hide under the table and squeak, "Grandpa, he's looking at me."'

'Well, who can blame her?' said Silvia. 'It's horrible.'

'Horrible? Nonsense!' cried Thomas. 'It's magnificent!'

'I always thought he was a villain from a fairy tale,' said April. 'Like the wicked uncle who captures the princess and tries to take over the kingdom.'

Thomas roared with laughter and reached over to squeeze April's hand affectionately. 'That is your ancestor, Princess, a very great man. He was known as the Black Prince.'

'Poppa, don't start with all this again,' said Silvia irritably.

'Why not? She should know her lineage – how else can she learn who she is? Especially now you live so close to your ancestors.'

Silvia shot her father a look, but Thomas ignored her and turned to April.

'I thought you knew our family has a vault in Highgate Cemetery?'

'No way!' said April, almost choking in surprise. 'Why didn't you tell me this before?'

'I thought your mother would have told you. You have a great-uncle and two cousins there,' said Thomas proudly.

'That branch of the family came to London many years ago. I wanted to bury your grandmother there, God rest her soul, but it wasn't to be.'

'Why not? What happened to Grandma?' asked April. Her father's parents were both dead and neither of her parents ever talked about their extended families, so she was very sketchy regarding her relatives. April noticed that look pass between her mother and grandfather again.

'Your grandmother went back to the Old Country,' Thomas said. 'It's what she wanted—'

'Not now, Daddy,' interrupted Silvia. 'Perhaps when April is older—'

Thomas frowned. 'Why do you always do this, Silvia? It's always "when she is older", "she won't understand". I think you underestimate my princess. She's a strong woman, like all Hamilton women.'

They stared at each other for a moment. April looked from her mother to her grandfather.

'What? What is it?' she asked. 'What aren't you telling me?'

'It's nothing, darling,' said Silvia, with a dismissive flap of her hand. 'Just some stupid myths and superstition.'

Her grandfather looked as if he was about to say something, then looked away and shook his head.

'So this Black Prince,' asked April, intrigued now, 'who was he?'

'He was a visionary and a revolutionary,' said Thomas proudly, puffing out his chest. 'This family owes him a debt we can never repay. We would be mere peasants begging for scraps were it not for your great-great-grandfather's bravery—'

'Poppa!' said Silvia with force. April had seen that look on her mother's face before. It was the 'don't mess with me' look she got when she had made up her mind about something. Only April's father dared to defy her when she looked that fierce – and he had the scars to show for it.

'Yes, yes, perhaps you're right,' said Thomas, smiling at April indulgently and reaching out to stroke her face. 'Maybe

I'll save the history lesson for another time. Ah, here come the florentines.'

They ate and drank in silence for a while, listening to the rain rattling against the windows. The weather had been getting steadily worse over the past few days and now it sounded like a storm was building.

'A toast, I think,' said Thomas, tapping a silver spoon against his teacup. 'To my dearest daughters and to family.'

They raised their cups and the mood lightened.

'So,' said Thomas, smiling at April, 'I hear you're going to a party?'

April glanced at her mother before answering. 'Yes, a girl from my new school has invited me to her Halloween party.'

'Well, that's good!' said Thomas with pleasure. 'Making friends already, it's important to have friends.'

'It's at a very big house in Highgate, Poppa,' said Silvia. 'April's friend comes from a very wealthy family.'

'Mum,' said April, reprovingly, 'like that's important.'

'Well, I certainly wouldn't be letting you out on a Sunday night if I didn't think they were the right sort of people.'

'Mum!' said April, exasperated. '"The right sort of people"?'

'No, your mother's right, Princess,' said Thomas. 'It's good to have wealth. Don't be afraid of money, it's a good thing. Only those who have never known poverty think money isn't important.'

'But I'm not going to the party because Davina's dad's rich,' protested April. 'Anyway, it's not even Davina's party, it's at Milo's house. Some of us aren't so shallow as to judge people only on their money,' she added, looking pointedly at her mother.

'But maybe you'll meet a nice rich boy there?' said Thomas with a sly smile.

'Grandpa, we're not all boy-crazy, you know.'

'Well, if you're anything like your mother ...' he teased.

'Poppa!'

'Oh yes, all the boys came running when my Silvia walked

97

by, I can tell you.' Thomas smiled proudly. 'She was the most beautiful girl in London back then. Still is.'

'Please, Poppa,' said Silvia, smiling despite herself.

'No, tell me more,' said April, glad to have the attention deflected away from her and her non-existent boyfriends. 'I've never heard what Mum was like when she was my age.'

'A wildcat!' cried Thomas. 'She would sneak out of the school window to go to all these stylish parties in Chelsea, meeting all these boys from Eton and Harrow. She thinks I don't know, but the headmaster told me everything.'

April was pleased to see her mother blush: another first.

'She was exactly the same at university, running around with the lord of this or the marquis of that. There was even an American she was very sweet on. Texas oil heir, isn't that right, Silvie?'

'Rhett's family—'

'Rhett!' April laughed. 'He wasn't really called *Rhett*, was he?'

'His mother was a big fan of *Gone with the Wind*,' said Silvia defensively. 'And it wasn't just oil, they had interests in electronics too.'

April found herself in fits of giggles, partly because of the mental image of her mother cast as Scarlett O'Hara, partly from the pleasure of seeing Silvia squirm as her dirty laundry was aired.

'Your mother was even engaged to a sultan at one point.' Thomas grinned mischievously.

'He wasn't a sultan.' Silvia sniffed. 'He was an emir, and we were never officially engaged. I think he was far more committed to his polo ponies than he was to me!'

They all cracked up with laughter at this, and it finally broke the ice. April watched with pleasure as her mother relaxed fully for the first time in a long while. The banter between her and her father as he raked over Silvia's old boyfriends and transgressions was warm and filled with genuine affection; a loving father and daughter reminiscing about the good old days. While she was happy to see them bond, it was tinged with sadness. April could vividly remember a time, not so very long ago, when this was exactly the way her parents had behaved towards each other; teasing and joking, enjoying the companionship and affection. How had it all changed? Why had it all become so tense and difficult? How could two people who loved one another become such a raw irritation to each other so quickly?

'Of course, your mother was never much good at picking the right man,' her grandfather was saying.

There was an abrupt frosty silence. April could suddenly hear the rain drumming on the windows and the traffic on the wet roads outside.

Brilliant, thought April, a sinking feeling in her stomach. *When it was all going so well.*

There was a long pause from the other side of the table before Silvia spoke.

'And what is that supposed to mean, exactly?' she asked quietly. To the untrained ear it was a simple enquiry, but to someone well versed in years of inter-family combat, it was a question loaded with history.

Thomas ignored his daughter and turned to April. 'Your mum could have had her pick of the men in London. A billionaire, a prime minister, maybe even a real prince, but no. She married someone who writes about dragons and mermaids.'

'Grandpa, please,' said April, her eyes wide and pleading. 'Don't go through this again.'

'No, I'd like to hear it,' snapped Silvia. 'It's always interesting to have someone tell me how I should have lived my life, especially when their own life has been so blameless.'

'What?' asked Thomas innocently. 'So I'm not allowed to discuss my own daughter's life? I suppose I'm only your father, who fed you and clothed you—'

'Oh, here we go,' said Silvia, casting her eyes up to the ceiling. 'The same old story, again and again.'

'Didn't I give you the best education money can buy?' he asked, colour coming into his face. 'Didn't I buy you a flat on the King's Road and give you a sports car, keep your wardrobe full of all those boutique dresses? And how do you repay me? By marrying some loser!'

'A loser? A LOSER?' yelled Silvia, slamming her hand down on the table so hard the bone china rattled. 'That's what you call my husband, the father of my child? How *dare* you?'

'I dare because I am your father, because I care about what happens to you.'

'It's a little late for that now, isn't it, Poppa? A little late to be worrying about "what happens" to me? Like you didn't have it all mapped out from the very start.'

Thomas glanced across at April. 'Silvia ...' he said, his voice quivering with fury. 'There's no need to—'

'Oh but I think there is,' hissed Silvia. 'I think there's every reason. You were the one who wanted to tell your granddaughter about her heritage,' she said, contemptuously gesturing at the glowering portrait above the fire. 'Well, why don't you tell her, if you're so proud of everything you've done? If my husband is such a bum and you're such a fine upstanding member of the human race, let's hear it. Let's tell her everything.'

April had never seen her mother more furious. She was leaning over the table now, glaring at her father. He was returning her gaze with defiance and she could see his shoulders quivering with anger. They were like a pair of dogs straining on the ends of their chains, desperate to tear at each other's throats. Thomas looked away first.

'This isn't the time,' he said quietly.

'That's what I thought,' said Silvia.

'Please!' said April. 'I don't know what you're arguing about, but I hate to see you both like this. We were all having such a nice time – why do you always have to spoil it?'

'See?' said Silvia. 'You've upset her now. You're always the same, like a bull in a china shop with people's feelings.'

'No, Mum,' said April, turning on her mother, 'it's not just Grandpa. You're as bad as each other, always picking at the same bloody scab, whatever the hell it is.'

'But, honey—'

'No, don't "honey" me, not this time.' April threw her napkin down and pushed her chair back. 'I asked you to be nice to Gramps today, but no, that was too much to ask, wasn't it?'

'Darling, your mum's a passionate woman,' said Thomas. 'She was only—'

April turned to her grandfather. 'And you're just as bad. You always have to say something about Dad, don't you? Even though you know it upsets Mum and upsets me. Well, you're both right about something – I am old enough to see that you're behaving like a pair of children. And I'm old enough to get a taxi home by myself. I'll leave you to discuss whatever it is you can't bear to tell me. I'm sure it's fascinating, but I think I can live without knowing.'

'But, Princess, honey—'

'Forget it, Grandpa,' she said, turning to leave, then swung back around. 'And don't call me Princess. From now on I'm April. Don't forget it.'

Chapter Ten

It was a perfect Halloween: gloomy and cold, enlivened by the odd sudden downpour. April gazed out of her bedroom window at the dark treetops whirling in the wind, then flinched as the glass was peppered with hail. Yesterday had been miserable, with her shopping expedition under grey skies and the lashing rain at her grandfather's house. By Sunday, the weather had wound itself up into a full-blown gale with the distant rumbles of thunder promising even more fun later on.

'It's pointless, Caro,' moaned April. 'Whatever we do with my hair, I'm going to end up looking like a drowned rat as soon as I go out there.'

'Stop being such a wuss,' said Caro, waving a huge can of hairspray. 'And come back and sit down – I'll make you look like a L'Oréal advert.'

'That's what I'm afraid of.' April pouted, but sat back down on the chair that was serving as their makeshift salon.

'Don't worry – my mum's a hairdresser, remember? I grew up with straighteners in my hand. Anyway, that's the beauty of a Halloween-themed party. No one knows if you're supposed to look pristine or like one of the undead.'

April glanced up anxiously. 'Can you steer away from the undead, please? I'd like to at least look as if I've got a pulse tonight.'

'I'd say that would be a distinct disadvantage,' Caro muttered as she tugged at April's hair.

'What's that supposed to mean?'

Caro tapped her on the forehead with her comb. 'Oh,

lighten up, buttercup. It's Halloween! Undead is hot! And stay still, or you'll turn out like Marilyn Manson.'

The truth was April was feeling uncomfortable about going to Milo's party. She didn't know anyone, least of all the party's host. Caro informed her that Milo and Davina's families were old friends, so it was sort of a joint party, but that didn't really help April, and anyway, even if she did find a semi-friendly face, what would she say? Caro seemed to pick up on her mood.

'It's all about state of mind,' said Caro between blasts of hairspray. 'Don't think of yourself as April the new girl, think of yourself as April the sex kitten. Here, take a look.' She turned the mirror to face April. 'Ta-dah!'

April gasped. If the dress complemented her figure, Caro's hair and make-up had worked a miracle. She looked amazing, with dark smoky eyes and artfully tousled hair falling in waves to her bare shoulders. She looked like a catwalk model in some gothic fashion show.

'Bloody hell, Caro,' she whispered.

'What? Don't you like it?' said Caro, chewing a fingernail nervously.

'Like it? I love it!' cried April, grabbing her friend and spinning her around. 'You're brilliant!'

'Hey, hey, careful, you'll smudge the blusher,' Caro scolded as she disentangled herself, but April could see that she was pleased.

'Caro, you're a genius!' said April, leaning in to the mirror to examine the make-up more closely. 'I look like a human being.'

'Well, that wasn't exactly what I was shooting for—'

'No, but I mean I look quite, well … nice. Grown-up, even. I barely recognise myself.'

'Don't sell yourself short,' said Caro. 'I can only work with what's already there.'

April beamed at Caro, then checked her reflection again. 'Seriously, this is fantastic. I feel like I can do anything dressed up like this, like it's a foolproof disguise or something.'

'Not that you need any help, of course, the way everyone looks at you.'

'Hey, I can't help it if I keep being in the wrong place at the wrong time.'

'That's not what I meant.'

April looked at her friend, frowning. 'So what *do* you mean?'

Caro shrugged and avoided April's gaze, concentrating on pulling strands of hair from her brush. 'You'll just call me paranoid, but haven't you noticed how all the boys look at you? It's like they're staring at you all the time.'

'Well, I'm the new girl, aren't I?'

'No, it's the *way* they look at you.'

'I don't know what you mean.'

Caro shrugged. 'No, neither do I, really. It's just there's something a bit … well, creepy about it.'

April began to feel defensive. 'What's this really about? Is it because you didn't get an invitation and I did?' she snapped. 'Are you jealous?'

Caro snorted with laughter. 'No,' she said. 'As if!'

'Hey, it's not funny,' protested April, feeling close to tears. She hadn't been feeling too confident about going to this bloody party in the first place and Caro's strange questions really weren't helping. Caro was the geeky type and she deliberately didn't fit in, but April wasn't a rebel by nature and she desperately wanted to settle down in this place.

'I can't help it if I'm suddenly the centre of attention,' she said, 'but I'm not going to turn down a party invitation just because you can't go as well.'

'Now, now, don't get all upset,' said Caro. 'Honestly, it's the last place on earth I'd want to be, getting trussed up in some expensive dress so I can hang out with airheads discussing lip gloss. Maybe I am just paranoid, don't mind me.'

April took a deep breath. She knew her temper could get out of control sometimes; one of the less appealing traits she had inherited from her mother.

'Okay,' she said. 'Sorry.'

Caro smiled. 'Apology accepted. So. Remember why you're there – it's not just to hit on boys, you know.'

'The spying thing?'

'The spying thing.' Caro nodded gravely. 'This is our best chance of finding out who's really in charge at Ravenwood. We need to work out if Milo's dad is really the power and money behind the school and, ideally, what the hell they're up to.'

April winced. 'Listen, I'm just going to a party. I'm not sure I'll be able to do much rooting around, I don't even know if we're going to be in the main house—'

'Hey, easy there, James Bond, I'm not expecting you to go safe-cracking or come back with an evil agenda mapped out on microfilm.' Caro smiled. 'This is more about you getting the confidence of those po-faced bitches, so maybe they'll let something slip about Daddy's business. You just go and have a good time. And no kissing.'

'I won't ... I will. I mean, won't. I hope.'

'Just don't get *too* friendly, huh? Don't want you going native. Remember who your real friends are.'

April looked at herself in the mirror one last time and then ran over and gave Caro a hug.

'I don't think I'll forget that.'

An unexpected knock at the door made April jump and squeal involuntarily.

'Only me,' said her father, opening the door a crack. 'Are you decent?'

'Dad, don't come in!' cried April, for some reason not wanting her father to see her in her party get-up. 'Go away, I'm getting ready.'

Caro, however, had other ideas. 'Hi, Mr Dunne,' she called, pushing April away and yanking the door open. 'It's lovely to meet you at last.'

'Ah, you must be Caro?' April's dad smiled. 'I've heard a lot about you. I understand you've been digging up an exclusive for me.'

'I'm working on it,' she replied. 'You'll be the first to hear about it when I've assembled all the evidence, don't you worry.'

'Sounds good.' He laughed indulgently. 'Now, I think it's time I gave you girls a lift ...' He looked across at April and fell silent.

'What? What's the matter?' asked April awkwardly, fingering her hair. 'Don't you like it?'

'I'm just ... shocked. I'm wondering what's happened to my little girl.'

'Aww, Dad ...'

'Sorry, honey, sorry. I can't help it. I know you're a grown woman and everything, but I still think of you as my cute little girl. Not that you're not still cute, it's just ... wow!'

'I think you should take that as a compliment, April,' said Caro.

'Yes, you should,' said her dad. He looked at April with glistening eyes. 'You look beautiful, love.'

April tried to swallow, but she couldn't, and her father looked away.

'Anyway,' he said with a sudden briskness. 'Let's get moving before the rain floods the streets completely, and you're stuck here with me, and that wouldn't be any fun, would it?'

As he turned to the door, William caught sight of Caro's jeans and T-shirt and frowned. 'Aren't you getting ready, Caro?' he asked.

'Haven't been invited to the swanky party, Mr D.' She smiled proudly. 'The burden of being a thorn in the side of the Establishment, you see. They don't want me around recording all their shady dealings – I'm sure you have the same problem. Anyway, I'm glad we'll have a bit of time in the car to ourselves, because I wanted to ask you about your theory on the war in the Middle East ...'

William made a 'save me!' face at April and headed down the stairs.

April made it from the car to the front door without the rain ruining her hair. *It's the next bit that's tricky*, she thought to herself, taking a deep breath as she looked at the big black door in front of her. She could hear the music pounding inside and suddenly she felt very alone. She glanced back to the car, but her dad had already turned around and was disappearing down the drive. He had given her the 'don't do anything I wouldn't do' speech as they drove to the party. 'I trust you, love,' he said, 'I know you're a good girl, but don't go getting drunk.'

April had winced, especially as Caro was in the car too, grinning at the cheesiness of the conversation.

'Yes,' Caro had piped up, 'and I've heard that some boys might try to kiss girls at parties. And they sometimes smoke cigarettes. Cigarettes are bad, aren't they, Mr Dunne?'

April reached up and pressed the doorbell.

Please don't let this be embarrassing, she said to herself. *Don't let me make a fool of myself, that's all I ask.*

The door opened and April found herself face to face with a gorgeous boy. Tall and dark-haired with hooded eyes that peered down at her, he was dressed in a black silk shirt and had a moustache pencilled onto his top lip.

'Zorro,' he said.

'I'm sorry?' said April, suddenly feeling a little off balance.

'I saw you looking at my moustache,' said the boy. 'I'm supposed to be Zorro.'

'Oh, sorry, I didn't realise ...' April stammered.

'Don't worry, I've spent the last twenty minutes explaining it to everyone else, so I thought I'd better get it in quickly. Sorry, don't stand out there in the rain, do come inside, I'll show you to the bar,' he said, stepping to one side and graciously helping April over the step. 'I'm Milo, by the way.'

Milo guided April down a dark corridor decorated with spray-on cobwebs and cut-out witches. To April's eye, the Asprey mansion didn't need much embellishment for Halloween – the dark wood panelling on the walls, carved wooden staircase and thick folds of the curtains at the windows already gave it a sombre grandeur, but the Faces – or, more likely, some party-planner they'd paid to look after the details – had clearly gone to some trouble to make it even more atmospheric, with glowing pumpkins, moody lighting and velvet draped over the furniture. *Or maybe it's always like this*, thought April.

'I think I over-thought the fancy dress thing,' said Milo as they threaded through the packed rooms. 'You'll see that everyone with any sense has gone for sexy Halloween outfits like you.'

April saw that the partygoers seemed to be a mixture of the most fashionable Ravenwood students – April nodded to a few as she passed and was surprised to be acknowledged with smiles and waves – and, unexpectedly, some of the more geeky element from school who were no doubt more comfortable in lab coats than dressed up as zombies.

'I think it looks good,' said April. 'The Zorro outfit, I mean.' *But then you'd look good in a bin-bag*, she added to herself, quietly admiring Milo.

'You're just being kind,' he said as they arrived at the bar. April had been expecting a table with a few cans and bottles on it, but this was a professionally catered event with a real zinc-topped bar and scantily clad bar-staff.

'So what can I get you, April?' he asked.

April gaped at him. 'How do you know my name?'

Milo laughed. 'You're pretty much the only thing anyone's been talking about for the last week.'

'Oh God …' said April, blushing.

'Oh no, don't feel bad,' said Milo, handing her glass of deep-red-coloured punch. 'New blood is always welcome at Ravenwood. Most of us have been hanging around together for, like, a hundred years. In fact, that's no exaggeration in my case; I've known Ben and Davina since we were tiny – our parents are friends. Speak of the devil, here's Davina now.'

Inevitably, Davina had been the only person to break her own dress code: she was wearing a stunning white silk sheath that trailed to the ground, with a white fur stole compliment-ing her luscious blonde hair. She looked like the White Witch from Narnia as she swept up with her boyfriend Jonathon trailing nervously one step behind her.

'Darling!' squealed Davina as she air-kissed April. 'Wow, look at you,' she said appreciatively. 'You look amazing! That must be Chloe? I had one just like it last season.' She looked over at Milo. 'And I see you've met our host,' she said. 'He's not as geeky as he looks.'

'Thanks, 'Vina,' said Milo sarcastically. 'I'll see you later, April,' he said, backing away, his eyes lingering on her.

'Don't let him get to you,' said Davina, shooting daggers at Milo as he disappeared into the throng. 'He's a bit of a sleaze, but he has hidden depths. At least, that's what my mother keeps telling me.' She turned to Jonathon and waved a regal hand towards April's drink. 'Get me one of those, would you, sweetheart?'

'This is an amazing place,' said April, when Jonathon had gone.

Davina shrugged. 'I suppose, I never really thought about it. I've been coming here for ever. Works for Halloween though, doesn't it? And so does *that*!' she said excitedly as a girl walked past. She was wearing a skin-tight catsuit and impossibly high heels; it took April a moment before she recognised this vision of slinkiness as Ling Po, the shy Chinese girl she had met a few days ago.

'Oh, doesn't she look amazing?' said Davina. 'We worked all day on this look, didn't we, Ling? Don't you think she looks sexy?'

April nodded. 'It's an amazing transformation.'

Ling didn't look quite so sure, putting one hand across her body and rubbing her arm nervously. 'Are you sure?' she asked. 'I'm not used to ... well, showing so much off.'

'If you've got it, flaunt it, baby,' said Davina enthusiastically. 'The boys are going to go wild for you tonight.'

'You think?' said Ling, looking to April for reassurance.

'Oh, I think you're turning heads all right.' April smiled kindly.

Davina took Ling's arm. 'Listen, I must introduce this sex kitten to the others,' she said over her shoulder. 'I'll see you a bit later, yeah?'

April nodded and watched as Davina strutted off confidently, waving and joking with the beautiful people. *She makes it look so effortless,* thought April enviously.

'Another drink?'

She turned to see Benjamin standing behind her. She had the odd feeling that he had been there for a while.

'Oh, no, thank you, I've just got this one,' said April.

'What is it, punch? I think we can do better than that,' he said, taking her elbow and steering her back to the bar. 'Megan?' he called, summoning one of the bartenders. She trotted over like an eager puppy.

'Ben, how can I help?'

'My friend here would like an Apple Pearl, could you do that for me?'

'Sure, no problem,' said the girl with a sexy smile, but as Ben turned away, April could almost see her eyes glow green with jealousy. *Hey, calm down, darling,* she thought, *he's not interested in me.* She glanced at Ben. *Or is he?*

There was certainly something quite compelling about Benjamin Osbourne and it wasn't just his good looks. Charisma, confidence, poise, all things he shared with his sister, she guessed. And he did seem to have perfect teeth.

'So, how's my favourite bad girl?' he said, one eyebrow raised.

'Oh, I'm afraid those rumours have been exaggerated. It's all been wrong place, wrong time.'

'Don't disappoint me, April Dunne,' said Benjamin, leaning in close. 'I've been looking forward to being corrupted by you.'

'I'm not sure I would know where to start.' *Am I flirting with him?* she thought with excitement. He was certainly bringing out a side of her she hadn't even known was there; and she was beginning to like the new, more confident April Dunne.

Smiling broadly, Benjamin reached back to the bar and handed her an elegant cocktail glass full of a viscous green liquid. 'Well, how about we start with this?'

April took a tentative sip of the drink. It was delicious, but she could tell it was also very strong.

'Umm, what's in this?'

'Ask me no questions …' drawled Benjamin. 'It's not Ribena, that's all I'm saying.'

April giggled. 'Aren't you having one?'

'Ah! You see? Trying to get me tipsy already.' He laughed. 'You *are* trying to drag me down to your level.'

'The night's young,' said April. *God, what's got into me?* she thought happily.

'So where's your friend?' she asked, steering the conversation into safer waters.

'Gabriel?'

April pulled a little face, annoyed to find that her heart jumped at the mere mention of his name.

Benjamin raised his eyebrows. 'He hasn't annoyed you too, has he? He has that effect on some people.'

'No, I … No, I meant the other one, Marcus?'

'Ah, he's around somewhere. Not too sociable, our Marcus, as I suppose you've noticed.'

'He doesn't seem to like me much.'

'Don't take it to heart. He's just slow to warm to people sometimes.'

'I won't hold my breath.'

'Don't worry – there are plenty of people around here who do like you. Believe me, even he's intrigued by you. We all are.'

She tried to look away, appear to be scanning the room for friends, but she could feel Benjamin's dark eyes examining her face curiously.

'So do you have a girlfriend?' she blurted out.

Benjamin threw his head back and laughed. 'You are direct, aren't you? I like that. I like it a lot.'

'I notice you haven't answered the question.'

Benjamin slowly leant towards her. *Is he going to kiss me?* she thought with a subconscious thrill. Despite herself, she suddenly realised she would like that very much. Benjamin brought his lips right up next to her ear, almost brushing her skin. She closed her eyes.

'The night is young, April Dunne,' he whispered. 'The night is young.'

Then she opened her eyes and he was gone. *Where the hell did he ... ?* She quickly turned around, but all she could see was the rest of the crowd. *How did he ... ?* April shivered and took a gulp of her drink. *Jesus.*

April was beginning to regret coming to the party. She only knew a handful of people, and none of them well enough to have a conversation with. She had only seen Davina twice the whole night and the last time was only to pass on some juicy gossip about Gabriel and a girl called Sara. Apparently she'd seen them going into the toilet together. 'And you know what *that* means,' she had trilled, watching April's reaction carefully. April's stomach was turning, but she wasn't about to let Davina know that, especially as she wasn't at all sure why. So she simply shook her head. Had they gone in to do drugs? To have sex? To work out some difficult equations? April had very little idea what was normal to pupils from Ravenwood. So she had spent the evening wandering around the house, trying not to look too lost, hiding away behind the paper umbrellas in a variety of drinks. Not wanting to let Caro down, she had tried opening as many doors as she could, but had only found empty bedrooms or necking couples, nothing even vaguely resembling a giant conspiracy. She had just decided to leave when she bumped into Gabriel coming down the stairs and, hemmed in on all sides, she couldn't get away.

'Hello,' she said frostily.

'Hello.'

'Enjoying yourself?'

There must have been something in her tone, because Gabriel frowned. 'Why do you ask?'

'Oh, no reason,' she said, surprised at how bothered she was by Davina's stirring. 'Just something I heard.'

'Really,' he said, holding her gaze as he walked past her, their bodies brushing against each other. 'I thought you might be the kind of girl who thinks for herself.'

'I am.'

He raised his eyebrows.

'What have you got against me, Gabriel?' she asked with annoyance.

He shrugged, not meeting her gaze.

'Why do you think I care one way or the other?'

'Well, you don't seem too happy to see me here. Not to mention you telling me to "get out" on my first day in school.'

He looked at her sharply.

'That wasn't what I meant,' he said. 'I was trying to … oh, it doesn't matter.'

April felt herself bristling.

'Why doesn't anyone around here say what they mean?' she snapped.

'I take it you don't like my friends?' said Gabriel with a hint of amusement that irritated her even more.

'Do you?'

Gabriel ignored her and took a sip of his drink.

'And what about Isabelle? Was she a friend?'

He turned to look at her, his dark eyes glittering. April held his gaze, her pulse quickening. She felt her skin tingle, as if an electric current was passing between them.

'Which Isabelle is this?' he asked.

'You know exactly who I'm talking about,' said April, lowering her voice. She still had no idea what had happened in Swain's Lane that night, but she was sure that Gabriel Swift knew more than he was saying; you didn't grab someone and shout 'Run!' unless you were pretty sure there was some danger. He *had* to be involved.

As if he was reading her mind, he said, 'Didn't DI Reece tell you who called them that night?'

'Was it you?'

Ignoring her question, he said, 'Has it occurred to you that I might simply have been in the wrong place at the wrong time, just like you? That maybe I was trying to help her? And maybe I was trying to help you?'

'So why don't you just tell me—' she began, but a tall blonde girl rushed up to Gabriel and, seemingly oblivious to April, threw her arms around his neck.

'There you are, baby,' she cooed, 'I thought you'd forgotten all about me.'

The girl looked up into his face and, seeing he was still observing April, turned towards her.

'Oh. Not interrupting anything, am I?'

'Not really,' said April contemptuously and walked down the last of the steps before pushing her way down the corridor, trying to put as much space between her and Gabriel as she could. *Men!* she thought. *Why do we bother? All they care about is their latest bimbo.* She slipped into a long room with floor-to-ceiling bookcases and took refuge in a tall leather wing-back chair where she couldn't be seen. Now that she was sitting down, April realised she was a bit drunk. She pulled out her mobile and checked for messages. One from Caro, one from Fiona. Caro's was predictable: *Don't forget the mission, Spygirl. Over and out. Xx*

Feeling guilty that she hadn't found anything for Caro, April stood up and walked around the library. There was nothing much to see here, just shelves and shelves of boring old books. She didn't even understand a lot of the titles, they were in some weird foreign language. She took one down and flipped it open. *Greek*, she thought, although it could well have been Cyrillic or something. April slid it back and shook her head. The whole plan was impossible; even if she had known where she was going, and what she was looking for, there was no way to get in and out of any of the rooms unseen, the party was too packed. Even the rooms and corridors upstairs, furthest away from the ballroom, had witches and ghouls sitting on the floor, kissing and drinking, some even lying down together. And anyway, she very much doubted if anyone connected with Caro's conspiracy, whatever it was, would leave files stamped 'Top Secret' out on top of a desk for her to find. International criminal masterminds tended to be a little more intelligent than that. She reminded herself that it was Caro's conspiracy, not hers, and quickly thumbed a response. *Working on it. Only found snogging couples so far. X.* She only had to wait a few seconds for a response. *Cool. Snogged any boys yourself?*

'If only,' she whispered to herself as she scrolled to Fiona's message.

How's the party? Everyone still horrible and mean? April smiled. Trust Fee to cut straight to the chase. She sent a reply.

Right first time. Horrible, mean and drunk. Think I'm heading home.

She closed her eyes and leant back. She really was feeling quite tipsy now, but not in an unpleasant way. Warm and fuzzy, but happy with it. She just wished she had friends here to share it with, possibly even a boy. She briefly thought about Benjamin, but immediately pushed him from her mind. He was just flirting with her; she'd seen him all over a number of other girls as the party had gone on. In fact, she'd seen him with his arm around two very geeky-looking girls. *Maybe he's into charity cases*, she thought. *God, maybe I'm a charity case.*

Her phone buzzed – a message from Fiona.

Don't go home yet! Send me photos of sexy boys first!

April laughed. There she was feeling sorry for herself when in reality Fee was probably sitting at home watching telly and wishing she could be at a glamorous Halloween party too. It wasn't that bad, even if Gabriel was an ass.

'Screw you, Gabriel Swift,' she whispered and began giggling. *God, I think I am drunk*, she thought as she wandered back into the ballroom. Positioning herself by a pillar to one side of the action, April held up her phone, hoping it looked like she was just scrolling through old texts, and quickly took a few snaps of the scenes before her. She wasn't at all sure people here would be happy to have their photos taken, given that they were drinking and smoking, but the underhandedness made April enjoy it more. Caro's ideas about spying might have been far-fetched, but April did feel the thrill of doing something a little forbidden. It was the first fun she'd had all evening; not quite James Bond, but a girl could fantasise, couldn't she? Speaking of which, there was Milo, spinning a girl around on the dance floor, a big cheesy grin on his face. *He is nice*, she thought, snapping off a shot, then quickly tapping in a message and sending it to Fiona.

'Forget it, sweetheart. He's out of your league.'

April turned around. The blonde girl, Layla, who she had seen with Davina on her first day, was staring at her with undisguised distaste.

'I shouldn't think Milo Asprey would be interested in someone like you,' she said, looking April up and down. 'He's not into slumming it.'

April's just gaped at the girl. She genuinely couldn't think of a response, so she simply turned and walked towards the back of the house.

How rude! she thought. *How could she be so mean?* It beggared belief. If she had been feeling out of place before, now, with her confidence crushed, April simply wanted to escape. She hurried along the corridor looking for the front door, but instead found herself in the doorway of the kitchen – or, to be more accurate, kitchen*s* plural. It was a huge space with stone floors and what looked like marble worktops; it was hard to be sure beneath the clutter of glasses and bottles and plates of nibbles. *Right, now send those photos and leave*, she thought to herself, quickly scrolling through the pictures. She had to admit, it did all look pretty decadent and happening – the dance floor with the girls in short skirts gyrating against floppy-haired boys, the bar area where the booze was flowing, the alcove to one side full of snogging couples. It looked like a cool night. She sent them to Fee with the message: *Like Studio 54, only with more bats.*

'Hey!' shouted a voice angrily. 'What do you think you're doing?'

As April had walked into the room, raising her phone for another picture, she had almost bumped into a group of four or five boys standing around a desk. One boy immediately jumped in front of her, deliberately blocking her view. 'Give me that!' someone shouted as her phone was snatched from her hand. April whirled around to find herself facing Marcus Brent. *Oh God*, she thought. *Of all the people …*

'And what are you doing with this?' he asked nastily, his dark eyes gleaming.

'Give it back, that's mine,' said April, making a lunge for her phone.

'Oh no you don't,' he said, holding it up in the air as someone else grabbed her from behind.

'Let me go!' she protested, struggling. 'I haven't done anything!'

'Let's see about that,' said Marcus as he looked down at the phone, scrolling through April's pictures, his expression changing from cruel amusement to outright anger.

'Oh really? And what are all these?' he asked, holding the phone up. 'I don't think we'll be needing these …' he said and pressed the 'delete' button.

'Those are mine!' said April, angry at his arrogance.

'No,' said Marcus with a superior air, 'they are *not* yours. Nothing here is yours and it never will be, you stupid little girl. I bet if I went through your bag I'd find half of Milo's family silver.'

'Piss off, Marcus,' said April, with feeling, but the truth was she was scared. It might have been a busy party, but this was an out-of-the-way corner and no one knew she was here.

'Oh, it's like that, is it?' Marcus smiled, reaching out to stroke her hair. 'I think we can show you what we do to thieves in our house.'

'It's not your house, Marcus,' said another voice.

Marcus's eyes opened wide and fear and anger flashed across his face as Benjamin stepped into the kitchen. The boy holding April instantly let her go and she stumbled backwards onto the floor.

'It's not yours either. And anyway, she was taking photos of us, Ben—' said Marcus petulantly, but Benjamin cut him off, snatching the phone from his hand.

'Out,' he said simply and April watched gratefully as Marcus and his friends disappeared from the kitchen.

'Come on,' said Benjamin softly as he helped her up and handed her phone back. 'Are you all right?' he asked, touching her shoulder gently. 'Nothing broken?'

'I'm fine,' she said, shaking off his hand. 'Just leave me alone.'

'Hey, I'm sorry if they—' he began.

'Leave me alone, Benjamin,' she said, rushing for the door. She pushed her way down the corridor, oblivious to the cries of people she bumped into or stepped on, just needing to get away and be on her own. She was furious with Marcus, furious with Davina for inviting her, furious at herself for being so vain she had believed she could fit in with these people. She ran blindly through the house, taking turns at random until finally she came to a glass door. She went through and found herself in a conservatory that no doubt looked out onto the grounds in the daytime, but now in the dark it only reflected the room back at her. *Christ, I look terrible*, she thought. She pulled a compact mirror out of her bag and looked at her face. Her make-up had smeared, her dress had hitched up and her cheeks were flushed. *It's Halloween, all right.*

'Okay, calm down …' she murmured to herself. Looking around, she saw a wicker chair and table by the window and sat down, fanning her face and trying to get her breathing under control as she fixed her make-up. There was an open bottle of white wine and some empty glasses on the table. Someone else had obviously found this spot earlier. She splashed wine into a clean glass and drank it down, wiping her mouth and grimacing as it burned her throat. *Urgh, not sure I'm a fan*, she thought, but it was for medicinal purposes. Suddenly April was aware that she wasn't alone. She turned to see Milo standing awkwardly in the doorway.

'Can I join you?'

April shrugged. Company was the last thing she wanted right now.

Milo sat down in the other chair. 'Sorry to intrude, but I saw you run past the ballroom. Are you okay?'

'No, I'm not okay,' snapped April. 'Your friends have been

shitty to me all night and I don't know why, I only came here to have a nice time and I've never done anyone any harm, but it seems that being civil to the new girl is too much to ask ...' All her frustrations poured out in a torrent and April was embarrassed to find that tears were beginning to trickle down her cheeks. She brushed them away angrily.

'Sorry,' she said, looking away from Milo. 'It's not your fault. I'm just not having that great a night, can you tell?'

Milo reached over and handed her a napkin from the table. 'Well, I wish I could tell you that my friends aren't arseholes some of the time, but I can't. It's just one of those things that comes with the territory, I'm afraid.'

April blew her nose and wiped her face, trying not to smear her mascara any more than it already had been.

'What territory?'

'Going to a posh school, having lots of money, knowing you may never have to work for a living and, even if you do, it will make you a packet just like Daddy. Being taught you're part of the elite. All that tends to make people think they are somehow superior.' He grinned. 'And of course if you add a pretty girl to the mix, well, that only makes us fight over her.'

April blushed. 'So if all that's true, how come you're being nice?'

Milo smiled. 'I'm not sure I am, exactly, but I try not to fall into too many of the traps. I try to be a good guy when I can.'

April filled her glass and chinked it against the bottle. She was feeling even more drunk now and uncommonly bold.

'Well, here's to the good guys,' she said.

Milo put his hand on hers, gently taking the glass away from her. 'I don't think you want to drink that,' he said softly, looking into her eyes.

April felt her heart do a backflip. 'What do I want to do, then?' she asked, the alcohol making her reckless.

'This ...' he said and bent forward, his full, warm lips pressing against hers in a soft, soft kiss. April pulled back a little, thinking of Gabriel for a moment, but only for a moment.

Why am I thinking about that selfish idiot? Then Milo kissed her again, this time with more urgency, his tongue seeking hers, his hot mouth on hers, and she thought of nothing else.

'Oh God,' she murmured as he pressed his body against hers, his hand sliding behind her neck to draw her closer. She did nothing to stop him. It was so good, she never wanted the moment to end. He pulled his mouth from hers and began to kiss her neck, her ears, nuzzling into her hair.

'You're so sweet,' he whispered, his hands slipping teasingly over her body, her pulse racing in response. 'So beautiful ...'

Milo was kissing his way down her neck now towards the soft swell of her breasts. It felt so good, so right. Cautiously at first she slid her hand beneath his shirt, feeling the firm muscles of his chest. He moaned in pleasure as her fingers brushed his nipple.

'Let's find a bedroom,' he whispered into her ear.

Her heart pounding, dizzy from his kiss, she nodded slowly, closing her eyes as he kissed her again. When she opened them again, clinging to Milo, she froze on the spot. Gabriel Swift was standing in the doorway glaring at them. His eyes were narrowed, his jaw clenched, his whole body exuding anger.

April froze, her mouth open, unable to look away from Gabriel.

'What's the matter ...?' said Milo, before seeing her face and turning towards the door.

'What do you want?' he hissed at Gabriel, clearly angry at being disturbed.

'Let her go,' said Gabriel simply.

'I don't think she wants me to,' replied Milo with a smirk.

'Let her go,' repeated Gabriel in a lower tone.

'Don't tell me what to do, Swift,' spat Milo, getting angry now. 'What's this got to do with you? She's mine.'

'Milo, don't ...' said April, but he wasn't listening. He lunged towards Gabriel. All in a rush the boys were fighting, a blur of fists and arms, struggling against each other, sending furniture and plants flying across the floor.

'STOP!' yelled April. 'Stop it now!' Milo landed a sickening punch against Gabriel's cheek. 'Just stop!' shrieked April.

'Get out,' Gabriel hissed towards her, his dark eyes blazing.

She fled outside, slamming the door behind her, running down a path, the gravel crunching under her feet. She could feel the rain lashing against her bare shoulders and the wind whipping at her hair, but she didn't care, she just had to get away from them, away from the party, away from all of it. At the end of the path she turned left, away from the lights of the house and down a flight of stone steps, almost turning her ankle in her heels. The path, enclosed by hedges, led her to a stone structure – a folly or a mock-temple gazebo of some sort? Whatever it was, it had a roof and offered shelter from the weather. Best of all, she was alone. She slumped down on a cold stone bench. *Why do boys have to fight all the time? Do they think it impresses girls?* And what business did Gabriel have interrupting her kiss with Milo? Was he jealous? For a moment, April hoped very much that he was, then pushed the thought away. She pulled out her phone and thumbed out a message to Caro. 'Sorry, didn't find any secrets, kissed a boy, feel miserable. Going home.' She pressed send, wrapped her arms around herself and rubbed her arms, which were icy now. She sat there silently for several minutes wondering how long it would take her to walk home, desperately hoping that the rain would stop. She should call her dad of course, but she didn't want him to see her like this. Then suddenly she turned towards the temple's entrance. Somehow she knew that Gabriel would be standing there before he spoke.

'I'm sorry,' he said in a soft voice. 'I know you'll find it hard to believe this, but I was trying to protect you.'

'Protect me from what?' she replied, glaring at him. 'From being kissed? What's so bad about that?'

'I know it's difficult to understand, but—'

'Really? Well, why don't you try me? Come on, blow my mind.'

'April, I can't—'

'Oh yeah, right. I bet it's something my tiny brain could

hardly grasp. Well, I'm sorry I'm not as academically gifted as some of you at Ravenwood,' she snarled sarcastically. She moved to push past him, but Gabriel blocked her way. 'And who the hell made you my protector anyway? What makes you think I can't look after myself?'

'You don't know Milo, you don't know what he wanted to—'

'No, and I'll never find out now, will I? Anyway, it's not like you're any better, is it, going into the bathroom with girls and that other one throwing herself at you on the stairs.'

'April, it's not what it seems ...'

Gabriel stepped towards her and suddenly she was scared again. She had no idea who this boy was, and no idea why she should trust him.

'Look, if you're not going to tell me what's going on, I just want to go home!' she shouted.

Gabriel studied her with those strangely piercing eyes for a moment, then slowly nodded.

'Of course, I'll get you a cab.'

April hesitated. Why should she trust one complete stranger over another? But there was something about the sadness in Gabriel's expression that convinced her. She was sure he meant her no harm, even though he'd been behaving oddly. And anyway, right now, she really did want to go home.

'Alright, said April. 'But no funny business, okay?'

Gabriel allowed himself a ghost of a smile. 'I promise. No funny business.'

It took them ten minutes to walk down the windswept drive and onto the main road, and they walked in silence for most of it. April kept stealing glances at her companion, but he seemed to be staring fixedly ahead, as if he was trying to ignore her. What was his deal anyway? She realised how little she knew about him. Davina had said he was moody, and he was rarely seen at school. Yes, he had been there that night in Swain's Lane, but she didn't know any more about what had happened there either. He could be a killer or a knight in shining armour for all she knew. They walked down the deserted roads towards the A1 where they should be able to flag down a cab, but when they got there the main road was just as deserted as the side roads. 'Here,' said Gabriel, taking off his jacket and draping it over her shoulders.

'No, you'll get cold,' said April.

'I'm always cold.' Gabriel smiled.

April shrugged, glad of the warm fur-lined jacket. 'So you're not going to tell me what all that was about?'

'If you can take my word for it, Milo Asprey is bad news. I'm sure he didn't have any good plans for you.'

'Ever think that maybe I wanted him to do whatever terrible thing he had in mind?' she asked.

'I really don't think you did.'

'Maybe I'm not the good girl you think I am.'

'Maybe not.' He smiled. 'But I hope you are.'

She took a moment to observe him. 'So is that why you've been protecting me? Is that what was happening in Swain's Lane that night?'

'So many questions …' He shook his head, still smiling.

She stopped on the street and turned on him furiously. 'Don't you dare joke about this!' she shouted. 'You go on about protecting me, but I'm the one who's been protecting *you*, remember! I could have told the police you were there in the cemetery that night but I didn't, and the least you can do is tell me what the hell is going on. I think I've earned that much.'

Gabriel didn't reply and for a moment, she thought he was ignoring her. Then he nodded slowly.

'You're right,' he said, taking her hands and looking into her eyes. 'Okay, listen. I know you have no reason to believe me, but what I'm going to say is true. I can't tell you everything right now, but I can tell you this: I didn't kill Isabelle and I don't know who did, but when you arrived in that cemetery the killer was still there.' Gabriel kept his gaze locked with hers, his face earnest. 'I was trying to protect you, April. You were in terrible danger.'

'But so were you, surely?'

He shook his head ever so slightly. 'You should know there was nothing you could have done for that girl. She was already dead when you arrived and if you had got there any earlier then you would probably be dead too.'

April realised she had been holding her breath the whole time he had been speaking and let it out in a rush. She was just about to ask him more when he released her hands and stepped into the road. The glowing orange sign of a black cab appeared around the corner and Gabriel raised an arm in the air. Once inside the taxi, April turned the heater on full and huddled up next to it.

'Remind you of Edinburgh?' asked Gabriel.

'God yes,' said April, shivering. 'It's like this all year round, but I could never adjust to it. Have you been there, then?'

Gabriel nodded. 'A few times, not for a while.'

'Really? Did you go for the Festival?'

Gabriel shot her a playful half-smile. 'I don't think they were doing the Festival when I was there.'

She was about to ask more, but it seemed stupid to be making light conversation after all Gabriel had said, and they lapsed into silence. He was right, of course – she had no reason to believe him, but the honesty and the emotion with which he had answered her questions – some of them, at least – convinced April he was telling the truth. It was a real leap of faith, considering she had known him for a week, but for some reason she did trust him. Was that silly? And was it anything to do with those dark eyes, that silky black hair, those cheek-bones? *God, am I falling for this boy?* she thought with a stab of guilt. *What's wrong with me? Wasn't I kissing another boy half an hour ago?* Like a devil on her shoulder, another voice in her head replied: *Yes, but you were thinking of Gabriel, weren't you?*

She giggled to herself.

'What's funny?' asked Gabriel.

'Nothing,' she said quickly. 'So where do you live?'

'Close,' he said.

Mr Conversation strikes again, she thought, just as he leant forward and banged on the glass divider between them and the driver. 'Turn left here, please,' he said, 'then drop us at the corner.'

'But we're not home yet,' said April, frowning.

'I want to show you something,' said Gabriel, paying the taxi driver and holding the door open for her.

The rain had stopped and the wind had dropped to nothing more than a murmur. As they walked along the dark street, the thick clouds were already parting and the bright almost-full moon was peeking through, making the wet road glisten.

Warily, she followed him.

'Through here,' said Gabriel, shooting her a reassuring glance.

His fingers brushed her hand as he led her down a dark passage between two houses.

'Isn't this someone's garden?' she whispered.

'No one lives here,' said Gabriel as they crossed an over-grown lawn. At the back of the garden was a gap in the fence and an old iron gate. Gabriel held it open for her and she stepped through onto a dark path.

'Are you sure about this?' April whispered, getting nervous about being in a deserted spot with a man she barely knew.

'It's quite safe, don't worry,' said Gabriel, taking her hand.

'Where are you taking me?'

'Patience,' he said. 'Just a little further.'

April felt as if she were being led into a dark wood. The snatches of moonlight were unable to pierce the canopy of leaves and they were surrounded by creepy shadows. Gabriel was striding forward confidently as if he were walking through a shopping mall, but April was holding her free hand out in front of her, half-convinced she was going to walk into a tree or stumble over something in her heels.

'Gabriel!' she hissed. 'Where are we going?'

'Here.'

Just then, the trees dropped away behind them and they stepped out into a wide clearing. In front of them was a huge spreading tree surrounded by what looked like an open trench curving away in both directions. It was as if the tree was growing in an enormous plant pot – but what was down in that dark corridor surrounding it? Suddenly she felt a huge rush of déjà vu. *I've been here before*, she thought, a split second before the penny dropped: it was the cemetery. *Why's he brought me back here?* she thought with alarm.

'What is this place?'

'The Circle of Lebanon,' said Gabriel, his smile bright in the moonlight. 'It's the jewel in the cemetery's crown.'

He took April's hand and drew her towards a flight of steps that led downwards into the dark passageway surrounding the tree.

'Don't be afraid,' he said, as if sensing her growing disquiet. 'It's a good place. Not even the foxes come here.'

It wasn't logical, but April had a strange feeling that she would be safe with Gabriel. She allowed him to lead her to the bottom.

'Oh, wow,' she whispered. April had expected it to be dark and spooky down here, but it wasn't like that at all. The strong moonlight lit the gently curving walls as if it were daylight. Set into the walls at intervals were a series of wide black doors, some with names carved into the stone above.

'They're tombs? But it's beautiful,' said April. To her surprise, she felt warm and secure down here.

'They built these tombs in eighteen thirty-nine when the cemetery opened. They made them so grand because they wanted to encourage people to come out here to lay their loved ones to rest. This was their shop window, if you like.'

They walked slowly around the circle, peering at the doorways. They were tall and made of black iron; they should have been cold and scary, but April found she was drawn to them by a strange curiosity. What was inside? Who was inside? What kind of lives had they lived – had they been happy?

'There's nothing much to see in there,' said Gabriel, as if reading her thoughts. 'They interred the remains in lead-lined coffins, but whatever was left will have crumbled to dust by now. Despite that, I think you can still feel the love down here. After all, they went to a lot of effort to make sure their relatives were remembered. You don't do that for people you don't love.'

They stopped in the shadows and April closed her eyes, seeing if she could feel what he felt.

'I know it sounds weird,' he said in a hushed voice, 'but I think certain objects and places can absorb emotions. That's why churches work.'

April looked about her. He was certainly right that it didn't feel creepy or sinister down here. For some reason, she felt as if she had been here before. The grey curved walls, the carved stonework, even the way the moonlight fell in patterns across the path, it all seemed familiar somehow.

'I think you might be right,' she said. 'No one laughs when you say Stonehenge has a certain feel to it, or even that a wedding ring does.'

Wedding ring, April? she scolded herself. *What the hell are you doing talking about wedding rings? You don't want to scare him off!*

But Gabriel had moved closer and April almost gasped as he touched her shoulder, steering her towards a doorway closed off by a heavy gate.

'This is the Columbarium, the only place in the cemetery where ashes can be laid to rest – if you look inside you can see the urns.'

She held on to the cold metal bars and pressed her face in close. She could feel him right behind her, his hands still on her shoulders. April knew she should have felt frightened, standing outside a tomb with someone she knew so little about, but all she felt was a tingling sense of longing. She wanted him to turn her around and kiss her here in the moonlight; nothing she had ever done had ever felt so romantic.

'Can you feel it?' he whispered, his mouth close to her ear. 'All that love?'

April couldn't help herself. She giggled and Gabriel immediately stepped back, breaking the romantic mood.

'You're making fun of me.'

'I'm not. You just reminded me of my dad,' she said, turning around. 'He's always writing these books about the unexplained, like UFOs and Bigfoot and all that.'

Gabriel looked at her strangely. 'Has he ever written about Highgate Cemetery?' he asked.

'No, I don't think so. But I'm sure he'd love it.' She looked back at the stone circle behind them. 'And I think you might be right about this place too. It just has something about it. You know, our family has a tomb here.'

Gabriel's face moved into shadow. 'Where?' he asked.

'I don't know, I only just heard about it yesterday from my grandfather. He's from Romania, so they're really into all this family stuff. Sorry, I'm babbling.'

'I think maybe we should go,' said Gabriel, stepping away from her. *What did I say?* she wondered; it was as if someone had thrown a blanket over a fire. Only seconds before she had been sure he was going to kiss her, now suddenly he was striding off up some wide stone stairs and she was having to trot to keep up. She barely had time to think about it; beyond the steps he led her along another path, then he was helping her over a gap in the wall where some stones had crumbled.

'Oh, I know where we are,' said April as they emerged on a little residential street. They were coming up to the south side of her square.

'I'll walk you back to your house,' said Gabriel.

'Is Milo really bad news?' she asked suddenly.

Gabriel nodded slowly.

'In that case, thank you for rescuing me and for making the rest of the night magical,' she said, not wanting to forget that moment in the circle, even if he did.

'My pleasure,' he said slightly stiffly. 'It's one of my favourite places.'

'I hope I can return the favour.'

'You're going to rescue me?' His humour was returning a little.

'No.' She laughed. 'I mean showing you one of my favourite places,' she said, immediately regretting it.

Gabriel was silent as they walked across the square.

'Sorry, I'm a bit drunk,' she said, feeling her cheeks flush pink.

They were at April's gate now and she looked up at him, waiting for him to say something, anything.

'Okay then. Show me your favourite place. Tomorrow?'

'Excellent!' said April, hoping she didn't sound too enthusiastic. She paused, her hand on the gate's handle. *Is he going to kiss me?* she wondered, but Gabriel turned away.

'I'll call you, April Dunne,' he said.

'You don't have my number,' she replied.

'I'll find it,' he said, as he walked back towards the square.

'Hey!' she hissed, running after him. 'Your jacket!'

'Thanks.' He smiled. 'Now you're looking after me.'

Last chance, she thought, gazing up into his eyes. *Last chance to say goodnight properly.*

Their fingers brushed as he took his jacket, but he backed away and pulled it on.

'You'd better get inside,' he said and disappeared into the shadows of the trees. Shivering and disappointed, she reluctantly turned and ran up the path. Inside, she slipped off her shoes and began to tiptoe up the stairs.

'Psssstt!'

'Who's there?' gasped April, clutching at her chest in fright.

Her father put his head around the door of the living room. 'Hi, Dad,' she said, breathing out. 'God, you almost scared me to death.'

'Sorry,' he grinned, the smile quickly fading as he saw her wet dress, her smeared make-up and rain-flattened hair. 'God, what happened? You didn't walk home in the rain did you?'

'Just the last bit,' she shrugged, hoping he wouldn't make a big deal about it. 'But I'm fine, honest.'

He raised an eyebrow quizzically.

'A good night, then?'

'Yes, yes it was. In the end. I'll tell you in the morning.' She smiled, then ran back and gave him a hug.

'Hey!' he hissed as April ran back up the stairs. 'You looked amazing tonight. Before you got dragged through a hedge backwards, anyway.'

'Thanks, Dad.' She blushed.

'Okay, darling, sleep tight.'

I'm not going to sleep at all tonight, she thought as she ran up the stairs, peeled off her wet dress and jumped into bed. But she did sleep, and it was Gabriel Swift who filled her dreams.

Chapter Eleven

She tried not to think about Gabriel all of Monday at school, but by lunchtime, April had to admit defeat. She'd spent the morning mentally dissecting every last detail of every conversation and look from the night before, worrying over whether she had done the right thing asking Gabriel out, fretting that she had put him off by being too pushy, wondering why he hadn't kissed her, remembering how Milo had. Of course, she hadn't heard from either boy, but that hadn't stopped her checking her phone for a message or missed call every five minutes since she had woken up and she kept catching herself smiling like a lunatic when images from the party popped into her mind. To be accurate, it was mainly images of Gabriel in the moonlight, although April was also enjoying reliving the kiss with Milo; she got shivers just thinking about it. After all, what girl wouldn't enjoy having two boys chasing her when usually there were somewhere around zero? *There's no reason he would call me so soon, is there?* she had to remind herself. *I mean, it was only a casual arrangement. And it's not like it's a date or anything – or is it? Did I even really ask him out?*

By the time the midday bell sounded, April was desperate to talk to someone about it. She'd coasted through her History lesson, surreptitiously checking her phone under the desk. She'd had about six texts from Fiona, all variations on 'Must talk!', 'Urgent!' and 'Where are you?', but she wanted to talk to Caro about Gabriel first. Caro had been at Ravenwood for years – surely she must know something about him. She was sure Caro would be waiting for her in the dining hall, equally keen to talk about the party, so she was quick to gather up her books, grab her bag and head for the door. She almost made it.

'April? Can I have a word?'

Miss Holden was calling her back. *Oh Christ, not another lecture, surely?*

The teacher closed the door and took out a file. 'I want to talk to you about your homework,' she said, putting the folder on her desk. 'How would you say you are getting on in History?'

'Well, I'm trying to keep up, but it's been hard. I'm enjoying it though, I think.'

'You think?' said Miss Holden, pulling out an essay April recognised as her own. It was covered with red ink and April's heart sank. 'I'll be frank, April, this isn't good enough. It would be enough, perhaps even good, in a regular school, but Ravenwood isn't a normal school, is it?'

'You can say that again,' muttered April.

'And that sort of attitude is doing you no favours either, young lady,' said the teacher. 'I appreciate that you may not have chosen to come here, but you're here now and there's no point in wishing it otherwise. If today's lesson is anything to go by, you've had your head in the clouds all day. Again. Do you want to stay here, April?'

April couldn't think of anything to say, so she looked at the floor.

'I'll take your silence as a yes.' The teacher sighed. 'Now, I'll tell you what we're going to do.' She picked up April's essay and, in one brisk movement, tore it in half.

April looked up, her eyes wide. 'But I spent hours on that,' she gasped.

'Not enough of them, apparently,' said Miss Holden, dropping it in the waste-bin. She pulled another sheet from her folder and handed it to April. 'This is your new assignment, regarding the church's role in social engineering in the Middle Ages. I've included a reading list, most of which can be found in the school library. It would do you a power of good if you actually read some books, rather than paraphrasing whatever you find on the Internet. I expect much, much better, April, so show me what you can do.'

April looked from the sheet to Miss Holden and back again. There were seven or eight books on the list – did she expect April to read them all?

'That's it for now,' said Miss Holden, turning away. 'You may go.'

'But ...'

'Yes?'

April shook her head. 'Nothing. Well, actually there is something. What is the Circle of Lebanon?'

Miss Holden looked at April with a frown. 'Local interest, eh? Well, it's a start, I suppose.' She took the assignment sheet from her and scribbled another line on it. 'Oh, and April?'

'Yes?' She sighed.

'The library's that way,' she said, pointing to the right. 'Turn left at the end. Can't miss it.'

April was boiling with anger as she strode down the corridor. *That witch! How dare she? Aren't teachers supposed to help you with problems, not take the mickey? I should report that smarmy cow.*

'Hi, April.' She turned to see Sara Gold, a minor member of the Faces, the one Davina had supposedly seen enter a bathroom with Gabriel. She was standing with Layla and they both seemed to be highly amused about something.

'Oh, uh, hi,' said April distractedly as she hurried on.

'Have a good time at the party?' called Sara to sounds of laughter.

April stopped and turned to face them. 'Yes, it was fun,' she said.

'That's what we heard,' said Sara, a touch of spite in her voice. 'A *lot* of fun.'

'I'm sorry? What are you saying?' said April with a creeping sense of dread.

'Oh, nothing. We just heard how you like to spread the love around.'

Sara cracked up laughing at this and April was disturbed to see that a crowd was gathering around them.

'I could say the same about you, Sara,' said April. 'I heard you spent a lot of time in the bathroom.'

The smile faded from Sara's face. 'Who told you that?'

The double doors to the refectory sprang open and Caro came bowling through. She grabbed April's arm and dragged her back the way she had come. 'We need to talk,' she said from the side of her mouth.

'What? What's going on?'

'No big deal,' said Caro. She hurried April down the corridor and out into the grounds. When they were a decent distance from the building, Caro stopped. 'Someone is spreading a rumour about you and a whole bunch of boys at the party.'

'WHAT?' cried April, horrified. 'You're joking! Tell me you're joking?'

Caro shook her head. 'No, I'm not. I wouldn't make something like that up.'

April could feel her heart hammering. *God, I've only been at this horrible school a week and already everyone thinks I'm a slut*, she thought in despair. *I only wanted to fit in.*

'But why? Why would someone do that?'

'Well, you obviously pissed someone off last night and now they're trying to drag you through the mud.'

'But who?'

Caro led April over to a bench and sat her down. 'Okay, talk me through the whole thing. And leave nothing out – the tiniest detail could give us the clue.'

'For God's sake, Caro,' snapped April, 'this isn't one of your stupid conspiracies, this is serious. This is about me! What if people believe it? What if I become known as some kind of sleep-around slut?'

Caro looked as if she was about to object, but instead she nodded. 'Yes, you're right, but let's go through it all anyway. We need to find out who is behind the rumour, then torture them until they retract it. So what happened?'

Taking a deep breath, April slowly told Caro the story of her night, from meeting Milo at the door, flirting with Ben, through the incident with Marcus, then making out with Milo, the fight and the romantic walk home with Gabriel.

When she had finished, Caro whistled. 'Wow. You did have a busy night.'

'So what do you think? Maybe someone saw me talking to all those boys and decided I was doing more than talking?'

Caro pulled a face. 'That's not the rumour. The rumour is that you were throwing yourself at anything in trousers. In fact, none of those names were mentioned.'

'Oh God,' said April. 'But why? Who would do that?'

Caro thought for a moment. 'Did anyone see you kissing Milo?'

'Only Gabriel.'

'Definitely?'

'Definitely.'

'Hmm. Well then, the prime suspect has to be Marcus Brent, doesn't it? You obviously caught him out and he's trying to cover himself with this story about how you threw yourself at him and his chums.'

'Eww, don't ...' said April, screwing her face up. 'But why? I mean, I know Marcus hates me for some reason, but I assumed that was because he didn't like Benjamin talking to me.'

'It's obvious – you were about to blow his cover.'

'What cover? Cover for what?'

'Think about it: what were you doing just before Marcus grabbed you?'

'I was taking photos of the party.'

'Exactly! And then he deleted all the photos, right? So now we can't see what they were trying to hide.' Caro was looking at April as if the answer was blindingly obvious.

'What? What's all that supposed to mean?' she asked impatiently.

'I knew it all along!'

'Knew what? What have you known all along?'

'That they're vampires!'

April gaped at Caro. She began to speak but then found she didn't have the words. She shook her head and stood up.

'Okay, fine,' said April. 'You have your little joke too. Actually I came to you to ask your advice about Gabriel because I thought you were my friend and that you might be able to help, but it seems that you can't stop your silly little games for one minute. Thanks, Caro. I'll deal with it myself.' She picked up her bag and started to stalk back towards the school buildings.

'Hey, hey!' said Caro, running ahead of her and putting her hands up. 'I know it sounds mad, but hear me out, okay?'

'Caro, please,' said April, trying to get past her. 'This is ridiculous.'

'Okay, so explain it to me – why did Marcus go so crazy when he saw the camera?'

April threw her arms up in frustration. 'I don't know! Maybe they were doing drugs? They were all standing around a table, maybe they had some coke or they were rolling a joint or something. Maybe they were arm-wrestling for all I know. Whatever it was, it was definitely dodgy and they didn't want me having evidence of it.'

'Or maybe there's a simpler explanation.'

'What? Them all being vampires is a simpler explanation? Jesus!'

She pushed past Caro, shaking with anger and disappointment. True, she hardly knew Caro, but she had thought they had really connected, that Caro was the one person she could count on. Didn't she understand how serious this was? Getting a reputation for something like that – more to the point, for something she hadn't done – it was unthinkable. She'd never live it down. Never.

'Dammit, dammit, dammit.' April sat in the kitchen staring down at her phone and its unblinking display. No bars at all, no reception in this stupid house. Why did they have to move here? April had tried to call Fiona, but her best friend's phone had gone straight to voicemail three times before she got home.

'Think, April,' she muttered to herself. 'What would Dad do?' Scotland's top investigative reporter wouldn't give up after a few failed phone calls. She only had half an hour left if she was going to get back to school before the lunch break ended – if she could even bear to go – but ... Then it clicked. Of course! Fiona would be on her lunch break too. She sprinted up the stairs, taking them two at a time. April flew across her bed and rattled at the keyboard, bringing the computer out of sleep mode. At lunchtime, April and Fiona had usually gone to their form room in St Geoffrey's to use the computers under the guise of 'extra study'. They generally messed about on Facebook and looked up celebrity gossip, but she knew that Fiona would check her email accounts as a matter of course, especially as she had been trying to get in touch to gossip about the party. She quickly signed in to her account.

Fee, need to speak urgently, can you call? she wrote, stabbing at the 'send' button.

Almost immediately, a box popped up on the screen.

Been trying, you daft cow. Your mobile doesn't work and the landline's constantly engaged! Fx

April cursed and ran across to the phone extension she's had installed in her room. Fee was right – the handset was out of its cradle. It began to ring the moment she clicked it into place.

'Thank God, Fee ...' she began, but her friend was already talking.

'What's the matter with you, April?' said Fiona with irritation. 'I've been trying and trying to get in touch since about ten o'clock last night! Where have you been? I've been up all night worrying myself to death.'

'I'm sorry,' said April, a little taken aback, 'but the big story all happened this morning.'

Fiona paused, hearing the distress in her friend's voice. 'Okay, sorry, but I was imagining all sorts of things after those photos. So what happened?'

April quickly told her all about the party, then the rumours at school. She left out the fact that she'd fought with Caro, too – they had enough to discuss as it was.

'Listen, Fee, I'm sorry I didn't call you this morning, but I thought I'd see Gabriel at school and then all this stuff about the ... well, the lies they're spreading about me, it distracted me. So what did you want to talk about?'

There was a pause at the other end of the line. 'Nothing bad, but ... well, it's just a bit weird. Look, get back on the Internet, I'm going to send you something, okay?'

April frowned. What was Fee on about? Was she worried April had fallen in with a bad lot or something? Surely Fiona knew her better than that?

When she opened her inbox, there was already a message from Fiona waiting for her, with the subject 'Open!' There was no other text, just four jpegs attached.

April clicked on each in turn and waited as her computer downloaded them.

'Are you looking at them?' asked Fiona impatiently.

'They're opening now. Hang on, the first one's ... oh. Oh God.'

The picture was grainy, as mobile phone snaps always were, but it was clear enough. It was the picture April had taken in the bar area at the party, with all the decadent teens lounging on the sofas. It was exactly as she remembered it, apart from one detail. Right in the middle of the shot, there was an armchair. On either side, perched on the arms and leaning inwards, were two girls, both laughing. *Only at the party they weren't sitting on the chair.*

'Where's he gone?'

'Who?' asked Fiona.

'Those girls in the first picture, they weren't sitting on the chair. They were sitting on this gorgeous guy's lap. He had a red shirt on, and it was sickening how they were throwing themselves at him.'

'And ...?' prompted Fiona.

'And he's not in the photo! It can't be, it can't ...' said April, almost to herself. The other pictures had downloaded now and she clicked on them quickly, looking for the one that was making her stomach turn over. Not that one: a shot of the crowded corridor; not the next one either: a shot of the entrance hall. And then, there it was.

'Oh no, no, no ...' moaned April.

'What's up? Are you looking at the one you sent me of Milo?'

'But this is stupid!' snapped April. 'Have you been messing about with them? You Photoshopped them or something?'

'No, April, I didn't.' Fiona sounded annoyed. 'I thought you had.'

April looked back at the screen. Her heart was beating too fast, too hard, it felt like it was wedged in her throat. The picture in front of her was of the ballroom. April had sneaked off to the side with her camera because she had wanted to send Fiona a picture of Milo. She had snapped it off, and sent it with the message: 'This is Milo dancing – sexy huh?' But Milo didn't look sexy in this picture. He didn't look like anything, because he wasn't there. Just like the guy in the armchair wasn't there. April tried to swallow, but she couldn't. Maybe she had made a mistake with that first shot – maybe the girls *were* sitting on the arms of the chair. *But they weren't, they weren't*, her mind insisted. But she hadn't made any mistake with the picture of Milo. He had been in the centre of the photo, dancing, a huge cute grin on his face because he was twirling a girl around in the air. And now, here, that girl was in the photograph alone. Whirling through space, no partner, no Milo. Just a weird black smudge where he should have been.

'Where has he gone?'

'That's what I wanted to ask you,' said Fiona. 'At first, I thought it was a joke, but I couldn't figure out why you'd bother airbrushing someone out of a photo right in the middle of a party. And then I started to worry. I don't know what's going on down there, but I do know it's pretty strange. And now you're telling me about this Marcus guy spreading rumours – it does sound a bit wrong.'

Wrong. That's exactly what she had been thinking. *All wrong.*

'So what do I do now, Fee?' said April desperately.

'I don't know, sweetie. Get a new phone?'

She couldn't explain it to Fiona, she hadn't been at the party. To other people it just looked as if she had a faulty camera, or like some weird light effect, but April had *been* there. She had seen those boys. She had touched them. *Oh God, I kissed a boy who isn't there*, she thought.

'April? Are you still there?'

'Sorry, Fee, I've got to go,' said April suddenly.

'But what are you going to do?'

'I'm going back to school. First I've got to make a grovelling apology, and then ...'

'Then what?'

'Then I think I'm going to visit the library.'

Chapter Twelve

April barely made it back to school in time for her next lesson. She was flustered and red in the face, but she managed to slip through the door for her English Literature class with seconds to spare. Luckily there was still a desk free next to Caro, near the back. She glanced at her friend, but she was avoiding her gaze. April opened her book and scribbled a note, then passed it across to Caro.

Sorry for overreacting. Sorry I shouted. Forgive me?

Caro took April's pen and scribbled under it, *Buy me cake and it's forgotten.*

April grinned and nodded. *Americano, tonight at seven?*

Caro gave a thumbs-up, then wrote: *Got a plan re: evil rumours. Now pay attention, some of us are trying to listen.*

April stifled a giggle. They were reading *Hamlet*, which, despite all the killing and ghosts and the weird Shakespearian language, seemed quite reassuring and normal after everything April had been coping with recently.

'Many critics have argued,' said Mr Andrews, their English teacher, 'that Hamlet is the embodiment of a man's journey from adolescence to maturity – birth to death, if you like.'

April wrote it all down, although she personally thought the 'many critics' were talking cobblers. As far as she could tell, the story was simple: Hamlet's uncle has murdered his dad, who appears to him as a ghost and demands he take revenge on Bad Uncle Claudius. Then Hamlet drives his girlfriend to suicide, there's a big sword fight and everyone dies. *Frankly*, thought April, *Hamlet's having a pretty easy time of it.*

April wished she had a ghost telling her what to do, telling her what those photographs meant. Was Caro right? Were there really vampires on those photos? Is that what her father's notebook was getting at? She shook her head. *Just listen to yourself, April,* she scolded herself. *Just because you took a couple of rubbish pictures on your mobile phone doesn't mean the undead are walking the earth. There are dozens of better explanations, if not thousands.* A couple of wonky photos, especially when she'd drunk about eight cocktails, were hardly proof of the supernatural.

'It's one of Shakespeare's most enduring plays because the majority of the audience identify with Hamlet's struggle,' said Mr Andrews. 'He doesn't know whether or not to believe the ghost, he's surrounded by people with ulterior motives, and then, when it comes to doing something about it, he finds all sorts of excuses not to act. That's what's at the heart of the play: which is better, thought or action? Head or heart? And those are questions we have to deal with every day.'

Tell me about it, thought April.

She was out of her seat almost the second the bell rang. She muttered a goodbye to Caro and sprinted to the front of the room. She wasn't going to stick around while everyone stared at her and discussed the rumours about her supposed orgy with Marcus Brent and his idiot friends. Besides, she had better things to do. She turned right along the corridor, keeping her head down, pretending to fiddle with her bag so she wouldn't have to make eye contact with anyone. Finally she turned into a long corridor with a wooden door at the end, a sign next to it reading 'Chandler Library'. She pushed it open and found herself in a surprisingly large space with a high ceiling and a balcony around the walls. It was very modern-looking with steel-fronted shelves and banks of computers.

'Big, isn't it?' said a voice to her left. April turned; a grey-haired old lady was sitting behind the desk, stamping a big pile of books in front of her. She guessed she must be about eighty – she had deeply lined waxy skin and horn-rimmed glasses in a style that April thought had slipped out of fashion in about 1956.

'Sorry?'

'I saw you looking at the room, dear.' The old lady smiled. 'A lot of people are surprised at the size of the library when they first walk in. They added it on to the original building when it was converted into a school. I suppose they thought all those mighty young brains would need more books.'

April looked around. There were two Chinese girls sitting at a long table in the middle of the room and she could see a couple of pupils browsing the shelves, but it wasn't exactly the popular destination she'd assumed it would be.

'Oh, it's all done over the Internet these days, lovey,' said the lady, looking towards the computer terminals with distaste. 'Or the wealthy families buy their children all the books they need. People don't read the way they used to any more. So the Chandler has become a repository for a lot of rare and specialised books. Which is nice, but I do prefer it when people read them.'

April nodded politely and began to move away.

'Library card?'

'I'm sorry?'

'I suppose you'll be needing a library card?'

'Oh, yes, of course.'

The woman pushed a white form towards her. 'Fill that out and I'll snap into action.'

April stared at her in surprise; she really didn't look as if she could move faster than a snail's pace. The woman kept a straight face, but there was a distinctly wicked gleam in her eye. 'I'm Mrs Townley, by the way. If you need any help, just yell. I'll probably hear you.'

April murmured her thanks and headed towards the history section. *Is everyone around here crazy?* she wondered as her eyes scanned the shelves. Military history, social history, international, political; each section was amazingly well stocked, but none of it quite fit the bill. She found one promising book – *The Inquisition in Britain* – but beyond a few engravings of heretics being tortured and burned at the stake, it didn't have much else of relevance. April had researched vampires on the

Internet after Caro had first mentioned them a few days before, but it was frustrating and repetitive with endless sites trotting out the same old 'garlic, mirrors, sunlight' stuff that everyone had seen in the movies and on TV. She was most interested in the mirror thing, as it seemed to be the same principle as cameras – something to do with the silver they used on the back of old looking glasses – but most of the information on the Net was contradictory, mainly because most people were getting their information from different movies and books. She found the worst offenders in the online discussion groups were incredibly serious teenagers who felt they 'were' vampires, despite the fact that they weren't immortal bloodthirsty killers. They all confidently claimed they knew the 'real truth' about vampires, but most of it seemed connected to various rather sad sexual fantasies. Ironically, April realised that she was looking for something like one of her dad's books – for a work by someone who had sifted through all the silliness and the rumours and could give her the hard facts, if there were any. But she couldn't really ask him, could she? She imagined the conversation: 'Dad, you know those vampires you're looking for? Well, I've found them. They go to my school. And you know how you told me not to kiss any boys at the party? Well, I didn't, technically, because it turns out he's actually a vampire.' *I would be so grounded, if he didn't cart me off to the loony bin first.*

'Ah-ha, this is more like it,' she whispered as she finally found the mythology section. Working backwards, there were books on zombies, witches, werewolves, even a book detailing the folklore of the will-o'-the-wisp. And then – her heart leapt – there were four or five books on vampires. She pulled them down and carried the pile to a table out of sight of the Chinese girls. There were enough rumours going around about her already without adding fuel to the fire.

April eagerly flipped through the books, but she was to be just as frustrated as she had been with the Internet. Vampires in the movies, vampires in romantic literature, vampires in folklore, it was all the same tired stuff: vampires don't like silver, crucifixes or holy water and you could kill them by staking them through the heart, exposing them to sunlight or beheading them. Some could turn themselves into bats or wolves. The end. There was nothing relating to her father's theories and nothing she would regard as serious – a scholarly dissection of folk myths, for example. And nothing on Highgate or the Highgate Vampire. She had felt sure a library of this size would have had something on local legends, but there was nothing. Dejected, April was putting the books back on the shelf when she noticed a volume that had been left on top of the book case. Curious, she picked it up and her heart leapt again.

London's Cemeteries: A Guide, by Ian Montgomerie.

Excited, she sat down and began reading:

In the early 19th century, London was booming. Almost overnight, the population doubled, with unchecked immigration and impoverished workers pouring in from the countryside, but the streets were not paved with gold, as many thought. Disease, overcrowding, poor sanitation and starvation all contributed to a massive rise in the death rate, so much so that in 1832 the government, fearing an epidemic, passed a bill designed to encourage entrepreneurs to set up private burial plots outside the city. Their plan worked and within the next decade, seven new cemeteries were built at Kensal Green, West Norwood, Abney Park, Nunhead, Brompton, Tower Hamlets and Highgate. They became known as the 'Magnificent Seven'.

April skim-read the chapter on Highgate and, although it was interesting – the Victorian attitudes to death, the use of pagan and Egyptian imagery, the famous burials – there was nothing she wanted. She flicked through the rest, but there was no mention of vampires or any sort of supernatural occurrences at all.

She took the book back to its shelf and headed towards the front desk where Mrs Townley was now sitting with her eyes closed, her knitting on her lap, listening to an iPod. April sighed theatrically, leaving her filled-in library card form on the desk and heading towards the door.

'Didn't find what you were looking for, eh?'

April almost jumped in the air. 'God, you scared me!' she gasped, clutching a hand to her chest.

The old woman chuckled. 'Been doing that trick for donkey's years. Gets 'em every time.'

April gazed at her, amazed. The old woman really was crazy. 'No,' she said, unable to keep the disappointment from her voice. 'I didn't find what I was looking for.'

'Well, stick with it, lovey. Whatever you're after, it's out there, it's just a matter of looking in the right place. And I can always find time to help anyone who's really looking for answers.'

April nodded weakly as she headed for the door. 'Thank you.'

'Oh, before you go, I thought you might like these,' said the old lady, picking up a huge pile of books from the shelf behind her and thumping them down on the desk. 'Miss Holden's reading list—'

'Wow, thanks!' said April. 'How did you—?'

'No magic to it, dearie. Miss Holden's very efficient. She sent me an email.'

April pulled out the sheet Miss Holden had given her and pointed to the title the teacher had added at the bottom.

Mrs Townley peered at it through her glasses, then looked at April. 'For that you'll be needing Griffin's.'

'Griffin's? Is that a reference book?'

'No, the bookshop on the High Street. Mr Gill is the owner, tell him I sent you and that you're one of my "special students" – he'll know what you mean.' Mrs Townley leant forward and beckoned April closer. 'I don't send many students to Mr Gill,' she whispered. 'He's a dear man, but he's very old and I don't like to wear him out. So let's keep it our little secret, yes?'

'But why do we ha—' began April, but Mrs Townley had already turned away.

'You!' she yelled at one of the Chinese girls. 'Break the spine on one of my books and I'll break yours!'

As April walked away, she heard Mrs Townley turn on her iPod again. Iron Maiden's *Number of the Beast*.

Crazy, April thought to herself as she walked out of the library. *Completely crazy.*

Griffin's looked like it had been abandoned, a curiosity from a bygone age left behind as the rest of the world modernised and moved onwards. It's a miracle it's avoided becoming a Starbucks, thought April. From its tiny windowpanes to its narrow entrance with its firmly closed door, it was the absolute opposite of the bright, welcoming, open-plan shops on either side. Griffin's bowed shopfront may well have been painted an interesting colour once upon a time, but whatever it was, it was now buried under decades of grime from the High Street traffic. It was a wonder you could even read the dull gold lettering on the shop sign: R. J. Griffin, Purveyor of Fine Books.

There was a hand-written sign on the door – 'Please ring bell' – but it took half a dozen goes before a little old man shuffled up to let her in: Mr Gill, April presumed. He had ruddy apple cheeks and was bald but for the tufts of wild white hair sticking out horizontally from just above his ears. His half-moon glasses and moss-green cardigan added to the impression of a studious but forgetful Cambridge don. But he didn't look particularly friendly.

'Can I help you?' he asked suspiciously, still holding on to the door. 'We're not sponsoring anything.'

'No, no,' said April, 'I'm looking for a book.'

The man raised his eyebrows and looked April up and down. 'Oh well.' He sighed. 'I suppose you'd better come in, then.'

He opened the door just enough to let April squeeze in. She had to duck under a clump of strange dried flowers hanging from the doorframe and step around an old full-length mirror. It was an incredibly cramped shop, every available surface covered with worn, dusty old books. She didn't hold out much hope of finding anything here, let alone the book she needed.

'Is there something specific you'd like?' said the old man sceptically. Clearly they never had any customers under seventy in here. April fumbled out her reading list and showed him the book title Miss Holden had scribbled at the bottom.

'I'm a pupil at Ravenwood,' said April, almost apologetically. 'Mrs Townley sent me.'

At the mention of the librarian, Mr Gill's whole demeanour changed. 'Mrs Townley?' said the old man, straightening up. 'Well, why didn't you say so? How is Marjorie?'

Marjorie?

'She seems, um, very well,' said April dubiously.

'Splendid times we had by the Serpentine,' said Mr Gill, almost to himself.

April waited for a moment, but Mr Gill was lost in his memories.

'The book?' she asked.

'Ah yes, the book,' said the shopkeeper, returning to his previous hostility. 'I dare say we have something like it in the local history section. You'll find it through the reading room,' he said, indicating a small door behind his counter.

Beyond the doorway, April found herself in a miniature version of an old-fashioned library, the kind you'd expect to find in a nineteen-twenties country house or an Agatha Christie novel, with wooden floor-to-ceiling bookshelves and two sloping reading tables in the middle of the room. Little hand-written signs were tacked to the front of the shelves: 'Classical Rome', 'Natural History', 'Psychology' and so on. Slowly she walked around, reading the spines of the books. She was no scholar, but even she recognised some of the titles: *Origin of Species* by Charles Darwin; George Stubbs' *The Anatomy of the Horse*; *Relativity: The Special and General Theory* by Albert Einstein.

'Wow,' said April. She wasn't exactly sure how rare or valuable these books were, but she knew they were probably worth thousands each, if not more. The little corridors formed by the shelves had lots of twists and turns; it was quite a maze back there and it seemed much bigger than the shopfront had suggested.

Hidden around a corner she finally stumbled across the 'Local History' section. It was crammed with picture books, full of old maps and sepia photographs of the area a hundred years ago, and books with faded gilt titles like *Dr Crippen, the Holloway Poisoner*, *The Battle for Churchyard Bottom Wood* and *The Life and Death of Samuel Taylor Coleridge*. It was all murder and death everywhere. She pulled out some books and checked their indexes, but there was no mention of vampires and no sign of the book Miss Holden had recommended. Still, April felt she was making progress of a sort, and she had the thrill of discovering a place she knew her father would absolutely love. Making a mental note to tell him about it, she walked into the section labelled 'Medicine'. Her eye was drawn to one ancient-looking book bound in black leather with hinges on the outside. There was just one word on the outside: *Necronomicon*.

'Don't touch that, please,' said Mr Gill abruptly, making April jump. She hadn't even been aware he was behind her. He pushed past her and draped a cloth over the book. 'Some of these titles are very delicate,' he said.

Okay, keep your hair on, she thought, *I wasn't going to set fire to it.*

'Is there anything I can help you with?' he asked pointedly. April was reluctant to tell him, but she had the distinct feeling Mr Gill was about to throw her out if she didn't say something intelligent.

'Well, I'm looking for something on diseases and myths, something along those lines?'

The old man walked over to one of the bookshelves and pulled out a slim volume with a green cover. 'This may be of some use,' he said, indicating a reading table and stool.

April nodded her thanks and sat down. The book was called *The Healing Word: Folk, Myths and Medicine*. April turned to the index and was almost overjoyed to see the entry under 'V': vampires, p. 124. She quickly turned to the page:

Vampirism has always been linked to disease. It is often dismissed as allegorical tales about the Black Death – undead strangers coming to remote villages and killing everyone – creating a story people can understand to make sense of the inexplicable. To simple peasants the idea of strange zombie creatures drinking blood makes more sense than the idea of some invisible bacteria carried in the air. But all the traits of the vampire – marks on the neck and wrists, lust for blood, hypersexuality, enlarged teeth, sensitivity to sunlight and even garlic – can all be explained in other ways. They are the symptoms of rabies and porphyria, to name but two of the diseases common at the time that could have added 'proof' to the rumours and speculation about vampirism.

Feeling disappointed, April carefully replaced the book and returned to the front desk.

'Not what you wanted?'

'Not really.'

'You were looking for something about the Highgate Vampire, I take it?'

April almost gasped and Mr Gill gave her a slight smile. 'One needn't be Sherlock Holmes,' he said. 'You were looking for information on the cemetery and on old myths. Fairly easy to see the link.'

'Oh,' said April, a little embarrassed. 'I thought I might find a book on it here.'

Mr Gill scoffed. 'Cobblers, the lot of it, I won't have them in the shop.'

'I'm sorry?'

'Books about the Highgate Vampire, they're not worth the paper they're printed on,' he said. 'But if you really want to know, it's all up here.' He tapped a finger against his forehead.

April's eyes widened. 'Really?'

'When something that exciting happens on one's doorstep, it would be churlish to pass up the opportunity to get your feet wet, as it were. All happened in the early seventies, you see.

I'm sure Marjorie – Mrs Townley – will remember it as well as I do.'

'Can you tell me what happened?'

Mr Gill indicated a tall stool facing his counter and April sat down.

'I'm only telling you this because of our, uh, mutual friend, you understand?' he said, pouring her a cup of tea from a tartan flask.

April nodded.

'As long as that's clear. Well, back in the nineteen-sixties, Highgate Cemetery was in rather a sorry state. I suppose many of the relatives of the ... ah ... inhabitants had died off themselves and the graves had become overgrown and somewhat neglected. It became a gathering place for some rather unsavoury characters, hippies and so on, and there were quite a few incidents of graves being desecrated, even bodies removed. Anyway, one night, a chap claimed he saw a "spectral presence" and wrote to the local paper asking if anyone else had ever had a similar experience in the area. Well, that was a red rag to a bull, of course, and they were inundated with reports, although none of them seemed to match: ghosts, blood trails, dead foxes—'

'Dead foxes?' interrupted April.

'Yes, there was a story that they were being found dead, with their throats torn open. But, of course, it was probably just one animal killed by a dog and the numbers got steadily increased in the telling. Interesting though.'

'Interesting? Why?'

'Oh, interesting that they should have chosen foxes rather than cats or rats or birds. Foxes are quite important in folklore, you see. They're a symbol of cunning and deception and also of hunting, for obvious reasons. The pagan Welsh believed witches could transform themselves into foxes.'

April stared down at her cup, her brow furrowed. 'I saw one,' she said very quietly. 'A dead fox, I mean.'

Mr Gill frowned. 'When was this?'

'Last week. Just inside the north gate of the cemetery.'

The old man couldn't hide his concern. 'Well, it was probably hit by a car, poor thing. People do drive up there like demons. Probably just crawled off somewhere quiet to die.'

April nodded noncommittally. 'I suppose.'

'Don't look so worried, dear child. After all, remember that none of this vampire hoopla has ever been substantiated and the people who claim to see them are the sort who call in to radio shows claiming to have seen Lord Lucan in their local supermarket. There are a lot of people who think it was all a hoax.'

'And are you one of them?'

'When it comes to vampires, you do find most of it is … well, not to put too fine a point on it, it's rubbish. Personally I think "vampire lore" is often a case of people seeking out Eastern European folklore and making it fit their story, rather than the other way around.'

'But how did they get from ghosts and folklore to vampires?'

'Now that's the interesting part of the Highgate story. The week after the original letter, someone else wrote in to the paper claiming that the original spectre had been a vampire, brought over from Eastern Europe in a coffin. The claim was completely unsubstantiated, but the media picked up on it, it made the six o'clock news and the story grew and grew. There were tales of a woman being beheaded and even a vampire being staked in a tomb and a nest of them being cleared out of the cemetery. All very unlikely, but that never stops journalists in search of a good story.'

'So you think it was all nonsense?'

'Oh no, quite the contrary.'

April looked at him, feeling cold all of a sudden. 'You think there were vampires in the cemetery?'

'I don't think there *were*. There *are*. Present tense. And not only in the graveyard.'

'I'm sorry?'

'Oh yes, my dear. It's my belief that vampires are real and that they are living among us.'

Chapter Thirteen

By morning break on Tuesday, it was all around school. By lunchtime, a buzz of rumour had mutated into the gospel truth and the original story had been embellished beyond all recognition. In fact, Simon's plan had worked so brilliantly, even April was beginning to wonder if there was some truth behind it. They had hatched the plot in Americano the previous evening. April had still been reeling from her conversation with Mr Gill, but as Caro had brought Simon along, she hadn't been able to discuss it. She had been so troubled by Mr Gill's revelation – she wanted to dismiss him as a mad old eccentric, but he was so sincere it was hard to doubt him – she couldn't concentrate on the job in hand.

'Hey! Sleeping beauty!' said Caro, snapping her fingers at April. 'Get with it, we're here to work out how to combat these rumours about you, remember?'

'Shhh …' said April, looking behind her to check they weren't being overheard. 'I don't want it spreading to the whole village. It's bad enough as it is.'

'Don't worry, honey,' said Simon, leaning in to whisper. 'We're going to fight fire with fire. Give them a taste of their own medicine.'

His plan was simple and, as it had turned out, devastatingly effective, working on Simon's theory that gossip was currency; people always wanted new angles on the same story, and having the latest angle was like gold dust. By the end of the day, the whole school believed Caro and April's version of events: that April had wandered into the kitchen at the party and had stumbled on Marcus Brent trying to 'debag' one of his friends. Frankly, it was the sort of horseplay that often happened among members of the rugby team, but when Simon had insisted on adding the phrase 'gay scrum', it had taken off like wildfire. It had been the girls' intention to imply there had been something a bit suspect about the boys' behaviour, but they had reckoned without the power of a juicy rumour to multiply. By the time the story came back to them at the end of the day, it appeared that the boys had been involved in some of the most extreme practices available to the imagination. April was shocked that the rather strait-laced pupils of Ravenwood could come up with such filth, but overjoyed that people were now looking at her with pity rather than disgust.

'Why didn't you tell me, darling?' said Davina. She had run into the Faces in the Ladies by the refectory, which was something of an office for them. She didn't often see them in the canteen. 'I knew that Marcus was a dirty boy, but I had no idea! It must have been terrible for you.'

'And you so innocent and all,' said Layla with a sneer. 'It must have been quite a shock to see what boys really look like.'

'Is it all true?' asked Chessy eagerly. 'Did you really see him do that thing with his tongue?'

April had shaken her head to it all and maintained an aloof 'I don't want to talk about it' position, but that had only added fuel to the fire.

'Golly, if she can't even bring herself to describe it, it must have been truly revolting,' she heard Chessy say to Davina as they left the bathroom.

Funny how people are always prepared to think the worst of someone, thought April as she looked into the mirror. Of course she was delighted that the plan had worked so well, but she was beginning to feel a little guilty. Not that Marcus and his cronies had had any qualms about spreading a rumour about her, but somehow April couldn't feel too pleased about their success. The truth was, the one thing she had really wanted to happen hadn't: Gabriel hadn't called. It had been three days now and she hadn't heard a peep from him. She'd hoped to bump into him at school, but he never seemed to be there. In fact, she'd only ever seen him in school twice, both times on her first day: once in Philosophy, and once heading for the gates. *Maybe I'll see him on his way home today,* she thought with a jolt of excitement. *Not that he's about to fall in love with this.* She looked in the mirror, pulling at her cheeks. *God, I look tired. Does everyone else see these rings under my eyes too?*

She put down her bag and pulled it open, rummaging around for her concealer. It was forbidden for girls to bring make-up into school, but like most of the other rules, it was openly flaunted. She certainly couldn't imagine any of the teachers stopping the Faces from touching up their lip gloss or mascara, which they did constantly, even during lessons. In fact, now she came to think of it, those girls were given an awful lot of leeway. *I guess it's just an unconventional school. Which is the understatement of the year.*

April stopped, make-up forgotten. She could hear a noise coming from one of the cubicles. *Crying?* She crept a little nervously along the line of cubicles, her ears straining. A muffled sound came from the cubicle at the end.

'Hello?' she whispered, tapping gently on the door.

This time she heard a definite sob and she pushed at the door, surprised when it opened. It was Ling Po, sitting on the toilet seat lid with her feet tucked under her, her arms crossed defensively.

'Are you all right, Ling?' asked April softly. The Chinese girl shook her head and looked at the floor. She seemed to be cradling her left arm.

'What's the matter? Are you hurt?'

She shook her head again and pulled her cardigan tighter around her. April frowned. 'What's wrong with your arm?' she asked. 'Can I see?'

Ling pulled away angrily. 'Don't!' she cried. 'It's nothing to do with you.' Then she looked up at April with frightened eyes. 'Don't tell them,' she pleaded. 'Don't tell them you saw this!'

'Okay, okay,' said April, a little confused. She could see

Ling was clutching a paper towel to her wrist. She reached out, meaning to help her if she could, but Ling jumped back as if April had struck her.

'Please, Ling, is there anything I can do?'

'You can leave me alone!' whispered Ling, pushing past April and running out of the bathroom.

'Sorry I spoke,' said April, staring after her. She was just stepping out of the cubicle when something caught her eye: there were little red spots on the white plastic toilet seat. *Blood?* She leant closer. Yes, it was definitely blood. For a fleeting second, April thought of Mr Gill and his claim that vampires were everywhere, but then she dismissed it. *Oh no*, thought April with a feeling of horrible pity. *She's a cutter.* April's friend Rachel in Edinburgh had been through a phase of self-harm when her parents had divorced and she recognised the pattern. God knows, April could relate to Ling's experience – the upheaval of coming to a new school, plus the pressure of trying to fit in with the Faces – she felt for the poor girl.

Shaking her head, she walked back to the sink and picked up her concealer. *I'll ask Caro who she thinks I should speak to about it*, she thought, leaning in to the mirror. Suddenly, April had a thought and almost laughed out loud. *Imagine if the Faces were vampires*, she thought, *they wouldn't be able to use mirrors, would they? That would mess up Davina's beauty regime.*

Suddenly her head was jerked backwards by her hair.

'Making ourselves pretty, are we?' hissed Marcus, bringing his face up close to hers. 'I think it will take a little more than that.'

'What are you—' began April, but her sentence ended in a squeak as Marcus tightened his grip on her hair and used it to yank her backwards across the room, banging her head hard against the tiled wall. She cried out in pain and fear, but Marcus grabbed her throat and squeezed.

'I suppose you thought it would be funny, didn't you? Hmm?'

'I don't know what you're talking about,' said April through gritted teeth. Marcus was really hurting her, but she didn't want to let him know that.

Marcus grabbed another handful of her hair and twisted her head down. 'Oh, I think you do,' he whispered. 'You and your freaky little friends have been spreading lies about me.'

'We wouldn't—'

'Don't!' he yelled. 'Don't even think about denying it. I saw your pathetic friend Caro all chummy with that disgusting fag in the refectory. It doesn't take much intelligence to put two and two together,' he said, his voice quivering with anger. 'And intelligence is what this school is famous for, or hadn't you heard?'

'You've made a mistake,' said April, tears of pain running from the corners of her eyes.

'Oh no, you're the one who's made a mistake.' He stared into her eyes and all she could see was pure fury. 'You have no idea what you're dealing with at Ravenwood.'

He put his arm around her neck, dragging her along the wall towards the toilet cubicles. *Oh God, help me, please, please*, thought April desperately, kicking out, trying to tear his arm away, but he was too strong. She was genuinely terrified now. Marcus was vibrating with rage, completely out of control.

'You want to spread rumours that I'm gay?' he spat. 'Want to find out if it's true? Want to see if I can do some of those things to you?' His mouth split into a wide grin. It was horrible, like a wolf about to rip the throat from a lamb, and April knew she had to act before it was too late.

'GET OFF ME!' she screamed, driving her knee upwards as hard as she could. With a surprised, breathless 'Oof', Marcus crumpled to the floor and she pushed past him, scrambling for the door just as it burst open.

'What the HELL's going on in here?' yelled Mr Sheldon, striding in, his eyes blazing, his jacket flapping behind him. 'How DARE you!' he roared. 'I won't have this kind of disturbance in my school!'

Then he saw April, her clothes dishevelled, her face

scrunched and tear-stained. 'What on earth ...?' he began. 'April, what's happened?'

April could only shake her head and gesture weakly behind her. Frowning, Mr Sheldon stepped past her and saw Marcus slumped on the floor, moaning. The teacher swore under his breath, then shot April a look. 'Get out, April,' he said quietly. 'I'll deal with this. Go!'

April didn't need telling twice. She turned and fled.

Chapter Fourteen

'He'll call. They always call in the end.'

April shook her head and flopped back on her pillows. 'Maybe they always call you, Simon,' she said sadly, 'but they don't always call me.'

'He'll call, honey,' said Caro. 'It's only been two days since the party, that's nothing. A boy doesn't take you to his favourite place in the moonlight then forget all about you.'

April tried to smile, but the truth was she was finding it hard to feel too positive about anything. It wasn't just the fact that it was Tuesday evening and Gabriel still hadn't been in touch, it was more a build-up of all the negative things that had happened in the last ten days and after her run-in with Marcus she just couldn't seem to keep her chin up. April had tried to tell herself she was overreacting, but she had been genuinely terrified; Marcus had been out of control, and there was no telling what he might have done if she hadn't been able to get away. She shivered at the memory of his eyes. They were horrible. She never wanted to see them again, but then she went to school with him, the chances of putting Marcus Brent out of her mind were slim. All in all, April was feeling pretty low. What with Marcus, Gabriel and her general homesickness for Edinburgh, she felt as if she was wandering around under a black cloud. She knew she had plenty to be happy about – she had friends and she was doing okay at school. It didn't help that her parents were constantly fighting, but that was par for the course these days.

'If he said he'd call, he will. Boys just aren't so time-orientated as girls,' said Simon as he combed his hair in April's bedroom mirror. 'He's probably doing other things, like playing football or *Grand Theft Auto* or something.'

'Does Gabriel Swift strike you as the sort of boy who would own either a pair of football boots or an Xbox?' said Caro.

Simon glanced over and shrugged. 'No, probably not, but that doesn't mean he's not tied up, writing deep poetry and listening to My Chemical Romance. Maybe he's fallen down a well.'

Caro threw a cushion at him. 'Yes, and maybe he's caught the Black Death,' she said sarcastically. 'Come on, this is serious.'

'Okay, so what do we do when things get serious?' said Simon, putting his comb down purposefully.

'I don't know, hide under the bed?' asked April.

'No, we get dressed up!' said Simon triumphantly. 'When the going gets tough, the tough get fabulous,' he added, striding to April's wardrobe and pulling a few things out. 'Ooh, this is nice,' he said, holding up a black dress.

Caro shook her head. 'That's the one she wore to the Halloween party. Too formal, anyway.'

'Well, what is this, then?' asked Simon. 'Is it a date or are you meeting as friends? Is he just lonely and needs someone to go to the supermarket with him, what?'

April shook her head. 'I wish I knew,' she said sadly. 'I was a bit drunk and I asked him out. I said I'd show him my favourite place. I don't even have a favourite place.'

Caro held up one finger to stop Simon from saying anything inappropriate and turned to April. 'All right. If it was me some boy hadn't called, what would you tell me to do?'

April sighed.

'Come on,' prompted Caro impatiently.

'I'd tell you to call him.'

'Exactly! So why don't you?'

April gave her a bleak look. 'I don't have his number. He said he'd call me, remember?'

Caro's face fell. 'Oh. I don't have it either. Simon?'

'Nope. In fact, I don't think I've ever seen him with a phone.'

'I thought you were the best-connected man in Raven-wood.'

'Honey, I am, but I can't force every pupil to join the twenty-first century. It's hard enough getting some of them to join the twentieth.'

They all sat staring at the floor.

'Well, can't we just engineer a meeting?' said Caro more brightly. 'Couldn't we stake out his house and then April could just conveniently bump into him?'

'Oh yes, and she could be wearing a miniskirt and a studded bra!'

'WHAT?' chorused Caro and April.

'Just in my mind,' Simon sniffed. 'I'm thinking of her as a kick-ass kind of woman, a real bad-girl vibe.'

Caro slapped him on the arm.

'Well, okay, assuming for a moment I even have a miniskirt, where does Gabriel live?' asked April.

Caro and Simon looked at each other.

'No idea,' said Simon.

'Me neither,' said Caro. 'Now I think about it, I haven't really seen him anywhere except school. And he's not there very often.'

'Actually, I've been meaning to ask about that,' said April. 'Why is he never in school? In fact, a lot of the sixth form seem to come and go as they please – am I missing something?'

Simon laughed and shook his head. 'Uh-oh,' he said, 'don't get her started on this one.'

April looked at Caro. 'What does he mean?'

Caro shot daggers at Simon. 'It's nothing, A, honestly. He's just stirring, he can't seem to help himself.'

April looked back at Simon.

'Hey, ask Miss Marple here, it's nothing to do with me.' Seeing that April wasn't going to give up, Simon sighed and said, 'Caro has a theory that the Faces and the rugby boys are all somehow linked to this massive conspiracy behind Ravenwood. She thinks they have some sort of agreement that they can sit around gossiping and doing their nails and that the school board will guarantee them sparkling Oxbridge-level results at the end of the year.'

'And what do you think?'

'For once, I think Caro's got a point. You don't see those rich kids doing any work and they do seem to turn up whenever they like.'

'Maybe they're just geniuses.'

'You have met Davina Osbourne?' Simon looked at his watch. 'Oh God, is that the time? All this talk of dates and I forget my own.'

'Who is it this time? A biker? A cowboy?' said Caro cattily, but April knew she was masking her true feelings. She hadn't missed the fleeting look of disappointment cross her face when he'd said 'date'.

'Ask me no questions,' said Simon, tapping the side of his nose. 'And I think I'd better escort you home too, young lady. The streets aren't safe these days.'

They both hugged April and she saw them to the door.

'Don't worry, honey, he will call,' said Simon as she closed the door. 'Boys are only interested in one thing and believe me, you've got loads of it.'

April smiled as she waved them off, but she still couldn't shake the sinking feeling in her stomach.

Her mother was sitting in the kitchen, watching a soap on the little portable TV on the corner of the breakfast bar.

'Your little friends have gone, darling?' she asked, without taking her eyes off the screen.

'Yes.' April sighed, opening the fridge, seeing nothing she wanted, then closing it again with a thump.

'That's nice,' said her mother vaguely, reaching for the glass of white wine in front of her. 'Have a good chat?'

April glared at the back of her mother's head. 'No, we had a massive orgy and smoked a huge pipe of crack, thanks for asking.'

She waited for a reaction, but her mother's eyes seemed glued to the screen.

Shaking her head, April turned on her heel in disgust and headed towards the stairs. As she reached the door, April heard a click as the TV shut off.

'I hear what you say to me, you know,' said her mother quietly.

April's mouth was open as she spun back around.

'All the jokes about axemen and drugs?' said Silvia. 'I hear it all. I'm not a geriatric quite yet.'

'So why don't you ever say anything?'

Her mother gave a hollow laugh. 'I thought you preferred it that way.'

April bristled. She wasn't in the mood for any of her mother's games. The truth was, if her parents hadn't forced her to move down to this horrible little village, April would still be happy. Mooning over Neil Stevenson, no doubt, but that was better than being assaulted in the toilets of some weird new school and being ignored by some strange boy who loved graveyards and couldn't seem to make up his mind about her. When it came down to it, it was all Silvia's fault.

'I can't believe I'm hearing this,' said April angrily. 'You really think I want a mother who ignores me?'

Silvia smiled and sipped her wine slowly. 'I thought you preferred me to fulfil the role of the ignorant mother, so you can be the long-suffering daughter.'

'No, I'd rather have a mother who talks to me and who seems to care what I do.'

Silvia put her glass down. 'What makes you think I don't care?'

'Why would I? When have you ever said anything nice to me or encouraged anything I do?'

'But you're always so good at everything—'

'That's such crap!' spat April. She knew she was being unfair, but she was spoiling for a fight. The Marcus thing, her father's notebook, the dead fox, it had all been building up. And now Gabriel's rejection, someone she'd been sure she'd made a connection with, was enough to make steam blow from her ears. 'I bet you don't even know what subjects I'm doing at school, do you?'

'No, but your father was always the one who got involved with your schoolwork.'

'See? See! You have no interest in your own daughter. I've always been a disappointment. I'm not pretty enough, not popular enough, I can't even choose my own party dress.'

Silvia jumped to her feet and came across the kitchen towards April, her arms open. 'Oh, darling, please don't talk this way,' she said, but April backed towards the door.

'Leave me alone,' she said, trying to duck her mother's embrace. 'Don't try to pretend you care how I'm feeling.'

Ignoring her, Silvia pulled April into a tight embrace and she immediately burst into tears.

'It's not fair,' April sobbed, 'I try so hard to do my best but no one cares, no one sees that this is hard on me too, all you care about is going out and shouting at each other.'

Finally April cried herself out and collapsed on her mother's shoulder. Silvia waited until her sobs stopped, then plucked a fresh tissue from a box on the kitchen counter and handed it to her daughter with a smile. 'Come on,' she said, rubbing April's back, 'I think this calls for hot chocolate.' She sat her daughter down on one of the barstools and April blew her nose as her mother busied herself at the stove. By the time she had placed a steaming mug of thick hot chocolate in front of her, April had dried her eyes. She sipped the hot drink slowly and regarded her mother warily.

'Why do you and Dad have to argue all the time?' she asked.

Her mother gave a short laugh, then blew her cheeks out. 'I … I don't know. He and I are too alike, maybe.' She glanced at April and seemed about to say something, then shook her head slightly. 'It's complicated, darling. There's some things your dad and I need to sort out, I suppose, but somehow life always gets in the way.' She looked at April with a soft smile. 'I know it can't be easy for you, with the move and the new school and everything. I guess you could do without your dad and me arguing as well.'

April snorted into her chocolate. 'You've got that right.'

Her mother nodded. 'I'll try harder. We both will, I promise.'

They sank into an agreeable silence for a minute or two.

'So, what else is bothering you?' asked her mother softly.

April sighed. 'How long have you got?'

Silvia smiled. 'As long as you need.'

April still wasn't in the mood to discuss her relationship disasters, especially not with her mother, who was completely beautiful and glamorous and – according to her grandfather at least – had dated princes and billionaires. Anyway, what was she going to say? 'You're way too good for that boy, forget about him'?

'I know what you're thinking,' said Silvia.

'Oh yes?'

'You're thinking, "What can this old hag know about men?" I mean, what with me being so close to death and all.'

'Hang on, how do you know this is about a man?'

'Darling, it's *always* about men. Nothing else can get you so upset and confused. Why do you think I spend so much time arguing with your father? So who is he?'

April thought for a moment. *Oh, what the hell ...*

'His name's Gabriel. He's in my Philosophy class.'

'Ah. And is he good-looking?'

'Mum!'

'What? I'm assuming you're not going to get all weepy over some ugly troll.'

April giggled despite herself. 'Yes, he is good-looking. Gorgeous, actually. And infuriating.'

'Didn't call when he said he would?'

April looked at her mother with new eyes. It was as if she could read her mind all of a sudden. Silvia reached out and gave her daughter's hand a squeeze.

'It's not magic, darling. Men have been the same way for hundreds of years. Girls in crinoline skirts worrying why some dashing soldier hadn't sent them a scented note. It'll be the same for your daughters, too.'

'Chance would be a fine thing.'

'Okay, here's what you have to do – positive visualisation.'

'What?'

'Come on, I know it sounds crazy, but humour me, okay?'

Silvia stood up and took April by the shoulders. She fixed her eyes on April's and stared at her intently.

'Mum,' she complained, wriggling away.

'Just close your eyes, okay?'

April smirked, but she did as she was told.

'Right, now picture yourself looking super-glamorous. You're the ideal version of April – even prettier and cleverer than the real you. The sexiest you can be.'

'This may take a while,' said April.

'Don't do yourself down, darling. Give it a chance. Okay, have you got it?'

April nodded. She was imagining herself as a femme fatale in a long black dress, her hair swept up, diamonds around her neck. A slight *Breakfast at Tiffany's* vibe, if she was honest.

'Right, where are you?'

'On the Riviera, walking along the seafront, stopping traffic.'

Silvia laughed. 'Excellent. Now there's a man coming towards you – who is it?'

'Robert Pattinson.'

'What's he wearing?'

'A blue pea coat.'

'Interesting. Does he have anything else with him?'

'He's brought me a present.'

'Perfect. What is it?'

'A box of chocolate éclairs.'

They both laughed.

'So, what are you going to do now? I'm your mother, keep it clean.'

'We're going for a walk along the beach, eating the éclairs.'

'Then what?'

'R-Pattz stops to collect some shells for me. Just because he thinks I'd like them.'

'Lovely. Now remember those images, print them in your mind. When you're ready, open your eyes.'

April blinked at her mother and pulled a 'what now?' face. 'That's it.'

'That's it? How is that supposed to solve all my problems?'

'Whenever you're feeling down or you're convinced you'll never get anywhere with boys, you just jump back to that image in your mind and you'll remember how fabulous and sexy you are and what kind of relationship you deserve to have.'

'But if he doesn't call, I won't have any sort of relationship.'

'If he doesn't call, sweetheart, then you don't want a relationship with him anyway. The boy's a moron.'

April instantly felt herself jumping to Gabriel's defence. *Don't call him a moron, he's not a moron*, she thought. But then, maybe her mum had a point. It was his loss; if he didn't want to go on a date, then he was the one missing out.

'Thanks, Mum,' she said, giving her a hug. 'You're a bit weird, but I do feel better.'

Her mother smiled. 'Men are very simple, darling,' she said. 'They always want the thing they can't have. You just have to convince them that you're that thing.'

April nodded and, taking her hot chocolate, headed back to her room.

'And April?' said her mother as she was about to close the door. 'He will call. They always do.'

Why does everyone keep telling me that?

Chapter Fifteen

Tap.

Tap-tap.

Tap.

April opened her eyes and looked around her bedroom. *What was that?* Had she really heard that tapping sound or was it part of a dream? She screwed her eyes up, trying to adjust to the gloom. Before going to bed, she had emailed Fiona with an update on the day's events, or rather non-events, and had fallen asleep without shutting the computer down, leaving the blue-white swirls of her screensaver to illuminate the room with a slightly eerie glow.

Tap.

Tap-tap.

There was a pause, then another tap, followed by a muffled voice cursing.

She definitely hadn't imagined *that*. Quickly climbing out of bed, April crossed to the window and peered into the darkness. She couldn't see anything except the shadowy, deserted square. Was someone down there? The house was too tall for her to see into the garden below.

Tap.

'Hey!' She jerked her head back as something – a pebble? – bounced against the glass about an inch from her nose. 'What the ...?'

Fiddling with the lock, April yanked at the little sash window and with a rasp it opened enough for her to stick her head through.

'Who's there?' she hissed.

Now she could see a dark figure standing by the gate.

'It's me!' came a whisper.

'Who's "me"?' replied April. *It had better not be the murderer,* she thought randomly, *that'd just cap off my week.*

The figure moved back across the road, into the yellow cone shining down from the old streetlight, and her heart leapt. It was Gabriel.

In the space of a few seconds, April's emotions swung from joy to anger, then back to breathless anticipation. She finally settled on irritation and annoyance.

'What the hell are you doing here?' she hissed. 'Do you know what time it is?'

'No.'

'Well, neither do I, but it's the middle of the bloody night.'

'Oh. Well, I just thought ...' he said, holding something up.

'What? What do you want, Gabriel?'

'Our date.'

She stared at him incredulously. *'Our date?'* She puffed out her cheeks and told herself to keep calm. 'Wait there.'

She ducked back inside and closed the window as quietly as she could, then threw on a jumper over her pyjamas. *If he doesn't like it, then tough,* she thought. She ran to the mirror, fumbling with some make-up, thinking of all the reasons why she should simply slam the door in his stupid, handsome face. He said he'd call. He hadn't. He had let her lie to the police. He had interfered with the one kiss she'd had since she'd left Scotland. And worst of all, he had forced her to turn to her mother, of all people, for advice! Maybe she was still groggy from sleep, maybe it was just a build-up of everything she had been through over the past week, but April found that now Gabriel had finally come, she just wanted to tell him to leave. She had thought of nothing else since the Halloween party and, if she was honest, had taken her disappointment with Gabriel's disappearance out on her friends and family, becoming a snappy, anxious mess. Perhaps her mother's positive visualisation had worked better than she had thought, but now he was here, she wasn't convinced she wanted him to be. Quietly, wincing at every sound – the last thing she wanted to do was wake her parents up – she crept down the stairs and opened the front door just a crack.

'What?' she said.

'I brought you something.'

'What is it?'

'Come out and look.'

Sighing, April opened the door a little more and shuffled out onto the step, crossing her arms. Gabriel looked every bit as gorgeous as he had that first time she had seen him across the road. His hair was a little more dishevelled, as if he had just got out of bed, and the collar of his pea coat was turned up against the cold, but basically it was the same good-looking guy with the same amazing eyes. *Yeah, but what else?* she thought. *Eyes aren't everything.*

'Here,' he said, holding up a cardboard tray. It held two coffees in styrofoam cups, steaming up into the cold air, and next to them were a selection of what looked like doughnuts.

'Coffee and doughnuts?' she asked.

He looked at her nervously. 'Well, I wanted to get you flowers or something, but the only place open at this time is the taxi drivers' all-night cafe down on Archway Road.'

'Gee, it's nice to think you planned all this just for me,' said April, a little more sarcastically than she had intended. Gabriel nodded, looking crestfallen.

'I meant to call, April,' he said sadly. 'I really did. But I just—'

'You just what? Couldn't be bothered?'

'It's complicated.'

'It sounds pretty simple to me. You said you'd call, you didn't. Listen, Gabriel,' she said, moving back inside the house, 'thanks for coming, but I can't stand here in the cold all night.'

He gestured back towards the square. 'Couldn't you just come out for a minute? I'd like to apologise, to explain, at least.' He smiled at her. 'The doughnuts are better than they look.'

April shook her head. She shouldn't, after the way he had treated her, but he *had* come. She let out a long breath, puffing in the cold air.

'It's freezing.'

Gabriel put the tray down, then quickly pulled off his coat and held it out to her. 'Please, April?'

Reluctantly she took the jacket and wrapped it around her, feeling his body heat and catching a hint of his personal scent. For a moment, it was like being wrapped in his arms.

'Okay, two minutes. But if my dad wakes up, you kidnapped me, okay?'

She ducked back inside and slipped on her dad's old trainers, clumping down the steps and across the road.

'God, I look like a bag lady.'

Gabriel grinned. 'I think you look adorable.'

Yeah, yeah, save the compliments and start grovelling, thought April. Gabriel sat down on a bench and April perched on the edge, her hands deep in his coat pockets, shivering.

'Here, this should warm you up a bit,' said Gabriel, handing her a cup. 'They don't exactly do decaf skinny lattes at the all-night cafe, but it's hot at least.'

She sipped it in silence.

'Listen, I'm sorry I've messed you about,' said Gabriel after a pause. 'I should have called, I really should. It's just ...' he trailed off. Then, after a glance at her, he continued in a rush, 'It's just there are things I can't explain right now, things you probably would rather not hear, and altogether it means I think we'd be pretty bad for each other.'

Oh great, thought April. *He's dumping me before we've even got off the ground.*

Then Gabriel turned to face her, those dark eyes glittering in the streetlights. 'But I *want* us to be bad for each other, I want us to be ...'

'What?'

'Together,' he said softly. 'I want us to be together. Like

this, like now, just the two of us, no one else. But believe me, things would always be difficult, there would always be things I couldn't explain.'

His words were so fervent and he seemed so sincere that April was starting to feel terrible about giving him such a hard time. Her heart was pounding in her ears and her fingers were tingling. He wanted them to be *together*.

'That's partly why I haven't been in school so much,' continued Gabriel, looking away. 'And that's why I've dragged you out onto a park bench in the middle of the night. Sorry.'

April shrugged, although the movement was lost inside the huge shoulders of his jacket. 'It's okay,' she said. 'Well, it's not okay, but it is okay, if you see what I mean.'

Gabriel laughed. 'Thanks. At least we're here. On our date.'

'So this is a date, then?' said April with a flutter in her stomach.

Gabriel held up a doughnut. 'It's not much, I know, but I've never been too good at the big romantic gestures.'

'You don't say.'

'Ouch.'

She took the doughnut and had a bite. It was actually pretty good, one of those squirty jam ones with the sugar all over it. Suddenly she loved jam doughnuts more than anything.

'Well … It's almost midnight, which means the cinema, dinner and the pub are all out of the question. So what did you have in mind for our date?' she asked, her mouth curling up into a smile.

'Go for a walk?'

April waggled her feet in the air, the oversized trainers wobbling about comically. 'I'm not sure I'm dressed for it.'

'Come on,' said Gabriel, standing up and offering her his arm. April jumped up and slipped her hand into the crook of his elbow and they began to walk slowly around the outside of the square. April had to admit it was romantic, strolling arm in arm with a boy in the moonlight while everyone around you was fast asleep.

'I like it at night,' said April, her breath making little clouds in the air. 'It's so calm and quiet.'

Gabriel nodded. 'It's the best part of the day,' he said. 'It's like getting away from the city into the countryside, only you don't have to move. I hate all the noise and the rush and it's too ... too bright.' He shrugged, but April nodded.

'I know what you mean. You can imagine what it used to be like when it really was a village, before all the cars and stuff.'

They fell into silence again, just walking slowly past the Scientific Institution and then the United Reformed Church.

'Shall we walk down to the Heath?' said Gabriel.

April shook her head reluctantly. 'I should get back. I don't want my dad to come down and attack you with a golf club.'

Well, not any more, she thought to herself.

'I'd better walk you back, then.'

'So that's it?' she asked, not wanting the moment to end, but feeling her face start to go numb. That wasn't a good look, whatever the Botox addicts claimed.

'I wish you didn't have to go,' he said in a low, quiet voice.

'If you'd come a bit earlier ...' she teased, but his expression was serious.

'Believe me, it would be better for both of us if I had stayed away, but I just couldn't stop thinking about you, I was miserable, I needed to see you. And –' he smiled '– if I'm going to be your protector, I need to be here, don't I?'

They were back outside her gate and she reluctantly shrugged off his coat. Handing it back, their eyes locked.

Please kiss me, please kiss me, she said in her head, hoping the positive thinking would work again. *This time, he has to,* she pleaded. For a moment, the wish seemed to hang in the air and in slow motion, April watched Gabriel's lips part slightly. Then he reached out and brushed her cheek with the tips of his fingers. She tilted her head towards his touch, loving the warmth on her skin.

'What is it?' he said.

April couldn't speak; she just shook her head and frowned.

'What's your favourite place? D'you remember? You said you were going to show me your favourite place.'

'Oh,' she said, a little disappointed. 'Covent Garden. There's a little patisserie there I love.'

'Good doughnuts?'

'Chocolate éclairs, actually.' She smiled.

'Well, you'll have to take me there one day, soon.'

'Maybe,' she said, turning towards the door, but he caught her arm.

'No, definitely,' he said. 'Definitely.'

April slipped back inside the house and closed the door, leaning her back against it. *Good God, what was all that about?* she wondered, putting her hand to her cheek where Gabriel had touched it. Then she slipped off the borrowed shoes and ran all the way up the stairs, grinning like an idiot.

Chapter Sixteen

For once, April didn't need an alarm; she was out of bed and into the bathroom before the sun had made it above the horizon. Despite the grey light, April felt perky and full of energy and, after a brisk shower, was ready for the most important task of the day: getting ready for school. Today, what she wore had taken on a whole new dynamic; not only did she need to look studious and clever, she also needed to be devastatingly sexy. Obviously, whatever she wore was going to be better than her impromptu date outfit, but even so, she wanted to look amazing in case she bumped into Gabriel, which was highly likely as this was Wednesday and she had Philosophy first thing. Tops, skirts and trousers were tried and discarded and her entire wardrobe was soon piled up on the bed. Finally she decided on black leggings, a navy and white striped T-shirt and ballet pumps, which she thought looked very Kate Moss chic but at the same time didn't look as if she'd spent an hour picking it out. She skipped down the stairs and was surprised to find her father already sitting at the breakfast bar, bent over a bowl of Rice Krispies.

'Hey, rabbit,' he said, 'you're up bright and early.'

She gave him a kiss and waltzed past to pop some bread into the toaster.

'What's all this?' Her father said. 'Has your mother been feeding you her Prozac? Yesterday you had a face like a wet weekend. Why the bouncy mood?'

'Why not?' said April playfully. 'Can't I just be happy?'

William looked at her with amusement. 'Of course, be my

guest.' He smiled. 'But if you see the real April, let her know she's welcome back here any time.'

April stuck her tongue out at him and went to get a plate from the cupboard. 'So what's on at work today?' she asked.

Her father shrugged. 'More on these murders. It's not often you get a murder in this neck of the woods, let alone two, so I'm under pressure to come up with something solid and exclusive pretty quick before the national boys do. It's tough being on a weekly, with no crime desk and a fraction of the tabloids' resources.'

'And are you getting anywhere?'

'Dunno, maybe. I'll know more tonight. I've got one pretty strong lead. If it's genuine, it might well be a big break in the case.'

'Sounds exciting.'

'Hmm, perhaps. Might also tie in with the book I'm writing. And you? What's on at school?'

'I've got Philosophy first – oh no!' April's sunny mood melted away as she realised two things in quick succession. First, she hadn't read the book she was supposed to be discussing – and given her performance in the last class, Hawk was bound to ask her something – and secondly, Benjamin Osbourne was going to be there. And where Benjamin went, Marcus Brent was sure to follow. She shuddered involuntarily at the thought of seeing him again.

'What is it, honey?' asked her father.

'Oh, uh, nothing,' said April quickly.

'It doesn't look like nothing.'

'I, um, I forgot to read that story. You know, that John Wyndham one?'

Her dad put down his spoon and reached for his briefcase. 'Ah, well, that's where I can help you.'

She looked at him with hope. 'Have you read it?'

'No,' he said, opening up his laptop. 'But I bet Wikipedia has.'

'Oh, Dad, you're a genius!' she said, throwing her arms around him from behind.

'Steady on.' He laughed. 'I'm not sure I should even be doing this. It's not exactly in the parenting handbook – "help your child cheat on homework".'

'Maybe just this once it's okay.'

The phone rang. April's heart leapt. *Gabriel?* 'I'll get the phone, you keep on the homework,' she said as she ran towards the hall. She skidded to a halt by the hall table and realised that the phone wasn't in its cradle.

'Dad! Where's the phone?' she cried.

'It might be in my study,' her dad called from the kitchen. *Damn this wireless technology.* She ran into the study and began rummaging through his mess. *Why can't he keep this place tidy?* she thought, picking up handfuls of paper and books desperately. She finally tracked the insistent chirping to a shape hidden under a copy of *New Scientist* and snatched it up.

'Hello?' she almost shouted.

'Hey, my ears!' It was her grandfather.

'Oh, hello, Gramps.' She was unable to hide the disappointment in her voice. There was no reason why Gabriel would call this soon, but at least, after last night, she was pretty sure he *would* call. Wasn't she?

'Is that all the hello I get?' said her grandfather testily. 'Have I upset my granddaughter in some way? Have I insulted you by calling to see how you are getting along?'

'Sorry, Gramps.' April sighed. 'I didn't mean … I was expecting someone else.'

'That much I know!' roared Thomas. 'That I can see! And who is more important than your own flesh and blood, hmm? Tell me that!'

April held the phone away from her ear as he continued to rant. It wasn't an unusual situation; her grandfather's phone calls often descended into anger and shouting over imagined slights. Last week, he had yelled at April's father for taking five rings to pick up the phone. 'Why does it take you so long? Am I not important enough to leave your stupid work for one minute?' It was easy to see where her mother got her hair-trigger fuse from. April knew it was just the way her grandfather was and, at his age, it was futile to expect him to change, but this morning she just didn't have time or patience for it.

'Listen, Gramps, I love talking to you,' she said firmly, 'but I've got to go to school right now and before that I've got to do something important for my coursework.'

'So I am not as important as your school—' he began, but April wasn't listening.

'Love you Gramps, speak later,' she said and pressed the 'end' button.

April was overcome by a wave of guilt. It wasn't her grand-dad's fault that he wasn't Gabriel of course, but why did he – and every other adult in her life – have to give her a hard time about nothing? She stood there tense and anxious, annoyed that her previous buoyant mood could be so easily shattered by one disappointment. Sighing, she bent to pick up the papers that had scattered onto the floor during her frantic phone search. As she was scooping them up, one caught her eye. It had a familiar logo on the headed notepaper: *The Sunday Times*. Curious, she picked it up and before she knew what she was doing, she had read the first few lines.

Dear William,

I'm so glad you were able to come in for interview last Thursday. I'm sure you're well aware how highly you are regarded here at the ST – our editor Peter Noble is a particular fan of yours. I was hugely impressed by your ideas for setting up a dedicated investigations team in Glasgow and your vision for revamping the reportage in the Scottish edition of the paper.

What's this? April thought as she read. *Why didn't he tell us he was going for an interview with* The Sunday Times? She quickly read the rest, the last paragraph making her gasp.

... on that basis, and subject to agreeing a mutually beneficial remuneration package, I'd like to formally offer you the position of Senior Editor, to begin immediately. Please let me know your decision as soon as possible. I look forward to hearing from you.

Yours sincerely,

Paul Bingham,
Publishing Director

April felt as if she had been punched in the stomach. Her brain scrambled to make sense of it. Why, if you've been offered a top job on one of the most prestigious papers in the country, would you turn it down for some crappy reporter's role on a local rag covering parking issues and village fetes? It just didn't make sense. Then she spotted more of his brightly coloured Post-it notes stuck to the shelves. 'Vampire hierarchy?' read one, with the words 'Three nests? Four?' scribbled beneath it.

'Bloody vampires!' she growled, ripping the note down and striding back into the kitchen.

'Who was it?' said her dad, looking up from the computer. Then he spotted the letter in her hand and his eyes widened.

'What's this?' demanded April, waving the letter in his face. 'Why didn't you tell us about this?'

His face paled. 'Listen, April, I was going to talk to you about that.'

'Oh yes? When, exactly?'

'I can see that you're upset, but it was something I had to decide on my own.'

April couldn't believe her ears. 'On your *own*?' she shouted. 'Aren't I part of this family? Doesn't this affect me too? I suppose I'm not allowed an opinion?'

'It's not that—'

'Well, what is it then? What? You think it's perfectly okay to choose to take me away from my life and my friends and dump me in some freaky backwater without even asking me how I feel about it?'

Her dad got up and walked towards her, but April backed away.

'Come on. Calm down and we'll talk about this.'

'Talk about it?' she snapped. 'It's a bit late for that, isn't it? We're here now. You've got exactly what you wanted.'

'Look, I didn't want to leave Scotland any more than you did.'

'Then why did we? It's only forty minutes from Edinburgh to Glasgow, you could even have commuted!' Hot tears of frustration were rolling down her cheeks now.

'Sometimes you have to make sacrifices, April,' her dad began, but she angrily interrupted him.

'Sacrifice! What sacrifices exactly? I've given up my whole life to come down here. I've had to leave all my friends, I've been forced to go to a horrible school where they all look down on me and where I don't even understand half of the things they say. And now I discover it's all because you didn't like the job on offer ...'

'Honey, there's more to it than that. Your mother—'

'Mum? Don't use her as an excuse. It's obvious she didn't want you to take this job in London, you've been arguing about it non-stop. This is all about you and don't pretend it isn't.'

William shook his head and looked down at his feet. April felt a new burst of anger. Even now, when she had put the evidence in front of him, he couldn't look her in the eye and admit he had lied to her. She felt her nails bite into the palm of her hand as she clenched her fist. She couldn't remember ever being so furious. It was the injustice of having her whole life decided for her, of being forced to change everything – *everything* – about her life, without her father even having the decency to tell her there was an alternative.

'So why did you bring us here? Because of *this*?' She held up the Post-it note and her father's face changed from confusion to shame to anger in seconds.

'Give me that!' he shouted, lunging at her. 'How dare you go through my work!'

'Here, have it!' she yelled, screwing the paper into a ball and throwing it at him. 'At least I know what's most important to you now.'

He picked it up off the floor and began smoothing it out. 'You shouldn't be poking your nose into things that could be dangerous.'

'Dangerous?' spat April. 'That's if your stupid theory on the Highgate Vampire is right. That's if they even exist.'

At the word *vampires* he looked at her sharply. 'Highgate Vampire? What do you know about that?'

'Everyone knows about it, Dad!' she said, her voice dripping with derision. 'It's not a secret, it's a tourist attraction. That's what you brought us here for?'

'Don't you dare speak to me like that!' shouted William. 'How could you think I'd be so selfish? We came here because it was best for the family, for all of us. For you.'

But April was far too angry to let him wriggle out of it. 'Okay, so look me in the eye and tell me we didn't come here for the bloody vampires.'

William stared at her and his face was a mixture of guilt, defiance and something else she couldn't quite put her finger on. No, she *did* know what it was: it was sadness. He closed his eyes and for a moment she thought he was actually going to cry. April's first reaction was to want to hug him. William Dunne had always been her hero, her warm and approachable father who, unlike most of her friends' dads, was fun and funny and involved in her life. She had always felt she could talk to him about anything because he was strong and clever and, above all, he was usually *right* – she knew that whatever happened, he would know the answer. He could always make her feel safe. But now the tables were turned and she was being asked to forgive him, tell him it was okay, whatever he did – and she couldn't do it, she didn't even feel she knew him any more. It was as if the picture she had built up of her father was crumbling away, leaving behind a sad, lonely man who didn't have all the answers after all, who made mistakes and avoided tough decisions just like everyone else. He wasn't Superman, he was just an ordinary, everyday suburban father. And that broke April's heart.

'I'm trying to get close to them,' he said quietly. 'We had to be here. It's more important than you realise.'

'Them? *Them?*' she repeated. 'The vampires, you mean? God, you're pathetic!'

Her father looked up, his eyes blazing. 'You will not speak to me like that!' he yelled. 'I am your father!'

'Really?' shouted April. 'To me you look like a grown man who believes in fairy tales! And you ruined my life for this crap? Jesus, Grandpa's right about you!'

William barked out a bitter laugh. 'Well, he should know.'

Even though she had just dismissed Thomas as a crazy old man, now she leapt to his defence. She was dimly aware she was overreacting, being unreasonable, but she couldn't help herself.

'Don't turn this back on Gramps,' she snapped. 'At least he wants the best for me. What's he got to do with this, anyway?'

William ran his hand through his hair wearily. 'More than you'd believe,' he said.

April felt a lurch in her chest as a piece of the jigsaw fell into place. It *was* her grandfather. That's why her father had refused a brilliant job in Scotland and moved them all the way down here – William was trying to impress his father-in-law.

'Oh my God,' she said. '*That's* what this is about? Jesus!' She laughed ironically. 'You want a best-selling book to show Grandpa he's wrong about you? And I suppose if they make a film out of it, you'll be able to throw it all his back in his face.'

William shook his head. 'Don't be ridiculous. We're just try-ing to give you the best life we can. I know you feel completely grown-up, April, but you still need protecting – more than you think you do. There are some things you don't understand.'

'Well, I do know this,' she croaked, the tears beginning to

flow again. 'If you truly believe there are bloodsucking vampires in Highgate, you're not just pathetic, you're disgusting.'

'April Dunne!' shouted her father. 'You do not and you will not speak to me like that!'

'Stay away from me!' she cried, backing towards the door. 'People are being murdered around here. You deliberately brought your family to a place of danger just to impress an old man? You'd risk us all being killed for a story? What does that say about you?'

'I'm doing the best I can for you and your mother,' he called after her. 'Maybe you're right, maybe it is time you were told what's going on. But you have to believe me, I thought I could make things better, give us all a better life.'

'Yeah, if we live that long,' she yelled at him as she wrenched the front door open.

'April, please,' he said, running down the hall after her and blocking the door with his arm. 'Let me explain!'

'Get off!' she screamed, pushing past him. 'I'll never forgive you for this – never! I hate you!'

She ran down the path and through the gate, not even looking for traffic as she sprinted across the road and into the square. As she reached the corner of Swain's Lane, she finally glanced back towards the house, a part of her hoping that her dad – the old, safe, protective dad – would be running after her. But there was no one behind her. The door was closed and her father had gone.

Chapter Seventeen

The ponds were beautiful despite the rain. Whatever light was pushing through the dark clouds seemed to be catching the fine droplets as they fell, forming a shimmering, misty curtain across the water. April shivered. Pretty as it was, she wished she'd thought to grab an umbrella before she'd run out of the house. She turned up the collar of her thin coat she had snatched as she ran out and huddled closer to the trunk of the willow tree she was sheltering under. 'Thanks, tree,' she said, patting the bark. At least something was looking out for her, keeping the drips from running down her neck. *Shame it's just a tree*, she thought. After her spectacular fight with her father, she'd run down West Hill, not really caring where she ended up. Following her feet, she had splashed through puddles on her way to the Heath and found herself standing by Highgate Bathing Ponds. Aside from a few very dedicated dog-walkers in the distance, the weather had kept everyone else indoors and April had the whole park to herself. She slid down the tree trunk and hugged her knees, suddenly letting out a loud sob. *Oh God*, she thought, *how has my life become such a mess?* Only a few weeks ago, she had a secure, safe, cosy life with friends who loved her, a house with a garden and, if she was really lucky, a good chance of getting together with Neil Stevenson. She had everything she wanted, pretty much. But now? She sobbed again, her shoulders heaving, the warm tears mingling with the drips coming through the leaves. Now she had nothing. Her mother was barely there, her father was a selfish fruitcake and the only friends she could rely on were hundreds of miles away, getting on with their lives. What did she have left? She stared at the green water of the pond, stippled with raindrops, and wondered vaguely if it would be cold. *Very, very cold indeed,* she decided, shuddering. But it would serve them all right if she was found floating in the weeds like Ophelia in that Pre-Raphaelite painting by What's-his-name. Or would they even notice she had gone? Letting out a long breath, April began to walk slowly around the pond and up onto Parliament Hill. *I bet it's lovely here in the summer,* she thought, but the notion of sunbathing and frisbees only made her feel more sad, more alone. She pulled her phone from her pocket. No messages. There hadn't been any messages five minutes ago, either. She wished she could make some great passionate gesture, like throwing the phone into the lake, but that would mean giving up all hope. And anyway, she loved her phone. She sighed: she was as pathetic as her father. He was clinging to the crazy notion that he might find supernatural beings in Highgate, while she was clinging to the hope that Gabriel Swift might become her boyfriend. No, if she was honest, she was hoping that Gabriel Swift would decide he wanted to marry her, sweep her off to the Bahamas for a beautiful beach ceremony, and then, after a bout of amazing lovemaking, reveal that he was stupendously rich and personal friends with Justin Timberlake. She snorted at the ridiculousness of it and had to scrabble in her pocket for a damp tissue. Now she thought about it, she honestly didn't know which of the scenarios was the most far-fetched. Vampires? Justin Timberlake? *Who knows? Maybe Dad's right,* she thought. *Caro seems to believe it, so does Mr Gill in the bookshop.* And then there were those horrible eyes on Swain's Lane and the photos from the party. It wasn't exactly overwhelming evidence, but then anything was possible, wasn't it? Three weeks ago she would never have believed she would be out walking in the rain, playing truant from school, but here she was. The church on West Hill began to sound the hour and April stopped to count. One, two, three ... ten o'clock. Her Philosophy lesson would be halfway through and she doubted anyone had noticed her absence. *Gabriel, perhaps?* Perhaps.

April instantly felt bad for thinking that. Why was she so down on Gabriel all of a sudden? Okay, so he hadn't called like he'd promised, but he had turned up eventually – for that perfect midnight moment – and while he was still maddeningly vague about what was going on, he had respected her enough to tell her there were things he couldn't explain. At least Gabriel wasn't pretending to be something he wasn't. It wasn't his fault her father had dragged her down to this horrid soggy place to play Indiana-bloody-Jones. She gave a short ironic laugh as she walked on, her shoes squelching on the grass, suddenly aware that she was cold, she was wet and there was snot dripping from the end of her nose.

'Right, bugger this,' she said, and turned back towards the school.

By the time she had dried her hair under the hand-driers in the Ladies toilet and sponged most of the mud from her shoes with wadded-up paper towels, Philosophy was over and it was far too late to go to her English lesson, so April walked down to the library instead. At least there she would get a little peace to gather her thoughts and do some reading; cutting class didn't come naturally to April and she felt she ought to make up for missing lessons. Plus she didn't want to look like a complete idiot, again, in Miss Holden's class that afternoon.

April was surprised to find the library completely deserted.

'Duh, everyone's in lessons, aren't they?' she whispered to herself, actually pleased that she wouldn't have to speak to anyone. She dumped her wet coat on a chair and wandered over to the History section.

Right, the Renaissance, she thought to herself as she read the titles. *Dates versus culture and all that.*

She picked out a few books and leafed through them, but they were either dry or difficult to read or both. *Why can't they do a 'Modern History For Dummies'?* she wondered, before spotting a stack of magazines piled up at the end of a shelf.

'Ah, now magazines I can understand,' she said, picking one up. It was a dusty academic journal called *Modern History*.

She flicked through the pages without interest. Stuff about the Iron Age, stuff about Roman baths, stuff about the Russian revolution. But then she stopped, as a few words – or rather, a name – caught her eye. In the introduction to a feature on bodies preserved in peat bogs, the author's name jumped out at her: Professor Annabel Holden. It was *Miss* Holden, her teacher – she had written the article! April quickly scanned the text, but was disappointed to find it was a dreary piece about the preservative qualities of mud. Not much use for her next lesson.

Hmm, I wonder… thought April, taking the whole stack of magazines back to a table. Flipping through them, she swiftly discovered that her hunch had been right; Miss Holden was in there quite a lot. She had either written a lot of rather boring features for the magazine or had been interviewed for one. Nothing, however, was of much interest, until April began to read a piece in the second to last magazine on the pile.

Wow, this is fantastic. It was an essay entitled 'The Past Will Eat Itself'. The introduction read:

New academic research is turning the way we think about history upside down, changing the focus from rigid timelines and dates to contemporary sources. It's an exciting new approach that may even force us to reconsider some of our most dearly held assumptions about the past.

It went on to debate the pros and cons of approaching history as a living organism rather than a series of events or decisions made by kings and politicians. It was exactly what Miss Holden had been talking about in their last lesson! Even better, April's teacher was actually quoted in the piece:

As Professor Annabel Holden, of Harvard University, says: 'People in the eighteenth century didn't think of themselves as a historical fact, they thought of themselves as cutting-edge technologically advanced intellectuals. They had sailed the seven seas, discovered new lands and mapped the heavens,

they had worked out how to power the railways, they were
God's chosen people. So if we view them as museum pieces
or historical curiosities in funny hats, we miss so much. We
need to reverse the whole polarity of history and think of them
as the living, breathing people they were. In many ways the
kings, queens and politicians of history were the pop stars of
their day.'

April heard someone approaching from behind her and
she turned, expecting to see Mrs Townley the librarian. Her
shoulders tensed as she saw that it was Layla. She was dressed
in a short pleated skirt and a tight roll-neck top, a fixed smile
on her face, and she slid into the seat opposite April.

April glanced around nervously. The library was still empty
and the clock said a quarter to twelve.

Layla followed her eyes. 'Free period,' she said with a smirk.
'Anyway, I'm glad I've caught you when there's no one else
around. I've wanted to have a quiet word with you since the
party.'

'What about?' asked April uneasily.

'Oh, just wanted to ask how you're fitting in, see if there's
anything I can do to help?'

April was beginning to feel uncomfortable. Layla had never
been particularly friendly to her; in fact, almost everything she'd
ever said had been loaded with a cruel subtext or bitchiness.

'I'm fine. Everyone's been really nice, really welcoming,' she
said. April wasn't going to talk about the dead fox, those evil
party rumours or Marcus Brent. Not with Layla, anyway.

'Yes, I saw that,' said Layla. There was an edge to her voice
that worried April. 'Lots of people seem to be very interested
in you, don't they? I wonder why that is?'

April shrugged. 'Because I'm the new girl here, I suppose.'

'Mmm,' said Layla, her head tilting to one side in a sympathetic way. 'I should think you've been working quite hard to
fit in, haven't you?'

'Well, as I say, most people have been kind. Davina especially. It was nice to be invited to the party.'

Layla's eyes narrowed. 'Yes, although I hear you had a terrible time there,' she said in a way that suggested quite the opposite. 'But you shouldn't read too much into it, especially if you think about why you were invited in the first place.'

April frowned. 'I'm sorry? What do you mean?'

Layla glanced around and lowered her voice to a whisper. 'Stop playing dumb, you stupid little cow,' she hissed. 'Davina didn't want you at the party because you're friends, did she? Even you must have realised that?'

'Uh, no. I didn't think—'

Layla reached out and grabbed April's hand, squeezing hard. 'Well, think about it, new girl. And while you're at it, think about the way you're making moon-eyes at all the boys in school. They all seem to be fascinated by you, don't they? Even poor Marcus Brent can barely keep his hands off you.'

'Don't you—' began April angrily, but Layla cut her off.

'Why is that?' she said nastily. 'It can't be because of your looks, can it?'

'I ... I don't understand— Oww!'

Layla dug her manicured nails into the back of April's hand. 'I'll make this as clear as possible,' she spat. 'Stop throwing yourself at my boyfriend. He's taken, do you understand? I won't tell you again.'

April's stomach turned over and she suddenly felt terribly cold. *Is that true?* She had been so sure everything Gabriel had said last night was sincere and from the heart, but suddenly his words rang hollow and cheap. She felt like melting into the floor. First her dad, now this. *Can't anything go right?* Her whole life was crumbling around her ears. With a last haughty look, Layla stood up, her chair scraping across the wooden floor.

'Don't let's have this conversation again, hmm? You obviously don't know how things work at Ravenwood and we wouldn't want you to get hurt, now would we? Oh, and do something about your hair,' she said with a cruel smile. 'You look like a tramp.'

*

Caro was all for throwing soup in Layla's lap. Or poisoning her Diet Coke.

'Violence is the only language that lot understand,' she said in a low, determined voice, as she stared across the refectory. The Faces were sitting at their usual table, preening and picking at their tiny salads. 'A nice bowl of hot tomato soup would be a good look on that skirt.'

'Now, now,' said Simon. 'We don't want to sink to her level.'

'Oh, but I do,' said Caro. 'Look at the talon marks she's left in April's hand.'

'I'm okay,' said April, touching the scrapes Layla had left on her skin. Physically she was fine, but emotionally she was stung. She didn't want to believe Layla was seeing Gabriel, but then she was right – April was just the new girl and Layla had been at Ravenwood for years. What did she really know about Gabriel or how they did things here? Not even Caro and Simon knew much about him outside of the school, and they could usually be relied on to have the most up-to-date gossip.

'So do you think she's really Gabriel's girlfriend?'

'I've made some discreet enquiries—' began Simon, before being interrupted by Caro's snort.

'Sorry.' She giggled. 'It's just that the idea of you being discreet about anything makes me laugh.'

'Play nice, children,' said April. 'Focus on my problem, okay?'

'Yes, well,' huffed Simon. 'My enquiries drew a blank about Gabriel specifically, but Layla definitely has a boyfriend. Apparently they've been keeping it very low-key, which certainly isn't like her, but ...' He looked at April sadly and she nodded.

'But it does sound like Gabriel,' she finished for him. 'He is the sort of boy who keeps secrets isn't he?'

'I'm sorry, honey,' said Caro, touching April's hand. 'But he's not exactly been giving the impression that you're an exclusive thing, has he?'

'But he called it a date,' said April. 'It was midnight. There were doughnuts.'

Simon sighed. 'That's men for you, darling. We're ruled by our urges, I'm afraid. And look at her.'

Layla was whispering something to Davina and then they both laughed.

'Layla's the sort of girl who helps men with those sorts of urges. Usually in the toilets.'

'Simon!' said Caro, slapping him on the leg and raising her eyebrows towards April. 'Too much information!'

'Sorry.' He shrugged. 'Maybe you had a point about the discreet thing. Anyway, what are we going to do?'

April looked at him blankly. 'What do you mean, do?'

'Well, we can't let Little Miss Fingernails win, can we?'

April looked at the scrapes on the back of her hand, then at Layla again. 'No,' she said. 'No, we can't.'

Thanks to her time in the library, April had managed to get through her History lesson unscathed. As she had expected, Miss Holden had singled her out and asked her a difficult question about the role of politics in medieval society. April had used the 'kings and queens were just like pop stars' line, arguing that they were simply reacting to the mood of the time in order to keep or to gain popularity. That spiteful girl Chessy from the Faces crowd had stolen her thunder by smugly saying, 'But isn't that just a lazy definition of politics?', but April could see that Miss Holden had taken note of her answer. Not impressed, necessarily – after all, April had stolen her own theory – but satisfied that April wasn't a complete idiot. She had also managed to slip out of class when the bell rang without getting another lecture, which April counted as a bonus. She was heading for the school gates where she was due to meet Caro for a post-Layla powwow when she suddenly stopped and ducked behind a pillar. Gabriel was waiting by the entrance, stamping his feet against the cold. Was he waiting for her? Had he heard about the confrontation in the library with Layla? Did he want to explain? She held her breath; from this angle she could watch him but he couldn't see her. He seemed to be scanning faces as the students filed out onto the road, looking for someone. Finally he gave up and, with a scowl, strode off out of sight. April exhaled, relieved. She didn't want to see him right now, not so soon, not before she had a chance to work it all out in her own head. She stepped out from her hiding place and immediately heard her name called. She turned to see Mr Sheldon standing by his car at the main entrance and her heart sank.

'A word, Miss Dunne, if you would be so good,' he said, beckoning her over, his strange eyes boring into her as he indicated that she should get inside. It was some sort of swish sports car, like something James Bond might drive, and April opened the door carefully. She didn't want to scratch anything.

'Now, let's get straight to the heart of it, shall we?' he said once she had gently closed the door. 'You didn't attend my lesson this morning and I'd like to know why.'

April was actually shocked by his direct approach. She was used to teachers pussyfooting around, asking if 'things were okay at home' and so on.

'I've had some personal problems.'

'I see. And what sort of personal problems would these be?'

Again, April found herself on the back foot. No teacher at St Geoffrey's would have dared to probe into her – or anyone else's – 'personal problems' for fear of having to listen to tales about bad periods or abusive parents.

'I had an argument with my dad.'

'Indeed? And this was enough to keep you from discussing the works of John Wyndham with the rest of the class?'

'Yes.'

Mr Sheldon nodded, seeming to mull this over for a moment. 'You are, of course, aware that Ravenwood is a school for gifted pupils?' he asked.

'Yes,' said April.

'Well, as you'll imagine, Ravenwood gets some of the most

spectacular results of any school in the country and, consequently, children are lining up to attend. Now, some strings were pulled to get you into this school.'

April made to object, but Mr Sheldon held up a hand. 'There is, of course, nothing inherently wrong with that. Plenty of pupils have paid their way into the school or have parents with influence. Your family has – shall we say – more influence than most.'

April looked up in surprise, but Mr Sheldon was ploughing on.

'We do, however, have a reputation to uphold and if a pupil isn't meeting our exacting standards, please believe that, however influential their relatives, we will ask them to leave. Is all of this clear?'

'Yes,' said April quietly.

'Splendid, then we understand one another,' he said, putting his key into the ignition.

April opened the door and climbed out. As she walked around the car, the driver's side window buzzed down. 'One last thing, April,' said Mr Sheldon, beckoning her back over. 'You'll be aware that it is standard teacher practice to conclude one of these little talks with something along the lines of "if you're having any difficulties or want to talk about anything, my door is always open".'

April looked at him and was discomfited to see that his intense eyes were even more powerful up close. She was reminded of a science experiment in middle school where they had explored the attraction and repelling properties of magnets. For some reason, his eyes reminded her of the small, powerful magnets they had used that day.

'Personally, I couldn't think of anything worse than having an office full of teenagers snivelling about how their boyfriend has run off with someone else,' said Mr Sheldon. 'But in your case, April, I do feel I have a certain responsibility to you.'

April shook her head. 'Why? Because of what happened with Marcus?'

For a moment, Mr Sheldon looked at her as if he had no

idea what she was talking about. 'No, not because of that – although you can rest assured that that particular issue has been dealt with in the strongest terms. The *strongest* possible terms. I won't allow that sort of behaviour in my school. However it is perhaps an object lesson in the dangers of spreading malicious rumours, whatever the provocation.'

April gaped at him, a slow blush spreading across her face. *How the hell does he know about that?*

'The thing to do would be to take it to a teacher, don't you think? We don't encourage vigilantism at Ravenwood.'

'But I don't see …' she began falteringly. 'If it's not that, then why do you feel you have to look after me?'

The teacher looked at her for a moment, then burst out laughing. 'Good Lord, they haven't told you, have they?' he said as he twisted the ignition key and fired up the engine.

'Haven't told me what?' asked April over the roar.

Mr Sheldon paused, as if weighing something up, then when he spoke, there was a half-smile on his face. 'That I'm an old friend of the family,' he said.

Chapter Eighteen

Caro was waiting for April when she came out of the school gates.

'Lizzie Welch told me Hawk was telling you off, so I thought I'd stick around.'

'Ah,' said April, distracted. She was still reeling from the conversation with Mr Sheldon. She had pressed him further about the 'family friend' comment, but he had simply said, 'Perhaps you should ask your mother.'

'Gabriel was waiting for a while too, looked a bit pissed off about something, but he seems that way most of the time. I didn't like to ask if he was waiting for you, anyway.'

April nodded and they began to walk slowly up Swain's Lane, heading towards the coffee shop on the High Street.

'So what's up? Did he tell you off for cutting classes? Or was it about that git Marcus? What's going on with him anyway?'

'Mr Sheldon gave me the impression that he had dealt with Marcus pretty harshly.'

Caro shivered. 'Ugh, I wouldn't want to be on the receiving end of that – not that a bastard like Marcus doesn't deserve all he gets.'

'He had the cheek to say that I should have taken "my problem" to a teacher instead of "provoking" Marcus. He might as well have come out and told me I was asking for it.'

'But that's ridiculous!' said Caro. 'That just shows how out of touch teachers are. They have no idea how things work at school. God, I hate everyone in that damned place.'

'I know what you mean,' said April, with feeling. 'Anyway, it wasn't about Marcus, it was about missing lessons this morning.' April sighed. She had been reluctant to go over the whole sorry mess of her row with her dad and its aftermath at lunch, especially when they'd had the Layla incident to discuss, but now she found she wanted to talk about it. So she told Caro about finding the job-offer letter and the vampire note and how she had confronted her dad. She even told her about the fight between them before she stormed off into the rain.

'I was so mad,' said April. 'He just didn't seem to see that there was anything wrong with bringing your family to an area you believe might be full of bloodsucking killers.'

Caro pulled a face. The vampire issue was still a sore point between them; they hadn't discussed it since their fight after the party. April had apologised for overreacting, of course, but she had subsequently avoided talking with Caro about the supposed vampire thing, partly because so much had happened in the past few days and partly because, crazy as it was, April was embarrassed by her father's investigation into the undead. It was one thing for a conspiracy nut like Caro to believe in monsters – she was an excitable sixteen-year-old, after all – but it was quite another thing to have your forty-something father fall for such an idea. April was used to her dad's eccentricities, but this was quite a different story: she didn't want to admit that, if he really did think Highgate was dangerous – and to be honest, recent events seemed to be proving him right – he was knowingly putting his family at risk for his story.

'I can see your point,' said Caro thoughtfully. 'I mean, you expect your parents to make sound, rational decisions, don't you? But then my dad spent all his life savings on one of those enormous Winnebago motorhomes last year. We can't afford to get the boiler fixed, but he's got a mobile chemical toilet parked outside in the street.'

April giggled despite herself.

'The point is, adults can be idiots too,' said Caro. 'Your dad might well have come here to research his book, but I doubt he really thought it was dangerous. Maybe he bit off more than he could chew, no pun intended.'

'I guess.' April smiled. She was glad she had shared her burden with Caro; maybe she was right, maybe he had expected the vampire story to be another silly hoax like crop circles or something and then, with the murders, sensed he might be on to something big. April shook her head. It was hard to see your parents as real people; she wasn't sure she liked the idea much.

'Actually, that reminds me of something odd Mr Sheldon just said.'

'Odd?' asked Caro. 'What did he say?'

'He said he was a friend of the family.'

'Ugh. That sounds more creepy than odd. I wouldn't want Mr Sheldon babysitting me.'

'Well, it's even more odd because I'd never heard of or seen him before last week. I'd remember those eyes. And then when I asked him about it, he went all mysterious, like it was some big secret.'

'You're right, that is odd. Better ask your dad.'

April pulled a face. 'Might not be the best time to have a cosy chat with my dad right now. I did just tell him that I hated him.'

'Oh yes, I was forgetting.'

They walked a little further up the lane. April always made sure they stuck to the left-hand side, away from the cemetery railings, but the white gravestones still looked ominous in the failing light, poking out of the undergrowth like elbows and fingers.

'So no texts or calls from Gabriel?' said Caro.

April shook her head. 'Actually, I'd forgotten all about it. I mean, you've got to move on, haven't you?'

Caro looked at her with a sly smile. 'Really?'

April tried to smile, but couldn't. 'All right, so I've only checked my phone every five minutes or so.'

The truth was, she had thought of almost nothing else. A few short hours ago, she had been so sure of Gabriel Swift and his feelings for her. He had come to her, with doughnuts, and said he wanted them to be together, however difficult it got.

The way he had spoken to her – his reluctance, his awkwardness – she had believed those words were coming from his heart. It was the most romantic date of her life, not that that was saying much. He had been gallant and sexy and kind. And now, ever since Layla had stuck her claws in, it hurt even to think of him. For that one bright, shining moment Gabriel had been the best thing in the world and now ... now the memory was like a blunt knife in her heart.

She took a ragged breath. 'I just feel so stupid,' she said. 'I thought all that stuff with the coffee and the pebbles at the window was him being spontaneous and lovely, but the truth is he'd probably just had a fight with Layla or something and was looking for a back-up. I guess that's all the stuff he couldn't explain – why he said it would be difficult.'

'Hey, don't beat yourself up, honey,' said Caro, rubbing her arm reassuringly. 'You can't help it if he's a two-timing rat, can you? It was pretty romantic. I'd have been swept off my feet too and you know how cynical I am.'

April shook her head. 'Anyway, the reality is I'm not going to hear from him if he's with Layla, am I? Unless she suddenly decides to become a nun.'

'Not likely,' said Caro.

'And even then, do I really want to be second best?'

Caro smirked. 'He *is* pretty fit.'

April managed a wan smile. 'Maybe I'd consider it. We'll have to see.'

They were passing the main gates to the cemetery now and April couldn't help peering in, half-expecting to see some weird apparition with dark eyes lurking in the shadows or beckoning her in with a bony finger.

'You okay?' asked Caro.

'Yeah, it's just that ... no, I'm not. I know it sounds silly, but after that evening with the fox, and then Isabelle's murder, I don't like walking past it.'

'Don't be daft, of course it's not silly. Something like that would shake anyone up.' She grabbed April's hand and ran across the road and into the park, pulling April along behind her.

'What are you doing?' April laughed as she was virtually dragged up the hill towards the pond.

'I'm saving you!' shouted Caro. 'Now come on, we have to get to Americano before they run out of that squirty cream.'

They ran through the park, cackling with laughter, past the aviary and the tennis courts before dashing out onto the High Street, completely breathless.

'Stop! Stop! You'll kill me!' shouted April, bending over with her hands on her knees, panting. Caro trotted back to her and hooked her arm through April's.

'Lightweight.' She grinned. 'You'll never make the Ravenwood track team.'

'Does Ravenwood even *have* a track team?'

'No, I don't think it does.' Caro laughed as they headed up the hill, peering into the shops and catching their breath.

As they came to the zebra crossing between the High Street and Bisham Gardens, they heard the unmistakable sound of a police car racing up the hill. They turned to watch as it tore past, its whirling blue light bouncing off the shop windows. Hard on its heels came an ambulance, then another police car. The heavy evening traffic had to swerve and even mount the kerb to clear a way for them and April covered her ears as they shot past, sirens blaring.

'Blimey!' Caro shouted over the noise. 'They're in a hurry.'

But the sound of the sirens didn't diminish. Even though the cars were out of sight, the clamour continued.

'Hey – whatever it is, it's close. Let's go and see what's happened!' said Caro, pulling at April's elbow.

'No, Caro, people are probably hurt and they don't need spectators,' said April, hanging back.

'Oh come on!' shouted Caro over the sirens. 'How often do you get to see a real emergency? Just for a minute? Come *on!*'

Caro sped off across the road and April followed reluctantly behind her. She caught up with Caro as she was turning into South Grove and cutting across towards the square.

'Wow, it's right on your doorstep,' said Caro excitedly, running on.

Yeah, like that's a good thing, thought April, *like I need any more drama in my life.* She dodged around a white van, which swerved and the driver honked his horn angrily.

'Sorry!' she said, sprinting over the road. When she got to the other side, it was as if the whole of Pond Square had been lit up for Christmas, with red and blue lights spinning off the buildings and trees. The emergency vehicles were parked higgledy-piggledy in the road and there were people running back and forth between them, shouting above the noise. It was only then that she noticed Caro had stopped and turned back towards her. Her friend's face looked pale and serious in the weird pulsing light. April instantly sensed that something was wrong, pushing past her friend when Caro tried to grab her.

'April, stop ...' she said, worry in her voice. 'I think it's your house.'

'What? No, it can't be,' said April, smiling uncertainly, her feet already moving across the square. But between the cars she could see that the yellow front door was open. 'Oh God,' she breathed, wrenching herself out of Caro's grip.

'April!' her friend shouted desperately. 'Wait ...'

But April wasn't stopping for anyone. Traffic forgotten, she dropped her bag and ran as fast as her legs would go, crossing the distance in seconds. A uniformed policeman saw her approach and tried to block her, but April was moving too fast. She barged him out of the way and shot through the front door, almost tumbling over a man in a bright green jacket crouching in the doorway to her dad's study. She went down on one knee, pain shooting up her thigh.

'What's going on? What are you doing?' she rasped, the words coming out in a harsh whisper. The corridor seemed to tilt to one side as her wide-open eyes tried to take in the scene. To her right, she saw the living room; it looked as if a bomb had exploded inside. Papers and books were strewn across the floor, even the shelves and pictures had been smashed. The hallway table was lying at an angle across the corridor with the phone next to it, the handset looking as if it had been used by someone with ink on their fingers. *I bet I'll get the blame for that*, she thought randomly, her mind scrabbling to get a grip and knowing, deep inside, that it wasn't ink. Slowly, with a detached fascination, she let her eyes follow the dark smears across the floor and up the wall. There was a wide daub – *a handprint*, her mind corrected – on the doorframe, tailing off into a long smear, as if someone – *your dad, your dad* – had reached out for support and then slid to the floor.

'NOOOO!' she screamed, and everything flashed back into full speed. Caro and the policeman were grabbing her, trying to pull her back as she pushed past the paramedic hunched over the thing on the floor.

It wasn't a thing. It was her father – her *father*. He was lying on his back, half-in, half-out of the study, staring up at the ceiling, a black pool spreading around his shoulders. The paramedic was working on a deep wet wound in his neck. It looked as if his neck had been torn open.

'No, no, no, Dad, no,' she whispered as she fell to her knees, trying to hold him, clutching his wet hand. *It's blood*, she thought in her vague, detached way, *I'm covered in my father's blood.* His eyelids fluttered and a horrible rasp came from his throat. *He's alive! He's alive!* thought April, looking up at the paramedics desperately, but they were oblivious to her, their concentration fixed on the job in front of them. The hands behind her were still trying to pull her back, but again she shook them off.

'Honey ...' gasped her father, squeezing her hand, his head turning, a slight smile on his lips. 'Don't ...' He coughed with an ugly rattle and bright red bubbles appeared on his lips. 'Don't ... worry.'

The paramedic pushed April aside and shone a light into her father's eyes. 'Can you hear me?' He touched William's face. 'Come on, mate, stay with us.'

April's father gave the slightest of nods and the man went back to work, pressing a dressing to his throat which immediately became dark with blood.

'April,' whispered her father, his voice a barely audible croak, his gurgling breath getting weaker. 'April ... you need to know. Your mum ...'

Suddenly his body tensed and he moaned in pain.

'Dad, no,' sobbed April. 'Please, don't talk ...'

He smiled with red lips and gave her hand another squeeze. 'I love you, April. I'll always be here for you.'

'I love you too, Daddy, don't leave me, please!'

She looked up just in time to catch a glance exchanged between the medic and the policeman: a slight shake of the head.

'No, no, no!' she screamed as the policeman got a hold of her and yanked her backwards.

'Let them do their job, love,' he said in her ear; urgent, but not unkind. 'Let them help him.'

'No, no, I can't leave him,' she cried, fighting the policeman, her arms reaching out for her dad as she was pulled away, screaming for him, hands clawing against the doorframe, her own red fingerprints mixing with her father's, her tears falling uselessly on the steps.

She knew he was dead when they brought her the blanket. A female police officer draped it around her shoulders as she sat on a bench in the square, Caro close beside, holding her tight. She could see the open doorway, she could see the paramedics wheeling the stretcher up the steps. They were doing all the right things, going through the correct procedure, but there was no urgency to their movements. There was no rush to get her dad into the ambulance and down the hill to the hospital. And she could feel it deep inside her, though she didn't know how or why – she could feel that he had gone.

'Your mum is on the way,' said the policewoman softly. 'She'll be here soon.'

April stared straight ahead, her face expressionless.

Caro looked up at the woman and nodded. 'Thanks,' she said.

The police had taped off the whole square, but the curious

rubberneckers seemed to be keeping a respectful distance anyway. Perhaps they sensed that something terrible had happened. The ambulance slowly rolled out of the square and April followed behind in a police car. She sat in silence, Caro on one side, the policewoman the other. She supposed it should feel weird or tragic or surreal, but she couldn't conjure up any of those feelings. She was numb and empty, as if she was one step away from the world, could see it but not touch it.

'Why would someone do that?' asked April, as much to herself as to the policewoman.

'There are some pretty nasty people out there, love,' said the officer, 'but you can be sure we'll do everything we can to catch him.'

April wanted to say something, to tell her to get out there and find the killer straight away, but she couldn't seem to open her mouth, it was as if she was encased in ice. Then they were standing at the hospital entrance, blinking in the harsh fluorescent light, watching as the paramedics wheeled the stretcher quickly away down a corridor, getting smaller and smaller, until it bumped through some double doors and disappeared.

She looked around her, the bustle and purpose of the doctors and nurses somehow rendered ridiculous by the broken patients around them, shuffling along in their backless gowns, pushing walking frames or trailing drips, not a trace of joy or hope in their faces.

'What is this place?' whispered April. *Is this hell?* The policewoman came and ushered them into a private waiting room and sat them down on wipe-clean plastic chairs.

'I should be crying,' she said flatly.

'You are, honey,' said Caro. April touched her face and found it was true. Tears were quietly rolling down her cheeks, wetting her collar.

'He tried to tell me something, before he … before …'

Caro nodded and pulled her tight. 'We know. We know, honey.'

'What did he say?' asked the policewoman.

April glanced at her; she was young, perhaps only a few years older than her and Caro, quite pretty in a scrubbed, pink-cheeked way, but there was a look in her eyes when she asked her question that put April, even in her numb state, on her guard. She was ambitious, eager to uncover some vital piece of evidence. April couldn't blame her for that, but even through her fug she knew she needed to think, needed to work things out before she said anything else to anyone. She wanted to get it all straight in her own mind first. April felt a sob welling up in her throat.

'That he loved me,' she said, her voice cracking.

'Of course he did,' said Caro, hugging her tighter. 'Of course he did.'

But April knew there had been something else in her father's last words. Something vital he was trying to communicate in the serious look on his face when he had spoken to her: 'There's something I need to tell you ... your mum ...' And had there been another half-word he was struggling to get out?

She shook her head. Her father's last words. April felt a horrible sickness spreading from the pit of her stomach as she remembered her last words to him that morning: 'I'll never forgive you!', 'I hate you!', her spiteful, selfish words. Words designed to hurt him, words she had meant, really truly meant. She had screamed that she hated him. Yes, she had said she loved him in those last terrible moments on the floor of the study, but she knew those horrible, childish, petulant words were the ones that would haunt her for ever.

'Oh, God. Forgive me,' she whispered, feeling as if someone was twisting a knife in her heart. 'Please, Daddy, forgive me.'

The waiting room door burst open and her mother flew in, her arms wide, her face creased with concern.

'Darling, darling!' she cried, scooping April up, squeezing her tight, her arms wrapped hard around her. And then the tears came for real and April finally gave in to it, crying so hard she choked, unable to breathe, her body sick with the pain, her face contorted, feeling as if she could never stand it, as if she must die too. *Why him? Why, God, why? Can't you turn back time? I want my daddy back.* And through it all, she clung to her mother like a rock in a storm, and Silvia cradled her like a baby, whispering soothing words, kissing and stroking the tears away, crying with her. Then, when April finally surfaced from her grief, completely wrung out, head pounding from crying so hard, Caro and the policewoman were gone. She wiped her eyes and looked up into her mother's face.

'Who would do that to him, Mum?' she asked. 'Who could hate him so much?'

'I don't know,' said her mother forcefully, 'but we'll find them and we'll make them pay. Believe me, they will pay.'

Her eyes were glittering and fierce and there was a look of determination on her face April hadn't seen before.

'Do you think it was something he was working on? Like an investigation?'

Silvia shook her head. 'I really don't know, but whoever it was, they will wish they had never touched that sweet man ...'

That was too much for April; she began choking on her tears again, to think of her kind, gentle father lying somewhere nearby, lifeless and cold. It was ridiculous, absurd and so very, very unfair. Silvia held her again, whispering soft, comforting words that could never help.

'Has he really gone?' asked April, finally looking up.

Her mother nodded slowly. 'It's just us now,' she whispered, stroking the hair from April's damp face. 'We've got to be strong for him. He would have wanted us to be strong.'

April shook her head. 'I'm not strong. I just want to lie down and die.'

'No,' said Silvia, lifting April's chin and searching her eyes. 'Never say that. You are so, so precious, my darling.'

She said it with such intensity, such passion, that April looked at her mother again. Her face was lined with pain, her eyes still bright with tears, and suddenly April felt ashamed. She had been so absorbed in her own agony that her mother's hadn't even occurred to her. Silvia had loved William Dunne long before April was even a twinkle in her father's eye. She had lost her husband, her one true love, and she must be torn up inside. April hugged her mother fiercely.

'You're right, Mum,' she said. 'We've got to look after each other now.'

But in her heart, April Dunne had never felt more alone.

PART TWO

Chapter Nineteen

It was a beautiful morning in Swain's Lane, for other people at least. April sat on the wall opposite the cemetery gates, watching the little spots of sunshine pushing through the trees swing and sway back and forth across the pavement, wishing she could enjoy the unusually good weather. Wishing she could enjoy anything. The wall was still cold under her legs and April knew she would be stiff when she got up. These days, though, she couldn't bring herself to care too much about such things. She supposed it was Wednesday, which meant it had only been a week since she had found her father on the floor of his study, but since then, time had lost its meaning. Sometimes a minute would drag horribly, threatening to leave her stranded in the grip of a twisting, grating pain, but then sometimes she would look up and realise that an hour had passed and that the bath had gone stone cold.

An elderly couple walked out of the park and across the road, shuffling to the closed gates. They peered at the sign and the woman checked her watch. Seeming satisfied, the old lady produced a fold-out chair and sat down to wait.

April was fairly sure she shouldn't have come here. It was basic first aid: before you can expect a wound to heal, you have to stop poking it. Stay well away from the area where your father was killed – no – the place where her father was *murdered*. The police had been pretty definite about that, so definite, in fact, that they had organised a press conference and read out a statement announcing that 'Journalist and acclaimed author William Dunne had been attacked and murdered in his home'. They had described it as a 'shocking incident', which had angered April. 'Shocking' was something you said about the weather or a football result; it seemed a wholly inadequate word to describe the full horror of what had happened to her father. They had also called for calm and reassured the public that they were 'doing their utmost' to catch the killer. Their 'utmost' seemed to be knocking on a few doors in Pond Square and asking the Dunnes' neighbours if they had seen anything. The answer, it seemed, was no. Consequently April had been ringing Detective Inspector Reece – the detective in charge of the case, the same one who had interviewed her in Mr Sheldon's office – bombarding him with questions, asking for updates on the investigation, but while he had been sympathetic and polite, he had told her nothing. 'Trust me, April,' he had said, 'we will get whoever did this.' But that was the problem: she didn't trust them. She didn't trust anyone any more. Her father had been killed in his own home – *her* own home – and no one seemed to know why. Was it because of something he was investigating, was it a burglary gone wrong, had he known the killer? April felt vulnerable and hunted, as if she was being constantly watched; which, in many ways, she was. The police were posted outside the house to discourage the ghoulish public and the unscrupulous press who had been camping out in the square all week. The papers, predictably, had gone to town on the story: three violent murders in one week, all less than a mile apart, was juicy news. Her father's paper, the *Ham & High*, had run eight pages on it, almost all speculation and supposition; they clearly had no better idea what William Dunne had been investigating than April or the police did. Unsurprisingly, the police had asked April and her mother to go into hiding. Not officially of course – the Metropolitan Police would never be so dramatic as to whisk them off to a safe house – but they had strongly suggested that 'for the girl's sake' it would be better if they left Highgate Village. So April and her mother had moved in with Thomas; it wasn't as if they had much choice. Her grandfather had been glad to have them, and April had been pleasantly surprised by how sensitive he had been, giving them space and defending them from press, police and well-wishers alike. He had even been kind about her father – prompting another storm of tears. Even so, the gothic splendour of the Hamilton mansion with its dark corners and narrow windows was not exactly helping April's mood. What she really wanted was to go back to Edinburgh and see Fiona and all her friends, surround herself with familiar things and memories of happy times. But she couldn't leave, not now. The police were keen to talk to her again, and appeared to be working on some theory that her father's death was linked to the Isabelle Davis and Alix Graves murders. More importantly, April was worried about her mother. Silvia had held herself together just long enough to check that April was okay, then she fell apart. She had spent most of the last week in bed, refusing to eat, her skin grey, her hair unwashed. But worse, she was refusing to talk about it. Whenever April went into her mother's dimly lit room, it was as if she was waiting for William to pop in to wake her up. It was as if she could wish it all away. So April had been forced to deal with it alone, sitting in the courtyard garden or wandering through Covent Garden Market, looking in the windows at the gaudy pre-Christmas displays, trying to distract her whirling mind with shoes and trinkets, just letting her feet take her where they wanted; anywhere so long as it was away from her grandfather's gloomy house. Which is why she had found herself on the Tube, heading back almost by instinct to the one place that reminded her of her father: Highgate.

By now there were about a dozen people standing by the gates, clustering together in little groups of two or three. Apart from one young touristy couple in high-tech walking gear, they were all elderly and dressed in a combination of tweeds and M&S basics. *Why do they come here?* wondered April. *Is it because they're so close to the grave themselves?* Of course, April could have asked herself the same thing and, if she was honest, she didn't have a good answer either. Just then a portly, middle-aged lady in a floaty print dress opened the gate and beckoned everyone inside. April wavered for a moment: *Is this really a good idea?* she wondered. *Am I just making things worse for myself?* But once again, April found her feet making the decision for her, placing themselves in front of each other until she was through the gate.

'Please pay the young man to your left,' cried the woman with that unmistakable I've-been-teaching-in-an-all-girls-school-for-forty-years-so-don't-mess-with-me tone. *Great*, thought April as she joined the queue without really knowing why, *it's a tour with Enid Blyton*. They were all shooed across a wide courtyard to a row of benches next to a war memorial where the schoolmarm introduced herself as 'Judith', although April could tell it killed her to use such an informal name. Judith greeted each of the tour party individually, asking where they were from.

'Um, Edinburgh,' said April haltingly, suddenly very conscious of the police warning her to stay away from the area.

'Scotland indeed?' said Judith, peering at her over the top of her gold-rimmed spectacles with disapproval then quickly moving on to probe the rest of her customers, clearly hoping for more civilised visitors. There was a trio from Esher and a couple from Norfolk; the blue-rinsed lady with the fold-out seat and her husband were from 'a small village in Cheshire'; and the super-hikers turned out to be tourists from the Ukraine. The stand-out visitors for April were an old couple from Milwaukee who, despite being in their late sixties, wore denim and leather as if they'd just climbed off a Harley-Davidson. Perhaps they had. Either way, Judith clearly didn't appreciate this deviation from the norm and directed her stern warnings against walking on graves, videotaping and 'straying from the path for any reason' at them. Rules clearly stated, money collected, Judith raised one arm in the air as if she was starting a Grand Prix and trilled, 'This way!', leading the slow-moving group up a marble staircase at the back of the courtyard. They crested the rise and, almost as one, the whole group gasped. The cemetery was magnificent, an almost perfect balance of menace and beauty. In front of them was a meandering path lined on either side with headstones, crosses and teetering caskets, all struggling to remain upright as the undergrowth clawed and choked them.

'Wow!' said Biker Lady. 'That's neat.'

April couldn't have put it better herself. It was at once glorious, moving and frightening and, to April, easily the most wonderful place she had ever seen. And she immediately felt bad for feeling that way. Since her father's death it felt wrong to be happy, any pleasure obscene. What right had she to enjoy looking at the view when her dad would never see another sunset or a spider's web or a flower? He wouldn't see anything ever again. April fought back the tears that were threatening to fall. Judith certainly wouldn't approve of public displays of emotion. Instead, April concentrated on the cemetery and tried to view it as a detached observer. She thought of Miss Holden and her idea about the past – that to understand history, first you have to understand how the people in it *lived*. If this was the Victorians' idea of remembering the dead, their way of life must have been spectacular.

Judith smiled in satisfaction at the open-mouthed reaction her baby had evoked.

'Let me take you back, if I may,' she began, 'to the beginning of the nineteenth century. The population of London was one million. Twenty years later, it had jumped to two and a half million souls. We get headlines about unchecked immigration today, but a hundred and fifty years ago people were pouring into the city. Cholera was rife, families routinely starved to death and the graveyards were literally overflowing, contaminating the water supply. Something needed to be done and this—' she swept a grandiose hand at the view '—was the solution. Highgate Cemetery was built in 1839, one of seven cemeteries in key spots outside the capital, all opened between 1832 and 1841. Highgate was the smallest, but by far the most spectacular.'

Judith carried on in this vein, talking about notable graves – a coach-master, a boxer, a general – and pointing out the grandest examples of 'funerary art' – the pillars, the upturned torches, the urns draped in cloth – and explaining how, one hundred years before, the cemetery would have been alive with colourful flowers and plants.

'It was a Victorian Disneyland, if you like, and fashionable ladies would come here to promenade and take the air.'

'So why is this place so ...' began the Ukrainian man, clearly struggling to think of the right word, 'so ... dead?'

'I believe you are referring to the "managed neglect",' said Judith with an indulgent smile. 'We have attempted to strike a balance between what it was and what it became. The cemetery fell into disrepair after the First World War. All of the burial plots had been sold – fifty-two thousand of them – and as a result the money stopped coming in. By the late sixties, it had become badly neglected and vandalised and in 1973 it was closed altogether.'

Walking slowly up the hill, April wondered again why she had come here to surround herself with death. She had expected it to be painful, but it wasn't. Quite the opposite, in fact. It was soothing somehow, as if she wasn't alone in her grief. Thousands of daughters had suffered the same loss, not to mention the pain of broken parents who had to bury their children. Perhaps she was doing the same thing as her mother – avoiding looking the reality in the eye. If she looked at other people's graves she wouldn't have to imagine the freshly dug hole for her father. She had been looking out for the family tomb, of course, but it was hopeless trying to spot a tiny name chiselled on overgrown stone in all this muddle. She didn't really want to ask Judith about it either as she was sure the woman would make a big deal about it and April didn't want to draw any attention today. Perhaps the truth was that she wanted to see the Circle of Lebanon again, stand in the spot where she had held Gabriel's hand, feel that closeness again, even if it hadn't been real. At least, while it had lasted, it had made her happy, made her feel alive. That was something to take comfort from. It went without saying, of course, that she hadn't heard from Gabriel. There had been texts and messages from distant family, close friends and people she'd barely even spoken to at St Geoffrey's, so many in fact that she had turned off her phone. *Anyway, why would Gabriel call me when he has Layla to talk to?* she thought with a dull ache. The truth was, obsessing over Gabriel seemed silly and pointless now she understood real pain. Gabriel didn't even come close.

'And this, ladies and gentlemen, is where the architects really started to show off,' said Judith. They walked around the corner and an amazing gateway appeared from behind an overgrown tree, its huge pillars carved from the rock, set into the hillside and opening onto a wide pathway.

'Welcome to the Egyptian Avenue, a masterpiece of funerary art, reputedly based on the original mausoleum of King Mausolus at Halicarnassus.'

It was incredible, a long corridor of stone climbing up the hill, the trees on each side so overgrown it gave the impression they were looking into a dark tunnel with sunlight at the far end. They walked inside and found that the walls had black iron vault doors set into them, all the way up the hill.

'Are these tombs still used?' asked April.

'Heavens no,' said Judith. 'Of course they could be – the families own these plots in perpetuity and we have a key for each one in the office. Grave-owners, or "key-holders" as we call them, can come to the cemetery at any time. But as for interments in these tombs, none of them have been used for decades.'

They walked up the avenue, examining the doors and the carvings in mute awe. April noticed that the keyholes in the iron doors were upside down. For some reason she found that unsettling.

Biker Lady had also spotted it. 'Why the crazy keyholes?' she asked.

'Ah, a silly superstition. Some people believe it confuses the devil,' she said, forcing herself to smile. 'Leaves him unable to unlock the door.'

'But the Egyptians didn't believe in the devil,' said Tweed Lady. 'They had a whole host of different gods.'

'Yes, but some of those gods were – how shall we say it? – troublesome.'

Waving away any more questions, Judith hurried up the path and out into the sunlight.

'And this is the jewel in the cemetery's crown,' said Judith proudly as they stepped out into the Circle of Lebanon. April looked at her sharply; those were the exact words Gabriel had used to describe it. Had he been here, on this tour? Maybe he had brought Layla along as some sort of horrid foreplay. April knew it wasn't Judith's fault Gabriel was a two-timing rat, but she found herself getting irritated with the woman all the same.

'Why doesn't this tomb have a door?' she asked, pointing to a vault with a boarded-up entrance.

'Vandalism, I'm afraid. In the sixties and seventies we had a terrible time of it, people breaking into coffins, stealing bodies, it was a disgrace.'

Mutters of agreement rippled around the group, until April innocently asked, 'Was that when the vampires came to the cemetery?'

There was a communal gasp.

'Vampires?' said Blue-Rinse Lady's husband.

'Yes, there was a lot of silliness going on,' said Judith, glaring at April, 'people claiming to have seen all sorts of things in the cemetery. Not surprising given the level of damage that had been done to the tombs, with coffins ripped open and so on. And the fuss contributed to the closure of the cemetery. But I assure you, there have never been any real ghosts or spectres here. Shall we move on?'

'Some spooks would liven these stiffs up though, hey?' Biker Lady whispered to April with a wink.

Judith hurried them around the circle. It seemed much wider and more open in the daylight. It was impressive still, but it didn't have the same magic April had felt that night. *Perhaps it's just the company*, thought April.

She watched with detachment as they trooped into the catacombs and inspected the death mask of the child in the Beer mausoleum, the owner of which had paid the equivalent of £2.5 million for the plot.

'Where's Dickens?' asked Blue-Rinse Lady.

'If you mean *Charles* Dickens, you should be in Westminster,' snapped Judith with some asperity, as if it was a personal irritation that the author had failed to be buried here. 'It was his wish to be interred in Highgate, of course, but Queen Victoria had other ideas. She wanted him in Westminster Abbey, and what her majesty wanted she tended to get. His wife and daughter are here, however.'

'Ooh, can we see them?' asked Tweed Lady.

Judith looked awkward. 'I'm afraid not.'

'Is it because of the murder?' asked Tweed Lady.

'What murder?' gasped Blue-Rinse Lady.

'There was a terrible murder here only a fortnight ago,' said Tweed Lady knowledgeably. 'Some poor girl. Police are baffled, apparently. The killer could strike again at any moment.'

A concerned twitter went around the group and April could see people glancing from side to side as if a knife-wielding maniac was about to jump from the bushes.

Judith patted the air in a calming gesture. 'Please, ladies and gentlemen, don't be concerned, you are quite safe. Despite some inflammatory reports in the press, I can assure you, there is nothing to see.'

'Have you been to look?' asked April.

'No,' said Judith through thin lips.

'Where did it happen?' pressed Tweed Lady.

Judith cleared her throat. 'By the east wall, in what we call the dissenters' section.'

'Dissenters?' said Blue-Rinse Lady, her hand jumping to her throat with alarm. 'Were they pagans?'

'No, no.' Judith smiled, pleased to be back on safer ground. 'Dissenters was the term used to describe any non-Anglican burials,' she said, 'although burials in that section were not necessarily non-religious, or even un-Christian—'

'So why can't we go there?' interrupted Biker Lady.

'We can't go there, dear lady,' said Judith, summoning up the last of her thinning patience with her unruly tour group, 'because there is a funeral today and, out of respect for the recently bereaved, today's tours have been slightly diverted.'

There was a pause.

'But I thought you said the cemetery was full?' said April.

Judith was definitely getting uncomfortable now. 'Some monuments and paths have been moved to make a little space.'

'It must be someone important, then?'

'I don't know.'

'Really?'

'They don't tell us everything,' said Judith firmly. 'Now, as I'm sure you all understand, funerals are a private matter, so if you would step this way, we can see the last resting place of a very interesting man ...'

April didn't know she was going to do it until it happened. She hadn't planned any of this when she had caught the train to Highgate, but when the moment came, as the tour group turned a corner and April was shielded by a curtain of leaves, she moved decisively. Stepping off the path – *Judith expressly forbade this*, she thought with a little thrill – she darted behind an angel and hid, listening to her own breathing and the fading voices as the tour ambled on. April stood up and stepped back onto the path, quickly walking up the hill away from the others. It was hard to keep her bearings on such winding, twisty paths with all the thick undergrowth preventing her from seeing where she was headed, but when she glimpsed the spire of St Michael's at the top of the hill she knew she was going the right way: east, towards the forbidden zone of the dissenters' graveyard. April didn't know what she was going to find there, but for some reason she wanted to see the place where 'it' had happened for herself in the daylight. If she was honest, she still felt guilty that she hadn't done more for Isabelle and felt that she owed her something – maybe she could find a clue the police had overlooked. A clue to Isabelle's murder might even be a clue to her father's. She walked along the path, lost in her thoughts, wondering what her dad would have made of this place, whether he would have ... She stopped. For a moment April thought she'd seen a ghost, a disembodied face floating above a half-toppled gravestone. She instinctively ducked down out of the line of sight, then slowly crept forward. There was no ghost, but rather a group of about twenty people all dressed in black – the funeral, of course. April kept her distance, but she'd never been to a funeral before and she found herself curious: how did people behave? Did they cry and wail? Did they keep a stiff upper lip? She craned her neck to peer through the leaves at the mourners' faces. The answer seemed to be that people were generally looking down at the ground with serious expressions, while a white-robed priest said words she couldn't hear. One woman was weeping into a handkerchief, but everyone else looked either sad or slightly uncomfortable, as if they would rather be somewhere else. April backed away and walked down the path, strangely reassured by having seen the funeral. In fact, she felt remarkably calm, almost cheerful, being here among the long-dead. She had expected – if she was honest, had *wanted* – her visit here to be depressing and morbid. She had anticipated a general atmosphere of gloom and despondency around the cemetery in which she could immerse herself, but it was quite the opposite. It was calm, picturesque and charming. More importantly, it was near impossible to walk through such an old graveyard without reading the inscriptions and be unmoved by words such as: 'Beloved daughter Charlotte Gosling, 1897–1919'. 'In loving memory of Elizabeth Sexton 1878–1899, rest in peace'. 'Joseph Cottingham, fell asleep, 10th May 1888'. April thought the sentiments were lovely. 'Eternal peace', 'joined in heaven', 'passed away', 'lives on in our hearts'. It was hard to be cynical about so many heartfelt markers of remembrance. Each one of these people had touched the lives of their families and friends, each one had a resonance and a positive energy. April thought back to Gabriel's words about the ability of objects to hold feelings and emotions long after the owner had gone, and she knew that he was right. She should have been freaked out with so many dead bodies just beneath her feet, but the horror of death seemed to be cancelled out by the endless love and affection that was displayed on the surface of the stones.

April was so lost in her musings that she almost stumbled into the crime scene. Turning a corner hidden behind dense ivy and a chestnut tree, she found her way barred by black and yellow police tape fluttering in the breeze. April ducked under it and continued along a narrow path near the east wall. The tape was protecting a wide area extending about fifty metres to either side of where she was standing. *Does that mean I'm standing right where Isabelle was killed?* she wondered. Gingerly she looked around her feet, half-expecting to see pools of congealed blood, but all she saw were leaves, twigs and gravel, not even the heavy footprints of the forensics people. The thought of their light blue moon-suits suddenly made April's heart lurch as she realised that the same men had probably been walking around her house only days later. She shivered and hugged herself. Suddenly she wanted to get away from here. She turned right and could immediately see the sunlight out on Swain's Lane through the old iron gate right next to that curious little white stone cottage; the North Gate, the one she had come through that night. Seeing the road out there, only a few hundred metres from bars and cafes, it looked so strange, like staring down the wrong end of a telescope. Back in the enclosed world of the cemetery, it was still the Victorian era and April could feel the gentle presence of the departed, tipping their hats as she passed, polite and welcoming. But here, where the ancient wall ended and the modern world leaked in, bringing its harsh light and blaring traffic, April felt the mood change, darken. It was colder here, the overhead sun pushed back by a thick tangle of branches and creepers, the decrepit tombstones leaning in towards the path, leering somehow. She couldn't say why, but there was just something different here, like that picture on her grandpa's wall. It felt … bad. Even so, she wanted to stop where she had stood before, where the fox had lain, to measure out how far she had been from Isabelle. From what she could tell, April had been very close. She walked carefully towards the gate, the little white house to her right. *What the hell is that, exactly?* It was like a miniature cottage, with little windows, even a chimney. The coldness felt even more intense here. Yes, it was autumn, but it was also a sunny afternoon – there was no way it should feel this icy. Slowly she approached the building and its white walls seemed to glow in the gloom. *Come on, scaredy-cat*, thought April, *what's the matter? It's only a little house.* She peered into the dusty black window – and jumped straight back. A white face loomed behind the glass. 'Jesus!' she shrieked and was running before her brain could react.

'Stop!' came a cry. A voice. A strong, angry voice. A *real* voice, not a ghost or a vampire. 'What the hell are you doing?'

April skidded to a halt and turned back as a tall man in work overalls ran out of the house.

'You do know you're not supposed to be in here, don't you?' he called.

He didn't come any closer, but April could see he was angry. *As if he had been caught doing something he shouldn't have been?* she thought suddenly.

'I was with the tour and I got a bit lost,' she said.

He raised his eyebrows sceptically, but didn't say anything. 'Well, perhaps I'd better take you back before you damage something.'

He walked slowly up to her and April could now see the man was about forty, with untidy hair and the weathered complexion of someone who had always worked outside. He gestured along the path and she warily fell into step with him.

'So what do you do?' she asked.

'Do?'

'You work here?'

'I look after the graves.'

'Don't you get scared?'

'What of?'

'Oh, you know, ghosts, that sort of thing – it must be spooky at night.'

The man looked at her sharply. 'No one comes here at night.'

'Really? Isn't there any security or anything?'

'Why would you want to know that?'

'I'm just curious.'

'Curiosity killed the cat.'

They turned left onto the main pathway and the man increased his pace, as if he was keen to get rid of her. He certainly wasn't one for small talk. *Maybe doesn't see many people in his line of work*, she thought.

'Hey, what's that?' said April, stopping at the corner where the path twisted away. There was a waist-high stone vault and carved into the top was an exquisite sculpture of a woman, lying down, one ear to the grave, as if she was weeping, or listening for signs of life. It had a powerful air of melancholy and sadness. 'What's that one?' she repeated.

The man paused before answering. 'They call her the Sleeping Angel,' he said quietly.

'Whose grave is it?'

Curiously, she noticed that her companion seemed to be avoiding looking at the monument.

'It's the grave of a girl,' he said. 'She was about your age. Francesca Bryne, her name was, laid here in 1894.'

'How sad.'

'Is it?'

April looked at him. There was an expression of distaste on his face.

'What do you mean? The poor girl was obviously loved if she was given such a lovely stone, wasn't she?'

Before he could reply, they heard footsteps and puffing, and Judith charged around the corner, her face almost purple.

'There you are!' she cried. 'I've been looking everywhere for you, I almost called the police out. You must never leave the tour! Never!' April could tell she wanted to say more, but she had completely run out of breath.

'I'm sorry,' said April. 'I was looking at an interesting headstone and turned around and you'd all gone. Then I got a bit lost.'

'In all my years I've never lost a guest, not ever,' said Judith. 'I've a very good mind to report this.'

'My father just died,' said April, stopping Judith in her tracks.

'I, uh, well I ...' she mumbled.

'It's been quite hard ...' She tailed off and pretended to sob, brushing away an imaginary tear. She could see that Judith was completely thrown; she certainly didn't want to get involved with an emotional teenager.

'Oh, well. Perhaps we shouldn't say too much more,' she said. 'I suppose we should just be glad you didn't get completely lost.'

'No, this man showed me the way back.' April turned around to indicate her companion and found she was alone. 'Oh. I met a man who showed me the way back, he was telling me about this grave, as a matter of fact.'

Judith looked even more perplexed. 'The Sleeping Angel?' she asked.

'Yes, he was saying it's the grave of a young girl named Francesca, very sad.'

Judith looked at her curiously. As if she had just realised she was dealing with a dangerous lunatic. 'No, that can't be true my dear. Now if you'd just like to step this way.'

'What do you mean?'

'Well, no one knows who the Sleeping Angel was laid here for. There are records of who bought it, but not who is interred here. We speculate it may have been a child, but no one knows for sure. And Francesca? No, no. We have researched the cemetery exhaustively. There is no one of that name buried here.'

'But he told me,' said April, as Judith guided her back towards the gates. Her attitude was now more like someone steering a monkey towards a cage than a guest back to their tour. 'He said he'd worked here for years. Tall man in overalls?'

Judith smiled indulgently. 'I'm sure that's what you think you saw, my dear, but let me assure you I have never seen anyone like that.'

'He was in that little house ...' She trailed off, knowing she had made a slip.

Judith tensed. 'The gatehouse? No one has been in there. It's been locked for decades, not even the police could get in when they were investigating that unpleasantness. You certainly shouldn't have been over there.'

'But he said—'

Judith was losing her patience. 'Young lady, in the fifteen years I have been here, no one has worked when there's a funeral,' she snapped. They came down the steps into the courtyard. 'Now, out of respect for the cemetery, I'm asking you to leave.'

'I *saw* him, I did!'

'Believe me,' said Judith with mounting irritation, 'no one who works at the cemetery fits that description.'

'Are you sure?'

'Quite sure. There is no one else in this graveyard, and I will be locking the gates behind you.'

Chapter Twenty

The polystyrene cup had left a ring on the table. If she moved the edge of the cup very slightly, the cold tea would run around the bottom of it like a little river. By tilting it just the right way, she could make little bubbles.

'April, don't.'

She dipped her fingernail into the tea, watching the way the fluorescent lighting reflected on the milky surface.

'April, will you stop doing that?'

She looked up and blinked, as if she was seeing the room for the first time. Not that there was much to see – the police interview room had bare off-green walls, one Formica-topped table and four chairs, that was it. Her mother was sitting next to her, shifting uncomfortably on her plastic chair. She had been irritable since they had arrived at the police station and that had been hours ago. She was swinging from listless to frantic and back again. April wanted to tell her mother to calm down; tutting and bristling wasn't doing anyone any good.

'It's as if they think we've nothing better to do,' said Silvia with irritation. 'I've got to talk to the coroner again before the end of the day.' She glanced at her watch for the second time in as many minutes and clicked her tongue. 'It's Friday afternoon, if we don't get an answer now, we're going to be sitting on our hands again all weekend.'

'Calm down, Mum, fretting about it's not going to help.'

'But if I don't fret about it, who will?' said Silvia. 'These people move at a snail's pace – if we leave it to the bloody authorities they'll spend weeks on the post-mortem, and then where will we be?'

April looked at her mother sadly. 'Dad's not going any-where, is he?'

'But how are we supposed to move on when we have this hanging over us?' said Silvia, her eyes beginning to sparkle with tears. 'We can't even bury him, we can't even say goodbye, I feel like we're in total limbo.'

April put her hand on her mother's. She knew what Silvia was going through, she knew she needed the funeral in order to let her grief out and that the delay caused by the post-mortem was driving them all mad, however necessary it was. At the moment, everything was bottled up inside her mother, all her pain and regret; it had nowhere to go. April could see the tension on her pale, lined face; despite spending most of the day in bed there were still heavy rings under her eyes. Not that April was exactly looking her best either. Since her off-piste visit to the cemetery two days ago, April had been plagued by bad dreams: faces at windows, sleeping angels that woke up suddenly and – the most disturbing, for some reason – an iron door with an upside-down keyhole which she couldn't unlock. It hadn't done wonders for her beauty regime; her hair had gone unwashed for the first time in years. There didn't seem much point any more. It wasn't like she had anywhere to be; she hadn't been able to face school or anything else – in fact, she liked it better that way. The difference between April and her mother was that April was in no hurry to bury her father. Right up until the vicar threw that first handful of dirt onto his coffin, she could pretend to herself that he wasn't gone, that he might be waiting for her when she got home, sitting at the breakfast bar, his nose stuck in a book. She didn't want to move on, she didn't want to face life without her dad. Yes, she knew he was dead. But to her, he wasn't gone. Not yet.

'Sorry to keep you waiting, ladies.' The door to the spartan interview room opened and Detective Inspector Ian Reece came in, balancing two fresh cups of tea in one hand. He was followed by his sidekick, Detective Sergeant Amy Carling, wearing the same badly fitting dark green suit she'd worn that day they'd interviewed her at school about Isabelle's murder.

'Tea for you both, thought you could do with it.' He spilled packets of sugar and plastic stirrers onto the table and pulled out a chair opposite them. 'Sorry for the delay, but you'll understand that in our line of work, when something important comes up, we have to see to it right away.'

'What I understand, Inspector,' said April's mother icily, 'is that we arranged to come in to assist your inquiries into my husband's murder. I had thought you would deem that "important".'

The detective was in his mid-fifties, stocky, with short salt and pepper hair. And shrewd eyes which April guessed had seen most things there were to see.

'Yes, you're quite right, Mrs Dunne,' he said kindly. 'I do apologise and we'll try to make this as quick as possible – I'm sure you have other things to be doing and we do appreciate your assistance at this difficult time.'

Silvia looked as if she was about to say something more, but April raised her eyebrows at her meaningfully and she just nodded instead.

'Fine, well, let's start, shall we?' The female officer set up a tape recorder and opened a large notebook.

'Now, obviously we've spoken to both of you before about William's death, but I wanted to get April in for a more formal chat to see if there's anything we've missed. I understand that going over this all again will be difficult for you, April,' said Reece gently, 'but can you tell me in your own words what happened that day? Tell us everything you can remember, and don't worry if it seems trivial or silly. We need to know as much as possible so we can find whoever hurt your dad, okay?'

April had been dreading this moment. She glanced at her mother who smiled reassuringly, but it wasn't reliving the day that was worrying April: she hadn't told Silvia about the fight with her dad yet. Her mother had left the house unusually early that morning to visit Grandpa Thomas, so she had missed the shouting match and April would have preferred that her mother never knew. It hadn't escaped April's notice, either, that she had no way to prove where she had been for that whole morning on a day when the police were going to find any change to her routine suspect. But that hardly mattered when, above all, April wanted to avoid recounting that horrible argument with her dad, to avoid explaining what it was about, making her look like a bitch and her father like a lunatic; she certainly didn't want that being the last thing anyone remembered about him. But April knew she was trapped – they were bound to have spoken to the school – so, haltingly, she began.

'I left the house at the usual time, I suppose,' she said, looking hard at the teacup, 'but then I walked down to Highgate Ponds. I didn't get to school until gone eleven, and when I got there I went to the library.'

'Just a minute,' said her mother, looking at April, then the two police officers. 'What's this? Why didn't you go straight to school?'

She glanced up at DI Reece. 'I had a free period,' she muttered, knowing it was futile to lie, but desperately hoping she could avoid an explanation.

DS Carling was shaking her head before April had even finished the lie. 'We've spoken to your teachers, April,' she said with some relish. 'We know you were supposed to be in lessons. What we don't know is why you skipped class that morning.'

It was that witch Layla, thought April angrily. *I bet it was, she was probably making the call to Crimestoppers the second she heard about Dad. 'No, she wasn't in lessons all morning, hair was wet, looked very guilty.'* Or maybe they just spoke to her teachers. April knew she was just looking for someone to blame when it was actually all her fault.

'I ... I wanted to be alone.'

'April? Why? What happened?' said Silvia.

'Nothing, I j-just ...' April stammered, 'I just had some things to think about.'

'At that time in the morning?' said Silvia. 'And what were you doing down by the Ponds?'

April frowned at her mother. Who was doing this interview, her or the police?

'I don't know,' said April lamely.

'Did you see anyone there?' asked Reece.

April shook her head. She could tell him before he started making any inquiries that no one had seen her there, not even the dog-walkers.

'Why did you go for this walk, love?' he asked her gently.

'Was it because of this boy?' asked Silvia.

'God, Mum!' cried April. 'Whose side are you on?'

April let out a long breath. She was loath to come across as some weepy airhead, but she supposed it was better to be a heartbroken teen cliché than a murder suspect. Much better than discussing what had happened between her and her dad that morning. She felt bad enough about that as it was. So she nodded, looking down at her hands.

'He was supposed to call and he didn't and I didn't want to go to Mr Sheldon's class because he would be there,' she said in a rush. 'So I walked around in the rain, then I went to the library for a bit.'

Of course only Layla can confirm that, she thought. *And I can't see her rushing to help me out.*

She turned to her mother. 'I'm sorry, Mum, I didn't mean to upset anyone.'

Silvia surprised her by squeezing her hand. 'That's okay, baby,' she said. 'I'm not upset.'

DI Reece looked down at his notes, tapping the pad with a pencil thoughtfully. 'And you didn't see anyone suspicious or out of the ordinary hanging around?'

April shook her head.

'What about the other time, the night Isabelle Davis was killed? Did you see anyone that night?'

'What's all this about?' snapped Silvia. 'April's already given you a statement about that night. I thought this interview was about the day of my husband's murder.'

Reece nodded. 'Okay, so let's go back to the start of the

day,' he said mildly. 'What time did you get up? What did you have for breakfast?'

'Oh. Well, I was up at about seven, I think.'

April winced as she thought of her excitement that morning, jumping out of bed, getting herself ready to see Gabriel.

'Did you wake up, or did your dad wake you?' asked DS Carling. April noticed that the chubby policewoman's manner was much less friendly, her eyes cold and cynical. *Good cop, bad cop so soon?* she thought.

'Er, I woke up myself.'

'Why's that?'

'Sorry?'

'Well,' said Reece, 'why do you think you woke up so early? I've got kids myself and most mornings a bomb wouldn't shift them.'

'I don't know,' said April, unsettled to see Carling scribble 'Doesn't know' in her jotter. *Is not knowing things an offence?* she wondered with alarm.

'Well, what did you do the night before?'

Her mind flashed on Gabriel, his face looking up at her window. They couldn't know about that, could they?

'N-nothing,' she stammered.

'Her friends came over,' said Silvia.

'And this would be –' Reece consulted his notes '– Caroline Jackson and Simon Oliver?'

Jesus, how did he know that? April was now seriously off balance. If they already knew about Caro and Simon coming round, what else did they know? Did they know she had lied about seeing Gabriel on the night of Isabelle's murder? If it had been Gabriel who had tipped the police off about finding her body, then he could well have told them she was there too. Suddenly she became really frightened. What if she couldn't prove where she had been at the time of either murder? What if they thought she had something to do with her dad's death? Nerves made her try to bluster it out, cover her fear up with anger.

'Yes, so what? Can't I have friends over?' she snapped.

'Of course, love,' said Reece. 'We were just wondering what the occasion was. Some problem at school? Or was it all about this boy?' he said, his tone jocular and amused, like it didn't matter much, but April could see the way his mind was working: if she hadn't been in school the next day, something must have happened the evening before or first thing in the morning to keep her away, something serious. Reece consulted his notes again. 'And I understand you had a talk with Mr Sheldon after school that day?'

Silvia looked at April sharply. She didn't need to speak to communicate her meaning: *You and I are going to have a little chat after this, young lady.*

'What did you discuss with him, exactly?' continued Reece.

'He wanted to know why I hadn't been in class that morning,' said April defensively.

'Look, what's all this about?' said Silvia impatiently, looking at Reece. 'I thought you brought us here to help you, not to have you grill my daughter like this.'

'We're simply trying to establish how April was feeling that day, Mrs Dunne,' said Carling with a slightly superior tone. 'It's important to know the state of mind of all the suspects—'

'Suspects?' snapped Silvia, her cheeks flushing. 'My daughter is a child grieving for her father, not a suspect!'

'Now, now,' said Reece, 'let's not get all het up here.'

'I think I'm well within my rights to get "all het up", Inspector,' said Silvia. 'April has told you everything she knows and you seem to be intent on insulting her. She is sixteen years old, for goodness sake. Her father has been murdered. We came here voluntarily, so if you're not going to ask any relevant questions, I think we'll leave,' she said, moving her chair back.

DS Carling cleared her throat. 'Actually, the meeting with Mr Sheldon was lucky for April. If she had left five minutes earlier, she might have been there when the attack happened. Their talk gives her an alibi.'

'An *alibi*?' hissed Silvia. The fury came off her like heat and DI Carling flinched. 'Do you really think that my little girl might go to her own home and *tear her own father's throat out?*' She was on her feet and screaming now. 'How *dare* you even consider such a thing?' she yelled, leaning forwards over the table and spitting the words out. Silvia turned to the detective inspector and her voice was suddenly cold and hard as stone. 'I will have your job, your career, your comfortable, cosy *life* for this. Mark my words, you have made a terrible mistake.'

April could see from his expression that DI Reece fully agreed with her.

With that, Silvia took April's hand and calmly walked to the door. 'Goodbye, Detective Inspector,' she said.

'Why didn't you tell me you missed school that morning?' asked Silvia.

April shook her head. 'Because you don't want to know.'

Silvia slammed the car door, breaking the silence. They hadn't spoken on the drive back to Covent Garden. April was still reeling from the grilling, Silvia was still fuming, and somehow in the space of the journey mother and daughter had turned all their anger and frustration towards each other. April had been grateful for her mother's fearsome protectiveness in the interview, but slowly that had turned to annoyance; why had she asked so many questions? It was almost as if she was trying to help the police catch her out. She guessed that Silvia was similarly annoyed that April hadn't told her about skipping school. But then why would she? She wasn't going to tell her mother everything, was she? Especially when her mother barely acknowledged her most of the time.

'What do you mean, I don't want to know?' snapped Silvia, unbuttoning her trenchcoat as they walked from her grand-dad's underground garage up into the house.

'Because you haven't been there for me, have you?' said April.

'What are you talking about? I've been here with you every moment since we left Highgate.'

'Oh, is that what you call it? Sleeping the day away, sitting in the dark? I came in to speak to you loads of times, but you just wanted to watch daytime TV with the curtains closed. I've not gone to school all week – is that news to you too?'

'I'm finding this hard as well, you know,' said Silvia as she pushed through the front door and threw her car keys on the hall table.

'I know, Mum! But this is what I mean – even now, now when I need you the most, you can't help being completely selfish.'

'You won't talk to me like that! I'm your mother!' she shouted.

'Are you? Well, it's a little bit late to start acting that way now.'

Silvia grabbed her arm, spinning her around. 'You will show me respect,' she hissed. 'Your father—'

'My father? Don't talk about him! You made his life a misery, yelling at him all the time, telling him how useless he was. Well, now you've got what you wanted, haven't you? I bet you're glad he's dead.'

Silvia's hand came flying out of nowhere, leaving a stinging mark on April's cheek. 'How could you? How *could* you?'

April ran through the house and out through the French windows onto the balcony looking down over the small court-yard garden. She needed to escape, to find some space, some air – she couldn't think, couldn't breathe. She leant on the white marble balustrade, watching as the tears plopped down onto the stone. April knew she'd gone too far, but she needed to strike out at someone or she'd explode, the pressure in her head was too much to bear. What if it was all her fault? What if the things she'd said to her dad that morning had made him do something that led to his death? What if she'd stayed at home, or ignored Mr Sheldon – maybe she could have saved him? *Or you'd be dead too*, her mind mocked her, *just like Isabelle Davis. And you didn't help her either, did you?* For a moment, April wished it *had* been her. She knew people said it in films all the time, but she genuinely would have swapped places with her father in a heartbeat. Death was preferable to this living hell. She pulled a raggedy tissue from her pocket and wiped her eyes, taking a few deep breaths. *It's all so unfair*, she thought, *why can't I have normal parents?* But she didn't have parents *plural*, did she? Not any more. April gasped and covered her eyes as it hit her what had happened the last time she'd had a screaming fight like this. *I can't cry again*, she thought, squeezing her nails into her palm. *I'm always crying. I've got to stop this, it's so childish.* But then April knew that was the real reason why she'd been so angry with her mother: she *wanted* to be childish, she wanted to curl up into a ball and have her mum hug her and kiss her and tell her it was all going to be all right. Some hope: hugs weren't exactly Silvia's strong suit, never had been. 'I'm sorry,' said a voice.

April turned around. Her mother's eyes were red-ringed and wet. 'Well, this is a first,' said April sarcastically. She knew she should relent, give her mother some credit, some compassion – after all, she was suffering too – but April was still too angry to be reasonable.

'Don't, darling, it's hard enough as it is.'

'Well, why shouldn't it be? Why should it be easy for you?'

Silvia shook her head. 'Because I need it to be,' she said quietly. The tears were now running down her face and she swiped them away angrily. 'Because I can't handle this, it's too much to bear. I mean, if it's all about ...' she trailed off. 'This shouldn't be happening to me.'

'To you?' shouted April. 'It's not just happening to you, or haven't you noticed? And what's with all these half-finished sentences, and all your stuff with Grandpa? What aren't you telling me?'

'Oh, and I suppose you tell me everything, do you?' snapped Silvia. 'Do you know how embarrassing it was to hear about your truancy from the police? To hear you *lie* to the police? If your father had been there—'

'Dad knew all about it!' shouted April. Even before the words were out of her mouth, April knew she had made a mistake.

'How did he know all about it?' Silvia's eyes narrowed and

she took a step towards her. 'Did something happen that morning?'

'No, I didn't mean—'

Silvia caught April's arm and squeezed. 'Tell me!'

'Mum, you're hurting me,' said April, pulling away. 'We had a fight, okay? That was it. I didn't see him again until ...' Her voice caught. 'Until I saw him at the house.'

'But what was it about? You've had fights, but you've never skipped a lesson before.'

April rubbed her arm and shook her head. Silvia had been right: it was too hard to bear on your own. But to tell her the truth, to tell her exactly what she had said to her father – no, what she had *yelled* at him – that morning would mean having to admit to herself that 'I hate you' and 'I'll never forgive you' had been the last real things she had said to her father. Could she stand that? Could she bear that? No. Not in a million years.

'I told you. We fought about the boy thing.'

'Why would you fight about that?'

April took a deep breath and told herself she was only protecting her mother. After all, what good would it do to say the truth out loud? *I found out Dad moved us to Highgate so he could investigate some stupid vampire story.* Would her mother really want to hear that her husband was deluded? Irresponsible? Downright reckless? Telling her about the job offer from *The Sunday Times* certainly wouldn't go down well either. That would definitely colour her memory of the man she loved.

'He told me I couldn't see Gabriel any more.'

'But why?'

April shrugged. She looked as if she was reluctant to talk about it, but in reality she was playing for time: why *would* he forbid her to see a boy he'd never met? She ran through a variety of possibilities and seized on the most likely.

'He said my schoolwork was suffering,' she said, trying to sound as petulant as possible. 'He thought ...'

'What?'

'That money was more important!' said April angrily. 'He

said that he was working every hour possible to send me to that stupid school for gifted pupils and that he wanted me to concentrate. Like qualifications are the only thing that's important!'

Her mother gave a small smile and nodded sympathetically. 'You shouldn't be so hard on him, love,' she said, touching April's hand. 'That boy *was* distracting you, remember? Your dad only wanted the best for you and he was working really hard trying to make ends meet.' She paused. 'I don't know if he ever told you this, but Grandpa offered to pay the school fees and your dad wouldn't hear of it. He was a very proud man. And he was most proud of you.'

April nodded sadly. She knew her mum was being kind, but she wasn't sure if it was true. She stared out over the garden, wishing he was here to tell her those things himself.

'Mum, can I ask you something? What do you think happened to Dad?'

Silvia avoided her eyes. 'I don't know. That's for the police to work out, isn't it? I'm sure they'll get fingerprints or fibres or something.'

'But you must have thought about it. Why would someone want to kill him?'

'It could have been anything, darling, a robbery gone wrong, some junkie out of their mind, maybe we'll never know.'

April frowned. Her mother was being very dismissive; did she know something?

'Did anyone threaten him?'

'What? No! He would have told me.'

'But he spent years investigating organised crime and drug trafficking, all that sort of thing. He must have angered people.'

Silvia shook her head. 'He wasn't MI5, darling. He was just a reporter.'

There was a strange faraway look on Silvia's face. Like she was remembering something, or something was falling into place for her.

'What is it, Mum? Do you know something?'

'No, no. I don't know what he was working on, we didn't discuss his work really. I'm sure the police will be following up all those leads.'

April wasn't entirely convinced. There was definitely something preying on her mother's mind.

'Mum, why did you and dad argue so much in those last few weeks?' asked April quietly.

'What? Why? Did we?'

'It's just all that stuff with Grandpa and the painting and I'd overhear the rows you and Dad used to have. I used to think—'

'What?'

April shrugged weakly. 'That I was adopted.'

Silvia laughed. 'No, darling, you're definitely ours. You've got so much of your father in you – you're clever and single-minded and stubborn.' She reached out to touch April's face. 'Oh, he loved you so much.'

'And what about you?'

'Of course I love you!'

'No, how much of you is in me?'

'Not so much of me,' she said sadly. 'And thank God for that.'

She walked over and pulled April into a hug, squeezing her tight. 'It's just us now, you know that, don't you? And I'll never let anyone hurt you, I promise.'

April nodded. It was all she had wanted to hear since her dad's death. She brushed a tear away. 'So what now?'

Her mother's face was bleak. 'I want us to go home, darling.'

April shivered, thinking of that pool of dark blood spreading across the study floor. 'Really? Go back there?'

Her mother looked at her and April had never seen her look so sad.

'It's the only place he still is,' she said.

Chapter Twenty-One

The kitchen was April's favourite part of her grandpa's house. Unlike the rest of Thomas's mansion, it was always warm and welcoming, the shiny black Aga at the far end of the room usually full of cinnamon buns or delicious casseroles courtesy of Mrs Stanton, the butler's wife and her grandpa's long-standing housekeeper. When she was a little girl, April would slip down to the kitchen and hide in the corner reading a book while Mrs Stanton bustled around mixing up scones or meringues. Sometimes her dad would even come to join her and play games under the big wooden table – he was probably hiding from the grown-ups too. Today, after her fight with her mother, April needed somewhere to hide herself and the kitchen was dark and deserted; the housekeeper had gone to visit her sister that morning.

No, not completely deserted …

'God, you made me jump!' breathed April as she saw her grandfather sitting at the table.

'Sorry, darling,' said Thomas. 'Sometimes I like to sit in the dark. Helps me think.'

She walked over and kissed his head. 'Me too. Can I join you?'

'Sure,' he said. 'Grab a cup, Mrs Stanton's left me a thermos. Hot chocolate, my grandmother's recipe.'

April took a mug from the cupboard and sat down next to her grandfather. He poured her some hot chocolate and they sat in contented silence for a while.

'I used to play with my dad under this table,' said April

quietly. 'We'd pretend it was a wigwam or the pirate ship from *Peter Pan*.'

'Ha! *Peter Pan*, that suits your father all right.'

'Gramps, please,' said April. 'He's dead. Can't you be nice about him even now?'

'I'm sorry, Princess,' he said, tapping her hand. 'You're right. He was a good man. I didn't agree with him on many things, but he loved you – and your mother. For that, I mourn your loss, I truly do.'

'I know you still think of me as a little girl with pigtails—'

'Not at all!' he roared, squeezing her tightly. 'You are a fine, beautiful woman, Princess,' he said, then quickly corrected herself. 'Sorry,' he said, evidently remembering her outburst before the Halloween party. 'No more Princess for you.'

'No, it's okay Gramps,' she said, touching his huge hand. 'You can call me Princess if you want. But I still need you to treat me like a grown-up. Especially now.'

He looked at her sideways. 'What do you need?'

'I need to know what actually happened to my dad.'

Thomas began to protest, but April put her hand on his arm.

'Gramps, I need to know. How can I let him go if I don't know what happened?'

'Some things are better left alone, Princess.'

'Please, Gramps. Please.'

He stared down at his cup, then nodded. 'I've spoken to my friends in the police and I can only tell you what they told me. They think that someone was waiting for him when he came home from work.'

'Oh no,' said April, her hand over her mouth.

'There was a struggle in the living room and your father's study. Then whoever it was … they cut his throat. Your dad bled to death.'

April was crying now and Thomas held her close. 'I'm so sorry, Princess, I wish it wasn't so. I honestly do.'

'But why, Gramps? Why would someone do that to him?'

'I think a lot of people ask themselves the same thing every day and I think the answer is always the same: we've moved too far from nature.'

'I don't understand.'

'It's simple. We surround ourselves with concrete, we walk on carpets, only touching wood when we sit at a desk, and so we assume we have all come such a long way from our caveman roots. But the animal is there, just under the skin, ready to kill someone for a crust of bread. Or in this day and age, for drugs or money. I know there's no comfort in this for you, but it's the truth.'

To her surprise, April found great comfort in it. She had been treated like an adult; her grandfather had assumed she could handle the truth. And she thought he was right about human nature. Since she had come to London she had encountered nothing but aggression and mean-spiritedness. Yes, she had made a few friends, but it was certainly easy to see the people he described just below the civilised surface: teeth bared, claws extended, ready to climb over each other to get what they wanted. And now, for whatever reason, those same animals had taken her beloved, gentle father from her. It wasn't a comfortable truth, no, but it felt good to face up to it nonetheless. Her tears soaked into her grandfather's shirt and strong shoulder and April breathed in his familiar scent; clinging to something real, something solid.

'Can I ask you something else?' she said, wiping her eyes on his handkerchief.

'Of course.'

'Why is the family called Hamilton?'

Thomas glanced at her, as if for a moment he was unsure of her meaning. Then he laughed. 'What a curious question,' he said, an amused smile on his mouth.

'Not really,' said April. 'I don't know anything about our family history, apart from the fact that we come from "the Old Country". Whenever I ask anyone about it, they say something vague about Eastern European royalty. I've never got a straight answer.'

Thomas shrugged. 'Like all families, Princess, we have

a few skeletons in our cupboards. That's why we don't talk about it much, but you can be sure you are from a good family with a noble ancestry.'

'But why Hamilton? If you came from Romania, then why such an English name?'

Thomas smiled. 'That was my doing, I'm afraid. When I came here in the sixties there was still a very strong class system and there was a lot of prejudice against anyone, well, *different*. I am proud of my heritage, make no mistake about that, but I took a practical decision: I guessed if I changed my name to something more English, lost my accent and put on a three-piece suit, I would be accepted.' He gestured upwards towards the house. 'I was right.'

April nodded. She could tell there was more to say, such as why did her grandfather come here in the first place if he was so family-orientated and what were those skeletons in the cupboard, exactly? But for now, April was happy that no one was ducking her questions. She had enough to deal with at the moment without finding out that her family were wanted by Interpol or something.

'So what do I do now, Gramps?'

'You go on. You may not feel it right now, but you are from a long line of strong women. Your mother, however? I think you know this is hitting her harder than she will tell you, so you're going to have to be strong for her. It's not what you want, but it's what families do, what they have always done. And the Lord watches over good families like ours.'

'That's nice, but I'm not sure I—'

'Believe in such things?' he finished her sentence for her. 'Don't worry, little one, it doesn't matter to Him, He will still protect you. Anyway, it's good to believe in things. That was something your father and I agreed on. *He* believed in something. It's too rare these days.'

'What did he believe in?'

'Many old-fashioned things. Honour, family, hard work. All good things. And he also believed in you, my darling.'

'Why does everyone keep telling me that now?'

'Sometimes it's hard to say what we really mean in life.'

For some reason, April suddenly thought of her afternoon in Highgate Cemetery, all those gravestones with their heartfelt words. Did all those people under the earth know how their loved ones felt about them? Probably not. Maybe it had always been this way; only the poets really said what they meant. Then she thought of Gabriel. *Well, I'm not going to make that mistake again*, she thought fiercely. *I'm not going to waste my time on something that isn't true.* It was time to dry her tears and do what she had to: find out who had killed her father – and why.

Chapter Twenty-Two

It was cold. Bitterly cold. The wind was rushing down from the north, being channelled into frigid, biting gusts by the winding streets, then cutting straight through April's coat. It had never been this cold in Edinburgh, or perhaps she had never felt it so keenly. Certainly there had never before been so little warmth to cling to. Which was why she was walking down West Hill towards Ravenwood on this wet Monday morning. No one had told her to go back – who would when something so terrible had happened? – but where else could she go? They had moved back to Pond Square over the weekend and April had no wish to stay in the house with its over-cheerful yellow front door and the sinister hunting scene above it. April had known that her mother needed to return, so she had gone back for her sake, but walking through that door had been one of the hardest things she had ever had to do. There was no outward sign of the terrible struggle as they had shuffled into the deserted hallway – April had offered up a silent word of thanks to the police cleaners – but the atmosphere was still claustrophobic and oppressive; it was as if the rooms and corridors were filled with a solid mist that they had to push their way through.

The only way to cope was to pretend life was going on as normal, but every now and then April would catch sight of something: her dad's coat hanging on a peg, his favourite coffee mug on the draining board, and she would remember that her dad was gone. And if that terrible revelation wasn't enough, she would instantly be gripped by anxiety, by the full knowledge that the killer had been inside this house. Had he got inside first and hidden, lain in wait, picking his moment to strike? Or had he pushed his way in, attacked her father in the hallway? The living room and study had been ransacked as if the intruder was looking for something, but no one knew what. Had he searched the rest of the house? Had he been into the kitchen? The bathroom? Her bedroom? There was nowhere inside those four walls April could feel safe; even her own room seemed smaller and darker. Perhaps it was fear, or perhaps that April could no longer fool herself that her father was coming back, that his laughter would fill this gloomy space ever again. The coroner had called late on Friday to inform her mother that they were finally releasing the body, so Silvia had thrown herself into the preparations for the funeral. April hadn't been surprised to learn that her dad was to be interred in the Hamilton family vault in Highgate Cemetery, but she had to admit it had upset her at first. To April, a funeral should be like the ones you saw on TV, on a green hillside under a tall oak with lots of people standing around in overcoats as the coffin was slowly lowered into the ground. But the more she thought about it the more glad she felt that her dad wasn't going to be buried under a ton of earth, but would be laid gently to rest on a shelf. At least this way if he woke up he could bang on the door or something. He had loved exploring the great unexplained in his lifetime; now he could wander about unravelling the mysteries of Highgate in death. And at least he would have company. April quite liked that idea. But there was no way she was going to hang around the house talking to her mother about it. The only place she could think to go was Ravenwood. At least in lessons no one would be able to talk to her and poring over books and problems might take her mind off things.

Ravenwood's facade looked even more forbidding than usual as she approached, and she turned up her collar. *I hope this wasn't a terrible mistake*, she thought to herself as she walked through the gates. April had timed her arrival so she would be among the last going into the school; she was trying to avoid the staring eyes and pitying looks, so she joined the final stragglers running in through the entrance and turned towards her English class.

'Oh hell,' she whispered, because right in front of her, chatting to that tramp Sara from the party, was Gabriel. April kept her eyes fixed to the floor and tried to walk past, but he had spotted her.

'April,' he said, 'I didn't know you were back.'

'Yes,' said April, still trying to step around him. 'But I'm late, so—'

'I was so sorry to hear about your dad,' said Sara, without an ounce of sincerity in her voice. Gabriel flashed her a look and she moved away. 'Well, must get to class,' she said.

'Me too,' said April, making to push past, but Gabriel put up a hand.

'Wait,' he said. 'How are you? I've been worried.'

'Have you?' said April, narrowing her eyes at him. 'Why's that?'

'Because— hey, what's going on?' asked Gabriel, a hurt and confused look on his face.

'Oh, just that I thought you had other things on your mind,' she said, nodding towards Sara's back.

Gabriel shook his head. 'Sara? Don't be ridiculous, you can't think—'

'Can't I?' April turned and pushed past him, but he caught her arm.

'April? What's the matter? Tell me!'

'Why do you care all of a sudden?' she asked.

He looked at her directly. 'I thought I made it clear how I felt the other night.'

'The only thing you made clear was that you were going to call me. It's been, what, a week and a half? That's ten days when I really could have used a kind word, Gabriel, but obviously you've been too busy.'

'I was going to call, I picked up the phone dozens of times—'

'I know, I know,' April silenced him. 'But you couldn't think what to say? Or perhaps you thought it might get complicated

247

and messy? It might all be too difficult? Listen, Gabriel, maybe you're right. Maybe it's better we keep away from each other. I know that works for me.'

She walked away down the corridor, leaving him standing there. April knew she should have felt empowered and full of self-confidence having taken control and told him where to get off. But she didn't. She just felt sad.

Mr Andrews, the English teacher, nodded to April as she rushed in and sat down next to Caro, but didn't make any other comment. April could feel the looks of the other people in the room.

'How are you, honey?' whispered Caro. 'Didn't think you were coming in.'

'I'm fine,' she replied, feeling that the complete opposite was the truth, especially after her confrontation with Gabriel. 'Just want to forget it all.'

Caro nodded and gave her knee a squeeze under the table.

April felt bad. She did have some good friends, but she had almost completely withdrawn from them since her father's death. Various people from Davina to Simon had been ringing and sending texts, but she hadn't wanted to talk to anyone, not even Caro or Fiona. What was the point? There was nothing to say beyond, 'Oh, it's all so terrible, I can't imagine how you must feel.' And that was the point: no one could understand what she was going through. Obviously, some people would have lost friends and relatives, but how many had died right in front of them? She knew they all just wanted to offer their support and a kind word, but to April, it was something she had to deal with on her own.

'The biggest problem with Hamlet is that he is always thinking too much,' said Mr Andrews. 'Now, that makes for some excellent drama and, in fact, some of the greatest soliloquies Shakespeare ever wrote, but it does have the potential to make Hamlet a tragic and sometimes quite annoying character.'

There was polite laughter.

'If you all turn to Act Three, Scene Two, right after Polonius has left, we can see Hamlet at his most angry. He's begun to suspect his mother's role in his father's death, plus Polonius has wound him up so much with his windbag sycophancy that Hamlet's almost spitting fire. Jacob, can you read the passage for us?'

A tall boy with sandy hair and freckles stood up and began to read in a strong clear voice. '"'Tis now the very witching time of night ..."'

'Drama club,' Caro hissed in April's ear. 'Thinks he's Kenneth Branagh or Mel Gibson or something.'

They listened while Jacob read the rest of the well-known lines:

> '"... when churchyards yawn and hell itself breathes out
> Contagion to this world: now could I drink hot blood,
> And do such bitter business as the bitter day
> Would quake to look on. Soft! now to my mother.
> O heart, lose not thy nature; let not ever
> The soul of Nero enter this firm bosom:
> Let me be cruel, not unnatural:
> I will speak daggers to her, but use none;
> My tongue and soul in this be hypocrites;
> How in my words soever she be shent,
> To give them seals never, my soul, consent!"'

As he finished, there was a ripple of applause.

'Very good, Jacob,' said Mr Andrews with a smile, 'although usually actors shout the line "drink hot blood"! But still, very well read. Now, can anyone tell me what Hamlet is talking about?'

'He's going to murder his mother, of course,' said a girl with a blue Alice band.

'Well, yes and no,' said the teacher. 'He does say "my soul and tongue in this be hypocrites" – he wants to kill her, but he knows he has to be clever and keep his mouth shut to find out what actually happened. But of course, it's just another excuse for inaction. A couple of scenes on we see Hamlet stumbling across his uncle confessing to the murder, then kneeling down to pray – the perfect opportunity to act out his revenge, but even then he manages to talk himself out of it.'

'But doesn't he kill Polonius straight afterwards?' asked a spotty boy at the front.

'Yes – it's as if he's so angry with himself for not killing his uncle and mother that he finally loses control. The point is, he wants to find out who killed his father and avenge the ghost, but he just doesn't know how.'

Amen to that, thought April. She was walking in Hamlet's shoes. She didn't know what to do right now, but she was determined to find out what had happened to her dad and then she could act. It was just a question of finding the proof. Evidently Mr Andrews was thinking the same thing, as he glanced nervously in April's direction and then abruptly changed the focus of the discussion, focusing on the safer ground of Hamlet's relationship with his mother instead.

If you only knew, thought April with a small smile. *If you only knew.*

As it turned out, April needn't have worried about the Ravenwood students' reaction to her as, to her surprise, they pretty much ignored her. As she and Caro walked along the corridors towards the refectory it was noticeable that people were deliberately avoiding making eye contact with her.

'What's going on?' said April as they sat down at an empty table. 'I thought everyone would be staring, but instead they're avoiding me. I suppose they don't know what to say.'

Caro raised her eyebrows and cleared her throat. 'It's not that so much, babe,' she said.

April frowned. 'So what is it?'

Caro sighed. 'You've been a bit out of the loop over the past week or so, so you won't have heard, but there's been a development.'

'What? Come on, tell me.'

Caro raised her eyebrows. 'Milo Asprey is in hospital and our dear old friend Layla is weeping at his bedside.'

'But why? Why would she ... oh God.'

Suddenly the penny dropped and April was overcome by a rush of conflicting emotions – hope, relief and despair. That confrontation she'd had with Layla in the library, when she had ordered April to 'stay away from my man', Layla hadn't been referring to Gabriel at all; she'd been talking about Milo. Which was good and bad. Good that Gabriel wasn't a two-timing ratbag, but bad that Milo had basically used her behind Layla's back. Thinking about it, April could hardly blame Layla for trying to warn her off if she had suspected what Milo was like, but even so it was still unfair – it was Milo who had hit on April when she was vulnerable, not the other way around! But none of that mattered now, what mattered was Gabriel and the very thought of his name made April feel as if her heart had dropped through a trapdoor. The way she had just spoken to Gabriel ... he hadn't been two-timing her at all and she had driven him away. She put both hands over her mouth and moaned. *What have I done?*

'What's the matter?'

'I think I just finished with Gabriel,' she said.

Caro's mouth dropped open. 'Because of the Layla thing?'

April nodded. Caro saw the look on April's face.

'And am I to take it that you gave it to him with both barrels?'

'Point-blank,' said April. 'Pretty harsh considering he *isn't* a two-timing back-stabber.'

They both looked at each other.

'What's wrong with him anyway?' said April eventually. 'Milo, I mean.'

'That's the strangest thing – no one knows,' said Caro. 'He's got some horrible skin condition, like it's blistering and falling off him. Apparently he's strapped to the bed because he's having fits too. Some people are saying he's in danger of organ failure, but that could just be another rumour.'

'That's horrible.'

'What's horrible?'

April looked up and there was Layla, standing with her

251

hands on her hips, her chin jutting out. Behind her were Chessy and Ling Po, who seemed to have been accepted into the Faces.

'Milo being ill,' said April. 'I've just heard, Layla, I'm so sorry.'

'Why are you sorry? You didn't care about him before.'

April looked at Caro nervously. 'No, well, he seemed nice, but it's bad he's in hospital.'

'Bad?' She laughed. 'Is that all you can say about it? My boyfriend is in intensive care and you think it's "bad"?' she mocked. Her friends all laughed.

'Listen, Layla,' began Caro, 'leave her alone, she hasn't done anything.'

'Stay out of it, Jackson,' said Layla, a nasty edge to her voice. 'We're just talking, aren't we, April? Just two friends talking about boys.'

April managed a weak smile.

'Of course, you haven't got much to talk about, have you, April?' sneered Layla. 'Not many boyfriends we can see, even though the guys are all over you. Maybe you prefer the company of girls.'

The Faces crowd cackled.

'Is that why you're so pally with each other?'

'Hey!' shouted Caro. 'What's she ever done to you?'

'Nothing.' Layla laughed. 'We're not all into that sort of thing, are we, girls?'

'Listen, I know you're feeling pretty bad about Milo, but—' began April, trying to calm the situation.

'Don't you *dare* tell me how I feel,' hissed Layla, jabbing her finger at April. 'What would you know about it? Oh, I suppose you think that just because your daddy's dead you feel my pain. Well, let me tell you – you have no idea.'

God, she's actually going to hit me, thought April, seconds before Layla made a lunge for her. April moved fast, but not quite fast enough. Layla clattered into her and they both tumbled onto the table, sending a pile of books flying.

'Get off me!' cried April, but Layla had grabbed a handful of her hair and was pulling her head down towards the tabletop.

'Shut up, bitch,' spat Layla. 'I'm going to rip your throat out, just like your dad.'

'*What?*' Suddenly April was overcome with a white-hot fury. 'Don't you dare talk about him!' she screamed, turning on Layla like a tiger. All April could think of was the injustice. It wasn't her fault Milo had a girlfriend and still hit on her. It wasn't her fault he was sick. And it certainly wasn't fair that she was getting the blame. But most of all it wasn't fair that her dad had been taken away. All the frustration and guilt that had been building up since her father's death spewed out and she screamed, pulling herself free of Layla's grip. She felt strangely strong as she did so, as if she had been shot through with electricity. Layla stumbled backwards, slipping on some spilled drink and tumbling onto her backside, and April was on her in a moment, pushing her down, grabbing her hair and banging her head against the floor.

'Stay away from me!' she yelled. 'Come near me again and I'll kill you!'

Strong hands grabbed her and pulled her away.

'I don't think that's a very good idea, Miss Dunne,' said a voice. She turned around and her heart dropped. It was Detective Inspector Reece.

Chapter Twenty-Three

The policeman didn't arrest her. He didn't even tell her off. Instead he took April to the headmaster's office and made her sit outside while he spoke to Mr Sheldon. Whatever was said, Reece obviously managed to persuade him that the fight was simply youthful high spirits between two high-strung students and that he would take her home. There were some advantages to being in mourning, she supposed. Besides, all the fight had gone out of her. At this point she barely cared what happened now, so she simply shrugged when DI Reece explained and then led her down to his car. Why bother kicking and screaming? April knew full well that even as they buckled up, Layla was already spreading her version of events: that the awful new girl had attacked her and threatened to kill her and now the police were taking her away.

'Good job I came in to speak to you today,' said Reece as he started the engine. 'If I'd left it until tomorrow, you might have strangled that girl.' His tone was light, but April could tell he was worried.

What the hell came over me? she wondered. *One minute we were talking, the next I was trying to kill her.*

'So what was it all about, April?'

April sighed. She was sick of keeping things to herself, trying to remember what she was or wasn't supposed to know. It was too much of a tangle and she suddenly felt very tired.

'Layla – that's the girl you pulled me off – thinks I'm trying to steal her boyfriend.'

'And are you?'

'Not really. He hit on me, but he didn't mention that he had a girlfriend.'

'Ah.' DI Reece nodded. 'I see.'

He backed the car up and they slowly drove through the gates and up towards the village.

'I heard the coroner released your dad's body,' said the policeman, glancing across at her, 'so I guess you'll be glad to get the funeral over, to start picking up the pieces?'

April just shrugged again and looked out of the window.

'But I don't suppose you actually want to go home right now, do you?'

April glanced at him. 'I s'pose not.'

'Well, how about I treat you to lunch?'

April lifted her hands in a gesture of complete indifference. 'Whatever,' she said. Then, after a pause. 'No McDonald's, though.'

Reece laughed. 'Okay, no McDonald's.'

He drove them out of Highgate, past the big houses on Hampstead Lane and then Kenwood House on the left. April had been wanting to see the big Georgian stately home on the hill ever since Hugh Grant had his heart broken there in *Notting Hill*, but somehow since arriving in Highgate she'd never had the chance to go. Now she thought about it, apart from the visits to her grandpa's place, she had hardly strayed from the village at all since they'd left Edinburgh, as if Pond Square had a giant magnet hidden beneath it and she had a metal plate in her head. *That would explain a lot*, she thought ruefully. They were approaching a bottleneck in the road – a strange white cottage seemed to have been plonked in the middle of the street. To April's surprise Reece didn't drive past; instead he turned off the road and into a car park next to a large white building opposite the cottage.

'A pub?' she said, with a little too much eagerness in her voice.

Reece smiled. 'I'm getting you a Diet Coke, young lady. But they do make an amazing goat's cheese lasagne.'

The Spaniards Inn was ancient and rambling, with low

beams, dark wood panelling and creaky floors. It even had a fire popping and crackling away beneath a polished copper chimney breast. It was the sort of pub American tourists believe lies at the end of every road in England. As Reece went to the bar to order their food, April wandered over to a chalkboard where someone had written up a few snippets of the pub's history. Apparently Charles Dickens, Lord Byron and the highwayman Dick Turpin had all spent time drinking here. According to the board, John Keats had composed 'Ode to a Nightingale' in the garden.

She heard a laugh behind her. 'It's probably a lot of old tosh,' said Reece, leading April to an alcove and putting the promised Diet Coke in front of her, 'but it's sort of nice to keep up the legends, isn't it?'

He settled into a squashy leather chair next to a window which looked out towards the strange white cottage in the middle of the road.

'It reminds me of that little white house by the cemetery gates,' said April. 'Is it true you couldn't get inside?'

Reece looked at her, his eyebrows raised.

'I went on a tour. The guide told me.'

'She's right, as it happens,' said Reece, rubbing his chin. 'It obviously hadn't been opened in years – door and windows painted shut, nothing inside – so we figured we'd leave it as it was.'

April thought of the tall man who had come out of the house – she was *sure* he had – and the tour guide's insistence that no one of that description worked there. She wished she knew what it all meant, but there was so much about this whole business that she couldn't grasp. It was like trying to juggle with one hand tied behind her back.

'So what is it?' asked April, nodding at the white house in the road.

'That's the old gatehouse where travellers had to pay a toll to use the road, and it's where Dick Turpin is supposed to have spotted his victims.'

'I bet you'd like to have caught him, wouldn't you?'

'No need,' said Reece. 'Contrary to popular belief, Dick Turpin was caught and hanged by a member of his own gang. But no, I'm not sure I'd like to be involved with that sort of thing. I'm more a rehabilitation than a hanging kind of guy.'

April sucked her Coke through the straw and looked at Reece. She wasn't so sure what kind of guy he was or what he was after, but she was glad to be out of school, and out of the house – and to be treated like an adult. Well, without the vodka, admittedly, but it was much better than the tea in the police station. Even so, she knew Reece hadn't brought her here for her sparkling conversation – this was an interrogation with beer mats.

'So do you think it's a good idea to bring a sixteen-year-old girl to a pub?' said April. 'Is this standard interview technique?'

'It's not really a standard case, April,' said Reece, his expression serious. 'There's far too much about it that's confusing. I was hoping you might be able to shed a little light on a few things and—' he indicated the empty bar '—I figured we might be free from eavesdroppers here.'

'You think there might be people listening in at the police station?'

Reece smiled. 'You're a sharp girl, April, but don't go creating too many conspiracies where there are none. Leave that to your friend Caro.'

It was April's turn to smile. 'Ah, you spoke to her?'

Reece rolled his eyes. 'Is there anything she *doesn't* think is linked to a shadowy global conspiracy?'

'Not much. Did she give you any ideas?'

Reece paused before answering. 'It's funny,' he said thoughtfully. 'Sometimes we get a bit blinkered in the way we investigate things, when we should think a little more laterally.'

'What do you mean?'

'Well, most crimes are pretty straightforward, especially violent crimes. Someone gets angry and hits someone else, then leaves a trail of blood back to their car. You'd be surprised how often it happens. That's why we have a better success rate solving murders than other crimes.'

April looked away, trying to concentrate on a picture on the wall as she felt her eyes becoming watery.

'I'm sorry,' said Reece softly. 'I often forget how hard it can be to talk about. It's my day job, I'm afraid. I assume everyone wants to talk about murder.'

'No, it's not that,' said April, blinking hard. 'I just can't think of my dad as a "murder". It just seems so weird, so wrong, really.'

'I understand. But we do need to talk about it, if you can. I think it's the only way we're going to catch whoever did this.' He looked at her meaningfully. 'Listen, April, I'll lay my cards on the table. We don't have the hard evidence to back this up yet, but I'm convinced that the three murders – Alix Graves, Isabelle Davis and your dad – are all linked. You've been close to two of them and in my world ... well, let's just say I don't believe in coincidences. So I think you may be the key to this case, whether you know it or not.'

April glanced at Reece. What was he saying?

'When you say you don't have the evidence, don't you have any leads? Like fingerprints and stuff?'

He looked a little embarrassed. 'No. Nothing. Which is why it's so odd. You see these TV shows about highly intelligent serial killers who plan their crimes in detail, but in my experience that just doesn't happen. There's always evidence, witnesses, something.'

'But not this time?'

'You, April, are the closest thing we have. I'll be honest, it's as if the killer was invisible. They got in and out without being seen on CCTV or by passers-by and they didn't leave the slightest trace behind, despite the destruction.'

April didn't want to think about the 'destruction'. She didn't want to think about someone coming into their house and attacking her dad, she didn't want to think about how he crawled to the phone leaving a smeared trail of his blood behind him. She didn't want any of it to have happened. But it had.

'We have to get him,' she said fiercely. 'We have to catch this killer.'

'We will,' said Reece, meeting her gaze steadily. 'We always do.'

Their food arrived and they ate in silence for a few minutes. April still didn't know what to make of the detective. He wasn't like the hard-bitten, hard-drinking cynics you saw in TV dramas. He was drinking Appletiser, for a start. And the goat's cheese lasagne was indeed delicious. Maybe he felt sorry for her, or thought she needed a friendly ear. More likely it was simply work for him: get the daughter off-guard and maybe she'll tell you something useful. April didn't mind that, especially if it got her free pasta. She would have been glad to help; she just didn't know what she could tell him.

'So what do you think? You must have some sort of theory?'

Reece gave her a half-smile. 'I'd rather hear what you think.'

April paused before she spoke. 'My dad is – was – a really nice man. I mean, of course you'd expect me to say that, but he was. My mum was always giving him a hard time and he put up with it, he didn't get angry. They'd shout at each other, but he was … calm, I suppose. Which is the reason I can't understand why someone would hate him enough to do that to him.'

She stopped and took a sip of her drink, trying to swallow whatever had got stuck in her throat all of a sudden. She put down her knife and fork and pushed the plate away.

'Sorry.'

'It's fine,' said the detective. 'Actually, that's what I've been thinking all this time: why? The most obvious idea is someone who has suffered because of something he wrote. An investigative reporter of his standing is always going to make enemies, but to be frank, retaliation almost never happens. You hear of journalists being killed in war zones, but not at home. Funnily enough, criminals can be quite moral about that sort of thing – they don't usually bear grudges against people who catch them fair and square. But then … perhaps if he was getting too close to someone or something, it's possible they would take action to shut him up.'

'But you don't think that.'

Reece pointed at her with his fork. 'I said you were a sharp girl. Well, it's still the most likely motive as nothing was taken from the house as far as we could tell, although you saw the state of the place and it's difficult to be sure. But we've been through all his notes and his computer and there's nothing there to suggest any ongoing investigation of that kind. In fact, there was nothing much there of any use, but I'd like you to have a look at something anyway. It might jog a memory.'

He opened his briefcase and pulled out a laptop, opening it on the table. As they waited for it to boot up, April thought about what Reece had said.

'So if you didn't find anything in the computer or at the house, maybe they *did* take something?'

'Yes, but again I come back to why?' said Reece. 'If it was me and I wanted to get at whatever information your dad had, I'd break in while he was out, steal his computer and make it look like a burglary.'

'So you think they planned to kill him?'

'Sorry, April, I don't want to worry you any more, but that seems the most likely conclusion. We just haven't got a clue why.'

He pulled the computer towards him and started opening files. 'Now, these are all the files we copied from your dad's computer,' said Reece, swivelling the screen around to show her. 'On the left-hand side is a rough draft of a story your dad was working on for the paper. It's about the Isabelle Davis murder, all the background to the case and the history of the murder site, Highgate Cemetery and so on. On the other side, I've opened a file your dad wrote a few weeks ago. It's a book proposal he was sending to his publisher. It was all about historic murders and violence in London, with particular reference to this area. Have a quick look: the similarities are superficial, but they are there.'

Nervously, April scrolled down. Reece was right: the similarities were there if you looked for them, but sitting side by side like this, they did look rather shaky. On the one hand, the

Isabelle Davis murder seemed straightforward – a young girl out on her own in a city, who tragically fell prey to a random killer. But when you compared it to William Dunne's research for his book, particularly the Whitechapel murders of 1888, it suddenly didn't look so random: Jack the Ripper's first victims would have appeared to be senseless and unconnected tragedies as well. There were other strong themes running through both stories: the cemetery, the sudden apparently random upsurge in violence, even the idea of a unifying conspiracy behind it all. But as Reece had said, it wasn't hard evidence, far from it. In fact, it all looked a bit silly.

'Now, I'm not suggesting for a moment that this case has links to Jack the Ripper or, God forbid, vampires or disease or whatever else your dad was writing about,' said Reece, 'but I have to consider all the possibilities, however strange they first appear. My job involves looking for patterns, hoping those patterns will eventually make a picture. But at the same time I have to ask: how can any of this be worth killing over?'

April's eye had been caught by one phrase on the screen and she frowned.

'You said earlier,' she began, 'that the only people capable of planning a murder like this are serial killers. There have been three murders in one village – couldn't that possibly be the work of a serial killer?'

Reece looked grim. 'Serial killers are incredibly rare in this country and they usually stick to the same type of victim: the Yorkshire Ripper, Fred West, Harold Shipman, they all did the same thing over and over again until they were caught.'

'But is this like that? Come on, Mr Reece, you've got to tell me.'

The detective looked at her for a while. 'There are similarities in the murders, yes. They all died from similar wounds to the throat, they all had strong links to the local area, the killings all took place either in or within a stone's throw of the cemetery. But beyond that, it falls apart. Different times of day, indoors and outdoors, male and female victims – it doesn't have the usual patterns we associate with a serial killer.'

'So how are you going to stop him?'

'Not me, April, us,' said Reece. 'I can't do this on my own – I need your help. I need to know what you know. I need to see what you saw, and that's why we're having this conversation. Take, for example, that night in Swain's Lane – are you sure you didn't see anyone else there?'

If Reece was watching her face, he may have detected a slight twitch in her expression. If he had, it would have looked like a flicker of fear; fear of the killer, fear for herself, fear that he might strike again. It was all those things, but in reality, April was afraid for Gabriel. April had been there, yes, but she had seen so little. Whereas Gabriel had stayed inside the gates with the killer. He could have seen the killer, which would make him a target. But ... *Oh no.* April had a sudden and terrible thought, something she hadn't considered before, and felt as if someone had punched her in the stomach.

'Oh God,' she whispered to herself, bending forwards hugging her middle.

'April? Are you okay?'

'I feel a bit ill,' she muttered and, pushing her chair back, ran for the toilet. Safely inside, she bent over the sink, dry-heaving. Why hadn't she seen it before? *God, I'm such an idiot!* It was so obvious. Gabriel Swift had been screwing with her head from the start. Yes, he'd behaved strangely – at school, in Swain's Lane, even the night of the party – but eventually he'd allayed her suspicions about his presence in the cemetery the night of Isabelle's murder. But what if it was all a big fat lie? What if Gabriel had killed Isabelle and *then killed her father?*

She looked up at herself in the mirror. The look of fear was definitely there now. Because it made sense. Why had she assumed there was anyone else lurking in the bushes when she had gone to help the fox? Yes, she'd seen those sinister eyes in the undergrowth, but that could have been Gabriel. It had all happened so fast, she wasn't sure of anything any more. And that would explain the rest, too. He had waited to see if she would pass his name to the police and when she hadn't, he had found her at the party and – *Oh no!* Had he taken her into the cemetery that night to *kill* her? She ran through it all in her head. *Think, dammit, think!* He had stood behind her in the Circle of Lebanon and she had thought he was going to kiss her, but maybe he'd had other plans. Had she spoilt them by turning around? And then she had mentioned her dad and he had rushed her out of there. He must have realised that her dad was on to something and decided to wait. Had she led her father's killer straight to him?

She shook her head. It was all too much. Her breathing was coming in sobs now and her heart was hammering. *How could I have been so blind?*

And then he had lured her out of the house in middle of the night, asking her to go for a walk down to the Heath. *What if I had gone?* And then the final piece of the jigsaw dropped in. Gabriel would have seen that she wasn't in Philosophy class that morning, he would have known Mr Sheldon would keep her back after school. In fact, she had seen him there, watching the road to make sure. *I gave him the opportunity to kill my dad!*

She jumped as she heard hammering on the door.

'April? Are you okay in there? Listen, I'm coming in,' said Reece, opening the door a crack and peering around. April grabbed a handful of paper towels and wiped her face hurriedly. She couldn't tell Reece about Gabriel, not now. No, she needed evidence first, real evidence.

'I'm okay, I'm fine,' she said quickly. 'Maybe it was the lasagne.'

'It wasn't me talking about that night in Swain's Lane—'

'No, no, just a stomach bug, I should think. There's always something nasty going around.'

Reece looked at her long and hard. Then he just nodded. 'You're right about that,' he said. 'Come on, I'd better get you home.'

The house was quiet when she got in.

'Mum?'

April walked into the kitchen. Her mother's coat and bag

were there, plus an empty wine glass with lipstick on the rim.

'Mum? Are you here?'

She tiptoed up the creaky stairs and along the corridor, opening her parents' bedroom door a crack to peek through. As she had expected, April found her mother sprawled out face down on the bedspread, 'star-shaped' as Fiona used to say. It wasn't much of a surprise; April had suspected that Silvia's long days in bed were due to a combination of wine and sleeping pills. She couldn't really blame her, there were times when April would rather blot it all out too; but not now. Now April wanted to be wide awake. She didn't want distractions, she didn't want to be cocooned from the pain, she wanted to face it all head-on, because more than anything she wanted to know the truth, however hard it was to bear. Gabriel as the killer – could it really be true? It made her physically ill to think about it, but it was time to stop thinking and start acting. She needed to work out why Gabriel had killed her father: did he know something about him? Had Gabriel come here looking for something? Perhaps something her father had uncovered? Either way, she needed evidence to back up her growing suspicions. And where better to start looking than right here? *The scene of the crime*, her mind taunted her. *The place where he died.*

'Oh shut up,' she whispered and walked back down the stairs, grasped the handle of the study door and pushed. And there was … nothing. April let her breath out slowly as she sat down on the corner of the desk. Aside from the conspicuous absence of the rug that had covered most of the floor, you wouldn't have known anything had happened here. That was precisely what was making her knees feel weak; in removing signs of the struggle, they had also removed all traces of her father. The study was neat and tidy, even the chair had been placed carefully back under the desk. She looked in the drawers: empty. There wasn't even a coffee cup or a half-read newspaper to show that anyone had ever been here. She ran a hand over the wooden surface of the desk, trying to feel some trace of him, some warmth left by his fingertips.

'I miss you, Dad,' she whispered, 'I miss you so much.'

She didn't know she was crying until she saw the tears drop onto the leather seat. It came over her in an unbidden wave, swallowing her up. 'Why did you leave us?' she moaned, gulping in air. She had lost the one strong, reliable thing in her life and he had been taken from her by the only other man she'd ever felt anything for. It was horrible. *Horrible.*

'It's not fair, it's not fair ...' She fell to her knees, almost hugging the chair. She wanted to be strong and full of purpose, but she was just a little girl and she didn't know what to do. 'What do I do?' she whispered. 'You always knew what to do.' She stayed like that, her back bent, head twisted to the side, letting it all flow out, and after a while the storm of tears passed; her breathing slowed and her body stopped shaking. So wrapped up in her grief had she been that she hadn't realised what she was looking at. Under the desk, at the back, she could see a tiny bit of sky blue. Frowning, she crawled further into the knee well for a closer look. There was a narrow gap in the woodwork between the back panel of the desk and the drawers and something was jammed in between them. She felt around with her fingers but it wouldn't budge. She shuffled back out and found a pencil in a pot on a shelf, then ducked back down. Using the pencil to wiggle the object, she slowly worked it out. Her heart leapt: it was the notebook she had pilfered from this very desk the night of Isabelle's death.

Eagerly, she sat back in the chair and flicked through the book. *This is it*, she thought, *this is what I need.* Her heart was racing now. The last time she had leafed through the book she had been annoyed by her dad's spidery handwriting and opaque references, but now they looked like lifelines, bright breadcrumbs to lead her along the path.

'1674 – 1886?' read one entry; 'Churchyard Bottom/Coldfall Woods' read another. At the top of another page was what looked like a book title: *Infernal Wickedness*, Kingsley-Davis, 1903, with the note 'nests?'

Her eyes opened wide. *Nests!* That was one of the words on the Post-it she'd thrown at him that last morning. Her fingers tightened on the pages, almost frightened the notebook would fly away. This was exactly what she needed; if not a road map, exactly, then at least a handful of possible places where she could follow in her father's footsteps. Of course, she knew she should probably go straight after Gabriel, but that could be dangerous to say the least and, besides, he was hardly going to break down and confess without some evidence to confront him with. No, this book was a sign. It was a piece of her father. It had his thoughts and his passion caught for ever between its covers. And he had obviously hidden it. Had he wanted her to find it here? She clasped it to her chest and whispered, 'Thanks, Dad.'

'April?'

She froze. *Oh God, Mum's awake*, she thought, jumping out of the chair and stuffing the notebook into her pocket.

'April? Is that you?'

Silvia was calling from the top of the stairs, her voice thick with sleep. April silently closed the study door and padded to the foot of the stairs.

'Hi, Mum,' she said.

'What are you doing down there?' said her mother grumpily. 'I thought I heard a burglar.'

'Just going out,' she said, taking her coat from the end of the banister and pulling it on. 'You want anything?'

'Where are you going?'

April thought for a moment. 'The bookshop. I need to do some research. Homework,' she added quickly.

Silvia scratched her messy hair. 'God, you're just like your father,' she said groggily. 'Be back for supper, I'll order pizza or something.'

April had almost made it to the door before her mother called her back.

'Oh, and darling? Could you pick me up some more wine? Say it's for me, they know me at the off-licence.'

I bet they do, thought April.

Chapter Twenty-Four

The little bell tinkled as April pushed through the door. Mr Gill looked at her with puffy, slightly pink eyes; she was fairly sure the ringing bell had woken him. In fact, she had a strange sense that the bell's chimes didn't just wake the shop's proprietor, they woke the whole shop: when the door was closed, time stopped entirely.

'Back so soon?' said Mr Gill suspiciously, setting his glasses on his nose. 'How can I help you today?'

'Well, I was wondering if you had some sort of index or inventory of the books you have here?'

Mr Gill clucked his tongue in disapproval. 'Oh no, no need for that. They are all stored up here,' he said, pointing to the wiry white tufts of hair on the side of his head.

'Then could you tell me if you have this book?' she asked, opening the notebook and pointing to the entry. '*Infernal Wickedness* by Kingsley-Davis?'

The old man peered at the note. 'Hmm ... well, we did have a copy. Rather popular, that one. But I think the young lady bought it only the other day.'

'Young lady? Who would that be?'

'Oh, a charming young thing. Shiny hair. No, no, now I think about it, she didn't buy it in the end. Yes, I think we may still have it. Shall we have a look?'

With some effort Mr Gill rose from his chair and gestured towards an alcove at the back of the shop, lifting the velvet rope that closed it off from the rest of the shop. April found herself climbing a wooden spiral staircase to the first floor, almost identical to the ground floor only crowded with even more books. Mr Gill followed her slowly then immediately began scanning the shelves at close range, tilting his head to read the worn leather spines through his tiny spectacles, tutting and muttering his way along the rows.

'Ah, now here we are,' said Mr Gill triumphantly, taking down a slim volume. It had a battered blue binding and faded gilt lettering. He handed it to April reverently.

'Very rare, that one. Never seen another copy, actually, and plenty of people have been looking, let me tell you.'

'Could I … ?' asked April, gesturing to a chair by the window.

'Oh, by all means, by all means,' said Mr Gill, tottering towards the stairs. 'I've plenty to get on with, rushed off my feet as you can see.'

When he was gone, she eagerly opened the book and began to read the foreword.

It is my unhappy duty to inform the reader, within these pages, of a true horror hiding in our very backyards. This is not an historical terror such as a young boy may thrill over while reading of dead kings and queens, but a very real present-day threat which may, if not handled with the proper vigour and dispatch, even undermine the already shaky foundations of our civilisation. It is not a disease that the wealthy classes can avoid with indoor plumbing and rich food, nor is it something education and breeding will unseat, for it is as present behind the doors of the finest houses in the land as it is in the dark streets of Clerkenwell and Bow. My dearly cherished hope is that, by setting these facts down in type, I can expose these fiends and rid our land of them once and for all. Please, dear reader, heed my words, for if this plague is allowed to spread, all that we hold dear will surely unravel.

J. Kingsley-Davis, St James, 1903

As she read the words, April felt herself shiver. It wasn't the comically dire warnings of the author, it was the fact that they were so similar in sentiment to the snippet of the introduction her father had written for his new book.

It was almost uncanny – unless, of course, he had read this obscure tome himself, but then Mr Gill had said it was super-rare, hadn't he? Still, her father was a journalist, he could find things that other people couldn't. She quickly turned back to the index page to look at the chapter headings. 'Chapter One – The Vampyre, A History', 'Chapter Two – Arrival On Sovereign Soil', 'Chapter Three –The Nests Are Feathered', 'Chapter Four – The Servants Are Recruited'. It was obviously a history of the myth, but presented as historical fact. In any case, it would be useful in April's investigation. She flipped back to the front page to see how much it cost and almost fell off her chair. 'Three hundred and thirty pounds?' she gasped. *How could any book be worth that? You can get anything off the Internet for nothing these days – why would you bother with these dusty old things?*

But then again, she had never found any information as focused and concise as this on the Internet. Certainly, everything she'd found written about the Highgate Vampire on the net was confused and a bit hysterical. *That's probably because vampires are made up*, April reminded herself. *It's not as if they're in the Natural History Museum.*

Sadly, April headed back down the spiral stairs to Mr Gill and put the book on his desk.

'Changed your mind?' he asked, peering over his glasses.

'More that I can't afford a book like that,' she said. 'It's a shame, because it's exactly what I need.'

'That's what the other girl said,' mused Mr Gill vaguely.

'Who was this other girl?'

'Oh, came in a while ago, asking for the Kingsley-Davis, said she couldn't afford it either. People don't appreciate the value of rare books any more, you see. Sometimes the books you find on these shelves are the last remaining copy of a masterpiece that took decades to complete and contains vital information that might otherwise have been lost.' The old man paused for a moment, seemingly lost in thought. 'Of course, many of them are utter rubbish,' he added.

'Well, thank you for letting me see it—'

'Isabelle,' said Mr Gill.

April looked up sharply. The shopkeeper was bent over a large ledger on his desk.

'Isabelle Davis, that was her name,' he said. 'I wrote it down in case a cheaper copy came in, although, as I told her, that's most unlikely. Yes, I remembered it because of the name. Apparently she and the author were distantly related.'

'Could it have been the same Isabelle Davis who was killed in the cemetery?'

Mr Gill's rheumy eyes opened wider. 'Do you think so?' he said. 'I read about it of course, a terrible business, but you never think of it happening to someone you've spoken to, do you? My word, the poor girl.'

April could feel the hairs standing up on her neck. 'Thank you, Mr Gill.'

She turned towards the door and pulled the handle.

'Of course, if you're not too busy, I could always give you a précis of the book,' he said, picking it up and waving it at her. 'I read it after she'd left. Very interesting, actually. Especially in the light of the, uh, murder.'

'Oh, that would be fantastic.'

'Well, sit yourself down over there and let's see what I remember, but not before I've put the kettle on, mmm?' he said, reaching for an ancient plastic jug. 'I'm sure you'd like a cup of tea?'

'Oh yes,' said April. 'Yes I would, very much.'

Chapter Twenty-Five

The gate clanged and a squeal rang around the square. Fiona was out of the taxi almost before it had stopped, throwing her arms around April and squeezing.

'Stop, Fee,' she moaned, half-coughing, half-laughing. 'You're going to suffocate me.'

'I'm just so glad to see you,' said Fiona, after they'd paid the bemused cabbie and lugged her case back to the house. 'I wish it was in better circumstances, of course. How are you?'

April almost laughed at her friend's dour expression; Fiona looked even more pale and gloomy than April. It didn't help of course that Fee was wearing her funeral garb of a black silk dress, long black gloves and a black pillbox hat with a veil, presumably the one she had bought to mourn Alix Graves' passing. Fitting her proud Scots heritage, Fiona had wavy red hair and creamy white skin, but her pretty face was more washed out than usual today. Fee always took an almost method-acting approach to choosing the right look for the right occasion, reflected April; she'd hit it spot on for the funeral.

'I'm okay,' said April sadly. 'It's better when I'm busy. I wish you'd let me come to meet you at the station.'

Fiona shrugged. 'I thought you'd have more important things to do today.'

April nodded. If it had been a normal day, she would much rather have been doing more digging into her Dad's death, especially with all the strange stuff she'd discovered in Mr Gill's shop the previous day. But then, if it had been a normal day, her Dad wouldn't be lying in a coffin at the undertaker's waiting to be taken to the church.

'I guess I should be helping Mum with stuff for the wake,' said April, 'but I'd rather spend time with you than hang around with her, fussing over the vol-au-vents.'

'How is she?'

April shrugged as she helped Fiona carry her suitcase up the stairs to her room. 'I think she's okay. She's coping by totally throwing herself into getting all the last-minute details right – like anyone cares about the cakes at a funeral,' she said with exasperation.

'What about your grandpa?'

'He's not coming until later. But we'll no doubt have a house full of weird relatives I've never met before when we come back here, so it's good I've got someone of my own to hold my hand.'

'Aren't you having any of your new friends over, like Caro and Simon? I'm dying to meet them,' she began, then stopped herself. 'Oh God, I'm sorry, I didn't mean—'

'Don't be silly,' smiled April. 'It's just a figure of speech. Anyway, Caro's coming to the wake – it's only a small cere-mony at the grave. And Mum's invited Davina and Ben because she wanted to invite Mr and Mrs Osbourne, her new BFF on the social circuit. Anyway, enough about that – can't we talk about something normal? Tell me what's happening in Edinburgh.'

They sat on the bed and Fiona filled April in on all the latest gossip: what was happening at school, who'd been spreading rumours about who, which boys Fiona and Julie had seen at the shopping centre and what it all meant. April loved every minute of it, constantly stopping Fiona to eagerly ask for more details. For a little while, it felt as if she had never left Edinburgh and that all these life-and-death scraps of gossip were everything that mattered in the world. *If only we had stayed in Scotland,* thought April. *Then this world Fee's talking about really would be mine. But it's not, is it?* But her ears still pricked up when Fiona dropped the biggest news of all: that Miranda Cooper was no longer seeing Neil Stevenson.

'According to Neil's friend Jake, Neil reckoned she was

'too immature",' said Fiona. 'Julie thinks that's boy-code for "wouldn't put out", but either way, he's single again.'

April tried to look enthusiastic, but the smile didn't quite make it to her eyes.

'Sorry, April,' said Fiona, squeezing her knee. 'I know it's difficult today.'

'No, it's not that,' said April. 'I dunno, it just all seems so – no disrespect to you, honey – but all this seems so silly. I really wish I could spend my days worrying about Neil and Miranda, but that's not where I'm at right now.'

'I know, you're making a new life down here,' said Fiona.

'No, it's not the place. It's all the weird stuff happening to me.'

'Those photos of the party?'

April shook her head. 'That's only part of it. None of it is much on its own, but when you add it to the Isabelle Davis murder and Milo being in hospital and then the whole Gabriel mess, and the police and now this vampire book thing, I don't know what to do.'

'Hang on,' said Fiona, frowning, 'rewind a bit. In fact, rewind a lot. The Milo in hospital – that's the one from the party? What's he doing in hospital? After that, we'll get to Gabriel and the vampires. Now, spill.'

April smiled. She had been so used to sharing every thought and experience with Fiona, yet since she had been in London so much had happened, and she had got out of the habit. Now she thought about it, they hadn't had a proper talk since a couple of days after the party and turning her phone off over the last week had left her friend completely out of the loop. So she made up for lost time, filling Fee in on everything: the fight with Layla, the Met-sponsored visit to the pub and the whole Gabriel story, including her growing suspicions, and ending with finding her dad's notebook in the desk and her visit to Mr Gill.

'Wow, let's have a look at the notebook,' said Fiona eagerly. April slid it out from under her mattress. She had been through it in detail and, although much of it was just a scrawl, it seemed that most of the entries were about two subjects: firstly, various 'real' sightings of vampires in Highgate, particularly in the sixties and seventies, and – and this was the exciting part – William's investigations into Ravenwood School. One particular entry had set her heart thumping: 'Regent = Ravenwood? Close.'

'The Vampire Regent' was the subject of one of the chapters in the book Mr Gill had shown her yesterday evening. The old man had clearly missed his calling; he would have made a brilliant teacher. He had told her how the book described the three vampire nests in London – Highgate, Covent Garden and Spitalfields – and how they were all ruled over by one all-powerful super-vampire known as the Vampire Regent. Mr Gill had emphasised that it was only a myth and that it was possible the author was under the influence of gin or syphilis or both, but he seemed convinced by the idea himself and, anyway, the fact that her father had been taking it seriously was enough for April. She still didn't know if her dad had actually read the Kingsley-Davis book, but he certainly seemed to know a lot about its contents: the Regent, the nests and the Highgate connection.

'So when he says "close", do you think he means that this Vampire Regent – assuming he exists – is close by? Like in Highgate?' asked Fiona.

'I've been wondering about that,' said April. 'Either that, or he felt he was getting close to uncovering the Regent's identity.'

Fiona flicked through a few more pages. 'What does this one mean: "Altar in C.F.WDS"?'

April shook her head. 'I wish I knew. The problem is he was making notes for himself – it wasn't meant for anyone else to read.'

'He hid it though, didn't he? So he must have thought what was in here was important and that it could lead to the people with the answers.'

'That's why I want to find out more about the school. He obviously thought whoever's behind Ravenwood is connected to the Regent. Maybe it was Ravenwood that wanted him out of the way.'

'So why did he send you there?' asked Fiona. 'I mean, if he really thought it was full of vampires?'

April nodded. It was something she had been struggling with too. It was one thing bringing his family to a dangerous area; it was another to send your only child to an establishment you thought might be run by bloodsucking freaks. Which was the strongest reason April had for thinking that her father couldn't have believed they were real.

'But whether this vampire stuff is rubbish or not – and it does sound unlikely – you can't really think Gabriel killed your dad, can you?' asked Fiona, lowering her voice. 'I mean, the way you were talking about him, I was expecting you to – you know – shag him, not shop him to the cops.'

April shook her head. 'Maybe I was wrong about him, Fee. I usually am about boys.'

Fiona made a face. 'Well, you sure can pick 'em.'

'What do you mean?' said April, offended at the implication.

'Well, remember that I'm your best friend and everything, so don't shoot the messenger, but you do have a habit of picking the most unattainable boys and then imagining a romance that might not actually be there.'

'You mean Neil.'

'Yes, Neil. But there was David Brody before that, and Baz from the market, remember? You were planning the wedding before you'd even had a text from him.'

April cringed. It was true. *Maybe I have some sort of deep psychological need to be rejected*, she thought. *Maybe I deliberately pick boys who mess me around. But I've never picked a potential serial killer before.*

'But don't you think it makes sense about Gabriel?' she asked.

'It's a bit far-fetched, honey,' said Fiona. 'Yes, it's odd that he was there the night of Isabelle Wotsit's murder, but that doesn't make him *the* murderer, does it? And the idea that he's been planning to trap you in the cemetery in order to strangle you is a bit gothic, even by your standards. Maybe this one actually does want to shag you, ever think of that?'

April threw a pillow at her, but Fee's opinion did make her feel a little better. It was true she didn't have any actual evidence against Gabriel apart from supposition and guess-work. After all, he had told her there were things he couldn't explain, he *had* told her he wasn't going to tell her everything. And she had got it wrong about Gabriel and Layla, hadn't she? April felt a sudden flutter in her tummy, but she tried to push the feelings away. Okay, so she didn't have any actual CCTV footage or anything, but there was too much coincidence, too many things linking him to Isabelle, to her dad, to *everything*. He *had* to be involved.

Fiona saw the faraway look in her eyes. 'Okay, Miss Heart-break, back to the vampire book,' said Fiona with a smirk.

'Well, apparently this author, Jonathan Kingsley-Davis, was like the Victorian equivalent of my dad,' said April, 'and he spent years investigating some dodgy goings-on in the East End.'

'Jack the Ripper, you mean?'

'Him, and a bunch of other stuff. Apparently, grisly mur-ders weren't all that unusual back then. Anyway, this guy claimed it was all down to vampires. And not just any random vamps running around biting people, they were organised into what he called "nests". There were three "nests" in London – Covent Garden, the East End and Highgate – all ruled over by a Vampire Regent; he gives the orders, chooses the new recruits.'

Fiona gasped. 'Highgate? So it's not just one of them hang-ing out in the cemetery – there's loads of them?'

April smiled. 'I thought I was the one with the gothic imagination. That's if you believe it, of course. His theory was that they'd been living among us for centuries and have been killing at will and using their influence in society to keep it quiet.'

Suddenly April had another thought: if the Vampire Regent

existed and was calling the shots, then it followed that he might have ordered her father's death for getting too close to the truth, whatever that was. Maybe Gabriel had been ordered to kill her dad – and Isabelle and Alix – so maybe it was the Regent she should be chasing. That's if he even existed.

Fiona was shaking her head. 'There's so much to take in, isn't there?' she said. 'What do you think? Do you think that book is right?'

'I don't know whether there are vampires or not, or if there's some king ruling over them all – frankly it could all be complete rubbish. What I'm interested in is why Isabelle Davis wanted the book. It's more than a bit odd that the last person wanting Kingsley-Davis's book is the same woman who was brutally murdered in the cemetery.'

'And maybe your dad saw it too,' said Fiona quietly.

April was nodding. 'And now I've seen it.'

'Now I'm scared,' said Fiona, pulling a queasy expression.

April found to her surprise that she wasn't at all frightened. The only thing that mattered to her right now was getting to the truth, and if that put her in danger, then so be it.

'The one thing I keep coming back to is that Isabelle and my dad were investigating the same thing.' She bit her lip and looked directly at her friend. 'You see, it doesn't really matter whether you believe in vampires or not. Clearly the people wrapped up in it do, so we can't dismiss it entirely.'

Fiona looked at April with dawning understanding, and then made a severe face. 'You're not thinking of tracking down Gabriel and confronting him?' She glanced around and dropped her voice to a whisper. 'If there's even a chance he's your dad's killer, you want to stay as far away from him as possible.'

'But Fee, whether he's the killer or not, he knows more than he's telling me and I need to know what happened to my dad.'

Fiona put her hand on April's arm. 'No, because in teen slasher movies, whenever the kids go after the killer, they always end up dead.'

'Not in *Scooby-Doo*.'

'*Scooby-Doo* is fictional.'

'So's Dracula, so are teen slasher movies – so what are you worrying about?'

Fiona's expression was serious. 'I'm worried because people are actually being killed here – or haven't you noticed?'

'Of course I've noticed,' snapped April, the light-hearted note gone from her voice. 'My dad is dead and I've got to find out who hurt him. I was kneeling down there while he was dying, with his blood all over me,' she said, her voice cracking. 'The police are clueless and if we don't get the killer, then I think I might go nuts, Fee. And you know what else? I think more people might die too.'

Fiona grabbed her and held her tight. 'Okay, honey. We'll do it. We've just got to be careful, okay? No heroics.'

April nodded. 'It's a deal.'

'One thing though?'

'What?'

'If this is *Scooby-Doo*, I'm Daphne.'

Chapter Twenty-Six

The weather was just right for the funeral. Overcast, with spots of rain and a cold wind swirling up the last of the autumn leaves. They all left the house, shoulders hunched, and walked slowly around the square and across South Grove. As April had predicted, she didn't know many of the people following them on the short walk to St Michael's church, each one in uniform black, each one looking grave and respectful, some dabbing at tears. April herself could not cry. Somehow it didn't feel real. But then, there at the end of the aisle was the coffin, covered in flowers, and suddenly her knees felt weak.

'You okay?' asked Fiona, taking April's arm, squeezing her hand tightly. She hadn't left April's side since she'd arrived that morning, and for that April was grateful.

April nodded and filed down to her seat at the front next to her mum and grandpa. Time stood still as the vicar went into his eulogy, recalling William's sense of humour, his dedication, his love for his family, talking as if he were an old friend. April knew he was being kind, trying to help them through this, but she couldn't help feeling annoyed. *You didn't know him*, she thought, *he was* my *dad. He loved* me. Even so, she went through the motions, saying the prayers, singing the hymns, but it all felt so remote, like some weird movie she was watching from a distance. It felt so wrong that a man who had been so full of life and excitement could be so quiet and still now. After the readings were over, they all filed out and climbed into a line of shiny black cars for the short drive down to the cemetery. April was glad that the one-way restrictions on Swain's Lane meant that they had to loop around down West Hill and back up, so she didn't have to watch the graves passing by on the other side of the road. Instead she concentrated on the rain dotting onto the window, the droplets joining together and forming little rivulets running down the windows. Finally, the hearse and the following car turned through the gates and parked. April stepped out and sucked in the cold air.

Fiona was there beside her, her arm linked with April's. She smiled and nodded encouragingly. 'You can do this,' she whispered. 'For your dad.'

April nodded. She had to be strong for her mum, too. Silvia was a wreck, walking unsteadily on her high heels, gulping at the air; Grandpa Thomas was virtually holding her up, one huge arm around her. The vicar came over to say a few words to Silvia, then approached April. He had a round face and red cheeks and his eyes were kind.

'I'm so sorry for your loss, April,' he said. 'William was a good man.'

April nodded politely.

'I always looked forward to our chats,' said the vicar. The priest saw April's quizzical expression and smiled slightly. 'Ah, perhaps he didn't mention it, but he used to pop by every now and then. A most engaging fellow. And of course, if you ever need to talk, I'm always here.'

He patted her hand and returned to April's mother, gesturing towards the steps.

What was all that about? thought April, frowning. *What 'chats'? We only moved to Highgate two weeks ago and Dad was never a particularly religious man. Was it something to do with the investigation?* She shook her head and forced herself to concentrate on the here and now as the pall-bearers hoisted William's dark wood coffin onto their shoulders and began to walk up the hill to the tomb. The priest leading the way, chanting the ritual words as he walked. 'Christ is risen from the dead, trampling down death by death, and giving life to those in the tomb ...'

April was concentrating on putting one foot in front of the

other, doing her best not to stumble, silently thanking Fee for persuading her to wear ballet flats not heels. She stared at her feet and tried hard not to think how, on the way back down this hill, she would have said goodbye to her father for the very last time.

She looked up at strangely familiar graves and statues as they slowly climbed the hill. Angels and animals and unhappy renderings of Christ. Where a few days before they had re-assured April, today they looked forlorn and powerless. Then she gasped and stumbled against Fiona.

'What is it?' she whispered.

'Nothing,' said April.

But it wasn't nothing. Standing half-hidden by the foliage twenty metres back from the path, April had seen the man from the little white gatehouse. The one who had disappeared, the one Judith had claimed was a figment of her imagination. April thought about asking Fiona if she could see him, but she dismissed the idea. *There's nothing wrong with me*, she thought, *I'm fine*. But when she looked up again, the man was gone. '*I look after the graves*,' that was what he had said. April could only hope he was as good as his word, because now she could see William Dunne's final resting place looming up ahead. The Hamilton vault resembled a tall Greek temple, with pillars to either side of an iron door and a pitched roof. To April, it looked like a miniature bank, and to her surprise the name above the door wasn't 'Hamilton'. It read 'Vladescu'. Of course, her grandpa had told her he'd changed his name, but it was still a shock to see. *Is that who I am?* thought April miserably. *Now he's gone, is that all I have left? Someone else's name?*

The door was already open and a table with a dark red velvet cloth laid over it was standing to one side of the entrance, while huge flower displays had been left to both sides of the steps. The pall-bearers gently laid the coffin down and the vicar began the ancient rites, the same words this hillside had heard over and over these past two hundred years.

'I am the resurrection and the life, saith the Lord; he that believeth in me, though he were dead, yet shall he live; and whosoever liveth and believeth in me shall never die.'

April began to cry.

'Into thy hands, O merciful Saviour, we commend thy servant William,' continued the priest. 'Receive him into the arms of thy mercy, into the blessed rest of everlasting peace, and into the glorious company of the saints in light.'

The mourners all mumbled 'Amen'; then, leaning on Grandpa Thomas's shoulder, Silvia shuffled forwards and, with a great sob, placed a white rose on the coffin as the vicar made the sign of the cross and began to intone: 'Man that is born of woman hath but a short time to live and is full of misery. He cometh up and is cut down, like a flower; he fleets as a shadow and cannot stay. In the midst of life we are in death ...'

April stepped forwards and placed her own flower on the coffin. 'I love you, Daddy,' she whispered.

'We therefore commit his body to this resting place; earth to earth, ashes to ashes, dust to dust, in sure and certain hope of resurrection to eternal life ...'

Each of the mourners stepped forwards in turn, then the priest signalled to the pall-bearers, who lifted the coffin into the tomb as they all muttered the Lord's Prayer over Silvia's sobs.

'Forgive us our trespasses ...'

Finally, the priest stepped forwards to close the vault door.

'Deliver us from evil ...'

And a terrible scream went up.

'Nooo!' cried Silvia, throwing herself against the door. 'I won't let you, I can't!'

'Dear lady,' whispered the vicar, and Silvia slipped down the door, as if in a faint. April jumped forwards, but her grandfather got there first, lifting Silvia to her feet and supporting her. The vicar, as gently as he could, finished the service.

'God of peace, who brought again from the dead our Lord Jesus Christ, through the blood of the everlasting covenant, grant eternal rest to his soul, O Lord. May his soul and all the souls of the departed, through the mercy of God, rest in peace. Amen.'

Chapter Twenty-Seven

Caro had painted her nails a pale, neutral pink. It was only a small thing, but April almost started crying again.

'Oh, honey, that's so sweet,' said April with emotion. She had never seen Caro with anything except black nails; it was almost part of her personality, a statement of intent to the rest of the world. But today she had changed it for April and for her dad.

Caro flushed a little and shrugged. 'Well, I just thought it was appropriate, respectful.' She lowered her voice. 'And I didn't want any of these weird people thinking I was taking the mickey.'

The 'weird people' were April's relatives. As William Dunne had no family to speak of, the mourners were mostly from her mother's side, so it was no surprise that like Silvia and Grandpa Thomas, they were tall and athletic. April had always assumed Gramps had been referring to character when he said Hamilton – or should that be Vladescu? – women were 'strong', but she could now see he was referring to their stature, too. Beautiful as well, which somehow gave April hope. Her mother had cheese-wire cheekbones, but April was still waiting in vain for hers to pop out. *Maybe there is still time*, she thought, casting a longing glance over at the Constances, Mariellas and Georginas sipping politely at their wine. *Maybe I'll get their legs too.* She wasn't particularly keen on inheriting their personalities, though. They were all polite of course, muttering that they were 'sorry for her loss' and that 'William was a good man', but overall, they were posh and aloof, observing the room with superior stares. Perhaps they were silently questioning Silvia's decision to hold a wake for her husband in the room next to the one where he had been killed. April certainly had.

'It wouldn't hurt them to smile, would it?' said Fiona under her breath. 'I mean, you don't expect stand-up comedy at a wake, but it is supposed to be a celebration of someone's life, isn't it?'

'I think they're worried they'll crack their make-up,' said Caro.

April was glad that Fee and Caro where getting on so well, as if they had known each other for years. Her life had been turned completely upside down in the last few weeks and it was nice to know that she had friends to lean on when it all went completely pear-shaped. *Like my bum*, thought April, and managed a giggle.

'What are you all sniggering about?' said a voice.

April turned to see another tall man about her dad's age. This one she recognised vaguely, possibly from photos at her grandpa's house. He had the standard-issue Hamilton frame; he looked like a gangster in his tight black suit, his neck bulging over his collar, but he had less of the frosty beauty with his broken nose and hooded eyes. Plus there was an amused arch to his eyebrow that April liked immediately.

'I'm Uncle Luke,' he said, holding out a hand. 'I'm sure April doesn't remember me, but I recognise her. I can see a lot of your mother in you.'

'Not too much, I hope.'

Luke laughed. 'Yes, she has many great qualities, your mother, but she does have a temper. Still, however much she drives you mad, imagine what it was like to grow up as her baby brother.'

'Did she torture you?' asked Caro eagerly.

'Not exactly.' Luke smiled. 'But I do have a few scars.' He pushed up his sleeve and showed the girls a white curved mark on his wrist.

'Did you try and commit suicide?' gasped Fiona.

'God, Fee!' cried April, looking at her uncle with embarrassment. 'I'm so sorry, she's not usually like this.'

Luke only laughed. 'It's quite all right – I can see why you might think that,' he joked. 'No, it's a bite-mark. I wouldn't let her have a go on my pogo stick so she sank her teeth into my arm. I let go of it quick enough then.' He chuckled ruefully.

They all looked at Silvia in silent awe. She was sitting on the other side of the room nursing what looked like a tumbler of vodka and talking to a grey-haired man April recognised as one of her dad's old newspaper friends.

'So is that why you haven't seen April for so long?' asked Caro.

April shot a look at her and Caro made an innocent face, mouthing the word, 'What?'

'It's okay.' Luke smiled. 'There's no excuse, really. I've been working abroad for the past ten years, so I haven't been over here enough. I'm back now though, and living in London, so I'll definitely be seeing more of you both. Anyway, I always knew your dad would look after you – and your mum sent me pictures and letters about you growing up.'

'Really?' said April, looking at her mother again, who was now blowing her nose on a lace hanky. It was a surprise; partly because Silvia had never seemed the sentimental type, certainly not the kind of woman who would swap baby photos. And also, now she thought about it, April couldn't remember many family photos being taken as she was growing up. She wasn't entirely sure whether either of her parents even owned a camera.

'Uncle Luke,' said April, 'are you a Vladescu or a Hamilton?'

Luke smiled. 'We've always been Hamiltons,' he said. 'Your granddad changed the name before your mum and I were born. I imagine it was strange seeing the old name above the door of the tomb, eh?'

April nodded. 'A little. Feels a bit weird that my dad should be in there with a load of strangers.'

'Oh, I shouldn't worry about that,' said Luke, that amused

eyebrow arch back again. 'Listen, I'd better go and check on your mum. I'll see you later, okay?'

'He seems nice,' said Fiona as Luke disappeared.

'Yes, I wish I had uncles like that,' said Caro. 'All mine are either villains or coppers.'

'I didn't know that,' said April.

Caro winked. 'Got to maintain my mystique, haven't I? Anyway, it's not like I'm going to boast about it. If this was my dad's wake, they'd all be drunk and fighting by now.'

'Speaking of which …' said Fiona, nodding towards April's mother. She seemed to be struggling to get to her feet while Thomas hooked an arm under hers.

'Leave me alone!' she snapped, slapping his arm away. 'I don't need your help, I can walk on my own, God knows I've had to for the last twenty years.'

'Excuse me,' said April, following her mother into the kitchen where she found her splashing more vodka into her glass.

'Mum, haven't you had enough? You're embarrassing us.'

'No, I do not think I've had enough,' said Silvia, defiantly taking a swig. 'I will never have had enough. Not ever. And if you think that's embarrassing, well, you can get out too.' She gestured unsteadily towards the living room.

'What do you mean, "me too"?'

'Your father,' said Silvia, slurring her words. 'He's gone off and left us again, hasn't he?'

'Again? What are you on about?'

'Ha! You always were such a little daddy's girl,' said her mother scathingly. 'He could do no wrong in your eyes, could he? But then how could he when his whole existence was built around protecting his little precious girl?'

April was feeling uncomfortable now, as if she had stumbled into a conversation she shouldn't have overheard.

'Protecting me? What from?'

Silvia threw her head back and cackled with laughter and swung her hand in a wide gesture, spilling some of her drink. 'From all of *them*, of course,' she said.

'Silvia!' said Thomas forcefully, striding over to April's mother and snatching the glass from her hand. 'This is not the time or the place.'

'Oh no? Well, when will be? When is the right time to tell her who her father really was? Surely now he's dead? Weren't you the one who was dying to tell her a couple of weeks ago?'

'I'm warning you,' growled Thomas in a low voice dripping with menace. April could see that he was gripping the glass so hard his fingers were white.

'Gramps, no,' said April, running across and trying to pull him back. It was like tugging on a tree. 'She's just drunk and upset,' she said, a pleading edge to her voice. 'She doesn't know what she's saying.'

Thomas glared at her and for a second April saw the fury in his eyes, a burning, raging fire, then suddenly his face softened and he put the glass down. 'Yes, of course. It's been a tough day for all of us.'

'Tough for you?' Silvia snarled. 'I should think you'd be popping the champagne.'

'Mum, please,' said April, her voice wobbling. 'Can't we all get along today? I'm sick of all this fighting. Please, it's destroying me. I've just buried my father, I don't want either of you ...' Her voice cracked. 'Don't leave me,' she sobbed, looking up at them with glistening eyes. 'Please tell me you won't go too.'

Thomas and Silvia exchanged a look. It was fleeting, less than a second, but once again April had the feeling that she had just seen something she shouldn't have.

'We're not going anywhere,' said Thomas, reaching out to hug April. 'You can count on that.'

At least Davina was enjoying herself. When April returned to the living room, she found the queen of the Faces flirting with all of the Hamilton men. She was wearing a short-short black satin dress with stockings and six-inch heels. *Jesus*, thought April, *does she think it's a wake or a party?* Clearly April's cousins and uncles weren't as dour as she had first thought, since Davina was leaning against one of them and laughing with a wicked expression.

'Oh hi, darling,' said Davina, seeing April walk in. She instantly changed her expression to one of sincerity, head tilted to one side. 'How are you? I'm so sorry about your dad.' She air-kissed April and whispered in her ear, 'Who is that gorgeous man behind me?'

'I think he's one of my cousins. I don't know really, we don't mix much.'

April realised that she hadn't really stopped to consider why. Her mother had always told her stories about how she had been forced to spend interminable holidays with endless elderly relatives as a girl and had sworn she would never make her child go through the same thing. April had assumed there was something more to it, especially given the spiky relationship both her parents had always had with Grandpa Thomas, but she had never asked about it. To her, it was just one of those things; some people at school had loads of cousins and half-brothers and some people didn't. As she had got older, of course, April had supposed that the Dunnes' lack of big family get-togethers was down to some sort of family feud her parents didn't want to tell her about. Given her conversation with her mother and grandfather in the kitchen, that was probably a pretty good guess.

'But what about Jonathon?' asked April.

Davina frowned for a moment, as if she was trying to recall the face of a distant acquaintance. 'Oh, him, he's gone,' she said vaguely, looking over April's shoulder. 'Now who is this? I love your hat!'

By the time April had turned around, Davina was fingering the lace veil on Fiona's hat.

'Erm, Davina, this is my friend Fiona from Edinburgh.'

'Delighted,' said Davina, leading a bemused Fee off to a corner for a fashion conflab. 'Now you must tell me where you get such yummy vintage ...'

April stood there, amazed at Davina.

'Sorry, she's always like this at funerals.'

Benjamin was standing behind her. *Why is he always sneaking up on me?* He stepped forward and handed April a glass of wine. She glanced around nervously.

'Don't worry.' Benjamin smiled. 'Your granddad's having some heated discussion with my dad and your mum's sitting on the stairs talking to Hawk.'

April looked up. 'Mr Sheldon's here?'

'Yes, I know,' he said, rolling his eyes. 'It's like this at my parents' get-togethers too – they always invite the last people you want to see. As we speak, my mother is in the kitchen talking to Miss Holden. We might as well have stayed in school.'

April took a long swallow of her wine and shivered.

'Looks like you needed that.' Benjamin reached out and gently stroked her arm. 'You okay? Can't be easy for you today.'

April shook her head. 'No, no, I'm fine.' She wasn't fine, of course. She still had her mother's words going round and round in her head. *When is the right time to tell her who her father really was?*

What the hell did that mean exactly? Was she implying her father wasn't the man she'd thought he was? But he had always been a good, loyal and hard-working family man. Hadn't he? Or was she saying something else – that William Dunne wasn't even her father after all?

'You sure you're all right, April?' asked Benjamin. 'You don't look too good.'

'Sorry, I just need a bit of air.'

She pushed her way outside. The backyard was just that – when the town houses had been built, the yards had been intended as a workspace for the house maid, not as a place for the owners' relaxation and enjoyment. Still, Silvia's friend Tilda had made the most of it, creating a little patio with wooden seats and raised flower beds around the edge. Not that it was terribly cheery in late autumn. April sat down on the seat and wrapped her arms around herself protectively. *God, it's cold here*, she thought. *Why is it so cold?*

The smell made her turn around.

'Sorry,' said the man standing by the door. He lifted his hand to show her a cigarette. 'Terrible habit, I know. Would you like me to put it out?'

April shook her head, but the man stubbed it out anyway.

'I can see you want to be alone – I'll go back inside. Just wanted to say hello though,' he said, leaning forwards and putting out a hand. 'Name's Peter Noble. I'm an old friend of your dad's.'

April shook his hand. *Why does his name sound familiar?*

'Actually,' said April, 'could I ask you something? About my dad.'

'Of course, if I can help. What do you want to know?'

'Well, am I like him?'

The man began to laugh softly. 'Oh yes,' he said. 'You're the dead spit of him, in fact.'

'Really?'

The man nodded and pointed towards the chair opposite April. 'May I?'

'Please. I'd like to hear about him.'

Peter Noble nodded. He must have been slightly older than her father, or perhaps it was the effect of his slightly-too-long grey hair and silver-framed glasses. *He looks like the sort of man who'd wear threadbare tweeds and have a Great Dane*, thought April. For some reason, she trusted him. After all, if he was an old friend of her dad's, he had to be one of the good guys, didn't he?

'I haven't seen your dad for a few years, not since you all moved to Edinburgh,' said Peter. 'But we spoke on the phone and exchanged letters and so on.'

The letter – that was it! Peter Noble was the man mentioned in the job offer April had found on her father's desk the morning they'd had their fight. The day he had died.

'Hang on, aren't you a newspaper editor or something?' said April.

'Yes, that's right – how did you know?'

'Oh, just something Dad said a few weeks ago.'

'Anyway, I haven't seen you or your mum for ages, but when I walked through the door and saw you talking with your friends, I knew it was you. You have his eyes. And his chin.'

'His chin?' April laughed.

'Yes, the way you stick it out when you're laying down the law – it's just like your dad.' He paused for a moment. 'I'm afraid I overheard you and your mum in the kitchen. Take it from me, I've known William Dunne since we were teenagers and you are his in every way. I also know how much he adored you.'

April looked away.

'I know, it's strange talking about him in the past tense, but believe me, it will get better. I lost my wife a couple of years ago and it was hard – really hard – but you'll pull through. Will was tough as old boots and if you've got half of that in you—' he chuckled '—and maybe half of your mother's fire, then I think you'll be fine.'

'I don't feel fine,' said April sadly.

'Listen, if you ever need anything,' said Peter, getting out his wallet and handing April a business card, 'advice, help with your homework, or if you just want to talk about your dad, give me a ring. Honestly, it'd be good for me too. I miss that old bugger, I really do.'

'Thank you,' said April gratefully, 'I think I will.'

When she got back inside, Davina, Fiona and Caro were standing in a huddle talking in low voices.

'April, quick!' said Davina, pulling her into their corner. 'We need your help.'

She looked around them, bewildered. 'What's going on?'

'Major intrigue,' said Caro. 'Okay, you know Mr Sheldon's here, right? Well, that's because he's a family friend. So Davina asked her mum about it and apparently *your* mum knew him at uni or something.'

Davina nodded eagerly. 'So that explains why Hawk's here, but why has Miss Holden come?'

'I don't know,' said April, completely confused now.

'Well, Fiona's got a theory,' said Davina, bubbling with excitement, 'and I think she might be right, but we need you to find out.'

'Find out what?'

'Whether Miss Holden is Hawk's date, of course!'

April almost laughed. Trust three teenage girls to find a romantic scandal at a funeral.

'Well, why don't you just ask her?'

'She's hardly going to talk to me,' said Davina, as if that should be self-evident. 'She knows I think she's a witch. She's not going to talk to Caro, either, because she thinks she's the Antichrist and Fee doesn't know her, so it has to be you.'

April couldn't believe how quickly Fiona and Davina had bonded. And she was already calling Fiona 'Fee'? *That's my pet name for her*, she thought indignantly.

'Come on, go,' said Davina, pushing April towards the hall. 'She's in the kitchen. And don't come back without the scoop.'

April reluctantly walked down the corridor and was relieved to see that Miss Holden was talking to a middle-aged couple. She turned to leave, but the teacher spotted her and waved her over.

'April, come and meet Mr and Mrs Osbourne, Ben and Davina's parents.'

Mrs Osbourne was wearing a calf-length fur coat and sporting an amazing jet-black back-combed hairdo that for some reason reminded April of the burning oil well footage on CNN. Mr Osbourne was tall with the same piercing blue eyes as Benjamin, and although he didn't quite look like the evil Bond villain Caro had made him out to be, April could certainly imagine him as a ruthless captain of industry, breaking strikes and stripping assets in his double-breasted suit. Together they made a formidable pair; even her haughty cousins seemed to be paying deference to them; it was almost as if royalty were in the room. Still, despite their impressive presence, the Osbournes weren't quite as dazzling as April had expected. Given that their children were so gorgeous, she had pictured them with movie-star looks. But then that was sometimes the way. When you saw the parents of top models it was sometimes as if the slightly wonky DNA on both sides had met in the middle to create a perfectly symmetrical whole.

'It's lovely to finally meet you, April,' said Mrs Osbourne, taking her hand and patting it. 'We've both met your mother a few times and she's always talking about you, and how well you're doing at school.'

April thought she saw Miss Holden's eyebrows rise at that comment, but she might have imagined it.

'If there's anything we can do for you, you need only ask,' said Mr Osbourne, touching her shoulder lightly.

April nodded politely, thinking, *I'm not sure you'd be quite so keen to help me out if you knew what my friend Caro and I have been saying about you.*

'Thank you for coming,' she said. 'My mother needs all the support she can get right now.'

'Of course, of course,' said Mrs Osbourne. 'I'll drop by next week when she's feeling, ah, a little better.'

Mr Osbourne pointed to his watch. 'Sorry, April, I'm afraid we're expected elsewhere.'

'Dinner with the Camerons, it's quite a bore but one must, mustn't one? We'll say goodbye to your dear mother and grandfather on the way out, and Ben will take Davina home later, so don't worry about rushing her off. You girls have a good old gossip.' She touched April's arm as she was walking past. 'And you must come to the Winter Ball on Saturday. I know you won't be in the mood to party but sometimes it's best to take your mind off things. I'll get Davina to drop off an invitation.'

When they had gone, April was left with Miss Holden. They smiled at each other awkwardly, then looked at the floor. Without the common ground of school, they didn't seem to have anything to say to each other.

'So did you come with Mr Sheldon?' blurted April, to fill the silence.

The teacher laughed. 'I did, but not as his date, if that's what you're asking. No, your mother asked Robert – Mr Sheldon – to bring me along. I met your parents a couple of times when they were choosing a school for you and I guess she assumed you'd need a bit of moral support. Of course, she doesn't know teenage girls like I do.' Miss Holden smiled. 'I think you've got all the support you need right over there.' She nodded towards the door where Davina, Fiona and Caro were watching them, trying to look casual and uninterested.

'Listen, April,' said the teacher suddenly, lowering her voice. 'I know this isn't the time, but there's something I need to talk to you about when this is all over.'

April's heart sank. She wasn't going to get told off for her assignments on top of everything else, was she?

'What is it? About school?'

'No, not about school. It's important,' she said quietly. 'I'll be in touch, and in the meantime you be strong, okay? Your dad was a wonderful man. You should be proud of everything he did.'

As she left, April remained standing alone in the kitchen, her head buzzing with thoughts. *What on earth was all that about?* But she didn't have much time to worry about it, because Caro, Davina and Fiona ran in, worried looks on their faces.

April laughed. 'Don't look so serious – it wasn't a date, my mum invited her.'

Caro shook her head. 'No, no, forget that,' she said urgently. 'This is something else.'

'What is it?' asked April with a sinking feeling.

The three girls exchanged looks.

'It's Gabriel,' said Fiona. 'He's outside.'

Chapter Twenty-Eight

He was sitting on the same bench. The bench he had shared with April the night he had brought her doughnuts, the bench she had sat on wrapped in a blanket as she waited for her father's body to be brought out on a stretcher. April didn't know how she was going to feel when she saw him and was surprised at the anger that immediately welled up. All her suspicions about Gabriel and his part in her father's murder sprang back into her mind and she didn't know when she had ever felt more furious. It was as if someone had poured boiling oil into her head.

'How *dare* he?' she hissed, moving down the path.

'April, don't,' said Fiona, holding her arm. 'It's not the right time – think of your mum.'

'My mum?' spat April, yanking her arm away. 'My mum would want him to pay. He killed my dad!'

'Come on, honey, you don't know that.'

'Well, he knows something about it, and I'm going to find out what.'

'Here, take this, it's freezing,' said Fiona, draping April's coat over her shoulders. April nodded her thanks and strode off across the road. Gabriel looked as if he had been sitting there for a long time; the shoulders of his jacket were dark with the rain and his hair was soaked, plastered against his head, but damn him, he still looked good. She cursed herself that he still made her heart beat a little faster despite her fury, and she turned all her mixed emotions on him.

'What the hell are you doing here?' she said, her voice trembling. 'Have you come back to the scene of the crime?'

'Hey!' he said, holding his hands up. 'Calm down, I meant no harm coming here.'

'Don't tell me to calm down,' she said, clenching her fists. 'You have no right.'

'Well, at least tell me what I've done.'

She glared at him. 'Don't pretend you don't know what I'm talking about.'

'I don't,' he said, 'I really don't.'

'So what are you doing here?' she said. 'If you're so innocent, why are you hanging around in the square?'

Gabriel looked at her, then glanced away. 'I wanted to check you were okay,' he said.

'Well, it's a little late for that, isn't it? My dad died ten days ago. Yeah, you're obviously really worried.'

Gabriel looked up at her and his gaze was intense. 'I tried to call you, April, but your phone was off, remember? You moved out, you weren't in school and then when I did see you in the corridor, you attacked me. I've been worried about you.'

'Yeah, right.'

'Look, can we go somewhere else to talk?'

A chill ran through April as she remembered him saying the same thing to her that night he had thrown stones at her window. That perfect romantic night when she had longed to spend more time with him, walk arm in arm in the moonlight a little longer. What if she had gone? Would she be here now? Would her dad? She looked back towards the house, but her friends had all gone inside and suddenly she felt vulnerable and alone. Okay, so she didn't have any hard evidence that Gabriel was the killer and if she was honest, she didn't *want* him to be the killer, but what did she really know about him? And at the same time she felt a terrible urge to find out what had happened to her dad that went beyond grief. She *had* to know.

'Why do you want to get me on my own?' she asked, a wobble in her voice. 'So you can do to me what you did to my dad?'

Gabriel shook his head, looking hurt and confused. 'I really don't know what you're talking about,' he said. 'Do you think I had something to do with his death?'

'You know I do.'

'But that's ridiculous. Why would you think that?'

'Okay, so tell me – what were you doing in the cemetery the night Isabelle was killed? Where were you the night before, when Alix Graves was murdered?'

Gabriel looked down at the floor. 'I've told you, April, there are some things I can't ...' he began, then trailed off.

'What? You can't tell me because I wouldn't understand? Or because then you'd have to tell me what you've done?'

He took her arms and stared into her eyes. 'I haven't done anything,' he said.

'Really? Then tell me what's going on! What is this big secret?'

'You wouldn't believe me if I told you.'

'Well, try me!' she shouted. 'I've just buried my father. The least you can do is tell me what you know about it. Who killed him?'

Gabriel shook his head. 'I don't know,' he said, but there was an evasive look in his eyes.

'But you know something, Gabriel – tell me!'

'I can't!' he roared at her.

'Well leave me alone, then!' she shouted back, shaking off his hands, and began stalking towards the house. Gabriel jumped up and blocked her way.

'Let me past,' she said.

'Not until you talk to me.'

'No,' she said, trying to sidestep him, suddenly remembering what Fiona had said about confronting murderers.

'April, please!' he said, anger flaring in his eyes. 'You're being stupid.'

'Why, because I've guessed your secret?' she said, trying to sound more sure of herself than she felt. 'Because I know you're a killer?'

'Because you're just putting yourself in more danger!' he cried.

Now April was starting to feel frightened. What danger? Danger of staying here with him? Gabriel was between her and the house. She looked past him at the bright yellow door; it was closed. *Why is no one watching?* She tried to push past him again, but Gabriel spread his arms out to stop her.

'Let me explain,' he said, stepping towards her.

At that moment, she heard a bus whoosh past and, impulsively, she turned and ran.

'April, stop!' he called after her. 'Where are you going?'

Away from you, she thought, but she was running too hard to reply. She ran across the square towards the church, not looking back.

'Come back!' he yelled, but she didn't stop.

The red bus was pulling into the stop outside the Flask pub and she sprinted for it, jumping aboard as the doors swished shut.

'You in a hurry or somethin', love?' said the driver genially.

'Yes, I'm escaping from a serial killer,' panted April.

The driver laughed and pulled away from the kerb. April watched as Gabriel skidded to a halt by the bus stop and stared after them.

'Where to, then?'

'Uh, sorry?'

'Where you going?'

April dug in the pocket of her coat and pulled out a handful of change.

'Anywhere but here.'

Once it had left Highgate and passed through Kentish Town and Camden, the bus slowed to a crawl, the rush-hour traffic in and out of London forcing them to stop and wait for a jam to clear every two minutes. Now she was sure Gabriel was a long way behind her, April relaxed for the first time that day. She had a window seat on the top deck and she was watching the city drift by, almost able to enjoy all the lights and decorations; the shops looked inviting and interesting and the people looked more glamorous than usual too, wrapped up in their overcoats and scarves, many of them carrying intriguingly shaped parcels, no doubt counting down the shopping days to Christmas. April felt something on her face and put up her hand; she was surprised to feel a tear. *God, I'm going to have to stop doing this*, she thought. *I can't keep crying at everything*. But it was hard to stop sometimes. This would be her first Christmas without her dad and – she knew this was silly – it would be his first Christmas without them. *I'm crying because I think my dad will be lonely up in heaven?* she scolded herself. *Get a grip*. Then again, if you couldn't cry on the day of your father's funeral, when could you? The thought of the funeral gave her a stab of guilt. She really shouldn't have left her mother like that, she would be worried. *Assuming she's not passed out already, of course*, she thought with a faint smile. She felt bad about leaving Fiona on her own too, after she had come all this way, but she knew Caro would take care of her. She just hoped Davina didn't get her claws too deeply into her friends while she was gone.

She felt around in her pocket. Thank God! Her phone was still there. She quickly texted Fiona.

Sorry, had to get away. Make excuse to Mum for me? Call later. xx

But the truth was, she felt better being on this bus, away from the wake and all those people – well meaning though they were – muttering their condolences. It was all so false, so tacky. She had been suffocating. And she was glad she had got away from Gabriel. The truth was he had frightened her. The look on his face when she had asked who had killed her dad was guilt, she was sure of it. And even if it wasn't, he hadn't denied it when she had accused him of being a killer. The bottom line was that he was keeping something from her. Too many people were doing that these days. Her mother, her grandfather, Gabriel, maybe even her father, if Silvia's outburst was to be believed. Why did they think she couldn't handle it? She wasn't some little kid any more. They were happy to lecture you about sex and drugs, but thought you were incapable of handling the boring details of their screwed-up adult lives. Well, if Gabriel wanted to play that way, April could play too. She would call Detective Inspector Reece and tell him what she had seen that night. Everything. She picked up her phone and scrolled through the numbers. There it was: DI Reece. She pressed the 'send' button. *Calling ...*

But then she suddenly stabbed the red 'cancel' button. What exactly would she say? 'Hello, Detective Inspector Reece. Hey, you know how I told you on two separate occasions that I didn't see anyone that night at the cemetery? Well, now I've changed my mind – the killer is my sort-of boyfriend.'

April smiled at the idea and imagined the policeman's response.

'So why are you telling me this now?'

'Um, because I've just had a public fight with him? Does that sound convincing?'

April had to admit it wouldn't have much credibility, and as Fiona had said, she really didn't *know* Gabriel was involved. There was just something wrong about the whole situation. The murders, the school, the way everyone acted around her, it was just, well, *weird*. Hopping off the bus at Kings Cross, she ran down the escalator and squeezed onto the packed Tube, riding shoved up against a pushchair along the Piccadilly line. She jumped off at Covent Garden and instantly felt better. Covent Garden was April's favourite station. She loved the old-fashioned green walls and the rickety lifts, the way they propelled you straight out into the middle of the hustle and chatter of central London. It almost felt like a conjuring trick. April had always looked forward to that part of the journey when her mum used to bring her here on shopping trips as a girl. But now, now she was on her own, and April felt human for the first time since the heavy iron door had closed on her dad's coffin earlier that afternoon. No one telling her what to do, no one looking at her with curiosity or pity, no one refusing to explain anything, she was just another body being swept along with the crowd. Somehow the lights seemed brighter and the smells sweeter here; she remembered her mum saying something about the metropolis having an energy all of its own. She agreed with her about that at least.

Drifting down past the Opera House and skirting around the busy market, she saw her favourite patisserie and walked over. She loved peering through the window at the marvellous cakes and pastry confections; it was April's version of Audrey Hepburn gazing at the jewels in Tiffany's. She jingled the coins in her pocket, wishing she had enough for a hot chocolate, her fingers pressed against the cold glass.

'I knew I'd find you here.'

April whirled around, her mouth open. It was Gabriel. He had found her.

Chapter Twenty-Nine

She pressed back against the window, her eyes darting around like a trapped rabbit's. Gabriel saw her expression and stepped forward.

'Hey, April, it's okay, don't be frightened,' he said, his hands outstretched. But April was already moving. She turned and ran, banging into a lady carrying a takeaway coffee which exploded on the floor in a spray of milk and foam.

'Hey!' shouted the woman angrily, but April couldn't hear anything except the wind rushing past her ears. She glanced behind and could see him following her. *No!* She pulled up her dress and her feet pounded the pavement, once again glad of her flat shoes, and she swerved to avoid tourists and shoppers. She dashed across a road, barely missing a black cab, and plunged into a narrow alleyway. *How close is he?* she wondered, not daring to look back. Little shops with cute Dickensian bow windows whirled through her vision as she looked for an exit. She skidded to a halt just as a bus whooshed past her nose in a red blur. *Left or right, left or right?* her brain screamed.

'April! Stop!' Gabriel's voice was close behind her. *Too close.* She went right, sprinting up the street, veering across and into another alley, hoping to lose Gabriel in the tangle of tiny streets. She plunged through a dark opening and along a narrow lane, no more than a pathway really, which hooked right and back onto the road. Where now? She followed the tide of people flowing downhill – where there were people there was safety, right?

She ran out into the road amid blaring horns and dazzling headlights. But then she was on the other side and to her right was the wide-open space of Trafalgar Square. It was teeming with tourists and pigeons, but it was too open, too exposed for safety. Besides, she had to stop, her legs, her lungs wouldn't take any more. She hurried as best she could up some wide white steps to her left and hid behind a pillar. It was a church, or a courthouse or something equally grand, but all April cared about was that she couldn't be seen. She slumped against the stone, gulping in air and trying to calm herself down. She ducked her head out and stared back the way she had come, scanning the crowd, looking for Gabriel in hot pursuit. *Maybe I've lost him, maybe he gave up*, she thought.

But no, there he was, walking casually towards her as if nothing had happened. *How did he get here so fast?*

'April, I'm sorry if I scared you back there. I didn't mean to freak you out, I just want to talk,' he said, both hands held out, palms down, as if he was trying to calm a skittish animal. 'Don't run, please.'

Out of the corner of her eye, she could see some tourists coming down the steps from the church, cameras in hands. So she screamed. A long high-pitched Hammer Horror-style scream. Every head within earshot turned in her direction and April took full advantage of it, quickly backing away from Gabriel, shouting, 'Help! Help me! He stole my purse and now he's trying to get my phone!' She waved her mobile to underline the truth of the claim.

A middle-aged fat man in a puffer jacket stepped between April and Gabriel.

'Hey, buddy,' he called in a gruff New York accent. 'You bothering this lady?'

'She's my girlfriend,' said Gabriel, not taking his eyes from April.

'I am not!' cried April.

'Hey, pal, why don't you give her some space, huh?' said the New Yorker. 'I don't think she wants you around right now.'

'Yeah, leave her alone!' shouted a black lady.

'I'm calling the police!' yelled someone else, stepping between them.

And April was off and running again, blindly taking the first road she came to, sprinting between towering white buildings, then taking a sharp left into an alleyway. As she ran she scrabbled with her phone, clumsily scrolling to Reece's mobile number and pressing the 'call' button.

'Come on, come on,' she panted, holding the phone to her ear without breaking stride.

'This is Detective Inspector Ian Reece ...'

'DI Reece! This is April ... April Dunne,' she gasped desperately.

'... leave a message after the tone.'

Dammit! Voicemail.

As the tone sounded, she tried again. 'DI Reece, this is April Dunne, I'm in ...' She looked around her desperately. 'Somewhere in London, near Trafalgar Square, I think I'm being foll—'

And then she was talking to the air. Her phone had been snatched out of her hand. She twisted around, stumbled and fell, landing on the ground with a jolt. Gabriel was standing over her, peering at the phone.

'Who were you calling? The *police*?'

April opened her mouth to scream again, but Gabriel was too quick. He jumped forward and before she could do anything, his hands were on her. *This is it*, she thought, *strangled at sixteen*. But to her surprise, he simply lifted her back onto her feet.

'What are you doing?' he said to her angrily, barely out of breath. 'Why are you running away from me?'

'Because you're a murderer!' shouted April and kicked him as hard as she could in the shin.

'Ow, Jesus!' he cried, doubling over, and April ran. She ran as fast as she could go. At the end of the alley were some wide steps where the lane became an arched tunnel and she jumped down them three at a time, her footsteps echoing, her breath rasping. Ahead of her she could see some people and she shouted out to them.

'Please help me! Please, he's after me!'

The first of them caught her as she ran into him. 'Hey, hey!' he said, laughing. 'What's the rush? Who's after you, love?'

The man was in his twenties, dressed in an expensive-looking polo shirt, his hair slicked back. His three companions were also young men similarly dressed in flashy retro trainers and short-sleeved shirts, despite the cold. One of them had tattoos running up his arms.

'Him!' gasped April, pointing to Gabriel, who was now standing at the top of the stairs, silhouetted against the light inside the tunnel.

'Who's that, your boyfriend?' asked one of the other men, sniggering.

'Or her pimp,' shouted another and they all laughed. April could now smell the booze on their breath.

'Having a domestic, love?' said the first man, the yellow light of the tunnel shining on his hair. 'Don't worry, we'll sort him for you.'

'Let her go,' said Gabriel, walking towards them. 'I won't tell you again.'

'Oo-ooh!' mocked one of the men, to more raucous laughter. 'He won't tell us again.'

Slick Hair stepped forwards and another of the men grabbed April's arms from behind.

'Well, how about I tell you something, pal,' said Slick Hair. 'She's with us now. We'll take good care of her, won't we, boys?'

'Yeah!' They all laughed and the man holding April twisted his head around to leer at her.

Slick Hair reached into his pocket and, with a flash of metal, he produced a knife.

'So unless you want some of this,' he began, waving the blade in front of Gabriel's face, 'I suggest you—' But he never got to finish the sentence. Faster than the eye could see, Gabriel grabbed his hand and twisted. There was a sickening crack that sounded horribly loud in the tunnel, followed by an even louder scream. The next few seconds were a blur: the man holding April tossed her to one side and she dropped to the floor. Then she heard a terrible guttural roar like a charging wolf and the man flew past her, his head cracking against the sloped wall of the tunnel. There were more thuds and another scream and then it was over; all of the men were lying on the ground and Gabriel was bending over April to help her up.

'It's okay,' he said softly, 'it's over now.'

'Get away from me,' she screamed, scrabbling along the ground until her back met the wall.

'April, they were going to hurt you,' he said, bending down towards her, but before he could touch her one of the men got back to his feet and grabbed Gabriel's coat, shouting obscenities. April spotted the knife, lying on the floor by her leg. She quickly reached out, grabbed it and stuffed it into her coat pocket as she clambered to her feet and ran up the steps, but Gabriel caught her at the top and pushed her into a doorway, his face cold with anger.

'You have to believe me, I had nothing to do with your father's death.'

'Why should I believe you?'

'Okay, you want to call the police?' he said, handing her back the phone. 'Go ahead, call your Detective Inspector Reece, ask him where *he* was when your father was killed.'

She looked up at him, then down at the phone. With shaking fingers, she dialled Reece's number.

'April?' said Reece urgently down the line. 'Where are you? What's happened? I tried to call you back, but it went to voicemail. Are you okay?'

'Yes, I'm fine,' said April. 'Look, I know this sounds crazy, but can I ask you something? Where were you when my father was killed?'

There was silence at the end of the phone. 'What's this about, April?' he asked suspiciously. 'Are you in trouble?'

'Please, DI Reece, can you just tell me? It's important.'

She could hear the policeman take in a deep breath and let it out. 'I was interviewing a witness,' he said. 'A lad from your school, actually, Gabriel Swift. Had to cut it short when

Carling got the call about your dad on the radio. Listen, what's going on? Aren't you with your mum?'

'I'm just going home now,' she said, looking at Gabriel. 'Hang on, he was a witness? To my dad's murder?'

'Another case,' said Reece. He paused for a moment. 'Isabelle Davis, in fact. He saw something that night too. Listen, April, do you need me to—'

'Sorry, Detective Inspector, I've got to go,' she said and hung up, immediately turning towards the Embankment Tube entrance only metres away.

Gabriel grabbed her arm, but she pulled it free. 'Let go of me,' she hissed, gripping the knife in her pocket. 'Do you want me to scream again?'

'Okay, okay,' said Gabriel, holding his hands up in surrender. 'But at least let me explain.'

'I'm not interested in anything you've got to say,' said April, turning back towards the station.

'I can tell you what's been going on.'

That stopped April in her tracks. She looked back at him. Was he telling the truth this time? He'd promised to explain before but hadn't followed through. Okay, so he wasn't there when her dad died – and she was more relieved than she thought she'd be about that – but he could still have killed Isabelle and he still obviously knew something he wasn't telling her. And April had to know. She *had* to.

'Okay,' she said. 'You've got two minutes.'

Gabriel nodded towards the little park next to the station. 'Maybe we'd better go somewhere a little more private.'

'No, first tell me why you're suddenly a police witness for the Isabelle Davis case,' said April.

Gabriel could see she wasn't going to budge and sighed. 'I called the police anonymously that night to tell them I'd found the body – and I didn't tell them you were there – I later found out that you didn't tell them I was there either. I've never thanked you for that, by the way.'

April shrugged. 'You're welcome,' she said, with slightly

more sarcasm than she intended. 'But why were you talking to Reece when my dad was killed?'

Gabriel paused before answering.

'I called them again, told them I'd thought of something else. I wanted to help them catch Isabelle's killer.'

'But what made you wait a week? Why did you suddenly get all public-spirited?'

'Because of the party,' said Gabriel. 'Because I saw what they were doing, what they were going to do, and I thought I might be able to help stop it.'

'Stop what?' said April. 'And who are "they", exactly?'

Gabriel glanced around him. 'Listen, I'll tell you whatever you want to know, but I can't talk about it out here. Come on, I promise I won't hurt you,' he said, walking backwards towards the park as he spoke.

April shrugged and followed. What was the worst that could happen? *He could kill you and eat you*, said a voice in her head. Considering how her day had been going, that didn't seem so bad to April right then.

'So what have you got to tell me?' said April impatiently as they walked through the gardens. 'You can start with that night in the cemetery. What exactly happened to Isabelle Davis? And what were you doing there?'

'I know you have no reason to believe anything I say,' he said slowly, 'but she was killed by a vicious animal and I was there trying to protect you.'

'What, the way you did back there with those blokes?'

'They weren't going to help you, April. Believe me, they had bad things in mind.'

'And how would you know that? Can you read minds?'

Gabriel walked on a few more steps, looking down at his feet. 'Listen, April,' he said. 'I still can't tell you everything, not all at once.'

'Oh Jesus Christ, forget it!' shouted April. 'I'm supposed to trust everything you say, however ridiculous, but you won't trust me with your precious secrets? Just forget it!' She turned to leave the park.

'I could smell them.'

April gave him a double take. He had said it in such a quiet voice, she wasn't sure she could have heard him correctly. She gave a nervous laugh.

'You could smell them?'

Gabriel nodded, his eyes hooded and faraway. He certainly didn't look like he was joking.

'Okay, and what did they smell of?'

'Violence, cruelty. Sex. The bad kind.'

April just blinked at him. He was serious, this wasn't a wind-up. Her stomach felt like an express lift dropping between floors. She looked back towards the bright entrance of the Tube station, but they were too far away now. No one would see them from this distance. She glanced behind her; the park gates were there, but they opened onto the Embankment, thick with roaring traffic. She was trapped.

'I can smell you too, April,' he said. 'I can smell fear, regret and ... something else – what is that?'

'Leave me alone,' she whispered, backing away horrified.

'You were right about me, April,' he said, matching her step for step. 'I *am* a killer. A hunter. We all are. Some of us are just better at it than others.'

And finally the penny dropped, finally she understood what he was talking about, what the real story had been all along.

'You are kidding me,' she said. April knew she should have been scared, mesmerised, rooted to the spot with terror, but instead she was furious. 'You are not *serious!*' she screamed, stepping towards Gabriel, her hand groping in her pocket. She pulled out her mobile phone, held it up and clicked the button. The flash lit up the little park and Gabriel jerked back, momentarily stunned.

'No way,' whispered April as she looked down at the screen, because Gabriel wasn't there. *He's not there. No trick of the light. No faulty camera. He's simply not there.* 'You're a vampire?' She looked up at him in disbelief. 'You're a bloody vampire?'

Gabriel took a step forwards. 'April—'

'You are! You're a bloody VAMPIRE!' she yelled, backing

away, but he was too fast. He was on her in a second, his hands gripping her arms. He pushed his face close to hers – and it was terrifying. His mouth was stretched back in a horrible grin, his sharp glittering teeth bared, his nose wrinkled and upturned, his eyes narrow and black. *Oh God, so black.* The very same eyes she had seen that night in the cemetery.

'Yes, I'm a vampire,' he hissed. 'I'm just a monster to you, aren't I?' He bent his head lower, his teeth moving closer and closer to her neck.

He's going to kill me too. April knew she wouldn't get another chance. Some older, darker primordial instinct took over and she gripped the knife in her pocket and thrust it upwards, screaming.

A look of confusion passed over Gabriel's face, then his arms dropped and he looked down at the handle of the knife protruding from his abdomen.

'You stabbed me,' he said. April watched in horror as he reached up and pulled the knife out and stared at the dark blood on the blade. Gabriel looked from the knife to April, but she didn't wait to see his reaction. She turned and ran, straight out of the park and into the road without breaking stride. She ran straight across Embankment, packed with speeding rush-hour cars, oblivious to the danger, not caring if she was smashed by a bumper or crushed by the wheels. A car passed in front of her so close it blew her hair out to the side, but she kept going, ignoring the blaring horns and squealing brakes. She was a gazelle being chased by a lion, a swallow chased by hawks, completely focused on putting that moving metal river between them. She almost made it. Her last step fell an inch too short and her toe clipped the kerb, sending her pitching forwards. Crying out, she landed on one knee, grazing it badly. As she staggered back up, she could feel the blood running down her shin, she could see the hole in her tights and the red wound beneath it. It didn't look good, but she didn't stop, half-limping towards the river. She knew she'd never make it to the Tube, but maybe there would be a boat or somewhere to hide. Hobbling badly, the pain sending little stars shooting across her vision, she staggered to her left. Towering above her was a huge stone column – Cleopatra's Needle. Almost hopping now, she made it to the foot of the monument and rested against the stone base for a moment. *Where now, genius?* she thought. April struggled down the steps at the back and sat down behind one of the huge sphinxes. It was the best hiding place she could hope for in the circumstances.

She felt her knee gingerly.

'Ouch,' she whispered to herself. She didn't think it was that bad, but it was stiffening up. If he found her she'd be unable to run. *Will he find me? Is he even alive?* It was just typical of her luck. *I find the boy of my dreams and he turns out to be a murderous vampire. I really can pick 'em,* she thought. She felt in her pocket for her phone, she had to call someone, but who? She couldn't very well call the police and tell them there was a vampire loose in Westminster and, by the way, I've just stabbed him. Reece! Of course, she would call Reece, he would know what to do. April glanced at her phone to pull up his number and saw the phone's screen, with the photo of Gabriel there in glorious Technicolor. Or rather, not there. Just like her photo of Milo from the party, there was a weird black swirly hole where Gabriel should have been. She knew she needed to act, but she couldn't take her eyes off it. *A vampire!* It was unbelievable, ridiculous. But in a funny kind of way, it all made sense. His sudden disappearances, the things he couldn't explain, the Circle of Lebanon, even the late-night date in the square, suddenly they didn't seem so crazy. *So why didn't I work it out before?* she wondered angrily. 'Because vampires don't exist, you idiot!' she whispered.

'But we do.'

April jumped, pushing herself back against the sphinx.

'Please, April, no more running,' said Gabriel quietly. 'It's too cold.'

'But I stabbed you ...' she whispered. 'You had blood.'

'Yeah, we have blood too, but ...' He lifted his dark-stained shirt up, wincing. There was a hole in his side, but the blood around it was congealed and dry. It looked like an old wound, one that was well on the way to healing.

'How ...?' was all April could manage.

Gabriel sat down on the step, keeping a little distance from April. 'I'm a vampire, remember?' he said wearily. 'We heal quick. Bloody hurts though.' He put his shirt down and cradled his stomach, as if he had bad indigestion.

'You were going to bite me!' she shouted indignantly. 'I didn't have any choice! I thought you were going to kill me, the way you did Isabelle.'

'I wasn't going to bite you,' he said. 'And I didn't kill Isabelle. I just wanted to scare you. I wanted to let you see what everyone else sees, to see what I really am.'

'But why didn't you just tell me?'

'How could I?'

April gave a short ironic laugh. 'I suppose, "Hi, I'm Gabriel, I'm a bloodsucking demon," might not win you many friends.'

'We're not demons,' he said angrily.

'Oh, it's "we", is it? There are more of you?'

'More than you'd believe.'

All in a rush, April realised that it was all true. *Everything.* The nests, the Regent, the Highgate Vampire, the book in Mr Gill's shop, it was *all true.* 'Oh my God,' she whispered, feeling a terrible sense of shame as she remembered the way she had spoken to her father, mocking his silly little hobby, calling him pathetic for believing in monsters. But he had been right all along.

'So where are they?' said April. 'Who are they? How can I tell who is and who isn't a vampire?'

Gabriel shrugged. 'It's not that simple.'

April felt another rush of anger. 'Listen, Gabriel,' she snapped. 'You're either going to have to kill me and eat me or you're going to have to stop talking in riddles. Seriously, it's getting on my bloody nerves.'

Gabriel threw his head back and laughed, then stopped, wincing. 'You're certainly different, April Dunne.' He chuckled, holding his side.

'What's so funny?' said April, still annoyed.

'Well, most people confronted by a vampire for the first time scream or beg for their lives. You, on the other hand, stab the vampire and then start telling him off.'

Despite herself, April started giggling too. She covered her mouth, but it still bubbled out with an edge of hysteria and the chuckles were replaced with great gulping sobs and her shoulders heaved with the effort. All the tension of the day was pouring out with the tears. Gabriel came over and held her and even though she knew she should push him away, she clung to him, her face pressed into his chest. Despite her fears, there was something comforting about his embrace.

Finally, the sobs became sniffles and she blew her nose.

'So you're really a vampire, huh?' she said, wiping her face.

'Afraid so.'

'So what's it like?'

'Difficult.'

She snorted. 'I'll bet.' She pushed herself up, trying to stand. Her knee didn't feel too bad. 'Come on, let's walk,' she said, reluctantly leaning on his arm. 'So long as you don't try anything.'

They walked slowly back along the river, silently watching the rolling black waters reflecting the lights from the buildings. April stopped and looked up at him.

'How old are you?'

Gabriel paused before answering. 'I was born in 1870.'

'Good God, but that's ... that's insane. So are you immortal? Can you never die? Have you always looked like this?'

Gabriel touched her hand gently and she was surprised that she didn't flinch.

'Don't try to take it all in at once, April,' he said. 'It's hard to grasp, but it's true. It really is.'

They were coming under the shadow of Hungerford Bridge now.

'How's the knee?' he asked.

'It's okay,' she said, doubtfully. 'More to the point, how's your side?' She lowered her voice and glanced around. 'Listen, I'm sorry I stabbed you.'

'Come here,' he said. 'I'd like to show you something.' Bending over, he effortlessly scooped April up in his arms and began running up the steps to the Jubilee Footbridge.

'Hey,' she protested, 'I'm not an invalid.'

'I know,' he said. 'Now shut up, I'm trying to be nice. And considering you just stabbed me, I'm also being very understanding.'

April shut up. She was still annoyed about being lied to, not to mention badly freaked out by the whole 'vampire' thing, but it was, well, nice being picked up by a boy. *RIP feminism*, she thought to herself. Gabriel put her down gently and they began walking across the river. The London Eye was a glowing disc on the South Bank.

'It's beautiful, isn't it?' said April softly. 'I don't think I've ever seen the river at night before. Not up close like this.'

Gabriel nodded. 'I used to live near the river,' he said. 'I'd come here at night and just watch it flow past. Of course, it was much busier then. And the London Eye wasn't there – it was all warehouses and pretty nasty slums, and living by the river was considered dirty and dangerous.'

April stopped and looked around to make sure no one was listening. 'So you're really telling me you're a vampire? A *vampire*?'

Gabriel nodded. 'I know, it's crazy, isn't it? But it's true, I assure you.'

'But what are you? Some sort of … ?' She wanted to say monster, but she was too polite. He might be a creature of legend, but calling him a 'monster' to his face still felt a little rude.

'I'm human, just like you, but I've been infected by the vampire virus. I won't blind you with science, but essentially the vampire disease is constantly destroying our cells and the body is constantly making new ones. That's why we have great skin and hair, and we never get ill. We age much, much more slowly because our bodies are constantly regenerating. So no,

315

we're not supernatural, it's just that science hasn't caught up with us yet. And no, before you ask, I can't turn into a bat.'

April smiled. They walked a little further. She had been right – her knee was stiffening up, making her lean on Gabriel a little more. She found she didn't mind that too much.

'So how did it happen?' she asked, looking up at him. 'How did you come to be a –' she whispered '– vampire?'

'I got bitten,' he said simply.

April shot him an impatient look and Gabriel shrugged.

'I chose to become a vampire,' he said quietly. 'And I did it for love.'

April still didn't know how to react to all this new information and she certainly wasn't sure how she felt about Gabriel Swift any more, but she definitely didn't like him using the L-word when it wasn't connected to her.

'Love?' she asked as they began walking across the bridge again.

'I know, it sounds crazy, but I was young and impetuous and ... anyway, I was a student, studying law. I didn't have enough money for a social life, though, so I used to come out here walking at night, that was my entertainment. Then one night, just over there—' he pointed downstream '—I heard a scream. A gang of yobs, just kids really, were roughing up a girl, trying to steal her pocketbook. So I waded in.'

'My hero!'

'Yes, well.' He coughed. 'That time it didn't really go my way. I got quite a beating. In fact, the young lady in question ended up pulling them off me. All very embarrassing.'

'And she became your girlfriend?'

He nodded. 'That was Lily, who became my girlfriend – fiancée, actually. She was beautiful and sweet, but she was also strong-headed. She hated the constraints of her sex, how she had to conform to certain old-fashioned notions of decent behaviour.'

'I'm with her there.'

'Her attitude was always "why shouldn't I go out walking

316

alone?" She was an original thinker. So we began courting, and we fell in love and I proposed.'

'So what went wrong?' April could hardly believe she was feeling jealous of a woman who had been born over a hundred years ago. But given the way this evening was going she wouldn't have been entirely surprised if Gabriel had suddenly produced his beautiful fiancée, still alive, still radiant and brave.

Gabriel shook his head and looked out at the river. 'She got sick. Consumption – tuberculosis. It might be hard to imagine what it was like in London a hundred years ago, but the conditions were terrible. Disease. Overcrowding. Whole families would jump into the Thames to avoid starvation and TB was the biggest killer of all. All it took was for one infected person to cough in an alleyway or marketplace and everyone who walked past would inhale it and contract the disease.'

They had come to the end of the walkway now and Gabriel helped April down onto the South Bank path. They walked into Jubilee Gardens where there was a small fair in the shadow of the big wheel. They stopped to watch the children going round and round on a Victorian-style carousel, squealing as the horses dipped up and down.

'It was so hard to watch,' said Gabriel. 'She was wracked with pain every time she coughed, blood spotting her handkerchief. Then it spread to her neck and leaked through her skin as a horrible pus. She lost weight and finally it spread to her spine and she found it difficult to walk. I so wanted to save her.'

He paused, looking up at the stars for a moment.

'There had been rumours about bad things happening around Christchurch even before Jack the Ripper. Bodies turning up. It was a dark place back then, even in the daytime with the fog blocking out the sun. People could do what they liked, then disappear into the shadows. I had a friend, another student, who boarded in Whitechapel because it was cheap. He fell in with a bad crowd, drinking gin, smoking opium, worse. One night he told me about the vampires. He spoke about them in hushed tones, as if he was talking about royalty. I was as sceptical as you were, but he showed me his scars. They were using him as a "feeder". That's what we call someone who allows a vampire to drink their blood. He was evangelical about it, he said his "master" would turn Lily – if he made her a vampire she would never be sick again. He wasn't just a powerful vampire, he was the Vampire Regent, the top man.'

Gabriel shook his head at the memory. 'I knew Lily would never agree. She was very religious, you see. But that night, it was worse than ever. I sat up mopping the cold sweat from her forehead, each cough and spasm like a knife through my heart. I couldn't stand it. I was weak.'

'No,' said April, touching his hand. 'It was a brave thing to do.'

'Was it? Or was I just scared to go through all that on my own? I don't know any more. Either way, I went with my friend to see the Regent. He lived in a big house near Bethnal Green. I knew the rumours about vampires were true as soon as I got there. The house was grand and luxurious, but dark and full of so many evil-looking creatures. I never saw the Regent's face, then or since. He was always in shadow. He asked me what I wanted and when I told him he sounded sympathetic. He bit me and ...'

'What happened?'

'I died, but I had to will myself to live. It's like clinging on to a cliff by your fingertips. It was horrible, truly horrible.' He shuddered.

'But you did it for her, for Lily,' said April. 'It was a beautiful thing.'

Gabriel shook his head. 'It didn't turn out that way. I was tricked. When it was over, the Regent laughed in my face. He said if I wanted to save Lily, I would have to turn her myself.'

'But why did he go back on his word?'

'Power. Vampires love power almost as much as the kill. I was a diversion, an amusing pastime. But I was angry, so angry with him.'

'So what did you do?'

'I attacked him. He hadn't expected it – too arrogant, I suppose. I think I hurt him pretty badly, but I barely got away alive – his guards came after me in force, chasing me across London. It was a stupid thing to do, it meant I had to grab Lily and flee. We didn't get very far.'

'What happened to Lily?'

'She died in my arms.'

He turned away from her and April instinctively reached out for him, then stopped herself. He was a *vampire*. A killer, a supernatural being. He had been born in 1870. She barely knew how to deal with human boys, she really shouldn't go getting mixed up with him. After a moment, they turned and walked towards Waterloo.

'So what did you do then?' asked April.

'Nothing. I wanted vengeance, but there was little I could do. They knew who I was, I wouldn't have got near the Regent. Plus I was weak physically. You need human blood to be a strong vampire and I had sworn to Lily that I would never kill anyone except the Regent. It's hard, the hardest thing anyone can ever ask of you. All of your instincts as a vampire are those of a hunter, a killer. However much you want to rise above it, the urge is within you. Sometimes it gets too much and vampires go rogue, like a fox in the henhouse.'

April thought for a moment, trying to visualise Gabriel killing. For some reason, she just couldn't. After all those doubts, all those suspicions, now she knew he was a vampire, a pure-bred killer, she just couldn't imagine him taking a life.

'But why did you vow only to kill the Regent? Why just him?'

'If you kill the vampire who turned you, then the virus he infected you with is neutralised. It's like putting a dock leaf on a nettle rash.'

April looked at him sharply. 'So you'd be cured? You could live a normal life?'

Gabriel smiled. 'In theory. It's very rarely happened. I've

only heard rumours of it, and it's not an exact science. It could just be another myth.'

'But if the Regent knows you're hunting him, how can you walk around London? Won't his guards find you?'

'That's just it – he doesn't know. That night, his followers chased me to a church in Spitalfields and I fought them. In the struggle, a lantern was broken and the vestry was set on fire. I escaped through the crypt but they believed I died in the fire.'

'Are you sure? What if they catch you?'

Gabriel smiled, but he looked troubled. 'Vampires are arrogant. They assumed I was dealt with, so why concern themselves with some nobody? I certainly gave them no reason to doubt they had killed me. I have stayed hidden ever since, but I have kept watch, biding my time, tracking them, making sure they still believe I'm dead. But recently ...'

'What?'

Gabriel shook his head. 'I can't put my finger on it, but I have this sense that I'm being watched.'

April felt herself go cold. It was hard enough to grasp all this craziness, but the thought that someone – some killer – might be watching them, following them was too much for her. 'Do you think it's the Regent?' she asked urgently. 'Do you know who he is?'

'No, I've never got that close,' said Gabriel. 'He's clever, he never stays in the same place for long and always travels under guard. He's deeply paranoid, always covers his tracks, and he's very, very good at it. So good, in fact, that I lost track of him about a year ago, but I can feel his presence – he's definitely on the move again.'

'If he's so good at hiding, how do you find him?'

'He loves power more than he loves anonymity, so he won't be able to stay hidden for long. Even now, he will be the head of a big international company or in some influential government think tank. He will start meddling in things, manipulating people and events – he won't be able to stay quiet for ever. And I think these killings are just the start of it.'

Gabriel looked into April's eyes and saw her fear. 'I'm sorry, I don't mean to frighten you, but I'm sure the Highgate murders are linked to him. Even if it isn't the Regent, there's definitely something going wrong – the balance has been upset.'

'What balance?'

'The balance between humans and vampires. Despite what you see in the movies, vampires are quiet, unassuming creatures. We don't wear red capes and live in big castles; we stay as hidden as possible because it's easier to hunt that way. You don't want your prey to see you coming.'

April shivered. 'And by prey, you mean us?'

Gabriel nodded. 'But recently, it's almost as if some of us have been stepping out from behind the curtain, as if they don't care that people will guess their secret. And now these three deaths—'

'You're frightening me, Gabriel.'

He looked at her. 'I think you should be frightened.'

They had reached Waterloo Road now; it was still busy, but the shoppers had gone home and the commuter crush had eased. A bus was just whooshing to a stop as they got to the stop and they jumped aboard, pushing their way to the top deck and finding a seat out of earshot of the other passengers.

'So where is Lily? I mean, where is she buried?' asked April as the bus set off, enjoying how the movement of the bus made her sway against him.

'Highgate. In the cemetery.' He paused, watching the lights of the city flash past. 'That's why I was in Swain's Lane that night. It was her birthday, and I always go to talk to her on the day. But there was someone – some*thing* – else there, another vampire. I could smell him, feel the danger. He'd killed foxes and birds, a cat, he was in a feeding frenzy.'

'God. So what did you do?'

Gabriel shrugged. 'We fought. He was strong, although I think Isabelle must have put up a fight because he was injured. But he would certainly have killed you if I hadn't been there.'

April had a sudden horrible thought. 'But did he see you? Does the killer know who you are?'

Gabriel nodded. 'That's my worry. It was very dark, but there's a good chance he saw my face when I pulled you into Swain's Lane. And then there's the other things.'

'Like what?'

'This sense of being watched, for one. That's the real reason I haven't been around much over the last few weeks, this feeling that someone is leading me into a trap. And then there was the business with the police. When I went in to talk to your friend DI Reece, I got the distinct feeling they were already aware of my involvement, as if someone had tipped them off.'

April felt a sinking feeling. 'The Regent?'

'I don't know, but it would be very convenient if I became the prime suspect in a murder inquiry and was therefore out of the way. But by the same token, if the Regent knows who I am, why hasn't he had me killed?'

'But do you know who the killer is?'

Gabriel looked out of the window. 'I told you: no. But the point is, if the Regent is behind the murders, then the killer's identity is almost irrelevant. If the Regent ordered Isabelle's death, it doesn't really matter *who* killed her. It's *why* he killed her that's important.'

April nodded and glanced around at the other passengers on the bus. A big black woman in a green raincoat carrying worn shopping bags; a young man in what looked like his first suit; two girls reading a magazine. They all seemed so far away, as if they were on the other side of a double-glazed window. They were in the real world, while April had slipped into this parallel universe where nothing made sense like it used to.

'So why don't all vampires kill the one who turned them?' she asked.

Gabriel gave an ironic laugh. 'Because you have to choose to be a vampire. If a vampire bites an innocent and infects them with the virus, the disease will kill them. Only if you choose to be a vampire, if you actively embrace the curse, will you survive, but you have to really want it. So those who make it through aren't about to murder their maker. They've embraced being a vampire. It's like the police or teaching, it attracts a certain type of personality.'

'Now you're teasing me,' said April, searching his face.

'A little bit.' He smiled.

'But vampires are killers, right? Don't they kill each other?'

'No. We're hunters, we choose weaker prey. Lions don't attack leopards because they're both predators. Not only would it attract attention, there's little in it for either party: we can't feed off each other. And that's why I'm worried about what's been happening in Highgate. It's against all the rules. Alix Graves, that could have been an accident, something gone wrong, but to follow that with Isabelle and your dad? Three high-profile murders in three weeks, it's against every vampire instinct. It makes me think there's got to be some purpose behind it.'

'Or some*one*, maybe?'

'Yes. I can't believe this could happen without the Regent's involvement.'

April caught sight of her reflection in the dark window. Serious and intense – desperately trying to absorb all this information and ask the right questions. *It's as if I've got a test on it tomorrow.* The thought made her laugh.

'What's up?' said Gabriel, frowning.

There was an edge of hysteria to April's giggles. Deep down, she was worried she was starting to lose it.

'What, April?' said Gabriel with annoyance.

'I've just been struck by how absurd this is,' said April, shaking her head. 'I've just buried my father and now I'm discussing the ins and outs of vampire lore, like it's all real.'

'It is real, April.'

April thumped her fist against the seat in frustration. 'But how can it be? Do you know how insane this sounds?'

Gabriel turned on her, irritation sharpening his tone. 'Insane or not, it's happening. Your father was killed because of it.'

April was angry now, edgy. She could feel a pressure building inside her, all the frustration, grief and anger in a growing knot at the back of her skull and tingling down her spine. The thought crossed her mind that this whole thing, the knife, the wound, was just some sick joke, that it was all a conjuring trick. Suddenly, she grabbed Gabriel's top and pulled it up.

'What the hell?' he said.

'Show me! Show me the wound!' she snapped. 'I want to make sure it's real.'

Gabriel grabbed her hand and pushed it against the red welt. It was raised and hot; it certainly felt real.

'Do you want to stick your fingers in it?' he said angrily. 'Will that satisfy you?'

She pulled her hands away quickly.

'And why should I believe you?' she demanded. 'Because you told me a sweet tale of undying love? You could have got all that from a Mills and Boon novel.'

'Don't insult me, April,' growled Gabriel, pulling his top down. 'I've told you the truth, something I've never done with anyone else, so don't throw it back in my face.'

'All I know for sure is that my father has been murdered because he was investigating something. Maybe he *had* discovered there were vampires in Highgate. Maybe he was after you.'

Gabriel shook his head. 'He wasn't.'

'Yeah? And how would you know?'

'Because he was investigating the school.'

April stopped and stared at him.

'How do you know that? Do you know who killed him?'

'No, I told you the truth about that. I really don't know.'

'But you suspect someone, don't you? Tell me! I have a right to know!'

Gabriel looked away and she grabbed his coat, pulling him around to face her.

'Gabriel, tell me! Who killed my father?'

Gabriel looked into her eyes, his gaze strong and unwavering. 'You have to believe me, April, I don't know. But I'll repeat what I said about Isabelle – if the Regent ordered his death, it doesn't matter who carried it out.'

'It may not matter to you,' she hissed, 'but I want to do

to them what they did to my father.' She began to get up, reaching for the button to stop the bus.

'Don't, April,' said Gabriel, pulling her back down. 'You've come too far to walk away from this now.'

'I'm not walking away,' she snapped. 'I'm going to find my father's killer, with or without you!'

Gabriel nodded slowly. 'All right. I'll tell you what I know, but you won't like it.'

She crossed her arms. 'Try me.'

'Okay. First, Ravenwood is a vampire school.'

'What?' April laughed mirthlessly. 'Now you really are joking, right?'

'Do you want to hear this or not?'

She nodded. She wasn't sure if she really did, but Gabriel was right: once you'd fallen down the rabbit hole and discovered Wonderland, you couldn't very well go back to normal life.

'Ravenwood is a recruiting tool,' said Gabriel. 'The vampires have formed a sort of shaky alliance between the clans.'

'The nests, you mean?' asked April.

Gabriel looked at her curiously. 'How do you know that term?' he said. 'I haven't heard it in a long time.'

'Something I heard from my dad,' said April lamely. She didn't want to tell him everything she knew – about the notebook and Mr Gill or even DI Reece's theories. She still didn't know if she could trust him, however much she might want to.

'Anyway, I don't know who's in charge at the school – they're way up in the food chain, well protected – but their plan is clearly very ambitious. They're gathering the cleverest, most influential and most able children in the country under one roof, then converting them to the cause.'

April couldn't believe it. Caro had been right all along.

'They're turning kids into vampires?'

'Some, not many. But they're all in danger. That was why I whispered "Get out" to you that first day at school. It was stupid I know, but I was angry. I couldn't stand to see someone else sucked into their scheme.'

He sighed. 'It was futile gesture. Vampires are hugely manipulative, they can control people in other ways than by conversion to vampirism.'

'How? Hypnotism?'

Gabriel laughed. 'No, simpler things than that – sex, drugs, blackmail, love, to name a few.'

'Love?'

'It's easy to love a vampire.'

Tell me about it, thought April, then shook her head to dismiss the thought. She couldn't get sucked in, not right now.

'But what are they going to do? What's the big plan?'

He shrugged. 'To take over, of course. They want their people at the top of every important part of society – doctors, barristers, politicians, soldiers, bankers, in all senior, influential positions.'

'But you can't have a vampire prime minister – he wouldn't show up on TV.'

'Which is exactly why they concentrate on seducing and manipulating people instead of turning them. You just have to persuade them that your way is the right way, whether it's communism, Christianity or vampirism. Make them believe in the cause. And those are the people they put in front of the cameras: the prime minister, the president. But the people pulling the strings stay in the shadows, out of sight.'

'Okay,' said April, mulling it over. 'So if the kids are being recruited, who's doing the recruiting?'

Gabriel looked at her, a genuine confusion on his face. 'You haven't worked that out yet?'

Her eyes were wide. 'You?'

'And my friends, yes.'

April looked at him, aghast. 'But if you hate the Regent, how could you become part of this?'

'For one thing, I'm still not sure the Regent *is* behind it. But that's why I'm there – getting close to them is the only way I'll find out what they're doing and who's calling the shots.'

'But you're recruiting? You're seducing a load of innocent science geeks, persuading them to become vampires?'

It was all too much. The man she was falling for was not only a vampire, he was part of the conspiracy. She had allowed herself to believe that he was one of the good guys, a lone wolf walking apart from the rest of the pack, but he was one of them. Then suddenly in a flurry, she thought of poor Ling crying in the toilets after Davina and her friends had left, her arm bleeding, and another piece of the jigsaw clicked into place. 'You're drinking their blood?'

Gabriel's eyes were blazing now. 'Oh, grow up, April!' he snapped. 'How else am I going to get their confidence? Besides, what would you prefer I do? Drink a little blood from some silly little schoolgirl or murder someone in their own home?'

'Silly little schoolgirl?' she said, barely keeping her voice level. 'Do you think they're your *playthings*? They're human beings! Are you saying that if you didn't bite Sara in the bathroom at Milo's party you'd have had to go and tear someone's throat out?'

'No, of course not,' he said. 'But I have to feed. We all do.'

April felt another piece of the puzzle drop in. 'Hang on, this "we"? Do you mean Davina? Benjamin? The Faces? They're all vampires?'

Gabriel nodded.

'Jesus,' she muttered, her head swimming.

'Oh God,' said April, reaching up and pressing the bell. 'Why didn't you tell me all this before?' She was already up and moving painfully down the stairs.

The bus doors swished open and she ran as fast as she could with her injured knee, pulling out her phone as she hobbled forwards.

'April!' called Gabriel, catching up with her. 'Where are we going?'

April looked at him and held the phone to her ear. 'To save my friends.'

Chapter Thirty

Fiona wasn't at the house. In fact, no one was. It was deserted, save for the mass of half-empty glasses littering the tables and kitchen worktops and the piles of uneaten food next to the bin. Someone had made a bit of an effort to tidy up after the guests had left, at any rate. Not her mother, that was fairly certain. Where *was* she anyway? April tried her phone again, but it went straight to voicemail.

'Hi, Mum, where are you? I'm home, but no one's here, I'm getting worried. Call me as soon as you get this, okay?'

'Have you tried your friend Fiona?' asked Gabriel.

April pulled a face at him. *Of course* she had tried Fee, but she called her again anyway. No, still voicemail: '*Hi, this is Fee, you know what to do …*'

She looked at Gabriel. 'Where would they have taken them?'

Gabriel shrugged. 'They could have gone anywhere. But I doubt they've been kidnapped.'

'How do you know?' snapped April. 'They could have ripped their throats out by now!'

Gabriel stepped over to her, but she pushed him away.

'April, think! They want to convert them, not kill them – what would be in it for them?'

'How should I know?' she yelled. 'You're the bloody vampire – you tell me! Isn't it *fun* killing people?' she asked sarcastically.

'I wouldn't know,' he said, glaring at her as he stepped over to the mantelpiece. 'Look,' he said, handing April a hastily scrawled note that had been propped up against a clock.

April, darling, gone to Euphoria, York Road. Your name's on the list, Davina. xx

April didn't say a word in the taxi, she was too angry: angry with Davina and Benjamin for trying to recruit/murder her friends; angry with Fiona and Caro for going with them and wanting to be friends with such airheads – such *vampire* airheads; angry with Gabriel for being a – *goddammit* – vampire; and angry with her mother for disappearing to God knows where in her time of need. Finally, she couldn't keep it in any longer.

'What the hell are they doing going clubbing on the day of my dad's funeral?' she snapped. 'What were they thinking?'

'I'm sure your dad wouldn't have wanted his wake to be all doom and gloom.'

'There's a big difference between "no doom and gloom" and "clubbing",' April said acidly. 'And what about me? Why didn't they wait?'

'Well, they didn't know where you were or if you were coming back,' said Gabriel.

'What's that got to do with it? They should have been out searching for me!'

Gabriel looked as if he was going to point out how unreasonable April was being, then clearly thought better of it.

'Listen, don't be too hard on them,' he said gently. 'This is what the recruiters do. They're brilliant at getting people to do what they want them to, they dangle temptation in front of their victims and before they know it, they're starting to believe all the "chosen people" crap.'

'"Chosen people"?'

'It's like the recruitment slogan,' said Gabriel. 'We tell potential recruits about all the benefits of "The Life": vampires are beautiful, powerful and rich. But for most people, that transition's far too big a step – it's terrifying, in fact. So, instead, we offer them the opportunity to hang out with us; not just at school, but beyond it. It's incredibly tempting, especially for kids who are naturally outsiders because of their intellect. They think they will be part of this elite, working with a super-race of divine beings. I mean, who doesn't want to be gorgeous and popular, part of the cool gang? That's the tastiest carrot for the kind of kids they target – the idea they will belong. The geeks and the misfits lap that stuff up.'

'Excuse me,' said April, 'but my friends are not geeks or misfits. Caro doesn't even *like* Davina.'

'If you say so,' said Gabriel, sitting forward in his seat to pay the driver. 'We're here.'

'Here' was a huge hangar-like building set back from the road in the middle of what looked like an industrial estate. There was a huge vertical neon sign fixed to the side wall, the letters running down it spelling out the name of the club, and there was a queue from the front entrance snaking around the building.

'God, we'll never get in,' said April as the taxi disappeared, leaving them on the road.

'That's exactly the point,' said Gabriel. 'That's the lure for the recruits. Stick with us and we will *always* get you in.' He turned to her, touching her arm, his face serious. 'Okay, April, this is important. You need to forget everything I've told you today about vampires, Ravenwood and conspiracies, okay? You don't know anything about it. You don't know what Davina and Ben really are either. And – and this is crucial – I'm just another of their snooty friends, okay?'

'But how can I—?'

'Are we clear on that?'

'Yes,' she said, fleetingly thinking that maybe all this was part of Gabriel's seduction technique and – even more quickly – deciding that she wouldn't mind that at all.

Gabriel saw her wavering and took her hands. 'This isn't a game, April,' he said fiercely. 'They might look like airhead bimbos, but these people are *monsters*. If you become a threat to them, they will kill you and your mother without a thought. If you give them the slightest clue that you know who they are and what they are doing, they will bathe in your blood.'

April stared at him, surprised by the sudden seriousness of his tone.

'Do you understand me?'

April nodded and Gabriel turned towards the club, but she caught his arm.

'Are you like them?' she asked urgently. 'Could you do that too?'

He looked at her for a moment but didn't answer her question.

'Come on,' he said, 'let's go in.'

She stepped in front of him, searching his face. 'Just answer me one question, Gabriel, then I'll do whatever you want, okay?'

He nodded.

'You promised Lily you would never kill a human, right? Have you kept that promise?'

Gabriel's intense gaze never left hers as he nodded. 'Yes, I have,' he said, turning back towards the club. 'So far, anyway.'

It was ridiculously loud inside the club. So loud, in fact, that when April looked down at her dress, she could see it moving in and out in time with the bass. She was glad she had taken time to change while they waited for the taxi. She had bandaged her knee and disguised it as best she could under a new pair of tights, but it was still throbbing and her feet were killing her after all that running. It didn't help that it was so amazingly hot and packed with writhing bodies damp with sweat and wet from the condensation dripping from the ceiling. Or at least, April hoped it was condensation. It was too dark to know for sure. Standing on tiptoes to peer over the crowd, April could see a raised dance floor surrounded by revolving lights and strobes, but the rest of the club was bathed in a dark red glow, like ultraviolet only more menacing. Gabriel took her hand and led her through the crowd, setting a cruel pace, barging people out of the way.

'Hey! Slow down, you're hurting me!' called April, hobbling

as fast as she could, but he couldn't hear her – or wasn't listening. They passed an enormous bar and went through an archway into a smaller room. Here, at least, it was slightly quieter and cooler. And then, across the room, April saw a horrible sight: Benjamin's mouth coming down towards Fiona's exposed throat.

'Fee!' she shouted and Benjamin stopped, looked up and waved, then went back to shouting in Fiona's ear. He wasn't biting her at all, just bending down to make himself heard.

'They're only talking,' she breathed to herself. 'Only talking.' *Play it cool, idiot.*

'April!' Davina waved a manicured hand from inside a raised seating area. 'Come on in,' she shouted, motioning them over and tapping one of the enormous security guards on the shoulder to lift the velvet rope.

'Isn't it fabulous?' she gushed. 'It's the hottest place outside Soho right now.'

'Hot is right,' said April.

'Absolutely.' Davina giggled, signalling to a waiter who brought over a cocktail in a champagne glass. It looked blood-red in the dim light, but then so did most things in the room. April knocked it back in one go.

'I like your style, darling,' said a voice to her left. April turned to see a gorgeous girl in skin-tight leather. April did a double take: it was Ling Po. Her long hair was shiny, her skin was luminous and her eyes glittered. *Has she been converted to the cause of day spas and three-hundred-pound blow-dries or has she been more permanently converted?* wondered April with alarm. Either way, there wasn't a trace of the shy, nervous mouse April had met only weeks before. Ling saw her reaction and beamed.

'You like?' she asked, striking a pose.

'Yes, well, I'm amazed ...'

'Oh, I know, I can't believe I spent so long as a sad-sack geek!' She laughed. 'Davina has brought out the woman in me,' she said, slipping her hand around Davina's waist and looking up at her with an expression bordering on adoration.

'It was always there, Bling-girl.' Davina smiled, then whispered something in Ling's ear that made her giggle as she walked away, hips swinging.

'Now tell me,' said Davina to April, 'did you make up with Gabe? Is it all back on? It's so romantic that he went to find you, isn't it?'

Remembering Gabriel's warning, April smiled. 'Not sure about the romance,' she said, 'but it was sweet he came. It was the least he could do, considering.'

'I know,' said Davina, pouting. 'Caro told me what a shit he's been, and it must have been so hard for you today, darling. Still, we're all here now and cocktails will cure anything, won't they?' She reached behind her and took a glass from a waiter, handing it to April.

'I'll drink to that cure,' said April, hoping this was what Gabriel wanted her to do; she wasn't entirely sure how a recruit was supposed to behave. Davina clinked her glass against April's and smiled wickedly.

'To the eternal cure!' she said and, with a wave, moved off to talk to a gorgeous boy in a leather jacket.

April looked around the VIP area. Over on the other side, Caro was talking to a handsome boy with black floppy hair. He seemed to be finding whatever she was saying hilarious. April walked over, all of her earlier worries that her friends had been hijacked spilling over into anger. For some reason, she was more upset with Caro than Fee; at least Caro had her suspicions about the vampires; how could she have been so stupid as to be sucked into their scheme?

'What are you doing?' she shouted over the noise.

Caro pulled a peevish 'what's it look like?' face.

'Can I have a word?' shouted April, tugging at Caro's arm.

'What?' said Caro as she got to her feet, a little unsteadily. 'I'm in here.'

April led her into a booth where it was a little quieter and they wouldn't be overlooked or overheard. She was incensed that Caro would agree to come to the club.

'What are you doing here with Davina?' she hissed into Caro's ear. 'It's my father's wake!'

'Oh, climb down off your high horse,' snapped Caro. Her eyes were glassy and her face flushed; she had clearly drunk more than a few cocktails. 'You disappeared without telling anyone where you were going. Were we all supposed to sit around wringing our hands?'

April felt her face flush with anger and hurt. 'I texted you to say I needed to get away and my phone was on the whole time,' she snapped. 'You could have called and asked, couldn't you?'

'Oh yeah, and what would Little Miss Sunshine have said?'

'Oh, sorry for being a killjoy on the day I buried my father!' shouted April. 'I just thought that today, of all days, you might be a bit more supportive. This is really, really tough for me.'

'Oh yes? And have you ever considered what I've been going through the last few weeks? No, it's all been about you, hasn't it?'

'What have *you* been going through?' she asked incredulously.

'Oh, forget it,' said Caro, turning away.

'No, tell me,' insisted April, really angry now. 'What is this terrible thing?'

Caro glared at her. 'You really don't know, do you? Jesus ...'

April grabbed her arm and shook her. 'What? Tell me?'

Caro pushed her away and held up her hands in front of April's face.

'Blood!' she yelled. 'Blood on my hands, all over me. Yes, he was your dad, and no, I can't imagine how much that hurts, but I was there too, April. I saw him die too!'

April saw Caro's hands begin to tremble, then watched fat tears run down her cheeks.

'I've been scrubbing and scrubbing, but I can't seem to get it off,' she continued, her voice cracking. 'And who can I talk to about it? You don't answer your phone. And everyone else is like: "Oh, how's April? How's she coping?" Well, what about me? How am *I* coping?'

April felt as if someone had slapped her. She had been so wrapped up in her own grief that it hadn't even crossed her mind. Caro had been there, just behind her, trying to pull her away from her dad. She must have seen everything over her shoulder. She reached out to her friend.

'I'm sorry—'

Caro shrugged her off. 'Don't,' she said. 'I *know* it's shitty for you right now, I *know* it's worse for you, but I reserve the right to get blind drunk and be kissed by some complete stranger once in a while, okay?'

April nodded. 'I wasn't thinking. I'm sorry. Really, I am.'

Caro gave her a twisted smile and wiped her face. 'Yeah, well, I'm sorry too.'

As she watched Caro go back to her floppy-haired boy, April couldn't remember a time when she had felt more wretched. Caro was right, of course. Losing her father had been devastating. Her life had changed in the most shattering, absolute and irreversible way, and right now she wasn't sure if she would ever get over it. But that didn't mean she should ignore her friends – and they were good friends. She looked around the VIP area. Fiona was sitting next to a guy who could easily have passed for a male model and seemed deep in earnest conversation with him. Gabriel was over on the other side of the room laughing with Benjamin, Marcus and a group of people she recognised vaguely from the Halloween party. *Which of these people are vampires?* wondered April. *And which of them are being recruited? Are my friends under their influence already?* To the casual observer, it was just a plush room in a nightclub, filled with pretty young things having the time of their lives, but now she knew better, it all looked seedy and sinister. Maybe if she could sneak her phone out and snap off a few shots, she would have her answer, but she couldn't forget what Gabriel had said to her: *'If you give them the slightest idea that you know who they are and what they are doing, they will bathe in your blood.'*

335

'You okay, honey?' April turned to see Fiona standing there, nervously stirring her drink with a straw. April took her arm and turned her away, so no one else could see their faces.

'No, I am not okay,' she said. 'I've just given Caro a hard time when I shouldn't have, so on top of everything else I feel like a terrible friend.'

'Why did you give her a hard time?'

'I got home to find the place deserted. I thought you'd all been murdered.'

Fiona laughed. 'No, Davina just thought it would be fun ...' Then she stopped. 'Oh, God, I can see why you might think that,' she said, covering her mouth with her hand.

April glanced around. 'So you know, then?' she whispered.

'Know what?'

'About the, you know, *vampires*.'

Fiona frowned and sucked on her straw. 'What? No – what vampires?' she said, clearly confused. 'No, I meant coming home to the place where your dad was, well, *you know* ...' She pulled a face. 'And then finding us all gone and your mum too, you could have jumped to any conclusion. I'm sorry, we should have waited for you, but Benjamin was so persuasive, he said it was the best thing to do and that Gabriel could bring you along later if you felt up to it.'

Damn, they are good, thought April, taking another gulp of her drink. 'What excuse did you give my mum anyway?' she asked Fiona.

'That Gabriel was taking you for a walk, she seemed to buy it, but then she's pretty cool isn't she? I mean, not many mums would come out with their daughter's friends, especially not on a day like today.'

'What?' said April. 'Are you saying my mum's here?'

Fiona watched as April looked around her wildly.

'Oh, I thought you knew.'

'No, I didn't bloody know!' she snapped, then strode off as she suddenly recognised the blonde woman talking with Davina.

'Mum!' she shouted, grabbing Silvia's arm and spinning her around. 'What the bloody hell are you doing here?'

'Oh hi, darling,' said Silvia, her words slurring. 'Just came for a little after-show party, glad you found us.'

'We've only just buried Dad!' shouted April. 'How could you?'

'It's only one little drink and, anyway, Davina said something very true.'

'Davina said … ?' April repeated, glaring at Davina.

'No, listen,' said Silvia, wagging a finger at her, her eyes glassy. 'Davina said that your dad would want us to have a good time today, to celebrate his life, because he was such a special guy, and you know what? He *was* a special guy. So I thought this would be a better way to remember him than sitting around in that house with a load of cousins and uncles who never liked him anyway.'

'You're pathetic!' shouted April, then stopped, hit with the sudden terrible realisation of what she had said. Those were the very same words she had shouted at her father the morning he was killed.

'Come on,' she said, taking her mother's hand and hauling her to her feet. 'We're going home.'

Silvia staggered dangerously, but caught herself just in time. 'You know, I think you're right, I don't feel too well actually.'

'Are you okay here? Need a hand?' Benjamin had come over, Gabriel just behind him.

'No, I think we've got it. Fee? Can you take her other side?' The two girls propped Silvia up between them and moved towards the exit.

'Here, I'll clear the way,' said Gabriel.

Remembering Gabriel's instructions, April turned back to Davina.

'Sorry about this,' she said. 'It was a nice idea, but …'

'Oh, I totally understand,' said Davina, doing her pout again. 'It's been a long, difficult day for you. See you in school, yeah?'

April forced herself to smile.

337

Outside in the blessedly cold air, they flagged a cab and bundled a now-senseless Silvia into the back seat. When Fiona was safely inside and out of earshot, April turned to Gabriel.

'Now get back in there and look after Caro. I don't want to hear she's been bitten, okay?'

Gabriel smiled. 'Whatever you say.'

'And be at my house tomorrow morning, eight sharp. We need to talk, okay?'

'But tomorrow's Wednesday, aren't we going to school?'

'I'm in mourning so I've got the day off school and I'm pretty sure skipping a few lessons won't harm your education.'

'Okay.' Gabriel grinned, and then suddenly leant over and kissed April on the cheek.

'Oh,' she said, touching the spot where his lips had brushed against her.

Gabriel laughed. In a daze, April turned and climbed inside the cab. Then she turned back and pulled down the window.

'Hey! You'd better show up this time,' she called, as the taxi pulled away, 'or you'll wish you *were* dead.'

Chapter Thirty-One

The doorbell rang at one minute to eight. April and Fiona had been sitting at the breakfast bar discussing the events of the previous day and picking at a couple of croissants Fiona had magicked from the oven. She had been up and about amazingly early, humming a tune and happily tidying away the wreckage downstairs; the kitchen surfaces gleamed. April had always been amazed – not to mention annoyed – by Fiona's powers of recovery. *And when did she become a domestic goddess?* she thought. *Is this part of the recruitment process?* April felt terrible for suspecting her best friend of having been seduced by vampires, but she had begun to find paranoia a useful tool; it was better to suspect everyone than wake up in a pool of blood. Fiona *had* been awfully pally with Davina and Benjamin the previous day. April had originally planned to discuss everything Gabriel had told her with Caro and Fiona, but now she wasn't so sure it was such a good idea. She wasn't sure about anything any more.

The doorbell rang again, more insistently this time.

'Oh God, he's early, he's here,' said April, leaping up and immediately regretting it as her knee complained. Even so, she straightened her skirt. 'How do I look?'

'You look amazing,' said Fiona. 'Now calm down, he's only a boy and if he's early he must be keen.'

Yeah, right, thought April as she walked to the door. *Come on, April, don't lose it*, she scolded herself. She reached up and opened the door.

'On time for once ...' she began, then stopped.

It wasn't Gabriel. It was DI Ian Reece and DS Amy Carling. Her heart dropped.

'Expecting someone?' said Carling with a nasty smile.

'Oh, no, well, just a friend,' stammered April before recovering herself. 'What's going on?' she asked, looking at DI Reece. 'Has something happened?'

'Nothing to worry about,' said Reece. 'I just wanted to have a word before school. Could we come in?'

April glanced over her shoulder. 'Well, it's not exactly the best time. What with the funeral yesterday and everything.'

'It won't take a minute, then we'll get out of your hair,' said Reece with a winning smile.

'All right,' she said, quickly scanning the square behind them for any sign of Gabriel. The last thing she wanted was for the police to start asking questions about their relationship, especially as she wasn't entirely clear on it herself. She opened the door and showed them into the living room. 'I can't be too long,' she said nervously as they sat down.

'I quite understand,' said Reece. 'Do you want to call your mum in?'

April shook her head. She wanted to get this over with as quickly as possible and dreaded to think how a badly hungover Silvia would react to being woken at this time of the morning, especially by a man she had threatened the last time she had seen him.

'No, that's not necessary,' she said.

'Okay,' said Reece. 'Now, first of all, I was rather concerned about your phone call last night, April. What happened there?'

April could feel herself blushing. 'Oh, sorry about that,' she said, 'I was a little upset. I thought someone was following me, but I was ... well, I was wrong.'

'But what were you doing in the centre of London, love?' asked Carling.

Don't 'love' me, you cow, thought April. The friendly older sister routine didn't ring true with the policewoman's personality and demeanour. In fact, April seriously doubted she had any friends.

340

'I, well, I suppose I ran away,' said April. 'The wake was full of all these people I didn't know and they were all talking about Dad as if they knew him better than I did. I just wanted to go somewhere where I remembered him being happy.'

'And where was that?' asked Reece.

'The patisserie in Covent Garden near my grandpa's house.'

Carling flipped open her notebook.

'And did you go in?' Reece asked.

'No. When I got there, I realised I didn't have any money,' said April. 'Listen, what's all this about? Have you learnt something new? What's going on?'

Reece and Carling exchanged a look.

'We tracked your phone call that night,' he said. 'You can be pretty accurate in the centre of a city, so we have a fair idea of where you were.'

April didn't say anything, so Reece continued, 'There was a violent incident near Covent Garden last night. I can't say too much, but there were details about it that are very similar to the cases in Highgate.'

'Like what?' asked April.

Reece shook his head. 'I'm afraid I can't tell you that at this stage.'

'Why not? Don't I—' began April, but DS Carling cut her off.

'Can you tell us exactly where you were?'

April looked down. 'Not really. As I said, I thought I was being chased, so I wasn't really looking where I was going.'

'Who did you think was chasing you, April?' asked Reece.

'I don't know.' She glanced up at him. 'The killer, I suppose.'

Carling eyed her sceptically. 'April? Did you see anything?'

'No, no I didn't,' said April, a little too quickly, feeling her stomach turn over. 'What happened? Was someone killed?'

Reece paused. 'I'm afraid so,' he said. 'It was pretty nasty.'

April put her hand over her mouth. 'Oh no,' she gasped.

DS Carling looked at her closely. 'What's the matter, April?' she asked. 'Do you know something about it?'

341

April closed her eyes and shook her head. 'No, nothing.'

But you do! her mind screamed. *You do! You were there!* That much was true, but beyond that, April really couldn't tell them anything. Did Gabriel kill those men? She had been sure they were still alive when she ran off. *But you didn't see what he did when you were running up the steps, did you?* mocked her mind. *Face it, he's a vampire – who knows what they'll do when your back's turned?* But why would he kill them? They were no threat to April by then, and what of Gabriel's line about vampires from the night before: *'Why kill them? What would be in it for them?'* Yes, when you applied logic to the problem, it seemed unlikely, but that was assuming vampires behaved logically. Weren't they bloodthirsty monsters?

Reece sat forwards and touched April's knee. She winced.

'What's the matter, April?'

April looked at him, anger sparking in her eyes. 'What's the matter?' she snapped. 'My dad was killed about six feet from where you're sitting – do you really have to ask? You told me that serial killers are rare, but here it is, happening right in front of me, in my house, following me around. I can't seem to get away from it.' She looked up at Reece, her eyes glistening. 'Do you think it's my fault?'

Reece returned her gaze for a long moment. 'No, April, it's not your fault,' he said seriously, standing up. 'Unfortunately, this sort of thing does happen. It's not pleasant, but it happens. And London's a very big place with a lot of people in it. I know it might feel as if it's following you around, but it's not. Sometimes these things are entirely random.'

'But what happened, DI Reece?' she said. 'I mean, don't you have CCTV footage or something?'

Again, the two police officers glanced at each other.

'Yes,' Reece said, 'but it's inconclusive. The incident happened in a tunnel near Covent Garden. Sadly, it doesn't have cameras. We have footage of you running from Trafalgar Square and then ...'

'What?'

Reece shrugged. 'It's probably nothing. We have a fairly

clear shot of you running into an alleyway as if someone is chasing you, but there's no one behind you.'

April frowned, feeling a horrible clench in her stomach.

'No one?' she whispered. 'No one at all?'

Reece frowned. 'No. Did you think there would be?'

April shook her head. 'Like I said, I thought someone was following me, but I guess I was just imagining it.'

'Exactly. So don't worry about it, it's probably just coincidence. There's a lot of it about.'

April did her best to smile at the policeman. She knew Reece was trying to be nice, but he didn't know the truth. He didn't know that Gabriel was there, he didn't know he might have killed those men in cold blood. And he certainly wouldn't have believed her if she had told him the rest of the things she knew about Gabriel Swift. April stood up and showed the officers to the door. She was just closing it behind them when she had another thought.

'DI Reece?' she called, just as he reached the gate. 'Can I ask you something?'

Reece glanced at her, then turned to Carling and told her he would meet her in the car.

'Why did you say "it's probably nothing"?' asked April when the other officer was out of earshot. 'You know, about the CCTV footage.'

Reece pulled a face. 'Oh, that. Nothing to worry about, probably just a fault with the camera.'

'But what was it? *Was* I being followed?'

Reece shook his head. 'No, it's just a shadow on the film, nothing more,' he said, and tried to laugh, but it sounded hollow. April could tell something was bothering him.

'Please, DI Reece,' said April. 'You're starting to worry me.'

The policeman looked at her for a moment, then sighed. 'Okay, just after you run into the alley, something else passes across the alleyway, like a thick shadow. For a while I thought it might be someone following you, but our tech boys assure me they can see the wall through it, so it's probably just a fault on the disk or something. I really shouldn't have mentioned it. Now, try not to worry,' said Reece. 'I promise you, we'll get to the bottom of all this.'

Not before I do, thought April as she closed the door.

Chapter Thirty-Two

April was trying her best to be brave, but it was breaking her heart to see Fiona load her suitcase into the taxi. It had been wonderful to have her to stay, even if she had spent most of her visit talking about vampires and notebooks and impossible goings-on, but it was still term-time and Fiona's parents wanted her to get back. April was glad they had let her come at all; she knew she wouldn't have got through the funeral without her; it was like having a piece of her old, sane life to lean on, one last scrap of normality to cling to, but now April knew she had to let her go. Much as she hated to admit it to herself, April Dunne had become a jinx. More than that: people around her were dying, and after last night, she couldn't risk the vampires getting any closer to Fiona. She couldn't lose her too. Not ever.

'Do you really want me to go?' said Fiona, pulling April in for a hug.

'I wish you could stay honey, I really do,' replied April, 'but I can't hang on to you for ever. I've got to start doing things on my own now. And anyway, you've a first-class ticket – you don't want to miss out on that free pastry, do you?'

Fiona smiled and hugged her friend tight. 'You call me every day, okay?'

'Are you kidding?' said April. 'I'll be on the phone every hour!'

She wanted to say more, but she was afraid if she did she would burst into tears again.

'You be safe now,' said Fiona. 'Seriously, it's dangerous around here. No running into haunted houses without at least one good torch.'

April giggled, but Fiona's expression turned serious.

'And watch yourself with Gabriel, okay?' she said, lowering her voice. 'I know he's gorgeous and everything, but he's still a boy and they're only after one thing. All right?'

April felt a flare of excitement at Gabriel's name, which was immediately quenched by the memory of her conversation with the police.

'I'll be careful,' said April as Fee got into the taxi. 'I promise.'

And then Fiona was gone, waving from the back of the cab as it turned the corner and disappeared out of sight. April stood in the road, staring at the place where her best friend had been standing. Now her last anchor to her old life was gone and she was left drifting in this bizarre fantasy world of beasts and bats. She didn't know what to do.

She felt a buzz in her pocket and pulled out her phone: one text message – Fee. She clicked it up and there were just two words: *Be Strong.*

April smiled. It was good advice; she only hoped she could follow it. She was just turning to go back inside when she saw him. Gabriel was standing across the road, looking at her, just like on that first night.

April looked quickly around the square. She didn't want the police to see him.

'Come inside,' she said. She led him in through the front door and into the living room, shutting the door. She turned and stared at him, anger making her shake.

'Gabriel, if I ask you a straight question, can you give me a straight answer for once?'

'Of course,' he said.

'What did you do to those men who were hassling me last night?'

He looked away. 'I did what I had to.'

'A straight answer, Gabriel!' she said.

He stared back her. His eyes were fierce. 'What do you want me to say, April? That I tore off their heads and drank their blood? Is that what you think of me?'

'Did you kill them?' she shouted. 'Tell me!'

'NO!' said Gabriel in surprise. 'Of course not! What on earth makes you think I would do such a thing?'

'What on earth?' mocked April. 'Just your being some sort of bloodthirsty creature of the night.'

'I'm not a *creature*!' he yelled, anger making his pale cheeks flush. 'And I did not kill those men.' He grabbed her arms and looked into her eyes. 'On everything I hold dear,' he said in an even, measured tone, 'and on everything *you* hold dear, I swear to you, I did not kill them.'

His gaze was so strong, so intense, April felt her heart pounding. She looked into his dark eyes and she saw no malice, no evil there. He was so genuine, so earnest, she knew in her heart he was telling the truth.

'Oh God, I'm sorry,' she whispered. 'After last night, I so wanted to believe you, but it's so hard. And then the police came this morning and told me those men were killed.'

Gabriel's face softened and he pulled her closer. 'I know, I know it's hard,' he said. 'But I need you to believe in me because …' He broke off and turned away.

'Why? What is it?'

'Because … you're important to me, April—' He stopped and took a deep breath. 'I want to walk away, but I can't help myself, I haven't felt this—'

'APRIL!'

It was her mother's voice.

'Oh crap,' said April and ran to the bottom of the stairs.

'What's all that shouting?' snapped her mother. 'I'm trying to get some sleep here.'

'Sorry, we were just … I'll keep it down.'

'Don't make me come down there,' said Silvia, shuffling back into her room.

April took a deep breath and walked back into the living room.

'Okay, so who did kill them?' she asked.

Gabriel looked at her warily. 'Is that what the police were here about?'

347

'Yes, they said the details were similar to the murders in Highgate.'

Gabriel frowned, thinking. 'Someone else must have been following you,' he said, almost to himself. 'Someone I didn't see.'

'What? You mean another vampire?' said April, a cold feeling coming over her.

'Yes. If the murders are similar then it must have been. I was worried this might happen.'

'Worried about what, exactly?' she said. She was scared now. 'Is someone trying to kill me too?'

'I don't know,' said Gabriel.

She grabbed his arm. 'Tell me! I need to know!'

He carefully took her hand from his arm, but kept hold of it. 'I don't know, April. That's the truth,' he added in response to her disbelieving expression. 'But what I do know is that something's going on here, something bad. The vampire clans have almost always been at war, but this is something different, something new.'

'So what's going on?'

He looked at her. 'We have rules. And someone is breaking them.'

April snorted. 'Vampires have rules?' she said sceptically.

'I know it sounds insane,' he said, 'but over the centuries, we have found that they keep us hidden, and for vampires remaining hidden is everything.'

She pulled a face. 'So what are these rules?'

He looked away. 'You won't like it.'

'Big surprise.'

'No children, no families, no one famous, never more than one kill per moon – per month. All these things draw attention. All the deaths in Highgate break the rules.'

'So what does that mean?'

Gabriel shook his head. 'Either the whole ceasefire is breaking down, maybe the Regent is orchestrating these attacks, perhaps both. And there's another possibility – that it's a rogue vampire acting on their own.'

'But why would they do that? What about the hunting thing? I mean, why attract so much attention?'

Gabriel shrugged. 'Maybe they're not in control of their urges, or they're killing for the sheer pleasure of it. Or perhaps they have a plan of their own, because they feel threatened in some way.'

'And if that vampire killed my dad ...'

Gabriel looked grave. 'That's what worries me. If a rogue vampire thought your dad was a threat, he could see you as a threat, too.'

April sat down hard. As if she didn't have enough on her mind without a killer stalking her.

'But how does the thing in Covent Garden link in?'

'He was obviously following you, waiting until you were alone.'

'No, I mean why is that against the rules?'

'Never kill more than one at a time. And never before midnight.'

April laughed nervously. 'Before midnight? Now that does sound like something from the movies.'

'No, it makes sense. After midnight people are more likely to be on their own, there are less likely to be witnesses, and you'd be surprised how few police are on duty.'

'Is that why parents always tell us to be home by midnight?'

Gabriel smiled grimly. 'Always be home by midnight, April,' he said. 'That's one of the few vampire myths that is true.'

'Or *was* true.'

'Exactly.'

Chapter Thirty-Three

'Okay, so you're telling me that garlic is useless?'

April was sitting in the kitchen getting a crash course in the finer points of vampire lore.

'Not if you're talking about pasta sauce,' said Gabriel. 'But if you're talking about killing a vampire, then yes.'

'So where did the garlic thing come from then? Why not parsley or coriander or something?'

'It's because garlic was used in medicine – it's like an ancient antibiotic that could "magically" cure people. If left untreated, some diseases can give you delusions, so administering garlic became seen as a way to drive out demons.' He saw April's raised eyebrow. 'Hey, I'm in the business, I know these things.'

'Holy water?'

'Nope,' said Gabriel. 'And we can go into churches too.'

'Sunlight?'

'There's a degree of truth to that. We can go out in the sun but we don't like it much, it irritates our skin, hurts our eyes. That's why some days we don't go into school – we don't want to be sitting in the refectory in direct sunlight. That's why vampires love nightlife and hate early mornings. We prefer the night and winter in the same way bleeders – sorry, humans – prefer the sunshine.'

April put up a hand. 'Wait, you call us "bleeders"?' she said incredulously, feeling both insulted and disturbed that vampires could talk about people as if they were just livestock.

'Sorry,' said Gabriel.

'Okay, so what about crossed candlesticks?'

'Now that's just silly, and so is the thing about not being seen in mirrors. We'd never be able to walk around a town centre for fear of walking under scaffolding or being reflected in a shop window.'

'So why does everyone believe it?'

'Because we want you to. All those myths were started by vampires.'

'What? Why?'

'It's simple, really. If anyone ever started to suspect someone was a vampire, all they had to do was turn up during the day, or eat some garlic or something. It's just another way to stay hidden.'

April paused for a moment, trying to take it all in. 'But if you're so good at hiding, can you spot another vampire?'

A troubled look crossed Gabriel's face. 'It depends. Turned vampires – the ones who have been turned by a bite, like I was – are easy to spot: they're too perfect. I mean, seriously, how often have you seen a teenager without spots? But true vampires are much trickier.'

'What's a true vampire?'

'The offspring of two vampires. They're much more power-ful because they've always been this way, it's a natural part of them. Manipulation and ruthlessness come effortlessly, they can kill without a second thought. Plus their powers of recov-ery are much greater, so it's almost impossible to kill them.'

'But why are they "true" vampires?'

Gabriel pulled a sour face.

'Arrogance. They believe they're pure-bred, superior to both humans and turned vampires; the ultimate predator at the top of the food chain.'

April shivered. 'How do you spot a turned vampire then?'

'Like I said, we're hunters, so our eyesight, hearing and sense of smell are much better than humans'. A true vampire looks and smells the same as a bleeder, but I would be able to smell a turned vampire.'

'Why? What do they smell of?'

'Death.'

'I shouldn't have asked.'

April looked down at her hands, trying to make her next question sound as casual as possible, but feeling butterflies in her stomach as she spoke. 'So what about feeding? What about blood?' she asked, torn between a morbid fascination and a flaming jealousy at the thought Gabriel licking some other girl's pretty neck. Gabriel seemed to pick up on her thoughts and grimaced.

'You're really not going to like this part,' he said softly.

'Try me.'

'Well, we can eat – our heightened senses of smell and taste make excellent food one of our great pleasures. But blood? We have to feed on human blood at least once a week, otherwise we start to get sick.'

Gabriel was right, April didn't like it, not one bit. She thought of Ling weeping in the toilets, blood seeping from her wrist, and felt her anger rise again.

'Who are you feeding from?' she asked tersely, unable to disguise the distaste in her voice.

'Feeders. People who allow us to drink a little of their blood. We don't need much.'

April put her hands around her throat. 'Don't even think about it,' she said.

'I wouldn't dare to presume,' he said with a smile. 'But seriously, that's part of the reason for the recruitment at Ravenwood – they have more humans to feed from and the more a vampire feeds, the stronger they will become.'

April took a deep breath. She hated what he was telling her, but knew there was no point in getting worked up; it was the way he was, he had to feed. And she knew she had to focus on what they could change, how she could help stop more innocent people becoming victims.

'So how can we stop them? A stake through the heart?'

'Yes, that would work. One of the few things the movies get right. Vampires can be killed by destruction of the body – of anything you can't do without, basically. So a pierced heart, suffocation or drowning, crushing of the body, decapitation, burning, anything serious like that, but smaller wounds can be regenerated and healed pretty quickly. As you saw last night.'

Gabriel pulled up his top to show her the wound. It was red and raised, but it was almost healed. April looked up into Gabriel's eyes and couldn't believe she had been so frightened of this boy that she had stabbed him. He was so beautiful and kind and gentle and ... she reached out and touched the wound, her fingers lingering on his skin.

'I'm sorry, Gabriel,' she said softly.

'April,' he whispered, placing his hand over hers and moving towards her. But suddenly, almost involuntarily, April pulled back.

'I ... I'd better go and check on my mum,' she said quickly and grabbed the door handle.

What are you doing? she thought furiously as she ran up the stairs. *He's totally hot and you had your hand on his skin and now you're running away?*

Cursing herself, she stuck her head around the door of her mother's room.

'Mmm, darling?' moaned Silvia, turning over sleepily. 'Is that you?'

'Yes, Mum,' she said.

'Could you be an angel and pass me my pills? Got a splitting headache.'

Sighing, April did as she was told.

'Thank you, sweetie,' murmured Silvia as she pulled the duvet over her head. 'And could you turn the TV down? I keep hearing voices.'

'Yes, Mum.'

She gently closed the door and padded back downstairs. She found Gabriel sitting on the sofa in the living room, a book on his knee.

'Sorry, I hope you don't mind,' he said, holding up the cover which read: *Beneath The Dark Waves: The Loch Ness Monster Mystery*.

'One of my dad's,' said April proudly.

'Looks pretty good,' he said. 'I was just reading that there is more water in Loch Ness than all the lakes in England, Scotland and Wales put together. Twenty-two miles long, one and a half miles wide. That's a hell of a hiding place.'

'My dad didn't find Nessie,' said April, sitting down next to him and peering at the photos, 'but we had a nice holiday up there. I remember there being an ice-cream van permanently parked outside our cottage, but that might be rose-tinted spectacles.'

Gabriel looked across at her. 'I wish I'd met your dad,' he said softly. 'But I promise you I will do everything in my power to find out who murdered him.'

April could only nod. 'I miss him,' she said finally.

'Why don't you tell me about him?'

April looked away. 'Nah ...'

'Come on, I'm serious,' he said. 'Tell me about Scotland.'

'Okay,' she said, secretly glad to be talking about happy times. She leant back against the sofa head-rest and began to tell stories, her fondest memories. The time on holiday in Skye, when they had found a boat washed up on the shore and he'd lifted her up to get inside and find pirate treasure but all they found were old nets. Or the time he'd tried to teach her to fish and she'd fallen over and got her wellies full of frogspawn. And the birthdays and the pantomimes and the bike rides. And as she talked, she felt safer and more relaxed than she'd felt in weeks, maybe years. She slid slowly down the sofa until she was resting her head on his shoulder and it felt good, it felt right. Gabriel slowly, gently began to stroke her hair, pushing it back behind her ears, and April felt a warm tingle spread all the way through her. *Kiss me*, she urged, closing her eyes, *for God's sake, kiss me.*

Suddenly Gabriel jumped in the air, hissing, as April's head fell back against the sofa cushion.

'What's the matter?' she said urgently, sitting up and looking at him. His face was a mixture of shock, fear and something else. *Revulsion*, that was it. April's heart was hammering in her chest. *Am I that horrible?*

'What is it? What have I done?' she asked.

Gabriel ran his hands through his hair in an agitated manner and paced around in a circle.

'Gabriel! What's going on? Tell me.'

He shook his head.

'What is it?'

He looked at her and there was a new expression there: pity. 'I shouldn't be the one to tell you,' he said.

'What? Tell me what?'

April's heart was pounding now because she had recognised the expression on Gabriel's face: it was the one her mother and her grandfather always had when they were talking about her family heritage, the face they pulled when it was obvious they had something they wanted to tell her but could not quite bring themselves to utter. Her stomach was on a spin-cycle now. What if all this wasn't about vampires at all? What if it was about *her*?

'Please, Gabriel,' she said, desperate now. 'What's wrong with me?'

He stepped over and took her hands in his. 'Okay, April, try not to freak – promise?'

'You're not making that easy,' she said, her voice shaking.

He nodded and took a deep breath. 'You have the mark.'

April put her hand to her face. 'What mark, where?' She jumped up and peered in the mirror above the mantelpiece. 'I don't see anything.'

Gabriel came up behind her and gently pulled the hair back from her neck. 'It's here, just inside the hairline, level with the top of your ear, do you see?'

April peered closer. *There was something.*

'What is it? A birthmark?'

Gabriel nodded and touched the brown mark. 'It's the north star, the sign of the regeneration, the bringer of light.'

She squinted. It looked more like an ink blot than a star to her, but she could see from Gabriel's face it was important. He looked stricken and hurt, like someone had just diagnosed her with cancer. She was getting really scared now.

'Does this mean something? Am I ill? And don't start with that "it's complicated" rubbish again.'

Gabriel shook his head. 'Okay,' he said, gathering himself. 'I know this sounds crazy, but it's a part of vampire lore. I suspected something when I heard about Milo, but now ...' He looked at her. 'But now I can see it's true.'

'You can see what?' shouted April. 'You're freaking me out, Gabriel, just tell me!'

'You're a Fury. You're the last of the Furies.'

She gulped at the air. It was as if someone had turned the heating way up.

'What the hell are the Furies?' she asked, her mouth dry.

'Vampire killers.'

'What? This is a joke, right?'

Gabriel put his hands on her shoulders. 'I wish it were, believe me, I do,' he said, leading her back to the sofa. He sat down next to her, keeping hold of her hand. She was grateful for his touch, but she didn't feel the warmth she had before.

'I'm not an expert on vampire lore and even if I was, many people think the Furies are a myth, a sort of bogeyman for vampire children. The Furies are supposed to be three females, all born within a generation, each with the power to destroy all vampires. Some think the Furies are a prophecy, a sort of mythological scourge, a sign that the vampires will be wiped from the earth. I think it's more like a genetic anomaly, almost like nature's counterbalance to the vampires.'

April's heart was still beating through her T-shirt, but Gabriel's touch and the feel of his thumb stroking the back of her hand were calming her slightly.

'I don't understand,' she said, trying to stop her voice from shaking. 'What have I got to do with vampires?'

'All right, I'll do my best to explain,' said Gabriel. 'Think of vampires as just being victims of a disease, a weird virus that has infected our systems. We're sort of suspended in a half-life state. We should have died, but the virus is keeping us here, halfway between life and death.'

April nodded. 'Okay, with you so far.'

'Well, you're the cure, the antidote.'

'I can cure you?' she said, reaching out for him. She was dismayed to see him flinch back.

'Sorry,' he said. 'I wish you could. No, Furies carry another virus in their systems that neutralises the regeneration mechanism in vampires. Once they get your virus, the disease is able to take its course and ...' He shrugged.

'What? What happens?'

'It eats them alive.'

April's hand flew to her mouth. 'Oh God! And you think that's what happened to Milo? You think I killed him?'

Gabriel nodded. 'The virus must have got into his body when you kissed him.'

'Oh no, oh no, oh no ...' moaned April covering her face with her hands. 'What have I done?'

'Don't feel sorry for that animal,' said Gabriel fiercely. 'You have no idea what he's done to girls like you over the years. He deserves everything he gets.'

'Don't talk that way!' shouted April. 'It's all right for you, you're not the one who killed him! I'm a killer, a murderer.'

Gabriel grabbed her shoulders and stared into her eyes. 'No, April, you are not a murderer. Milo is still in hospital, remember? He's still alive. And anyway, you didn't know what you were doing, you had no idea you could hurt him. You didn't make that choice, you're a good person.'

'Am I?' she said bitterly. 'So what about this?' She pointed to the birthmark behind her ear. 'You didn't exactly jump for joy when you saw that. You looked at me like I was carrying the plague.'

'April ...'

She shook her head. 'You know what I thought when you were stroking my hair?' She barked out a brittle laugh. 'I thought you were going to kiss me.'

Gabriel tried to hold her gaze, but finally looked away. 'I'm sorry,' he said, shaking his head.

She stood up and walked over to the door, holding it open. 'Get out.'

'What?'

'You heard me,' said April. 'You told me you cared for me, but all you cared about was finding out whether I had this weird bloody thing,' she said, gesturing towards her ear. 'You only asked about my dad so you could get close enough to look. How do you think that makes me feel?'

'But don't you see?' says Gabriel. 'You can't ignore this. If the vampires ever find out who you are, they will try to kill you. You have no choice, you have to fight, it's the prophecy.'

'Oh no,' said April, pointing her finger at him. 'No you don't. I'm not carrying out any bloody prophecy. I've got A levels to do.'

'But April, please—'

'No,' she said, handing him his coat and pushing him towards the front door. 'I'm not interested.'

As she hurried him out, he turned back and said in a low, urgent voice, 'April, whether you like it or not, you have a destiny.'

'I don't want a destiny!' she snapped back. 'I want a boyfriend!'

And she slammed the door.

Chapter Thirty-Four

Books were everywhere. Stacked on the dining table, in piles on the floor, even thrown higgledy-piggledy on the sofa. April stood on a chair and, reaching up, ran her hand along the bare shelves. *Where are they?* There had to be more. As soon as she had thrown Gabriel out, she had got to work, trying to find her father's notes; he must have hidden them somewhere and now more than ever she needed answers. She jumped down and grabbed another of her father's books, *Burning Desire*, a history of witches during the English Inquisition. Holding it by its spine, she shook it and riffled the pages, hoping for some notes or papers to fall out. *Nothing.* The boxes of papers the police had returned were, as DI Reece had suggested, pretty much useless, consisting of old research from previous books and articles, and some bland research stuff about medicine in the nineteenth century. The thin blue notebook she had found under the desk was too cryptic, too personal to make head or tail of. The lack of notes just didn't make any sense. Her father was good at what he did, he was dogged and thorough – you didn't get to be a top investigative reporter without being that way. So where were his notes on vampires? She desperately needed to find out more – about the vampires, the Regent, his investigation into Ravenwood – but right now, she wanted to know about herself. Was she a Fury? Was everything Gabriel had told her true? Could she really have killed Milo just by kissing him? And what was this destiny Gabriel was talking about? Whatever the answers were, April hadn't found them in the books. She had been hoping to find something slipped between hardbacks or at the back of a drawer, but she found nothing except the odd piece of paper used as a bookmark.

'Having a bit of a tidy-up, darling?'

She turned to see her mother, sleep mask on the top of her head, duvet wrapped around her, standing in the doorway. She looked terrible; grey skin, sunken eyes, even her lips looked thin and a little blue.

'Yes, I wanted to sort it all out. Things got a bit mixed up after the … you know, the struggle.'

Her mother just stared into space, as if she hadn't heard the answer.

'Mmm?' she said at length. 'Sorry, miles away. Not feeling too good today, I'm afraid.'

'Look, why don't you go back to bed?' said April. 'I'll bring you up a Lemsip.'

'Thanks, sweetie,' said Silvia, nodding slowly. 'You're a good girl.'

'Oh, before you go, Mum? Are these all of our books?'

Silvia blinked and shook her head. 'Your dad did all the packing, darling,' she said vaguely. 'He put a load of boxes in the cellar, though.'

Idiot! April thought, annoyed at herself. *The cellar. Duh!*

She put the kettle on, then nervously approached the cellar door under the stairs. April had never been particularly comfortable in dark enclosed spaces. *Who is?* she thought as she opened the door and craned her neck to peer down the stairs. *Spooky and dusty.*

'Where's the light switch, Mum?' she shouted.

'Doesn't work,' came the muffled reply. 'Torch by the step.'

Oh God.

She picked up the heavy orange torch and flicked it on – its beam was pathetically weak for such a big thing. *Be strong*, that's what Fiona had said and she was right, so April gripped the handrail and made her way down, stepping over the boxes that had been left on the stairs. Reaching the bottom step, she could see that the cellar wasn't that big – long and narrow, going back from the foot of the stairs and under the kitchen. There were bare brick walls and a smell of damp, but it was too cramped to be that intimidating; the whole of the floor was covered with stacked boxes. She looked in the first one: books, books and more books. Stuff on politics, stuff on economics, a collection of poetry, a biography of a painter she'd never heard of. The next box was even worse: wodges of paper, everything from a receipt for a lawnmower to a gas bill from 1998. She was never going to find anything in here. Dejected, she climbed back up the stairs, then flinched as she felt something on her skin.

She scrabbled something away from her face. *A spider's web?* April hated spiders.

'Ahhh! It's in my hair,' she cried, frantically brushing it away and dropping the torch in the process. 'Damn,' she muttered and bent to pick it up. And there, reflecting the light back from the weak beam, was an old Quality Street tin sitting on top of a pile of magazines near the top of the stairs. She tucked the torch under her arm and pushed the lid off and there it was, a little green book with one magic word stamped on the cover: 'Diary'. Her heart gave a little leap. Of course: it was the perfect place to put it – accessible, but hidden. She quickly leafed through the book, looking for the day of her father's death. 'Where is it? Where is it?' she muttered impatiently as she ruffled through the pages. And then there it was, with an appointment scribbled halfway down the page.

'Mum!' she shouted, running for the door. 'I'm going out!'

'What about my Lemsip?' came the muffled reply.

But April was already halfway across the square.

April peered through the dirty glass, cupping her hands around her eyes to get a better view.

'Mr Gill!' she shouted, rapping on the window frame with her knuckles. 'Are you there?'

She could see the old man sitting with his head back, his mouth open, presumably snoring, but April couldn't hear anything with the traffic roaring past on the High Street behind her. She knelt down on the steps and shouted through the letter box.

'Mr Gill!'

His head rolled slowly sideways and bumped into the bookshelf behind him.

'What?' he muttered, annoyed at being disturbed. 'What on earth ...?'

'Over here,' hissed April.

'What are you doing down there?' snapped the shopkeeper.

'Trying to get in,' she replied.

'Well, come through the door like everyone else, not the letter box,' he said irritably, rising stiffly and twisting the lock.

'I'm sorry,' said April, brushing down her knees carefully. 'I didn't mean to wake you, but I'm in a hurry.'

'Wake me? I wasn't asleep,' said the old man, patting his pockets for his glasses, then finding them on his nose. 'I was in the middle of an important inventory. Now then, what's all the fuss about?'

April pulled out her father's diary from her pocket and opened it to the relevant page. 'I found this in my dad's diary.' She pointed to an entry on the day of his death. Written in his scrawling handwriting and circled, it read: 'Griffin's, 2.30'.

Mr Gill adjusted his glasses and peered down at the entry. Then he looked up at April.

'Your father, you say? Is he a customer?'

April shook her head. 'Was, I'm afraid. He died a couple of weeks ago.'

'Oh. Sorry to hear that. Was it very sudden? I find at my age, sudden is all you have to look forward to.'

'Quite sudden, yes.'

'Well, I suppose you'd better have a seat and tell me how I can help you.'

April perched on a wooden stool and began to explain to Mr Gill how she was trying to find out what her father had been investigating before his death and how she had found the diary with Griffin's Bookshop listed as his last appointment. She didn't add that she had sprinted across the square the moment she had seen he'd had an appointment on the day of his death.

'Hmm,' said Mr Gill. 'We have been very busy of late, what with Christmas shopping and whatnot, I can't exactly recall who came in that day.'

'But the diary has you written in here as if it was an appointment.'

'An appointment?' he said, tapping his finger against his lips. 'I suppose that's possible. Let me check.'

He opened his brown leather desk jotter and laboriously turned the pages, licking his fingers and tutting until he finally found the correct one and then ran his finger down the entries.

'Yes, a Mr Dunne?' he said, looking up at April.

'Yes! Yes, that's him – what did he buy?'

The old man shook his head slowly. 'No, no, I don't think … no, I'm sure of it.'

'What?' said April impatiently.

'Your father made his appointment by telephone, said he was very keen to find a certain book, but I'm afraid he didn't arrive. I remember distinctly because there was a programme I wanted to listen to on Radio Four and I missed the start of it because I was waiting for him. Something else came up, perhaps? Another engagement?'

'Oh, yes. That's probably it.'

April wanted to cry. She had been sure this was the breakthrough she was looking for, but once again, it was just a dead end.

'Such a shame, really, it's a rather splendid book.'

She looked up. 'What book?'

Mr Gill reached under his desk and brought out a small volume with a faded red cover. April felt her heart flutter.

'This is the one he was interested in – *Folk Myths of the Ottoman Empire*. Very rare. Marvellous condition, though.'

'May I look at it?'

'By all means, please. Would you like to go through to the reading room? I think you know the way.'

April sat down and went straight to the index. *Furies, the, pp. 23-4, 112, 212-34.* Yes! There it was!

She quickly turned to the front of the book and read:

The earliest mention of the Furies comes late in the reign of Suleiman the Magnificent, around 1560, when the empire extended its borders deep into Europe, most notably Hungary, Transylvania and Wallachia. Some scholars believe that, as the vampire folk-myths were so ingrained within this culture, the Ottoman rulers created the Furies as a counter-myth. Others claim that the Fury is a folk-myth corruption of the Old Testament angel imbued with the power to act as the scourge of God. Either way, the story was the same: once every generation, three women will be born with the power to kill vampires, and they will be marked with a star symbol. The Furies' destructive power was variously explained as having the ability to detect vampires at a glance, to defeat them in battle by superior strength or to destroy them by breathing fire on them. Unlike vampires, there are no contemporary sources that claim to have seen a Fury, although there are reports of whole countries having been cleared of vampires by these creatures. Young (cf.) posits the theory that the Furies are either a personification of Muslim rule or of Islam itself – the light of the prophet literally banishing the creatures of the dark – especially as the Fury birthmark so closely resembles the star enclosed by a crescent moon used on the Ottoman flag. The curious thing is that four hundred years of imperial rule failed to completely dispel the rumours of either vampires or their mysterious nemesis.

'Bloody hell,' said April.

Is this me? April thought as she walked back across the square. *Am I really the scourge of the vampires?* She had read every reference to the Furies she could find in the book, but there was little hard information. *It's a book about ancient myths, April,* she reminded herself, *not a DIY manual.* Besides, just because one myth was true, it didn't mean they all were. *Anyway, even if I am this chosen one, it's up to me what I do about it. Not all tall people become basketball players.*

But April knew in her heart of hearts that she couldn't ignore it. The Furies were portrayed as superheroes who had been privileged with the power to overthrow evil. *But I'm not some ancient warrior queen*, she thought to herself. *I'm a sixteen-year-old schoolgirl.* As she closed the front door behind her, April felt small and vulnerable. She didn't want to go to war. She wanted to hang out with her friends and gossip about boys, then come home and have tea. The future of the human race seemed a little too much to bear, especially as she was already struggling with her father's death, a mountain of incomprehensible homework and a sort-of boyfriend who just happened to be a vampire.

'April? Is that you?' came the muffled voice from upstairs.

'Yes, it's me,' she said as she wearily climbed the stairs.

'Davina Osbourne called,' said Silvia as April walked into the bedroom.

'Did she? What about?'

'Oh, I'm sure she just wanted a chat, isn't that what you girls do all night? Anyway, she was very charming and invited you over tomorrow after school. I left the number on the side.'

April's face froze as a dozen thoughts went through her head. Was she being recruited already? Should she go along with it? Her mother saw her expression.

'Is something wrong?'

'I've got a ton of homework, that's all.'

'Don't be silly.' Silvia tutted. 'It's nice to make friends, especially from such a lovely family.'

Like hell they are, thought April.

'It never does any harm to be friends with some influential people. Take it from one who knows.'

Sighing, April trailed upstairs to her room. She dialled Davina's number but it was engaged, so she took out her dad's diary one more time.

If she was honest, April had been gravely disappointed by

both the diary and the notebook. She had, of course, been hoping she would find a name written in one or the other with an arrow pointing to it and the words 'Vampire Regent' in big capital letters. Then she could tell the police and it would all go away. But it wasn't going to happen like that. Even if she had found such a miraculous cast-iron clue, she couldn't tell the police about the vampires because they'd think she was crazy, and the Regent wasn't necessarily her dad's killer anyway. In fact, the diary had been even more obtuse than the notebook. Names were abbreviated to initials, phone numbers were scribbled down without any reference and it was all mixed up with things like 'Pick up dry cleaning', 'Don't forget Russia deadline!' and 'Lunch, Riva, 1.30'. She had to admit it appeared to be a normal everyday diary, the kind any busy journalist might carry around with him. But she kept coming back to the same thing: if it was all so innocent, why hide it? April knew she couldn't rest until she found out the truth about her dad, and it seemed most likely she would only find the answers she wanted by solving the rest of the puzzle and working out who, or what, was behind Ravenwood. Slipping the diary back under the bed, she called Davina again.

'Oh hi, honey, I heard the big news on the grapevine,' she said.

'What news?'

'That you kicked Gabriel out on the street, of course!' she trilled.

'How did you hear about that?' asked April, suddenly very suspicious.

'Oh, I don't know,' said Davina vaguely. 'Gabe poured his heart out to Ben, Ben told Marcus, Marcus told Sara, something like that. The point is you're young free and single, so ...'

'So?'

'So we need to make plans! You're such a hit with the boys that I'm sure we can find you someone gorgeous, especially with the party coming up. There'll be some *very* eligible guys there.'

'What party?'

Davina tutted. 'Daddy's Winter Ball, of course. You *are* coming? You know it's on Saturday?'

'Yes, of course. But—'

'I won't take no for an answer. It's the perfect opportunity to meet some amazing boys and totally take your mind off things.'

Despite the fact that April wanted to be as far away from Davina and her kind as possible, she knew it was also a perfect opportunity to find out more about the circumstances surrounding her father's death. Taking a deep breath, she tried to sound upbeat and excited.

'Well, if you put it like that, how could I miss it?'

'That's settled then. You pop over after school tomorrow and we'll work the whole thing out. Anyway, must fly, got to finish Ling's pedi. I've left her soaking in the foot spa. Ciao!'

'Jesus,' whispered April as she hung up. *Surely that girl can't be a vicious killer?* It was like asking her to believe Paris Hilton was going to invade Poland.

'Darling!' called her mother, interrupting her thoughts. 'Did I hear something about a party?'

Chapter Thirty-Five

Caro wasn't looking too healthy. Her face was white, her eyes red and sunken and she squinted and winced at the morning sunshine.

'You look like death,' said April as she sat down next to her on a bench in the deserted playground where they wouldn't be overheard.

'Well, I feel like death too,' said Caro, putting on a pair of sunglasses and pulling her coat tighter around her body. 'I think I've got a two-day hangover. I couldn't even get out of bed yesterday, had to get my mum to ring the school. What happened in that club anyway? All I remember is a throbbing red room and loads of fit boys in a booth.'

'That must have been after I left,' said April with a smile. 'What boys were these?'

'No, really – there were loads of gorgeous boys all wanting to talk to me and buy me drinks, then the next thing I remember is your Mister-bloody-Darcy turning up, scaring them all off and telling me it's time to go home. I mean, where's the fun in that?'

'Gabriel took you home?' asked April, failing to hide the jealous note in her voice.

'More like a kidnapping, actually, almost got me in a head-lock to drag me out of the club. Then he spent the whole journey home quizzing me about what Ben and Davina had been saying to me. I tell you, considering he's their friend, he doesn't seem to like them much.'

'Well, that's sort of why I dragged you out here. I've got something to tell you about him.'

'Oh God, April,' said Caro. 'You're not—'

'No, I am not pregnant!' said April indignantly. 'I can't believe you'd even think that,' she added in a quieter voice. 'Besides which, I might be naïve, but I do know you have to have sex in order to get pregnant. I've only known him two weeks, Caro!'

'Sorry, brain's not engaged today,' said Caro, waving a hand.

'Well, try,' said April seriously, 'because this is important. I don't know who I can trust any more but I'll go mad if I don't tell someone. So please tell me I can trust you.'

Caro sat up straight and lifted her sunglasses. 'What? Yes, of course,' she said, dismayed. 'Of course you can trust me. Why would you even ask that?'

April shrugged sheepishly. 'Well, you looked as if you were getting on very well with Davina and Benjamin in the club.'

'So? I'd had about a gazillion cocktails!' she said. 'And they knew some totally fit boys. End of story. Anyway, why would that mean you couldn't trust me?'

April looked at her. 'Because Davina and Benjamin are vampires.'

'I beg your pardon?'

April took a deep breath and started from the beginning. She told Caro about finding her dad's notebook, then visiting Mr Gill and the Kingsley-Davis book. She told her about the nests and the Vampire Regent. Then she told her about the night in Covent Garden and the chase along the Embankment.

'No way,' whispered Caro, her eyes wide. 'You *stabbed* him?'

Finally she told her about Gabriel finding the mark and the Furies.

'Wow!' said Caro, staring off into the distance. 'That's … that's mad.'

April waited for the questions and the mickey-taking and the suggestion she visit a shrink, but Caro remained silent, just staring back at the school.

'Well, this isn't the reaction I was expecting,' said April with a nervous laugh.

'Hey, you're preaching to the choir here, remember,' said Caro. 'I told you we were surrounded by vampires the first day you were at school.'

'Yes, but I thought you were talking figuratively. Like they were sucking the life out of you or something, not actual real-life bloodsuckers.'

'Well, that too. But the thing about this place? I've been trying to get to the bottom of that for years. I'm pleased that I'm so goddamn clever, honestly, I'm just a bit too sick to do cartwheels right now.'

April looked at her. She had been expecting laughter or derision or at the very least some whooping and 'I told you so's. She was disappointed and a little annoyed that Caro was so calm. After all, she was telling her that they were surrounded by the undead. To most people, this would be big news.

'Don't you think this is weird?' she asked with irritation.

'Of *course* it's weird,' said Caro soothingly, 'but you're missing the big picture, honey. Three people have been killed within a few hundred metres of each other in the space of less than a month, but there's been weird stuff happening here for ages. Something is wrong in Highgate and *very* wrong at Ravenwood. I know it's hard for you to get your head around, with it all happening so fast and, well, so horribly close to home, but some of us here – those who have been paying attention, anyway – have been living with this for years. You coming here and giving it a name, a proper explanation, it just confirms what I've suspected for a long time.'

'And what's that?' asked April.

Caro took off her sunglasses, and her eyes were terribly sad. 'That we're surrounded by evil.'

Fortified by strong coffee and two fizzy vitamin tablets, Caro was feeling more human by lunchtime. She and April had gone to the library to research the final days of Alix Graves on side-by-side Internet terminals.

'It's amazing what you can find, isn't it?' said April, staring at the screen. 'If you're a celebrity, it's like you're constantly under surveillance. You can find out where he went shopping, who he was meeting, everything.'

'I can even tell you what he had for lunch,' said Caro, swivelling her screen towards April. 'Have a look at this.'

It was a website called 'Celebstalking.com' which had a headline reading 'Grave Danger'. April read:

If you are what you eat, then drop-dead gorgeous singer Alix Graves is a heart attack waiting to happen. Spies in Soho yesterday spotted him coming out of Rancho Diablo, the Texas steak joint. Further investigation revealed that the Belarus frontman had gorged himself on a full rack of ribs followed by a very rare T-bone steak, all washed down with 'three or four' beers. Watch out, Alix, you'll be growing horns. Or love-handles!

'God, it must be awful having people following you everywhere,' said April.

'Well, it's lucky for us they did,' said Caro.

'Morning, ladies!'

They both turned to see Simon saunter in. He looked as fresh as Caro looked wrecked: hair perfectly combed across his forehead, casually dressed in a navy jumper and jeans with a silk scarf at his neck. He looked like he'd stepped off the back page of *GQ*.

Caro and April exchanged a 'what-the-hell?' glance.

'Well, isn't this all very exciting?' said Simon. 'I get a mysterious text in the middle of double Maths asking me to come to the library, and now I get here to find two gorgeous girls beavering away. What gives?'

'We were just wondering if you wanted to look at some pictures of Alix Graves?'

Simon pulled a face. 'Not really. Seems a bit passé, if you know what I mean.'

'I thought you loved Belarus?' said Caro, narrowing her eyes.

'Did, past tense,' he said airily, heading back out. 'I'll leave you to it. Want to meet for lunch with the girls?'

'What was that all about?' said April when he had gone. 'I thought he loved dissecting Alix's outfits and stuff?'

Caro had a frown line between her eyes. 'Did you see what he was wearing? And who are "the girls"? I thought *we* were his girls.'

'You don't think he's talking about the Faces, do you?'

Caro nodded. 'I think we should keep our investigations to ourselves for the moment,' she said.

April watched her friend form the corner of her eye as she got up and walked over to the printer. She was obviously upset by Simon's behaviour, but she just as obviously didn't want April to know about it. Caro picked up a sheet of paper and handed it to April.

'Have a look at this,' she said. It was a double-page spread from a German tabloid, published two days after Alix's death. The photos from the news story were of the outside of his house, showing an ambulance behind a police cordon as his body was brought out on a stretcher.

'Basically, the story says that Alix was having a big party on the night of his death,' said Caro. 'The Europeans aren't so hot on libel and all that as we Brits are so they can be as sensationalist as they like, and they're saying this party was a big goth orgy. Candles, incense, drugs, booze and ladies of the night – the other kind, of course – every decadent cliché you can think of.'

'Wow,' said April. 'But then I guess they can say anything now he's dead, can't they?'

'Exactly. It's not terribly reliable stuff, especially when they go on to suggest his death was some drugs-and-sex experiment gone wrong. Personally, I got the feeling it was a lot more violent than that. Anyway, that's not what I was looking at. Check out the big photo on the right.'

April's heart jumped. Alix Graves was stripped to the waist, looking moody and pouting at the camera. But it wasn't the singer's magnificent pecs April was staring at.

'See anything that looks familiar?' Caro asked.

She did. There was a tattoo on his right shoulder in the shape of a star, the exact same shape as the one on her head. April jumped up and rushed into the library toilets. Leaning in to the mirror, she scraped her hair back. *It's the same! It's the same!* she thought as Caro came in behind her.

'Oh, Caro, what does it mean? Was Alix part of this? Was he killed because he knew about the myth?'

'I'm sorry, honey, I wish I knew,' said Caro. 'Maybe they were trying to turn him, maybe he wanted out, who knows? But that isn't all. Ten days before the so-called Goth Orgy, he had a meeting at Transparent Media.'

'How do you know?'

'Because of this.' She handed April another page. It was a copy of a news story from the music industry newspaper *Music Week*. The picture showed Alix Graves shaking hands with a man in a suit, with a caption reading 'Graves plans to change the way Transparent sells music to the consumer'.

April looked up. 'So?'

Caro smiled. 'So Transparent Media is registered as a subsidiary of Agropharm. And who's the chairman of Agropharm?'

April gasped. 'Of course! Nicholas Osbourne.'

Caro nodded.

'Davina's daddy.'

Chapter Thirty-Six

Caro was fuming. When they got to the refectory, Simon was sitting with the Faces and the rugby boys, laughing and joking like they'd been best friends for years. He waved to Caro and April, but didn't make a move to come over to their table.

'Has he been recruited?' whispered April.

'Either that or he's just got really annoying overnight.'

'But he is a maths genius, isn't he? He's exactly the sort of brainy kid they'd target,' said April.

Caro turned to her and there was anger in her face. 'We've got to do something about this,' she said. She looked down at her watch. 'Come on.' She jumped up and headed for the exit. 'I've got an idea. I'll tell you on the way.' She pushed through the double doors and strode off.

'Well? Are you going to tell me?' asked April, trotting to keep up.

'To my mind, the way to stop them is to go to the source, find out who's behind Ravenwood, yes?'

April nodded. 'Yes, I think so.'

'Cut off the head, the snake will die,' she said. 'We might also flush out whoever killed your dad into the bargain.'

April grabbed her arm and pulled her to a halt. 'Is that supposed to be funny?' she snapped.

'What?' said Caro, surprised at the anger on April's face. 'What did I say?'

'What did you say? You said your stupid conspiracy is more important than my dad's murder, that's what!'

'Eh? No, I didn't mean—'

'Nothing – and I mean *nothing* – is more important than finding out who killed my dad, do you understand?'

Caro gaped at her. 'Yes, yes of course,' she stammered, taken aback by the sudden fury. 'I wasn't saying it wasn't important, honestly. But there is still a good chance that the Regent or whoever's behind Ravenwood may well have ordered your dad's murder, so we might crack both cases at once. I didn't mean to upset you.'

April nodded. 'Sorry, I guess I'm a bit sensitive at the moment.'

Caro smiled. 'It's understandable after all you've been through.'

'Okay,' said April, taking a deep breath. 'So where are we going?'

'To the source. Hawk always goes out for his lunch – blood probably – so we just need to sneak past his secretary.'

'Hang on,' whispered April as they pushed through the double doors and along the corridor towards the front of the school. 'You think Mr Sheldon is a vampire?'

Caro stopped and looked at her seriously. 'We have to assume everyone is now,' she said. 'Guilty until proven innocent and all that.'

'Guilty of what, exactly?'

April whirled around to find Miss Holden standing in the corridor, blocking their way.

'Oh, we were just talking about—' stammered April.

'Boys,' said Caro.

Miss Holden sighed. 'I'm not surprised. It would be too much to ask that you were discussing something constructive like schoolwork, something you could both do with paying more attention to.'

'Yes, Miss Holden,' said Caro, 'sorry, Miss Holden,' with just the slightest edge of sarcasm to her voice. Miss Holden simply stared at her until Caro looked away.

'All right, Caro, you run along and chase boys or whatever it was you were doing – I want a word with April.'

Caro looked as if she was going to say something more, but

the teacher flashed her a warning look and she sloped off.

'April. How are you?' said Miss Holden when Caro had gone.

'I'm fine.'

'You're sure? It'd only be natural if you were feeling a little fragile after, well, after everything that's happened.'

'No, I'm okay, honestly,' said April, itching to get away.

'All right, well, as I said to you the other day, I need to speak to you about something important.'

Something about the look on the teacher's face made April pause.

'Is it about my dad?'

Miss Holden smiled sadly. 'In a way, yes. Can you stay behind after school today?'

April looked at the floor and shook her head. 'I told my mum I'd be straight home. She's not very well at the moment.'

She didn't want to tell Miss Holden that she had arranged to go to Davina's house after school; she knew she wouldn't approve.

'I understand.' The teacher smiled. 'How about you come in early tomorrow? Say in the form room at eight-thirty?'

'I'll try,' said April. She hurried after Caro. As she turned the corner towards Mr Sheldon's office, Caro grabbed her and pulled her into a doorway.

'Shhh!' she hissed, pointing to the open door. 'Listen.'

Inside the office, they could hear laughing.

'Oh, you'll never believe what happened then ...' a woman was saying.

'Hear that?' whispered Caro. 'Mrs Bagly, the secretary, loves to gossip on the phone. I've been sent to the headmaster's office often enough to know. She'll be talking in there all lunch break.'

'So how are we supposed to get past?'

Caro pointed to the door. 'Mrs Bagly sits behind that door, but she has one of those high desks you can lean on, so if we keep low, she won't see us. Then, once we've sneaked past the desk, we go around the corner and through the door into

Sheldon's office. Mrs Bagly can't see the office itself from where she sits.' Caro glanced at her watch. 'I reckon we've got at least half an hour. Ready?'

'What?' spluttered April. 'We can't just walk straight into the headmaster's office!'

Caro looked up and down the corridor, then peeked around the corner.

'Not walk,' she whispered. 'Crawl.' She dropped down to her knees and shuffled towards the door.

'Caro!' hissed April, but Caro just motioned her onwards. Shaking her head, thankful she hadn't chosen to wear a skirt today, April crawled after her. The secretary's desk was to their right and had an elbow-height platform like a doctor's reception, thus blocking Mrs Bagly's view of the girls – unless she happened to stand up. They crawled across the outer office on their hands and knees and slipped inside the headmaster's office. Caro closed the door very, very slowly, so that it wouldn't attract Mrs Bagly's attention. When it finally, softly, clicked to, they both breathed out.

'This is crazy!' whispered April.

'Shhh!' said Caro.

April looked around; the office was just as impressive as it had been when she met DI Reece for the first time. Thinking about the police did nothing for her nerves, so she got to work, pulling open a filing cabinet, while Caro slid behind Mr Sheldon's desk.

'What are we looking for, anyway?' hissed April.

'I don't know,' said Caro. 'Something suspicious. Anything that tells us who's behind the school.'

April pulled out a file at random. 'Hey, I've got Mr Andrews' personnel file,' she said.

'Not exactly what we're looking for.'

'His CV is amazing,' she hissed. 'This guy could work anywhere. What's he doing here?'

'Maybe he likes blood,' said Caro. 'Now get searching.'

Quickly, April felt swamped with information. She found financial spreadsheets and costings for replacing the windows in the science lab with some sort of tinted glass, she found the exam results of the chemistry department going back six years, even a budget for a skiing trip to Austria, but there was nothing out of the ordinary, just things relating to the running of a secondary school.

'Anything on the computer?'

'Nah, it's all password-protected,' said Caro, 'and all these folders are locked ... Hold up. Bingo!'

April ran over. Caro had clicked on an email with an Agropharm logo at the bottom.

'Where'd you find that?'

'Mrs Bagly has her email account on here too and this was cc-ed to her. It was just there in the in tray. Yes!' she said excitedly as she read it. 'Listen to this: "It's frustrating that the school is not producing enough candidates for our industry. I don't have to tell you how high the stakes are. We need more results your end Robert, if you want to see any more funding for your expanding science lab."'

'Who's it from?' asked April.

Caro's eyes were wide. 'Nicholas Osbourne!' she hissed triumphantly. 'Could he be the Regent?'

A loud bout of coughing from the outer office made them both jump.

'Move!' whispered Caro urgently. 'Get behind the door.'

Out in the office, they heard Mr Sheldon's voice. 'Are you okay, lad? Do you want a drink of water?'

The coughing seemed to get worse.

'Mrs Bagly, can you give me a hand?' said Mr Sheldon. 'We'd better get him to the nurse.'

April had to clamp her hand over Caro's mouth to stop her from laughing out loud at their good fortune. She peeked around the door and, seeing the coast was clear, they ran out into the corridor.

Chapter Thirty-Seven

April saw him waiting for her as she crossed the square and cursed under her breath. *I shouldn't have stopped off at home*, she thought, *I should have gone straight to Davina's.* DI Reece was standing by her garden gate. More questions were the last thing she needed right now. *Answers, that's what I want.*

In particular, she wanted to know what their discoveries had meant. Could Nicholas Osbourne be the Vampire Regent? He certainly had all the power and influence you'd expect from someone in charge of a sinister conspiracy, and there were links to both Alix Graves and Ravenwood. Who was he expecting Hawk to 'recruit' for him? Was he choosing the brightest kids for the Regent to turn? April just didn't know and that was what was so frustrating; she kept stumbling on little clues, whispy bits of information that disappeared as soon as you clutched at them, but nothing concrete, nothing she could rely on. And even if she did find absolute proof that Davina's father was the Regent, what then? Tell the police? DI Reece was a nice man and pretty open-minded, considering, but honestly, who would believe such a crazy idea?

'Ah, there you are,' said DI Reece, throwing his cigarette into the gutter. 'Sorry to hang around in the street, but I didn't want to come to the school again and there was no answer at the house.'

'Have you got news on the case?' she asked, without much hope.

Reece shook his head. 'Only in a roundabout way. We've had the full forensic report back.' He nodded towards April's yellow front door. 'Do you want to go inside?'

April shook her head. 'I'd rather not if it's okay with you, Mr Reece,' she said, stifling a shiver. 'I don't really want to be talking about that stuff where ... well, you know.'

The detective nodded. 'Understood. How about I buy you a coffee?'

They walked to Americano in silence and settled into a booth at the back where they could talk in privacy.

'I'll cut to the chase, April,' said Reece. 'The report told us virtually nothing. No fingerprints, no fibres, nothing under the fingernails. To be frank, we don't know who was in your house or how they got there and the only unusual thing the post-mortem revealed was, well ...' He hesitated. 'It was rather unbelievable.'

April could see it was something he would rather not tell her. The policeman looked decidedly uncomfortable.

'What is it?'

'The cause of death. It seems your father's throat was torn out.'

'Torn?' she said, feeling bile rising.

'Yes,' said Reece, holding her gaze. 'I realise this must be hard for you to hear, but according to the coroner, it was as if an animal had got hold of him.'

April shook her head. 'I'm sorry, I don't understand. Are you saying it *was* an animal?'

'No, I'm saying it was a human bite. They attacked him with their teeth.'

April stifled a moan.

'Biting cases are surprisingly common, I'm afraid, usually in drunken pub brawls where ears or even noses are torn off. Those nasty primeval urges are still with us, just under the surface.'

'But to bite someone's throat—'

'Indeed,' said Reece. 'According to the coroner, it would take enormous strength. The jaws are the strongest muscles in the body, of course, but even so, the attacker would have to be extremely disturbed to do what he did, so we're starting to think that we're dealing with a lunatic.'

'Why? I mean, why do you think that now?'

The detective paused, running a finger along the rim of his coffee mug. 'This is very sensitive information, April,' he said, 'but I'm trusting you with it because I think you need to know, for your own safety if nothing else.'

April waited, screwing her hands into tight fists under the table.

'All of the murders – Alix Graves, Isabelle Davis and your dad – all have identical causes of death.'

April had to struggle to draw a breath. 'They were all bitten?' she whispered.

Reece nodded. 'Yes. All of them.'

April's hand went to her throat. She had guessed as much, of course; there were vampires on the loose – for God's sake, she had seen them with her own eyes, so it was only to be expected – but having a policeman spell it out to her was still a shock. Somehow, she had managed to stop herself thinking about it. She knew her dad had been killed, of course, but up until now, she had avoided thinking about *how*.

'So what now?' she asked, looking at him with pleading eyes. 'Can you stop him?'

'We'll have your house watched, of course,' he said. 'We're taking this extremely seriously.'

'That doesn't answer my question,' said April angrily. 'Can you *stop* him?'

Reece looked away. 'I have to be honest – I don't know. We'll do everything we can, of course—'

'Great,' said April, glaring at him. 'Just great. So that's your plan? Watch the house and hope this maniac turns up to rip our throats out?'

'Of course not,' said Reece firmly. 'I will never let that happen. Never.' But his face told a different story. There were dark rings under his eyes and the lines on his forehead looked more pronounced than the last time she had seen him.

'We'll catch him, April,' he said. 'And we'll catch him the same way we catch every other criminal – through good, solid police work. It might not be as spectacular or as fast as we'd like, but it always gets results in the end.'

'In the end?' she snapped. 'Do you think we can wait that long?' She knew it wasn't his fault, but she was frustrated and she was scared. She was jumping at every shadow, flinching each time the telephone rang. Gabriel had said he had the feeling he was being watched, led into a trap; April could feel it now too. There were eyes everywhere and she was convinced some of them were watching her.

She fixed Reece with a probing stare. 'Who could have done it, Mr Reece? Who could have killed my dad?'

'Well, as I said, it would take someone in a frenzy—'

'No, I mean who had the opportunity to do it? Who are the suspects?'

Reece put his cup down. 'Can't tell you that, April. It's privileged information. I've already told you more than I should have.'

'Exactly, so why not tell me this as well?'

'The information in the coroner's report related directly to your safety—'

April sat forward. 'But so does this, don't you see? If the killer didn't break in, the chances are my dad knew them and therefore the chances are I know them too. Putting a car outside the house isn't going to do a thing if the killer is popping around with a cup of sugar, is it?'

The detective sat for a moment, staring at his hands. 'I suppose there's no real reason not to tell you,' he said finally, 'but I don't think it's going to help.'

'Please, Mr Reece.'

He rubbed his hand over his chin. 'Okay, let's start with you. As we know, you were with Mr Sheldon in front of the school, then you left Ravenwood and walked up the hill with your friend Caro. You saw the ambulance and ran to the house. That eliminates you and Caro for a start. Your mother was with your grandfather all morning and was making her way home from central London when my sergeant called her and she went straight to the hospital. Your grandfather verifies her story, by the way, and vice versa,' he added, looking up at April. 'Now, I was with your friend Gabriel Swift at the time—'

'He's not my friend,' said April.

'Well, regardless, we know where he was and we've also checked out most of your schoolmates: Davina and Ben Osbourne, Marcus Brent, Simon Oliver, Ling Po Chan, Layla—'

'How do you know who I hang out with?' interrupted April, a little unsettled. 'Have you been watching me?'

Reece smiled slightly. 'We asked your teachers. They always know what's going on in their school.'

April blushed.

'After that, we widened the net to your dad's friends – all at work or in Edinburgh; your mum's friends – most of them were tucked away in various hairdressers'; and other possible disgruntled people who your dad may have upset in his work as a journalist, but again, our most likely suspects are either in prison or out of the country.'

'So you have nothing? No suspects?'

'Unfortunately, it's quite the opposite. Most of the alibis are full of holes: "I was at home watching telly" or "I was asleep at the time": very hard to prove, very hard to disprove. Take your own alibi, that you were with Mr Sheldon. We have other witnesses that saw you together, but we only have your word and his as to when it took place. Also, Mr Sheldon has a fast car, he could have driven up to the house, knowing you'd corroborate his story. If you want to get all Agatha Christie about it, you could be working together.'

April understood what he was saying, but she didn't like it at all.

'So you're saying anyone could have done it?'

Reece smiled without humour. 'Almost everybody has a weak alibi, April. Your friend Davina says she went shopping, Benjamin says he was "hanging out" with his friends: do you see? We check their stories as far as we can, but unless we stumble across a bloody knife when we question them, we need other evidence first.'

'So what do I do?' she asked, a note of desperation in her voice. 'How can I tell who might be the killer? Who can I trust?'

DI Reece's face was hard when he spoke. 'Trust no one, April. It sounds melodramatic, but it's the best advice I can give you. As I said before, I think we're looking for one killer – that's the logical conclusion – but then nothing in this case is straightforward. Normally I'd ask, "why would any of these suspects kill your dad? Why would they kill Isabelle or Alix?" And I'll be honest with you, I'm drawing a blank. Nothing I can see links all of the suspects and the victims, except Ravenwood – and only then in a very vague way. None of the usual rules apply here.'

'So what are you telling me, Mr Reece?' asked April, a horrible creeping feeling in her stomach. Reece shook his head and sighed.

'Any one of the people I've mentioned could have killed your dad,' he said, looking her straight in the eyes. 'And one of them probably did.'

Chapter Thirty-Eight

It was scary enough to visit the Osbourne mansion with its huge gardens and tall chimneys, but it was even more nerve-wracking when you had to pass a security checkpoint before you even got onto their property.

April pressed the intercom button and waited as a camera with a blinking red light swivelled around to look at her.

'Zzzzkkt. Yes?' said a robotic voice.

'Uh, hi, I'm April Dunne? I've come to see Davina.'

'Zzzrrt. One moment.'

She waited again, wondering if this was such a good idea. After the success of their audacious raid on the headmaster's office, Caro had been full of excitement about her 'play-date' with Davina. 'She's sucking you in like one of those tractor beams in *Star Wars*,' she said. 'It's only a matter of time before she tries to bite you.' *That's what I'm worried about*, thought April as the black gates to the mansion began to swing open. Her conversation with DI Reece had left her shaken. In one conversation, all her worst suspicions had been confirmed: her father had been killed by a vampire and in all probability she knew his killer personally. Could it be Davina? Benjamin? One of their friends or relatives? The sane thing to do would be to turn around and run away from this house as fast as she could, but April couldn't do that. She was committed; she had to find out who had killed her father, even if it meant putting herself in danger. The stakes became higher than ever as April felt herself pulled deeper and deeper into this disorientating labyrinth, fearing with every twist and turn that she would find herself at the very centre. The school was still buzzing with rumours about Milo's worsening condition. Apparently it was such big news that Caro's Biology teacher had taken the time to explain his condition – a variety of necrotising fasciitis, caused by the *Streptococcus pyogenes* bacterium, Caro had knowledgeably informed her – so people were now paranoid it was infectious. April put one hand up to touch the birthmark behind her ear and hoped that Gabriel was wrong.

'Bloody hell,' muttered April as her feet crunched along the gravel drive. She felt an awfully long way from the road. To her left was a pond – well, more like a lake, really – with a little oriental bridge over it and in front of her the house loomed like a medieval palace. She couldn't imagine what the Osbournes must have thought of her tiny house.

'Hello!' called a cheery voice, and Davina popped her head around the front door. 'Sorry about that,' she said, walking out to air-kiss April. 'The security's so annoying, isn't it? But we can't be too careful with Daddy's company, there's so many loonies about.'

Any demonstrators might get a surprise if they tried to protest here, thought April as she walked inside.

'Wow!' she said. The hallway had a domed glass ceiling and impressive-looking art was hung all the way up the stairs. 'It's amazing.'

'Do you like it? I think it's a bit, you know, old. Mind you, it's nothing on Daddy's place in Gloucester, that's like an Elizabethan nightmare, all creaky floors and horrid little windows.' She shivered. 'Still, it's great for parties. You are still coming to the Winter Ball? You have to, it's going to be full of so many of Daddy's horrid lechy friends, we need all the glamour we can get.'

April nodded eagerly in a way she hoped looked suitably air-headed. In truth, she was dreading it, being surrounded by strangers, not knowing who was who and indeed, who they really were under their masks, but aware that some, if not all of them, were killers. Her *father's* killers.

'Fabulous,' gushed Davina. 'Come on through to the drawing room, Ling Po's here.'

The drawing room was wide and open with high windows overlooking the terrace which was slowly dimming as the winter sun sank behind the horizon. Some interior designer had spent a fortune on the black and white upholstered Art Deco furniture and cream carpet. Even the chrome light fittings looked expensive.

'Hi, darling,' said Ling, trotting up and kissing April. 'Ben's just been teaching me how to play poker.'

Benjamin was sitting at a long dark-wood table, expertly shuffling a pack of cards.

'Not strip poker, I hope?' said Davina with a frown. 'Honestly, that boy's got a one-track mind.'

Benjamin ignored her and smiled at April. 'Hello, April, welcome to the madhouse.'

'It's amazing,' said April. 'I was just telling Davina.'

'April thinks it's marvy,' said Davina with a wicked smile that Ling returned, as if they were sharing a joke.

'Oh, I prefer modern architecture, don't you?' said Ling. 'I can't stand all this old stuff.'

'Philistines,' said Benjamin, cocking a thumb at them.

'Do you want to come for a dip, April? Dav and I are going in the hot tub in a minute.'

'No, Ling, April's here now,' said Davina.

'But you promised,' whined the Chinese girl.

'Well, only if April comes too,' she said, shooting a devilish look at April.

'Oh, I didn't bring a costume,' said April uncertainly.

'It's a hot tub, silly.' Ling giggled. 'You don't need a costume.'

'Do come, April,' said Davina, touching her arm. 'It's so nice to be outside when it's so cold.'

'But it's so hot inside,' said Ling, still giggling.

'Don't listen to them, April,' said Benjamin. 'It's freezing out there and they're only teasing about the costumes, *aren't* you?'

Davina pouted and held up her thumb and forefinger. 'A little.'

'You go and have your much-needed bath.' Benjamin sighed. 'I'll look after your guest.'

'Do you mind, April?' asked Davina, even as she started heading for the door.

'No, not at all, I'm fine,' she said, although inside she was feeling quite the opposite, as if she had just walked into the lion's den. If Gabriel was right, then she was being left alone with a vampire, a mythical killer. There were no witnesses, no one to call for help, she was completely alone. No, she was not 'fine' at all.

'Go on, shoo!' said Ben, shutting the door behind them.

He turned to April and rolled his eyes. 'She's going to have to learn a few more hostessing skills to have a hope of marrying into royalty.'

April forced out a laugh. 'Is that the plan, then?'

'Oh yes, hasn't she told you? She's been tracking all the eligible princes in Europe since she was old enough to play Barbie weddings. Her room is a shrine to *Tatler* and *Paris Match*.'

April frowned. Something didn't quite fit here. The marry-into-royalty plan certainly sounded like something Davina the vacuous schoolgirl would choose as a career plan, but if Davina was in fact a devious vampire, there was a big stumbling block: she couldn't be seen in photos. Surely as a high-profile society wife she'd be snapped by the paparazzi all the time? Yes, Gabriel had explained that the vampires' plan was to stay in the background pulling the strings, but for a woman like Davina, that would be impossible; she'd be in *OK!* and *Hello!* all the time. Or perhaps it's just her cover story.

Benjamin saw the look on April's face. 'What's the matter?'

'Oh, nothing,' said April. 'Just not very romantic, is it?'

Ben chuckled. 'You've met my sister, right? I don't think romance is high up on her list of priorities; things like "Bentley", "Cartier" and "couture" come much higher.'

April smiled, then remembered where she was and who

she was talking to. *Be professional, April*, she scolded herself. *Infiltrate.*

'So what's your long-term plan, Ben?' she asked. 'Finding yourself a nice little heiress?'

'God no,' he said. 'If I ever get married it will be for love.' His eyes twinkled mischievously at April, but then he quickly added, 'But I want to get into politics as soon as I can, so I suppose that's not very romantic either. I've been doing media training and getting experience at one of my dad's firms. All very dull, I know, but you've got to know what you want in life.'

And sometimes what you want is irrelevant, thought April ruefully. She wished she could imagine her own career in the same way, but apparently someone had other plans for her. April wondered if Benjamin would run into the same problem with photos and TV cameras as Davina, but perhaps that was what his media training was all about. Certainly in politics it was possible to stay in the shadows and still have influence, but even so, April was unsettled by these revelations. She couldn't be sure, but she had a feeling there was something more going on here, something she was missing – but what was it? She puzzled over it as they watched Davina and Ling scamper for the hot tub on the terrace.

'I bet it's an amazing view,' said April, walking over to the French windows. In the fading light, she could just make out the garden beyond the terrace and after that the park and the cemetery. It was like a slightly more stylish version of Milo's house, although the Asprey place backed onto the Heath instead. 'Although I wouldn't want to have the cemetery so close. Don't you find it a bit, well, creepy, having all those gravestones just beyond your garden wall?'

'I suppose.' Benjamin shrugged. 'I guess I've just got used to it. Never seen any ghosts or anything either. Anyway, since you've been abandoned by your hostess, how about I give you the guided tour?'

April smiled, forcing herself to look interested despite feeling she was being pulled in two different directions. The old April, the one who had lived in Edinburgh and had only seen vampires in rubbish late night movies, the old April wanted to run. She wanted to fling the French windows open and sprint off into the night screaming. But the new April, the one who had been unwillingly plunged into a world of murder and mythology, she wanted to make the most of this; to see if she could pick up some clues or leads, anything that might help her find her father's killer, because the new April wanted revenge, she wanted to make whoever had hurt her daddy pay. Even though the sensible, normal part of her knew that it was very likely she was being led into a trap, the grieving, hurt, broken part of her didn't care too much. She didn't want her throat torn out, but she knew it was a risk she had to take.

Benjamin showed her the library and the 'lower gallery' – a long room that served as a formal dining room – and the kitchens, which were even bigger than her grandfather's. The stairs to the upper floor curved all along one wall, and there were twelve bedrooms. The en suite to Ben's parents' room was bigger than the whole downstairs of April's house.

'And I thought we lived in a swanky house being in Pond Square,' said April.

'It's ridiculously big, isn't it? But my father's always bringing "important people" back here,' he said, framing the words with finger quotation marks, 'so we have to have the best of everything. It's a bit like living in a museum – well, until you get in here, anyway.'

He pushed open a door and April walked in.

'Good God!' she said, laughing. 'Your room, I presume?'

It was as if a whirlwind had whipped through it. Drawers hung open, spilling T-shirts and socks onto the floor, bookshelves were crammed with magazines and DVDs, and there was even a drum kit in one corner, a pair of jeans draped over one of the cymbals.

'I like to think it counterbalances the house,' he said. 'The chaos here makes the order of the rest of it look so much better.' He nodded to a door at the end of room. 'I wouldn't go into the bathroom, though. I can't guarantee your safety in there.'

'Gosh, I didn't realise you were such a big Alix Graves fan,' said April, pointing to the posters Blu-Tacked to the Cole and Fairfax wallpaper.

Benjamin gave a guilty smirk. 'Well, obviously for me it's about the music rather than his fine physique,' he said, putting his hand over a picture of the singer wearing only leather trousers.

April giggled, pulling his hand away to examine the picture. She managed to suppress a gasp as she realised it was the same picture Caro had shown her in the library earlier that day, the one with the star tattoo. *Deep breath, April*, she said to herself. *Don't show him how you feel*. 'Yes, he did have a fine collection of tattoos,' she said.

'Yes, it's the tattoos.' Benjamin grinned. 'It's definitely the tattoos I liked. Tattoos are manly.'

God, I wish he wasn't a vampire, thought April suddenly, then scolded herself for having the thought. *He's the enemy, remember!* But was he? Was any of this crazy situation true? It was certainly hard to believe when confronted with such a typical teenager's bedroom. But then she remembered the night on the Embankment, the photograph and Gabriel's face pulled back in a snarl. She remembered the knife – *Jesus, I actually stabbed him* – and the wound disappearing. So how come she couldn't believe it when presented with all those facts? She looked at Benjamin, so handsome and charming, lounging on his bed. It was because she didn't *want* to believe.

A scream from the garden had April running to the window, to see Ling and Davina splashing about in the hot tub, squirting water at each other.

'You learn not to get too excited about screams living in this house,' said Benjamin, peering over her shoulder. 'There's a lot of drama.'

Perhaps it was high spirits, but Ling did seem to be sitting rather close to Davina in the hot tub, although it was hard to see exactly what was going on under the bubbles.

'The hot tub is a tradition at our parties,' said Benjamin in a low voice. 'Especially at the Winter Ball. Everyone gets in at midnight.'

She realised that Ben was standing very close, could feel his breath on her neck. *Okay, so he's a vampire, but he is so hot*, said the rebellious voice in her head.

'You are going to come, aren't you?' he asked. He was so close she could feel the warmth from his body now. *If he's that hot, he can't really be a vampire, can he?*

'Yes, I ...' she said, turning to face him.

Then there was another scream, a real scream – a long, wailing cry of grief from somewhere inside the house. With a concerned glance at April, Benjamin ran from the room and along the corridor. April followed close behind. At the top of the stairs, he stopped and bent over the banisters.

'Mum! What is it?' he called.

April got there just as Mrs Osbourne stepped into the hallway, a phone in her hand, her face white. She looked up at Benjamin and shook her head.

'It's Milo,' she said. 'He's dead.'

Chapter Thirty-Nine

The whole school was in mourning. If Milo Asprey hadn't been the most popular boy in school, he still appeared to have had a lot of friends. Certainly, if 'Milo's Wall' was anything to go by, it looked like almost every Ravenwood student had been touched by his presence. The Wall was a long noticeboard just outside the refectory, usually only used for notes relating to the next meeting of the chess club or posters advertising a concert by the school band. But somehow, without any official assignment of the space required, by lunchtime on Friday, the wall had become a shrine to the boy's memory. Pictures, cards, poems, even some elaborate and presumably time-consuming artworks had appeared, eulogising Milo's humour, sensitivity and all-round brilliance. The school had caught on fast and announced that anything pinned up on the wall would later become part of a book of remembrance for Milo's family. The wall also had the knock-on effect of making Layla hugely popular by proxy. Previously seen as Davina's bitchy and cruel sidekick, her bedside vigil as Milo had fallen ill, slipped into a coma and died had transformed her into a tragic heroine with hitherto unseen depths. Even girls who had been on the receiving end of her sniping put-downs had been offering their condolences.

April had not been one of them. Leaving aside her feelings regarding Layla and her sharp nails, she was still finding Milo's death very difficult to deal with. She had tried, time and again, to convince herself that it was pure coincidence, that Milo had caught some tropical disease just after their kiss, whatever Gabriel had claimed, but in her heart she knew it wasn't true. She knew she was responsible. Of course, she hadn't planned it, hadn't known that she was anything special – let alone a Fury – but she had caused Milo's death nevertheless. It wasn't murder, but it was manslaughter and April felt it deeply. She'd enjoyed their kiss and had been disappointed to be interrupted; after all, Milo had been about the only one at the party to be nice to her. And now she'd killed him. She walked around in a gloom, dragging a black cloud with her wherever she went. A casual onlooker would think that April Dunne had simply been moved by Milo's passing, possibly feeling the tragedy more keenly because of her own recent loss, which was of course true. But April was also struggling with feelings of powerlessness. She had been moved down to London against her will, her father had been murdered and she was failing to find out who was responsible. And now, it seemed, she had another role thrust upon her, a role she had no stomach for. She felt even more isolated by Caro's seemingly boundless enthusiasm for the 'project', as she insisted on calling it, not least because she thought catching William Dunne's killer was a secondary goal, and because she had no one else but Fee to talk to – and she still wasn't sure if she could even trust her best friend. She hadn't heard from Gabriel since she'd thrown him out two days ago. *Par for the course*, she thought. But then April hadn't tried to contact him either, and it wasn't really because of their quarrel. After all, it wasn't Gabriel's fault she had the birthmark and, truthfully, Gabriel was probably the one person who would actually understand everything she was going through. But she still couldn't call him. *Not that I've even got his number.* Maybe she was being too sensitive, maybe she was burying her head in the sand, maybe she simply didn't want to face it; she didn't want to be a Fury, whatever the hell that was. She fleetingly wondered if she should go to her mother or her grandfather and ask them point blank if they knew anything about it: it had crossed her mind that their whispering and bickering about her 'heritage' might have something to do with this Fury thing, but she had almost no expectation of getting a straight answer from either of them – *they've kept it to themselves so far, so why would that change now I've accidentally killed someone?* – and besides, what if it *wasn't* about her being a Fury? She didn't want to open another can of worms if she didn't have to, and either way, April didn't need to bear that extra weight of responsibility on her shoulders at a time when she just wanted to curl up in bed and hide from everyone and everything.

April picked up her fork and stabbed it into her muffin. 'I hate cake,' she said.

Caro raised her eyebrows. She had brought April out to Americano on their way home from school in an effort to cheer her up.

'Now that's just silly,' she said, enthusiastically biting into her pain au chocolat. 'Cake is one of the greatest inventions of all time.'

It made April smile despite herself. She was very lucky to have such a good friend and, she supposed, the Milo business did have its positive side. By and large, people were leaving her alone, which was infinitely preferable to having them gossip about her, plus she had been able to dodge Miss Holden and her 'little talk' by claiming she was too upset. April wasn't the only one benefiting from the situation either. Davina, predictably, had also made the most of events, coming in to school wearing a classic black Chanel sleeveless dress and dark glasses which she would periodically lift to dab at her eyes with a lace handkerchief – and where Davina led, the Faces and indeed the rest of the school were sure to follow; you would have been forgiven for thinking that Ravenwood had a strict uniform code, with the emphasis on black. The one flash of colour in all this gloom was, equally predictably, provided by Caro who maintained her status as the school rebel by wearing an 'ironic' purple hoody.

'I thought we were supposed to be allowing ourselves to be recruited,' said April moodily. 'The Faces aren't going to want anything to do with you if you keep this up.'

April was now slowly picking her muffin apart, leaving all the blueberries in a pile on the plate.

'Well, that's where you're wrong,' said Caro, pointing at her top with a fork. 'This purple monstrosity is my ticket to the big time.'

April shook her head in confusion.

'It's basic psychology, m'dear. If I joined in with Milo-Fest and started going for manicures with Layla, the Suckers would smell a rat, wouldn't they? By keeping up my outsider persona, I come across as more genuine and they're more likely to want to draw me in.'

'Hold up,' said April. 'Are we calling the vamps "Suckers" now?'

'I thought it had a certain something.' Caro grinned. 'Plus if we're overheard, we could be referring to anyone: teachers, boys, anyone.'

April nodded her approval. 'I like it.'

'Anyway, it's worked,' she said, reaching into her bag and pulling out a gold envelope. 'One ticket to the Osbourne Winter Ball, hand-delivered by Head Sucker, Davina Osbourne.'

'No way!' April hugged her friend excitedly. This, at least, was some good news. She had been dreading attending another posh party alone, where she would feel like an imposter, an outsider – and more than that, she *would* be an interloper, seeing what she could find out, what clues she could pick up, all the time putting herself in danger.

'Oh Caro, that's brilliant – how did you swing it?'

'I casually dropped into conversation that I had already been offered places at Cambridge, John Hopkins and MIT. There was a slight pause while Davina went off to check that it was true, then all of a sudden she was eyeing up my jugular and discussing cocktail dresses.'

'Well, that's excellent work,' said April. 'Maybe we're getting somewhere.'

'Yes, and that's not all,' said Caro. 'I spent last night trying to track down the Disappeared.'

'The Disappeared' were six Ravenwood pupils who had abruptly vanished over the past few years, some supposedly to go overseas, some to different schools.

'I've tried all the schools you could think of and asked other people in their classes. So far, no one has actually heard from them. Not even a Christmas card.'

April sipped her coffee and tried not to despair. They had to catch a break soon. She'd got nowhere with her own research into her father's death. The diary had yielded very little beyond her father's appointment with Mr Gill and she still had no idea why he hadn't turned up at the bookshop. Her mother had been out with Grandpa Thomas on the day of her dad's death, so she was no help with information about his movements. The trail seemed to be going colder and colder. Even her research into the Vampire Regent and the Furies had barely got off the ground. Despite endless websites dedicated to vampire lore, she hadn't come across a single mention of either an internal hierarchy or any sort of ancient nemesis. According to received wisdom, all vampires were rogue vampires, roaming about and killing at random, but that couldn't be true otherwise the countryside would be littered with corpses. April felt like she was wading through treacle. Her resolve and enthusiasm of only a few days before had been sapped by Milo's death. Every glimmer of a clue led to another dead end, as if someone had come and wiped everything clean.

'Do you think we'll learn anything at the party?'

'Have faith,' said Caro kindly. 'You've got the A-team on it now.'

April wished she could take some comfort from that.

Chapter Forty

The house looked wonderful. Snow had fallen overnight and created the perfect setting for the Osbournes' Winter Ball. Only two days earlier, when April had visited Davina after school, the mansion had been a towering, intimidating fortress, but as the taxi drove through the open gates the snow on the hedges and lawns sparkled in the light of burning torches lining the drive, while the windows of the house glowed orange like a cat's eyes in the dark. At first, April had been dismayed to discover that her mother had also been invited to the Osbournes' ball, but now she was glad that she was acting as chaperone. There were security guards in black suits checking invitations at the entrance and party guests in sleek dinner jackets and white furs milling around, shouting hellos and laughing, their jewels glittering in the light of the smiling half-moon. The Winter Ball seemed so big, so important, she was glad to have her mum there. Not that she had been much use for the last week or so, lying in bed and complaining of headaches, but something – perhaps the prospect of tonight's party – had finally lifted her spirits. When April had got up, her mother had gone out, leaving a note reading 'Gone shopping' and when she had arrived home that afternoon she seemed utterly transformed. Her skin had its colour back, her hair was blow-dried and glossy and her eyes were bright. 'Been up West,' she said, dumping half a dozen shopping bags on April's bed. 'I did a little shopping for you too.' Which was why April was wearing an off-the-shoulder McQueen ball gown and Gucci heels and her mother was wearing an Ossie Clark column of sheer silk and *her* mother's diamonds. 'You can't take it with

398

you, baby,' she'd replied to April's objections and she set about doing April's hair and make-up. She hated to admit it, but the makeover had done wonders for April's mood, too. She still didn't feel right about Milo and Gabriel and her new unofficial status as the Nancy Drew of the underworld, but, for once, it was nice to get dressed up and forget all about it. Well, she was sure that Caro would be snooping around, but April had resolved to have a good time tonight. Especially if Benjamin invited her to jump into the hot tub.

'Now, are you going to behave yourselves tonight?' asked Silvia, as if she was reading April's thoughts.

'Yes, Mrs Dunne,' sang Caro. 'We'll be very, very good.'

'I'm glad to hear it, because I will be drinking champagne and whirling around the dance floor enough for all of us.'

'Mum!' said April.

Silvia gave her a warm smile and tapped her knee. 'I'm joking. I shall be the picture of elegance all night.'

April leant over and kissed her cheek.

'What's that for?'

'For being you again.'

The taxi let them out among the Bentleys and Porsches and they made their way to the entrance where they were waved through, but not before they were politely asked to surrender their cameras and mobile phones.

'Security, miss,' was the only explanation offered by the guard when Caro had indignantly asked what it was 'all in aid of'. They exchanged disappointed looks, but had no choice but to comply.

'Check it out!' said Caro as they stepped into the entrance hall. The interior designers had gone to town on the winter theme. Ivy and lush green pine boughs had been woven through the banisters of the staircase and red church candles placed on each of the steps, while strings of tiny fairy lights trailed down every wall, giving the impression of shimmering ice.

'Silvia! So glad you could come.'

Barbara Osbourne came over to greet them, embracing

April's mother warmly. She was wearing a silver ball gown with a plunging neckline.

'So nice to see you out among us again,' she said. 'And April – oh, you're looking lovelier each time I see you.'

Well, I was at my father's funeral the first time, thought April cynically, but she smiled politely.

'And this is Caro Jackson,' said Silvia.

Caro gave a sort of curtsey and mumbled a greeting, but her attention seemed to be elsewhere. April followed her gaze and saw the source of her distraction. Over on the other side of the room Simon was sitting at a piano, singing loudly with Benjamin, Marcus and the rest of the rugby boys.

'Sorry, just going to the bar,' said Caro vaguely and promptly disappeared into the crowd. Mrs Osbourne also made her excuses and left, waving to someone across the room.

'Quite good-looking, isn't he?' said Silvia, nodding towards Simon.

'Yes, but I think Caro might be out of luck,' said April. 'He plays for the other side.'

'Does he?' said Silvia sceptically, gazing at him. 'I wouldn't have thought it.'

A waiter approached and served Silvia with a glass of champagne – 'Just one,' she said with a wicked smile – and April with an orange juice. April had no intention of getting herself into the same state she had at Milo's party.

'Honestly though, Mum, it's great to see you looking happy again. Well, I don't mean happy, that wouldn't be right, but—'

Silvia put a hand on April's arm. 'I know what you mean, honey. Don't worry, I'm not going to run off with any men any time soon. In fact, I'm not going to run off full stop. I know this will be strange to hear, but your dad was the only man for me from the moment I met him. Yes, we had some hard times, things we had to work through, and I'm sorry you had to be in the middle of that sometimes, but I loved that man so much.' Her eyes began to sparkle and she stopped, pressing a hand to her lips.

'Oh, Mum,' said April sadly. She'd always had a spiky relationship with her mother – she was distant and hands-off compared to her dad, at least – but she felt for her now. April was hurting, but she really couldn't imagine the pain of losing your one true love, especially if you'd spent years giving him a hard time.

'No, it's okay,' said Silvia, taking a deep breath. 'The thing you need to remember is that your dad loved us very, very much. Too much sometimes. But he also loved life, he valued it and if he was here now, he would already have had two brandies and dragged me onto the dance floor.'

April laughed. It was true, he was always the life and soul of the party, always at the centre of things, laughing and playing jokes. If William had been here, she was sure she would have been mortified by his behaviour as he made a complete spectacle of himself. She wished more than anything she could see that now.

'I think that's how we should remember him,' said Silvia. 'Take a leaf out of his book and throw ourselves in feet first.' She raised her glass and clinked it against April's. 'To him,' she said.

'To him.' April smiled.

'Right, better get mingling, then. You don't want some old broad cramping your style, so you toddle off and find your friends.'

She kissed April on the cheek and disappeared into the crowd.

April put her empty juice glass down and began to make her way towards the back of the house, walking out through the open French windows and onto the terrace. Portable gas heaters glowed in a long line, taking the chill from the freezing night air.

'There she is!' said Davina, sweeping up the terrace stairs, her arms open wide for an embrace. She was wearing a strapless sheath dress completely covered with white sequins and a white fur stole, which made her blonde mane look even more glossy and luxuriant than normal. April had to hand it to her, vampirism certainly suited her. As they hugged, April saw that the lawn at the bottom of the stairs was covered by a huge marquee filled with the flashing lights of a disco.

'Is that "The Macarena" they're playing in there?' asked April with a smile.

'Oh God, I could strangle my father sometimes,' said Davina, casting her eyes to the heavens. 'It's his age, you see. He booked some cheesy Radio One DJ from the eighties. Cost him a fortune, apparently.'

'And is he here? Your dad, I mean?'

'Oh, Daddy wouldn't miss the Winter Ball for anything. He's down there shaking his stuff right now, so embarrassing. It's like for three hundred and sixty-four days of the year he's this arse-kicking take-no-prisoners corporate machine, then for one night he has to act like a teenager.'

April smiled sadly. 'I think it's nice.'

'Oh God, I've put my foot in it, haven't I?' said Davina, touching at April's hand. 'I'm so sorry, I didn't think.'

'No, don't be silly, I just meant it's nice he can be human.'

April realised the irony of what she had said about the man she suspected was the Vampire Regent and almost laughed out loud.

'I suppose,' said Davina, oblivious. 'I just wish he didn't have to do it in public.'

Glancing around, Davina took April by the elbow and led her back towards the house.

'Now, I don't want to ruin your night,' she said, 'but you've seen who's over there, right?'

Following Davina's gaze with a sense of inevitability, April saw a group of boys standing at the end of the terrace, drinking and laughing, among them Benjamin, Marcus and Gabriel.

'Don't worry, I don't think he saw you. I'm sorry, darling, but Ben insisted on inviting Gabe. I know he's not your favourite person at the moment, but I have asked Ben to keep you apart.'

'You didn't have to do that,' said April.

'No, no, whatever he's done, I'm completely on your side

and I don't want anyone upsetting you on a night when you should be enjoying yourself. Speaking of which, I think we both need a drink,' she continued, leading April back inside the house. 'I don't know if you're aware of this, but my useless brother has invented the best cocktail.'

April laughed and shook her head. 'I've already encountered the Apple Pearl, thanks. I think I'll stick to juice this time.'

Davina pouted. 'Killjoy.'

'On the subject of boys,' said April, 'I haven't seen Jonathon in a while.'

A flicker of distaste passed over Davina's face. 'Oh, ancient history,' she said airily. 'We broke it off when his dad had to move out of town. He was cute, but there's plenty more fish in the sea.'

April had almost been expecting the 'family had to move out of town' line. It was one she and Caro had been hearing again and again as they tried to track down the disappearing Ravenwood students.

'So where did he go?' she asked, as casually as she could.

'Somerset, I think,' said Davina with a sigh, 'or was it Devon? Nowhere with an airport, anyway. But he'll probably like being out in the middle of nowhere, poor boy, he always did spend so much time *reading*.' She snapped her fingers at the barman, then turned to April. 'You sure I can't tempt you?'

'Not right now,' said April. 'Anyway, I've got to visit the little girls' room. See you later.'

April followed the corridor to the left and through the door, locking it behind her. She slipped off her shoe and put her foot up on the closed toilet seat, then pulled up her long skirts. At the top of her thigh, there was a frilly sky-blue garter she had borrowed from her mother's drawer and sticking out of the top of it was April's mobile phone. She pulled it out, gave it a kiss and switched it on, then carefully placed it inside her bra.

'Good job they make these things so slim,' she murmured. No girl should ever leave home without her own personal vampire detection device.

'Right then,' she whispered to herself as she checked her appearance in the mirror. Caro had once again styled her hair beyond recognition: it fell in glossy waves to her bare shoulders. Her amazing violet ball gown and the dark red lips and blusher all made her feel like a 1930s Hollywood siren. 'Not bad,' she said, allowing herself a smile, 'not bad at all.'

She picked up her bag, winked at herself in the mirror and turned to unlock the door. 'Party time,' she said.

Caro was clearly having fun. As April watched her from the top of the stairs, she saw her drink two glasses of champagne in quick succession, before dragging a group of gorgeous men onto the dance floor, throwing shapes to some classics of the synth-pop generation. But she clearly hadn't forgotten her mission, because by the time April pushed her way through the throng, she found her friend sitting at a table deep in conversation with none other than Nicholas Osbourne.

'Hey, April, come and meet Davina's dad,' she shouted, waving April over. 'You'll never believe what a great dancer he is.'

'I don't know about great,' said Nicholas, shaking April's hand. 'I think my children are a little embarrassed.'

'They've obviously never seen you do the "Birdie Song" dance, then,' said Caro.

'Your friend here has just been giving me a lecture in corporate ethics,' said Mr Osbourne, clearly amused. 'She thinks she could run my businesses more efficiently than I do.'

'I simply pointed out that if you donated more money to charitable organisations, it could be a great PR coup worth millions in marketing.'

'What do you think, April?' he asked, turning to include her in the conversation. Behind his back, Caro was mouthing the word 'school'. April almost laughed out loud. 'Well, how much do you donate to charity? It's all tax-deductible, isn't it?'

Nicholas nodded. 'Some of it, anyway.'

'So why not copy the Victorians?' she said. 'The big philan-thropists used to build hospitals and schools.'

'Yes, you could call it the Osbourne School of Dance,' said Caro and Nicholas laughed.

'I like your thinking, girls, but I'm not sure it would work. People are much more cynical about that sort of thing these days. If Agropharm built a hospital there would be an outcry, people accusing us of exploiting the sick, forcing our drugs and equipment on them, even using patients as guinea pigs. It's a crazy topsy-turvy world we live in.'

'So what about a school?' said April.

'Same thing, I'm afraid. It's no secret I'm a big supporter of Ravenwood, but that's acceptable as my kids are students there. Anything more and the liberal press would accuse the company and me of brainwashing young minds and stealing all their best ideas.'

'And our young minds are so impressionable, aren't they, April?' said Caro coquettishly.

'But getting the best minds and stealing their ideas – that's what business does anyway, isn't it?' said April.

'Well, not the brainwashing part,' said Mr Osbourne. 'And we do pay people for their ideas.'

This guy is smart, thought April. She'd expected the Vampire Regent to be intelligent and charismatic, of course, but Davina's dad was as smooth as a politician, which only made him more dangerous.

'I bet you'd like to have Caro on your staff, though, Mr Osbourne,' said April. 'She's in the top one per cent of the country. She's going to study at Harvard.'

'MIT,' corrected Caro. 'Or Cambridge.'

Nicholas chuckled. 'You get your qualifications, then you come to see me, all right?' he said, patting Caro's hand. 'Now, I think I hear Duran Duran coming on. I'll see you ladies later, okay?'

'That man is pure evil,' said Caro when he had gone. 'He's got to be the Regent, *got* to be.'

'What makes you so sure? The love of Duran Duran?'

'I was asking him about his rivals and whether he'd ever consider a merger and he looked like he'd rather cut their throats. He's not the sort of man who would ever let anyone else be in charge.'

'That just makes him an alpha-male captain of industry, Caro. It doesn't make him a vampire.'

'What's made you Little Miss Benefit of the Doubt all of a sudden?' said Caro.

April leant in so they couldn't be overheard, despite the loud music. 'Because I'm the bloody Fury, remember?' she hissed. 'I'm the one who would have to kill him. Not that I've got a clue how I'm supposed to go about that – I can't very well go about kissing everyone at the party, can I? Anyway, if anyone's going to be killed, I want to make damn sure it's the right man.'

'Okay, okay,' said Caro defensively. 'I'm only trying to help.'

'Sorry. I know you are. So where's Simon?'

'Trying to shag anything that moves, as far as I can tell. I asked him what he was doing with all the rugby lot and he was like, "Oh, they're all right once you get to know them, they're a real laugh."' Caro rolled her eyes. 'When I tried to tell him he was in danger, he just called me a mad conspiracy nut. I guess he's got a point – if you don't actually know what they are, it does sound pretty crazy.'

'I'm sorry,' said April. She could tell it was killing Caro to see Simon going over to the 'dark side'.

'It's not like he's my boyfriend or anything,' said Caro, shrugging it off. 'Talking of boyfriends, I think that's my cue to disappear,' she said, nodding to the other side of the room. April looked up and her heart skipped a beat. Gabriel was staring right across at her.

'I'm not surprised he's staring,' whispered Caro, 'you look stunning tonight. But be gentle with him, huh? He is on our side, sort of.'

'We'll see,' said April as she stood up. She walked across the dance floor purposefully.

'April …' said Gabriel, but she ignored him and headed towards the far side of the marquee and out into the gardens. She walked around the ornamental fountain and stopped on the side furthest from the marquee, her arms wrapped around her against the cold.

'Here, put this on,' said Gabriel, coming up behind her and draping his jacket over her shoulders. She couldn't help enjoying the familiar warmth and smell, remembering the other times he had given her his jacket. Nor had it escaped her notice that he was looking gorgeous in his well-filled dinner suit, his bow tie and top button undone, his hair falling down over one eye. She stood there for a minute, staring out over the Osbournes' garden wall to where the gravestones and tombs were twisting from the ground, bleached white in the moonlight.

'It's so peaceful over there at night, isn't it?' she said quietly. 'So pretty.'

'It's not always that way,' said Gabriel.

She turned on him immediately. 'Oh, don't start with your cryptic bullshit, Gabriel. Aren't we beyond that by now? You're a vampire, I'm the saviour of all mankind, what more secrets could there possibly be?' She looked into his face and groaned. 'There are, aren't there?'

'Aren't there what?'

'More secrets.'

'April, you can't—'

'Oh, shut up!' she said. 'You, my mother, my grandfather, even Miss Holden – you all want to talk to me about some secret but never get around to it, and I'm sick to the back teeth of it!' She turned to walk back towards the house. He grabbed her arm and spun her around, so she was looking straight into his dark eyes. They were so fierce, so passionate.

'Look at me, April,' he said. 'I'm here to help you, but you can't keep pushing me away. I know it's hard for you to accept, but there's no point pretending this isn't happening. If we don't do something, the people who killed your father will win. They will go through with whatever they're planning.'

'And what if they do?' snapped April. 'What difference will it make? One more corrupt government, one more group of self-interested people in power? How is that any different from what we have now?'

Gabriel's grip on her arms tightened and he shook her once, hard. 'Oh, *wake up*, April!' he hissed. 'You're not a child any more, so stop thinking like one. These people are not just corrupt, they are evil. *Pure evil*. They will rape and torture you, they will starve you and burn you and laugh all the way. They enjoy pain and suffering, they love the taste of blood. They have no limits, no morality, they will do anything they think will benefit them: nuclear war, chemical weapons, maybe even something worse! Maybe they're planning on pushing the world back into a vicious feudal state with humans as their eternal slaves. *Anything*. How will it be different? It will be hell on earth.'

April was scared now. Scared of Gabriel and the anger in his eyes, scared of the threats and scared of what she might be forced to do. She pulled away from him.

'But I don't want this!' she yelled. 'I don't want to have to deal with any of this.'

'Well, get used to it,' he spat. 'I'm not happy about it either, but we have to work with what we've got.'

'Damn you!' shouted April, punching him on the arm as hard as she could. He dodged her next blow and caught her hands, pulling her into a tight embrace.

'April, listen to me,' he said urgently. 'I wish it was different, I really do, but we need you, *I* need you, I ...' He ground to a halt.

'You what, Gabriel?' she said angrily. 'Spit it out! You love me? You hate me? You want me? What? Tell me how you feel.' She was furious at him, at the whole situation. He was asking her to sacrifice her whole life to go to war with an enemy she couldn't even see. *Sacrifice*, that was the word her father had used the morning they had fought. Well, she didn't want to sacrifice anything, not when the one boy she wanted wasn't prepared to even tell her how he felt.

He looked at her then looked away. 'I swore,' he said. 'I swore I would never go there again.' Gabriel's grip didn't waver when he gazed down at her, his eyes burning like coals. 'You say you didn't ask for any of this, but neither did I,' he said, his voice like gravel. 'I thought that part of my life was gone for ever, yet here you stand in front of me, so ... so ... incredibly beautiful, so wonderful and yet so fragile and dangerous at the same time.'

April could barely breathe. She wanted to respond, but her mouth just hung open.

'All I want is you,' he said. 'More than anything in the world, I want to kiss you and never stop.' He stared down at her and his final words were little more than a whisper. 'But I can't.'

April wrenched herself away from him. 'So does this stupid Fury thing mean we can never be together? Does it mean you have to keep running from me?' she said, tears filling her eyes. Every part of her was yearning for his touch, his kiss, she wanted him to reach out to her, hold her, but to Gabriel she was an infection, an untouchable. It was breaking her heart.

'I don't care about any of that, Gabriel! Don't you understand? I don't care about my destiny or your broken heart or the balance between humans and vampires! All I want is for you to tell me how you feel. No legends, no lore, just two people who like each other, who want to be together. Is that too much to ask?'

Gabriel just looked at her, a terrible air of sadness and regret surrounding him.

'Oh great,' she said, throwing her hands in the air. 'That's just great. You want me to save the world, but you can't commit to a date? And *I'm* the one who's behaving like a child?' She turned and began to run back towards the house, ignoring the pain in her knee and in her heart.

'April!' he called. '*April!*'

But she was gone.

*

409

April sat at the bar, staring down into her second Apple Pearl. *God damn you, Gabriel Swift!* she thought. Everything about him was right: he was sexy, mysterious, serious and funny, he was like an addiction she just couldn't kick, but at the same time he was maddening, always throwing up barriers between them, always finding yet another reason why their love was doomed. The things he had said made her heart judder, but what use was feeling that way if it meant you had to live on either side of a glass wall? Logically, dispassionately, of course she could see that there was a sense to what Gabriel said, but why should they let something written in a dusty old book get in their way? They could move to Paris or the Caribbean or Alaska or something, where none of this mattered, where they could just *be*. Even as she thought it she knew they couldn't. Destiny and birthmarks and vampires and furies aside, April knew she could never be happy if she didn't find out what had happened to her father. *All right, Gabriel*, she thought, taking a long drink and banging the glass down. *If you won't do anything about it, I will.*

What would her father have done? He would have got up off his backside and done something, that was for sure. Action is always better than sitting around making excuses – reading *Hamlet* had taught her that. *Hey, who says schoolwork is a waste of time?* But what did she need to do exactly? Maybe she could call Fiona; she felt so strange keeping her best friend out of the loop, just on a vague suspicion Davina might have 'got to her'. *You have to trust someone some time*, she told herself as she leant forward and felt inside her bra.

'Can I help you with that?'

She looked to her left and saw that Benjamin had slipped onto the stool next to her.

She blew out a long breath. 'Ben! You almost gave me heart failure.'

'Is that what you were massaging inside there?'

April gave him a weak smile. 'Listen, Ben, you're very sweet but—'

Benjamin nodded. 'Hey, don't worry. I heard about the

fight with Gabe. Well, saw it actually. I've ... well, I've never seen Gabriel Swift like this over a girl before.'

She looked up at him, frowning. 'What do you mean?'

'April, you can't have a screaming match in the garden and not expect people to overhear.'

She swallowed. 'And what did you hear?'

'Nothing much, something about how you didn't want this, how you were sick of it, then I think "behaving like a child" was mentioned. Or rather shouted.'

April winced. 'Sorry.'

'Hey, don't feel bad. If Gabriel doesn't know when he's on to a good thing, then that's a bonus for those of us who do.'

April raised an eyebrow. 'Well, thank you, kind sir.'

'Look, I'm not about to give you advice, but it seems to me you're a grown-up and you should do whatever you decide is the right thing.'

April nodded, took a final suck of her straw and tapped her hand on the bar. 'You know what? You're right.' She slid off her stool and walked away, leaving Benjamin staring after her, open-mouthed. As April pushed her way through the crowd, she slipped a hand into her dress and pulled out her phone, keeping it hidden as she turned it on.

Sod Gabriel and sod his bloody prophecy, she thought, *and screw the Furies and their stupid virus. I'm here to find out who killed my father.* If he had been killed for asking too many questions about the vampires, it seemed logical that the man in charge of the Suckers might have a few answers. That was probably Mr Nicholas Osbourne, no less. But first she needed cold, hard evidence. She pushed her way out onto the terrace and down the steps; the dance floor was packed, everyone waving their hands in the air to some seventies disco classic. The perfect cover. She danced her way across to where Mr Osbourne was strutting his stuff with his wife and turned her back to him; then, checking that the flash was off – that would be a dead giveaway, in more ways than one – she slipped the phone under her arm and clicked the button. She danced back over to the tables and sat down, putting the phone in her lap. She scrolled through the menu to the 'pictures' folder and trapping her lower lip between her teeth she clicked 'open'. And there he was, as large as life, dancing away with his wife. Nicholas Osbourne was in the picture.

It couldn't be! *How could he be there?* He was supposed to be a vampire; not only that, he was supposed to be the top vampire! *How dare he be human!* He was clearly a bloodsucker, just not of the vampire variety.

And then she started to laugh.

Through the crowd, she could see Caro and Simon gyrating on the dance floor, as if they were oblivious that they were all teetering on the edge of the abyss.

It's all down to me now, she thought fiercely. *Someone's got to find out who killed my father. Well, if it's not Nicholas, who does that leave? Benjamin and Davina are vampire recruiters, but as far as I know, they don't have any connection with my father.* April felt another jolt of fear. Maybe it wasn't all linked. Maybe there was more than one conspiracy going on here. *God, please don't make this any more complicated,* she moaned to herself. Interesting though the idea might be to explore at a later date, April knew she needed to concentrate on what she did know. *So who else is involved?* Isabelle Davis? Davina knew of her, but she never said she met her. Alix Graves? *Alix!* And then another of those jigsaw pieces clicked into place. April could see Alix's photo on the wall of Benjamin's bedroom and she could hear him saying he had been doing work experience at one of his father's companies. Could it have been Transparent Media, the one Alix was connected with? *Well, there's only one way to find out,* she thought. She pushed through the crowd and up the stairs, then padded along the corridor.

She pushed open Ben's door and peeked inside. Where was the light switch? *No, better not turn it on.* She opened her phone, using the display's backlight like a mini torch. Moving over to Ben's cluttered desk, she started going through the drawers, pulling out papers and holding them up to the light. *Dammit.* The mobile's display just wasn't bright enough. It was impossible to read anything. She fumbled around on the

dresser and turned on a lamp. And then she heard a laugh
– no, it was more of a cackle – and she turned, just feeling the
slap of a blow across her face as she fell sideways.

'You!' said a male voice, high with glee, as strong fingers
seized her face, cruelly pressing into her skin. He twisted
her head around and her heart lurched. *Marcus!* In a blur,
she remembered Gabriel's words about hunters lying in wait,
choosing easy prey. *It can't be!* she thought. *He can't be … can
he?* But she didn't have chance to think any more as she was
pulled sideways.

'I knew it would be you,' crowed Marcus, pushing her back
towards the desk, forcing her face close to the lamp. She began
to scream, but he rammed her face downwards, catching her
cheekbone against the corner of the desk and sending a flower
of pain shooting out from her cheek.

'No, no, no,' he said. 'We can't have you screaming, can
we? Not until we've had our little chat. Now what were you
looking for in here, hmm?'

When April failed to say anything, Marcus slammed her
head forwards again, this time bashing her against the book-
case.

'Speak!' he commanded. 'What. Were. You. Looking. For?'
On each word, he pushed her closer and closer to the lamp
until the burning pain of the bulb against her skin was unbearable. She twisted to get away but he was too strong.

'Were you going to take another of your clever little photos
with this, hmm?' he said, dangling her phone in front of her
face, then smashing it against the wall. 'Tell me or I will make
the pain go on for ever. Believe me, you will wish you'd got
this over with quickly,' he hissed, pushing his mouth close to
her ear and whispering, 'Like your dear old dad.'

'NO!' she began to yell, but Marcus was too quick: he
slammed her head against the wall and little stars popped
across April's vision. She could feel blood running from her
temple.

'There's no rush, Angel,' he cooed, running a finger down

her face, then slowly licking her blood from the tip. 'Not when you taste so good.' He grinned manically.

He's a vampire, oh God, Marcus is a vampire, her mind screamed. *And he's trapped me. The hunter has caught his prey.*

'I'm *wait*-ing!' he sang, slamming her head against the wall again.

'Drugs!' she screamed.

Suddenly Marcus flung her to the floor.

'What? What drugs?'

April thought fast. She had a reputation as the school's bad girl with her visits from the police, so perhaps it had a shred of credibility. But only a shred.

'I wanted some, and I thought Ben might have hidden them in his room,' she said, drawing the words out, playing for time.

'Ben does not use drugs,' said Marcus, his voice dripping with disdain. Every word he uttered chilled April to the core. He was a vampire, a killer, he was going to drink her blood. *Oh God, please God help me*, she thought. But then something inside her clicked. Something Gabriel had said about predators, about leopards and lions.

'Do you?' she said quietly. 'Do you use drugs?'

'What?' hissed Marcus, outraged. 'No!'

'Well, what were you doing in Benjamin's bedroom, then?' she asked, edging closer to him. 'What were you doing in here, all on your own in the dark?'

He raised his hand again. 'I'm warning you!' he said, but April could see he was rattled.

'Does it make you feel sexy, Marcus?' she whispered. 'Do you like being close to Ben's things ... you *freak*!' she screamed, simultaneously grabbing the lamp and throwing it at his face. Marcus jerked back in surprise and gave her just enough space to jump over the bed and dive into the bathroom, locking the door behind her.

'You *bitch*!' he yelled, and she saw the door handle rattle up and down violently. April grabbed a chair and jammed it against the door just as it shuddered in its frame. Marcus was throwing himself against it.

'I'm going to kill you, you little bitch!' he screamed, followed by another thud against the doorframe. April looked around desperately. It was a small room – sink, bath, shower and two sash windows to one side.

THUD.

She pushed her face against the window and cupped her hands around her eyes, but she couldn't see anything but blackness down there. No way out. *I'm trapped. And Marcus is going to kill me.*

THUD.

She looked around quickly. Maybe she could find something to use as a weapon, but beyond a shampoo bottle and a disposable razor, there was nothing. This time, the thud was accompanied by the sound of splintering wood. Surely someone would hear the noise and come to investigate? But she knew, with the disco and the noise of the party and the size of the house, it was unlikely. She could scream her lungs out and never be heard. No, she had to save herself this time.

THUD.

She looked back at the windows. They were her only chance; she had to get out or he was going to kill her. She quickly undid the locks on the first window and heaved. *Damn!* It was stuck fast. She tried the other and it gave a little, enough to get her fingers under it.

'Nowhere to run, bitch!' yelled Marcus through the door. 'I'm going to have fun with you!'

She heaved with all her might and – *thank God* – it opened a little more. She heaved again and the gap looked just big enough. It had to be.

THUD.

She forced her bare shoulders through, the decades of layers of paint cutting into her skin.

CRASH.

She was almost through – until his hand closed around her ankle. He pulled hard, but he was too late. She kicked out, hit something, and then she was pitching forwards, down, down into the black, twisting, turning. *God, I'm going to break my neck.* And then *THUD!* Her own thud, this time. April had landed on something soft, yielding, wet and warm. And then she was flailing around, terrified, disorientated. *Am I drowning?* she thought. And then she realised. Her fall had been cushioned by the plastic cover of the hot tub and her lower body had sunk into the water. She scrabbled around and finally gripped the side of the tub, rolling over onto the floor, her wet dress clinging to her.

'Bitch! You bitch!' screamed Marcus in frustration. Surely he wasn't going to follow her.

SLAM-PLASH.

Wrong. April felt the spray from the hot tub as Marcus landed in it feet first. *My God, he's crazy!* She scrambled to her feet – only one shoe, kicking it off, tearing up the seam of her dress so she could move. *Mum'll kill me, that cost a fortune*, she thought madly as she looked around. *Which way?* She couldn't run towards the house because Marcus could easily cut her off in that direction, so she vaulted over the balustrade and ran across the sloping lawn, angling towards the marquee, feeling the snow on her bare feet, burning with cold.

'Gabriel!' she screamed. 'Anyone! HELP ME!'

'Too late,' hissed Marcus. He had moved so fast, cutting her off, unimpeded by dress and bare feet. For a moment, his face was caught in the light from the house: his lips were pulled back in a snarl, his eyes narrow and black, his nose upturned; he looked the way Gabriel had, that night by the Thames.

So you can see me as others do, that's what he had said. *So you can see me as I really am.*

April didn't have time to think, she was running for her life. She swung around and headed the only way she could – towards the graveyard wall. Without stopping to think or break stride she leapt for the wall, her bare toes digging into the bricks, skin tearing painfully, her nails splintering, all the time expecting to feel his hands grab her. And again she was falling, rolling over and over, this time landing in snow-bent bushes, the branches jamming into her thighs, her shoulders, her chest, her torn knee screaming with fresh pain. Desperately, she pulled herself free, not feeling the wounds now, totally focused on getting away. She ran forward blindly, her palms held out in front of her, thumping into gravestones and trees, their angles catching her knees, their roots pulling at her ankles. She ran and ran, until finally she ran straight into the side of a tall white monument, the stone slamming into the side of her head, dazing her and sending her careering sideways into a snow-filled ditch. She was winded, dizzy, gasping for breath, but instinct told her to stop, to play dead. To hold her breath *like a mouse hiding in his house*, sang her mind crazily. She listened, straining her ears for sounds of her pursuer, but there was nothing. Had she lost him? Had he failed to get over the wall? Had someone seen or heard them fall into the hot tub?

No.

'I can *hear* you,' sang Marcus, terrifyingly close. 'I can hear your little rabbit heart beating.'

Don't call me rabbit, thought April angrily. *Only my dad calls me rabbit.*

He was close, just to her left, but she was shielded by two splintered gravestones, fallen, broken fragments of them cutting into her back.

'I'm going to find you, you do know that, don't you?' called Marcus. 'And when I find you, Marcus is going to have all the time he wants with you, isn't he? No one will hear you scream out here.'

She could hear his footsteps crunching on leaves. *He's going away*, she thought, hope rising ...

'And when I'm finished with you, I'm going to do to you what I did to those bleeders in Covent Garden,' he said, a note of glee in his voice.

April almost squeaked in surprise.

'Oh yes, I tore their throats wide open, just where your boyfriend left them. You never knew it was me, did you? I was watching you, tracking you, waiting for my moment. But

Gabriel Swift got in the way. He's always getting in the way.'

April wanted to scurry away, she wanted to run. But instinctively she knew her only chance was to stay as still as she could, hold her breath, hope that he wouldn't find her, hope he couldn't hear her shivering bones. *Marcus is a vampire, Marcus is a vampire ...* she thought. He must be the rogue vampire Gabriel was talking about, the out-of-control killer, mastered by his urges, unable to stop. *A modern-day Jack the Ripper*, added her dangerously overstretched mind.

'But no one's going to get in the way any more, are they? No, because after I've dealt with you, next on my list is Caro Jackson, then your little friend Fiona, and then that meddling Gabriel Swift will be no problem at all.'

April wanted to scream, to lunge at him, to stop him before he hurt anyone else she loved, but all she could do was lie there, turn herself to stone. She could hear his footsteps, just on the other side of the graves, crunching in the snow.

'Can't you forgive me, April?' he whispered. 'I was only following orders, after all. Isabelle was getting too close, you see, he didn't like her asking so many questions. And your dad? Well, that was inevitable, wasn't it?'

Marcus, Marcus killed my father!

She could see him moving to her left now, creeping forwards, his arms outstretched, his silhouette like a horrible twisted tree come to life.

'Alix Graves, well, that was something different. Alix couldn't make up his mind. He wanted to join us, told us he could persuade all his little teenage fans that eternal life was better than living with Mum and Dad. But then Alix got cold feet. And now he's cold all over, isn't he?'

Marcus had stopped. Only his head was moving, slowly turning from side to side.

'But you know how I'm going to catch you?' he said.

She held her breath. Waited. Waited. And then she screamed. Because in one terrible rushing noise he was on her, his sharp fingers gripping her neck, his breath on her cheek. His crazy, crazy eyes staring right down into hers.

'Because I can *smell* you,' he growled, and his nose turned upwards, his grin stretched wide, his teeth bared. As his long fingers tightened around her throat she flailed with her arms and legs, trying to get a grip on something, tearing his shirt, nails sinking into his bare chest.

'Don't struggle, little rabbit,' he said. 'We've got all the time in the world.' He squeezed tighter and tighter and April could feel herself getting weaker. She reached out desperately with her fingers, the tips just touching something rough. She scrabbled, trying to get hold of it, of anything, before her breath finally gave out. With one last buck of her chest, she forced out a groan. 'Grrun ... Arllee ... Haaart.'

'What's that? Did you speak?' He chuckled nastily.

'GRRuN ... arllHee ... Hubt,' she tried again, her head swimming.

Marcus loosened his grip just slightly, curious as to what his prey was trying to communicate.

'What?' he whispered into her ear, his mouth opening, slowly licking her neck with his cold tongue.

'Don't ... call me ... rabbit!' she snarled and swung the rock in her hand with all her might. It caught him square on the temple, spraying blood and goo up her arm. Howling, he tried to roll off her, but she clung on, using his momentum to swing over on top of him. Straddling him, she raised the jagged rock again and smashed it down into his eye, feeling a twisted joy as he screamed, then brought it down again, smashing his mouth open, teeth pink and broken. 'Don't call me rabbit!' she screamed, crashing the stone into his face again and again. 'Only my dad can call me that,' she shouted, the rock rising and falling in a frenzy. 'And he's DEAD! Because you killed him, you BASTARD!'

Finally she could lift it no more and she collapsed on top of Marcus, her shoulders heaving with the exertion, her lungs choked with sobs, her throat raw from screaming and from Marcus's death-grip. She crawled away through the snow, pulling herself up on a gravestone.

Is this it? she thought. *Is this what being a Fury is? Beating out someone's brains in a cemetery at midnight?*

'Is this your prophecy?' she sobbed out loud. 'Is this my future?'

'What prophecy?' said a rough voice, and then with a great roar, she was flying through the air, her back slamming against the monument with a crunch. *He's still alive,* she thought with an almost amused detachment. *How can he be alive?*

'What prophecy?' Marcus yelled down into her face, spittle and blood flying from his shattered teeth. He lifted her again and threw her into the air as if she was a broken toy, and then there was sudden crunching, piercing pain as she landed on top of a fallen stone cross. Agony lanced through her side as he lifted her again and slammed her back down. Her head lolled around and she saw that he had dropped her on top of a flat coffin-shaped tomb. She couldn't move her right arm, could see it sticking out at a crazy angle, and she could taste the sharp metallic tang of fresh blood in her mouth.

Again he gripped her throat and she felt more pain, a terrible dark, sapping pain in her chest.

'Tell me about the prophecy, April Dunne,' he said softly, stroking her face. 'Tell me everything you know before I make you beg for death.' He wrenched her arm and she screamed, the white-hot agony filling her mind. 'How do you know about us? Was it your dear dead daddy? Who told you?'

This time he didn't give her chance to speak, instead squeezing his grip tighter. His voice was getting fainter, more distant. The cold from the tomb seemed to be seeping into her body, pulling her down into its embrace.

'Whoever it was, perhaps you'll know we can recover from wounds,' he was saying in an almost conversational tone, sounding as if he was walking away down a tunnel. 'And you'll know we gain strength from your blood, so your death won't be in vain ...'

Then it was as if a tornado had rushed into the cemetery. April heard a gurgling scream, like someone drowning in treacle, then she was bathed in white. She could see a kind face above her – was it Gabriel? – and the cold and the pain faded. She would have been happy to stay here and just sleep on this nice warm rock, let the black duvet wrapping itself around her swallow her for ever. And then it changed again and she was filled up, and up and up, like that man she'd seen at the circus who blew up a hot water bottle until it burst. And suddenly the pain came rushing back into her arm and her side and her head.

'No,' she tried to say, tried to stop him. 'You mustn't!'

But Gabriel was smiling down at her, bringing his lips to hers, kissing her so tenderly, so softly, so full of love. 'I've been waiting so long for this,' he whispered. 'I wouldn't want to be in this world without you.'

And, tears running down her face, she lifted her chin to join him in the kiss, feeling the warmth of his skin, wanting to pull him closer and closer, at once horrified at what he was doing, and so full of happiness that she might melt. She opened her eyes again and she could see fluffy white snowflakes falling towards them, landing on her cheeks and eyelids as his warm lips brushed against her ear and he whispered, 'I love you, April Dunne.' As if in slow motion she gasped, kissed, laughed, suspended in a perfect moment of peace and wonder and joy, then suddenly Gabriel was gone and the rest of the world was sucked in, with noise and movement and lights. Another face was there – it was Mr Osbourne, Davina's dad, the one who wasn't a vampire – and he seemed angry and he was shouting orders and pointing and talking into a phone. Then she turned her head and looked down at her arm. And then she was screaming again. The world was snow and blood and broken bone, and everything hurt. And she had killed Gabriel Swift, the boy who said he loved her.

Chapter Forty-One

Caro had eaten all the grapes again. April would have laughed if it didn't hurt so much. During the week she had been in hospital, Caro had come in every day after school bearing a plastic carrier bag of fruit, crisps and unhealthy fizzy drinks to 'help build up the patient's strength', despite having been repeatedly told that April was not allowed – was unable, in fact – to eat anything except the pureed hospital food. 'Ah well, can't let it go to waste,' she would shrug, reaching for the Wotsits. April actually enjoyed the routine and was glad to have her friend to distract her with stories of the world outside, particularly details of the aftermath of what Caro now referred to as 'The Winter Ball Massacre'. April was amused to hear that the school had bequeathed her a 'Wall of April' opposite 'Milo's Wall', which was crammed with cards and letters from well-wishers, the same well-wishers who had so recently been exchanging gossip about her supposed loose behaviour at the Halloween party.

'That girl Emily from your Philosophy class is now claiming that you and she are best buddies and that you're going on holiday together when you get out of here. Clacton, I think it is.'

April giggled and immediately winced. On top of the pain in her bruised neck, laughter would also bring on shooting pains in her side where she had broken three ribs. Considering she had been attacked by a bloodthirsty monster from hell, April considered herself to have got off lightly. She'd had eighteen stitches in her head, a bruised spleen, a broken little finger and damage to her larynx. Worst of all, her arm had not been broken, it had been bitten, torn open down one side. 'It looked like a Rottweiler had got hold of you,' the surgeon had told her later. It was currently stapled together pending another operation, and bound up in bandages two inches thick.

Apart from an awful lot of very dark blood, no trace had been found of Marcus and the police were working on the theory that he had somehow managed to skip the country. According to DI Reece, who had visited the day before, they were also keen to talk to him in connection with both the Alix Graves and Isabelle Davis murders, although April guessed that this was due to pressure from his superiors to clear up the unsolved cases, rather than from a wealth of evidence. April's statement was, she suspected, all the evidence they had.

'There are about fifty theories going around school about Marcus,' said Caro as she unzipped a banana. 'Crack addiction, radiation poisoning, some sort of gay love tryst.'

'I take it that last one was Simon's?' asked April.

'You know him too well.' Caro smiled. 'The funny thing is that no one's really going for the—' she lowered her voice '—*vampires* angle, especially considering it all happened in Highgate Cemetery. I was convinced the media would be all over it, but maybe Nicholas Osbourne has managed to hush the whole thing up.'

April smiled. Even now, Caro couldn't let the conspiracy theory go, despite the fact they had proven Davina's father was neither a vampire nor the heartless fiend Caro had claimed. In many ways, April owed Nicholas Osbourne her life. After Gabriel had carried her onto the lawn, Davina's dad had realised that it would take too long for an ambulance to reach the house, so he'd carried April to his car and driven her to A&E himself – mercifully close to the house – at high speed, running red lights and taking corners at sixty. Of course, without Gabriel, she would never have made it that far. Without Gabriel's sacrifice, she would be lying next to her dad right now.

Oh God, Gabriel, what did you do? she thought for the hundredth time. *Why did you do it?*

When she had come round, two days after the attack, the doctors had told her how the young man had used his shirt to skilfully bind her wound. 'An amazing job,' said the consultant. 'Without it, you would have bled to death for sure.'

But that wasn't all. No, Gabriel had done something else, something so wonderful and terrible it still made her heart lurch to think of it. He had given her the kiss of life, despite knowing it would kill him. He had put his lips to hers and breathed life into her, even as she stole his away from him, infecting him with the Fury virus. April had done little else but lie there and think over the past few days and she would swing from anger at his stupidity to amazement at the incredible, selfless, loving thing he had done. Because it *was* love, she was sure of it. He hadn't just resuscitated her, he had kissed her – he had kissed her there, half-dead in the snow of the cemetery, a full-on, passionate kiss that she had felt from her toes to the tips of her ears. And then – it made her heart leap so hard it hurt – he had told her he loved her. He *loved* her. More than that: *he didn't want to be in the world without her*, those had been his actual words. April had tried to bring it up, to discuss it, to dissect the meaning when Gabriel had visited over the past few days, but she had found that whenever she tried to repeat the words, her throat closed and she choked, and instead she had simply held his hand and whispered, 'Me too.' Right now, April decided to concentrate on simpler matters.

'So how's everyone else?' she asked.

'Ah well, Davina's thriving on the fact that it all happened yards from her bedroom and the fact that her dad was the unlikely hero. I was right about that too, by the way – the power of positive PR. Agropharm's share price has gone through the roof after his heroics. I wouldn't like to suggest he only saved you for the publicity, but ...'

April smirked. 'You're still miffed he didn't turn out to be the Regent, aren't you?'

Caro pulled a satsuma out of her bag and began to peel it. 'A bit.' She smiled. 'But it doesn't mean that the Regent, whoever he is, isn't the one behind the school. And there's still that email from Nicholas to Hawk to explain. I mean, what does he want Ravenwood students for, exactly?' She noticed April's troubled expression and pulled an apologetic face. 'Hey, you don't need to worry about all that now,' said Caro. 'You just concentrate on getting better. Besides, Gabriel and I had a bit of a pow-wow last night and Big Gabe reckons the suckers will back right off now. There's too much heat on them at the moment. Plus they must have loads of Christmas shopping to do. Capes, candles, that sort of thing.'

April giggled and winced again.

'So how's your mum coping?' asked Caro.

'It's ironic, but I think it's been good for her, having her daughter in intensive care,' said April. 'It's given her something else to fret about. She certainly looks healthier these days and she and Grandpa Thomas seem to be getting along better. They've promised to give me "a big talk" when I've recovered, God knows what that's going to be about. Stay away from crazy boys, probably.'

'Speak of the devil,' said Caro, looking across April's bed and nodding towards the door of her room. She turned to see Gabriel standing there and her heart did a cartwheel. He was wrapped up in a big coat and he looked tired.

'Hey there, hero,' said Caro, standing up. 'Your turn to cheer up the patient.'

'Don't go on my account,' said Gabriel, but Caro held up the empty goodie bag. 'I'm all out of supplies,' she said, leaning over to kiss April goodbye.

When she was gone, Gabriel pulled up a chair and they smiled at each other awkwardly. April was glad he had come, but it hurt her to see him looking so drained. There was so much she wanted to say to him, but she just didn't know how. She pushed herself up and swung her legs off the bed.

'We're going for a walk in the garden,' she said to a nurse as they left April's room, then took Gabriel's arm and they walked slowly down to a wide silver lift that opened into the same lobby she had stood in the night her father had died.

They walked to the rear entrance, into a garden overlooking Waterlow Park to the north and the East Cemetery to the south. Through the trees they could just see the top of the Osbourne mansion and April shivered. Gabriel draped his coat around her shoulders, almost a ritual between them now, and they walked along the path.

'So how are you feeling?'

'Not bad,' said April, gesturing to her injured arm. 'Apparently I'm healing really quickly. Not as quick as you, of course. Well, I mean, as quick as you used to heal. Sorry, I didn't think.'

Gabriel laughed. 'Don't worry,' he said. 'I'm okay. I quite like it in a funny way.'

'How can you like it?' said April with sadness in her voice. 'You're dying.'

Gabriel let a long breath out, his cheeks pink. 'I haven't been ill in a hundred years. Not a cold, not a headache, barely even a scratch. When you get used to being that way, it makes you complacent and arrogant. You lose touch with life.'

They stopped where the wall bordered the cemetery. There was a little green space with benches and they sat down. Gabriel ran a hand over the bare branches of a shrub growing next to their seat as if he was seeing a tree for the first time.

'Nature is all about things being born and dying, isn't it?' he said quietly. 'In a few months there will be leaves here and flowers in the beds. There's a flow to the world that you can only see when you're vulnerable. Normal people get sad when it rains, they worry about germs, they look forward to spring. None of that matters to a vampire, because nothing can touch us. It's funny, I feel more alive than I have in years, now that I'm dying. And now that I have you.'

'But maybe you're not going to die,' said April, tears springing into her eyes. 'Maybe there's a cure.'

Gabriel put his cold hand up to touch her face. 'There is, April.' He smiled. 'It's you. You are the cure.'

She was crying now. 'But I've only just found you,' she sobbed. 'Why does everything I love have to go away?'

He took her face in his hands and kissed her. His lips were soft and warm and April could feel him next to her, his heart beating as hard as hers. *God, is this how it feels?* she thought. *Is this really love?* Then suddenly she pulled back, pushing him away ineffectually with her one good arm.

'Oh God, what have you done?' she said. 'You can't kiss me!'

Gabriel laughed. 'Oh yes I can!' He chuckled, gathering her up in his arms and kissing her again. 'You can't infect me twice, can you?'

April looked unconvinced. 'But maybe I'll make it worse or something.'

He shook his head and placed two fingers on her lips. 'Trust me, I'm a doctor.'

'You're a *what?*'

He threw his head back and laughed, but there was a rasping sound to it that April didn't like at all. 'I'm over a hundred years old, remember?' he said. 'You stick around long enough, you can learn a lot. Got to fill your time with something – we don't all play the church organ in the dead of night, you know.'

April stared at him open-mouthed.

'You're a *doctor?*'

Somehow this was harder to believe than him being un-dead.

'Remember I was a student when I was turned? I switched from law to medicine. I needed to be near blood, so it seemed logical. Unfortunately, I have to keep doing the exams.'

'Why?'

'Because I look like this,' he said, pointing to his face. 'I can pass for early twenties, but I'm perpetually a junior doctor, so every few years I have to start again and requalify in a different place.'

'But doesn't seeing all that blood send you into a feeding frenzy or something?'

Gabriel shook his head. 'Just the opposite. Imagine you were a drug addict who ran a chemist's. You wouldn't spend your whole time off your head, would you? Having so much blood around makes it easier.'

'But aren't there other ways to get blood?'

'Well, most vampires have feeders, people who let them drink a little of their blood every day.'

'Don't you?'

'I have in the past,' he said, and April found herself feeling ridiculously jealous.

'So, what – you have access to the blood banks?'

Gabriel nodded. 'It's not like I'm denying anyone – despite what the blood donor drives tell you, there's always a huge surplus of type O.'

'So because of your training you were able to stop my arm bleeding?'

Gabriel nodded. April tried to remember it, but all she got was a jumble of images: the sensation of falling, gravestones and trees, Marcus's face covered with blood. She turned to Gabriel.

'Why did you do it, Gabriel? Why did you save me?'

He brushed the hair away from her face. 'Because I couldn't let you go,' he said softly.

'But you're going to have to now, aren't you?' she said, feeling tears sting her eyes. 'Now we'll be apart anyway.' It was all so unfair: she had found her perfect man, done everything she could to push him away, and now, when he had finally told her he loved her, he had given his life for hers.

'Hey, I'm not dead yet,' he said and pulled her in for another kiss.

'Ahem ...'

At the sound of someone clearing their throat, April glanced away from Gabriel and found herself looking at Miss Holden.

'Miss ...' she stammered, instinctively pulling away from Gabriel. 'What are you doing here?'

The teacher raised her eyebrows. 'It's visiting hours, April, the nurse told me where to find you.' She held up the bag she was carrying. 'I brought you some books I thought might help pass the time.'

Homework? thought April bitterly. *Haven't I suffered enough?*

'Well, I think I'd better be going,' said Gabriel, standing up.

'Indeed,' said Miss Holden. He nodded to the teacher, but then turned back to April. Slowly, deliberately, he planted his lips on hers, taking his time with the kiss.

Wow! was all her brain could come up with, hoping he might do it again, but instead he just turned and walked back to the hospital.

'Well.' Miss Holden cleared her throat uncomfortably. 'Are you allowed to drink tea? Because I could certainly do with a cup.'

In the ground-floor café, the teacher brought April a cup of warm soup and they settled down at an out-of-the-way table.

'Do I really have to do homework?' asked April, blowing on her soup.

'It is Ravenwood, April,' said Miss Holden. 'You can't get behind. Anyway, I thought you'd want something to keep your mind off things, since you've had an awful lot on your plate recently.'

April shrugged. 'I'm doing okay,' she said. 'I mean, it has been tough with the new school and my dad and everything, but—'

'Oh, I don't mean all that,' said Miss Holden, taking a sip of her tea. 'I mean the vampires.'

She said it so lightly, in such an offhand manner, that April didn't think she could have heard her right. 'I'm sorry, the vampires?'

Miss Holden smiled. 'Yes, April. I know all about it, and I've been trying to discuss it with you.' She raised an eyebrow. 'It's been rather difficult so far.'

April put down her spoon. Suddenly she didn't feel like eating any more.

'You … you know?'

The teacher nodded. 'I've been a little economical with the truth, I'm afraid. It's true that as a teacher, it's my responsibility to look after you, but my responsibilities actually go a lot further than that. I know that you've recently discovered your true place in the world and I'm here to help you however I can.'

April shifted in her seat. She felt uncomfortable and, frankly, a bit weird. Was this woman really telling her that she knew about the Furies thing?

'What place in the world?'

'You're a Fury, April. You have the mark behind your ear, don't you?'

April couldn't help reaching up to touch her hair defensively. 'I don't know what you mean,' she said.

Miss Holden nodded and looked down at her cup. 'I completely understand. This must be the strangest thing in the world for you at the moment. Not only have you discovered that vampires are actually real, you've discovered that some of them live in your town, in your street. Then, when you're getting your head around that, you find that they even go to your school.'

April genuinely couldn't think what to say. It seemed stupid to deny it when Miss Holden clearly knew so much, but even so, she had become used to being paranoid and careful. After all, she had no idea who this woman really was or what she wanted. She said she was here to help, but how could she possibly help?

'I don't know what you're talking about,' said April, as evenly as she could.

Miss Holden smiled slightly. 'Okay, fine,' she said, fixing April with a serious look. 'I'm guessing that no one has been straight with you up until now, so I will be. My name is Annabel Holden and I am a Guardian. I have known about the vampires since before I could talk, and I have been fighting them ever since I could stand. The Guardians are a secret society dedicated to gathering information on the vampires and doing everything we can to prevent their rise. We have been doing this since the first undead climbed from the grave, and many believe that moment pre-dates the Bible. My mother was a Guardian and so was my grandfather; the secret is passed down the generations. We have a network of friends around the world – police, church members, academics, even people in government – who let us know where the vampires are active. We go there to do what we can. That's why I'm here, that's why I teach at Ravenwood. At first, I thought I was here to learn about the Ravenwood organisation and do my best to protect the students, but now it seems I am here to train you.'

'Train me?'

Miss Holden smiled. 'Not like Rocky. I'm here to teach you everything I know about vampires. Who they are, what they can do, what they want. What you can do. Because without that knowledge, you'll be in serious danger.' She watched April's face carefully. 'I don't want to scare you, April, but it's pointless to pretend otherwise. There's something bad happening around us, a darkness is gathering.'

'A darkness?'

'Three high-profile killings, unprovoked attacks, an increase in recruitment, and I think that's just the beginning. The vampires are on the move. Maybe it's just a power struggle between the clans, but the rise of Ravenwood suggests a bigger plan, something much more far-reaching and sinister.'

'But wasn't Marcus acting alone?' asked April with a terrible feeling of dread. It had been hard enough to grasp the fact that she'd been half-killed by a vampire, but the idea that it might not have been a random act was too much to bear.

Miss Holden saw her frightened expression and softened her tone. 'Yes, it's possible Marcus was just out of control, although if he was involved in your dad or Isabelle's deaths, I assume he was acting on orders, but this –' she gestured towards April's wounds '– this was personal. I'm sorry. I should have guessed that Marcus would do something like this after you were targeted by Benjamin.'

'I was targeted?'

'Yes. All of your friends have been – you must have noticed that?'

April looked down at her hands, feeling guilt at having dragged so many people she cared about into this horrible mess.

'I can only think Marcus felt threatened by you when he saw how strongly Benjamin, Davina and the rest of the vampires were drawn to you. He felt the attraction too and I think he hated being so powerless; that's probably what sent him over the edge. Mr Sheldon disciplined him after he threatened you, of course, and I thought that would be enough, but I was wrong.'

'What do you mean, they were drawn to me?'

'You're a Fury, April. Like it or not, you're a part of nature, a counterbalance to the vampires. You're a honey trap for vampires. Everything about you is designed to draw them in: the way you look, the sound of your voice, even your smell. You must have noticed that people at the school were reacting to you in an unusual way?'

April felt cold; goosebumps ran up and down her unbandaged arm. She *had* felt it. Of course, she had assumed it was because she was new and therefore interesting, but perhaps ... It would certainly explain a lot: like why someone like Milo Asprey would want to kiss her. Like why Davina wanted to be friends with her. But could any of this be true? Was she really that different from everyone else? She knew one thing: she didn't *want* to be different.

'You're not saying much,' said Miss Holden.

April shook her head. She was reluctant to open up to the teacher, tell her how angry she felt at having been backed into this corner, having so much heaped upon her shoulders, having people around her get hurt. She wanted to tell someone, to let it all out before she burst, but she had no idea who Miss Holden really was and what she wanted from her. April shrugged. 'I'm finding it hard to get excited about any of it to be honest. My dad's dead, I've been mauled by a lunatic and ... well, I've got a lot on my mind.'

'Gabriel, you mean?' she asked.

April looked up and saw a kind expression on the teacher's face. 'For what it's worth, I don't think the Fury thing is what drew him to you,' said Miss Holden. 'I think there's a much simpler explanation.'

April could feel herself choking up and Miss Holden touched her hand gently. 'I know what he did for you, April,' she said softly. 'It was a wonderful thing, whoever or whatever he is. So maybe this will help: a Guardian's job is to know where the vampires are and what they're doing, and as far as I know, Gabriel Swift hasn't shown any interest in another woman since he buried Lily.'

April's eyes widened. 'How do you know about Lily?'

'I know the whole story, April – it's what I do. But you watch yourself with him, okay? He may have saved your life but he's still a vampire.'

April shook her head, tears pricking her eyes again. 'Not for much longer.'

Miss Holden lifted her bag onto the table and pulled out a book. 'Listen, I've got to be getting back to school, but I'll leave you this.'

She slid it across to April. It was an old linen-bound book, the sort Mr Gill had stacked up in their thousands. On the spine in faded letters was the title *Magick and Ritual*.

'This will answer a lot of your questions,' she said. 'It's a sort of *Rough Guide* to mythical creatures, written in 1840. You can take whatever you find in there as gospel, more or less.' She tapped the edge of the book where a bright pink Post-it note was sticking out. 'I think you'll be particularly interested in chapter six. I've marked the page, although as a Guardian, I really shouldn't be telling you about it. Think of it as a goodwill gesture.'

April looked at her quizzically, but Miss Holden just smiled.

'You'll see,' she said, rising. 'And I've written my numbers on the bookmark. Give me a call when you feel up to it, then we can have a proper talk. My door, of course,' she said with an ironic smile, 'is always open.'

April got up with her and walked back towards the lifts. 'So what happens when I go back to school?' she asked.

'Business as usual. I'm the teacher, you're just another student.'

'But how can I pretend nothing's happened?'

Miss Holden stopped and looked at April, her expression deadly serious. 'You *have* to, April, because your life depends on it and so do the lives of the people around you.'

April began to object, but the teacher held up a hand to stop her.

'Yes, I know you don't like it and I can sympathise, but the vampires will be looking for you – some of them will have worked out that there is a Fury in their midst –and it's vital that we stop them before they figure out who and what you are. The best way to do that is to stay in school, gain their confidence and try to get to them from the inside. Your friend Caro's theory is a good one. Only this time, we will be doing it together.'

April nodded. She wasn't sure she had grasped everything Miss Holden had told her, but she believed her when she said she was in danger.

'So does this mean I'll get an A in History?' she asked.

'No, April. It doesn't,' said the teacher as she turned away. But April could see that she was smiling.

April got back in the lift and returned to her room. Carefully laying Gabriel's coat on the chair, she clambered into bed with difficulty and opened the book. The chapter was headed *Mesapotamic Alchemy: Solve et Coagula.*

What is that? French? Latin? she wondered. She read on:

The great Persian alchemists were men of infinite wisdom and vast ambition, and among their myriad lusts were three primary aspirations, to whit: the transmutation of base metal into gold, the creation of a panacea – a universal remedy that held the power to cure all known contagions – and the discovery of alcahest, a universal solvent which could dissolve any material, even the hardest stones. The most ancient and secretive of all the alchemists were the Hermetic scholars whose dread experiments combined all of the magick and heretical knowledge to one end: the search for immortality. Many believe that the Muslim physician Muhammad ibn Zakariya al-Razi, or Rhazes, actually succeeded in his quest in the ninth century, inadvertently creating the vampire race, although another, equally lucid school believes the alchemists were searching for a cure to the vampire disease: a chicken and egg argument. What is indisputable is that by the early sixteenth century, with the rise of chemistry and biology as mainstream philosophical approaches, many branches of alchemy were forced to choose a side, go underground, or both – for example, the Guardian sect, direct descendants of the alchemist Rhazes, who had sworn to use their substantial knowledge to fight vampires and lycanthropes. The Guardians also swore to protect the Furies, a group of humans with the biological ability to destroy vampires. Guardian lore also contends that they held the antidote to the Fury virus, known as 'Dragon's Breath', suggesting that the sect had great magickal learning. Little is known of this elixir, except that it involved distilling the root of the Hawmarsh tree and the leaves of the Spirula plant, only found in a very few ancient English woods. The recipe is supposedly hidden in the Latin tract Liber Albus, one of the many spellbooks lost with the rise of materialism.

'What are you reading?'

April looked up to see Gabriel standing at the foot of her bed.

'Gabriel!' she cried and jumped up, throwing her one good arm around him awkwardly.

'Hey, steady!' He laughed, hugging her back, then helped her into bed.

'You came back.'

He shrugged sheepishly. 'For my coat. I'm feeling the cold all of a sudden.'

April threw a pillow at him. 'And there I was thinking you couldn't stay away from me.'

'That too.' He smiled.

'Listen, I've got some amazing news,' said April eagerly, quickly explaining what Miss Holden had told her, then showing him the book. When she had finished, Gabriel just nodded and looked thoughtful.

'What's the matter?' asked April. 'Aren't you pleased?'

'Of course. I want to stick around as long as possible now I've found you.' He smiled at her. 'But there's a catch.'

'What catch?'

'This potion – assuming we can find all the ingredients – may well counteract the Fury virus, but it won't cure me. I'll still be a vampire, April.'

'But you'll be alive!' said April with excitement. 'And where there's life there's hope, Gabriel. Once you're back to strength we can start looking for the Vampire Regent, but first we have to get you well. Please, Gabriel,' she said, the tears beginning to run down her face. 'Don't go away just when I've found you.'

Gabriel pulled her to him and hugged her tightly. 'I don't want to leave you. It's just that this past week, I've felt so alive, so connected with the world, with you, and I don't want to lose that either. But of course you're right. Let's find the book, wherever and whatever it might be. Let's find the Regent. Let's find the man who had your father killed. Okay?'

She looked up at him with shining eyes. 'Okay,' she said.

He pushed her back onto the bed and began kissing away her tears. 'Besides which, I've got some ideas of my own.'

April giggled and reached out for him, but instead he turned away.

'Hey!' she protested. 'Where are you going?'

He went over to the windows and flipped the blinds down, then locked the door.

'Well, if you're determined to find me a cure,' he said, grinning as he walked back to the bed, 'then we'd better make the most of it, hadn't we?'

Acknowledgements

Thanks go to Dr Jim Muir for his endless expert advice on psychiatry, psychology, psychoanalysis and the dark side, human and otherwise. Cheers to Danno for the title (although I'm sure you don't remember saying it), Diggo for the brainstorming and the promo video (www.thesourcecreative.com) and Will and Far for the transglobal book club. Big love to Tom for his endless nagging to get wrting and Bowie for the inspiration (seven books and counting!) and the suggestion that one character should be called 'Fang'. Also to Horse and Philip for the creative bitching sessions down Bodeans.

Huge thanks also to Sheila Crowley and Eugenie Furniss for faith, hope and the occasional sticky bun and to Gillian Redfearn for her vision, editorial wisdom and for all those firm-but-gentle 'suggestions'. Also to the Gollancz design team for their skill and patience. And thanks to Lucy Fleming Brown for being the first person in the world to read *By Midnight* and for her invaluable feedback.

But most of all, the biggest thanks go to Linda Butt for her generosity, kindness and patience, spending hour upon hour stuck on trains, making puppets and playing Cinderella. Genuinely, without her tireless support this book simply would never have been started, let alone finished.

BEAUTY
IS THE MOST DANGEROUS
WEAPON OF ALL

Set in a world of stunningly beautiful, exceptionally dangerous monsters, Fire is one of the most dangerous monsters of all – a human one. Aware of her power, and afraid of it, Fire lives tucked away in a corner of the world. Until the day comes when she is needed and has to take a stand not only against her enemies, but also against herself . . .

GOLLANCZ Fiction for young adults

For more information, proof giveaways, exclusive competitions and updates please visit: **www.orionbooks.co.uk/gollanczya**

WHAT IF EVERYTHING YOU TOUCHED WAS CURSED?

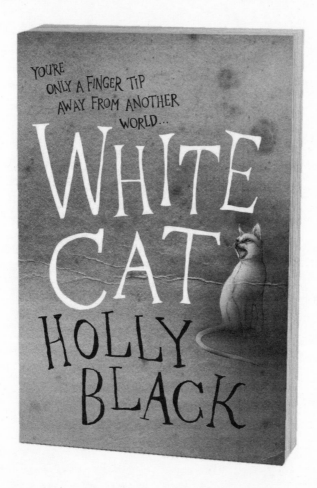

YOU'RE ONLY A FINGER TIP AWAY FROM ANOTHER WORLD...

WHITE CAT
HOLLY BLACK

Cassel is cursed. Cursed by the memory of the fourteen year old girl he murdered. No-one at home is ever going to forget that he is a killer or that he isn't a magic worker. But Cassel is about to discover a dangerous family secret that will change everything.

www.orionbooks.co.uk